WHERE WE BELONG

Catherine Ryan Hyde

BLACK SWAN

TRANSWORLD PUBLISHERS
61–63 Uxbridge Road, London W5 5SA
A Random House Group Company
www.transworldbooks.co.uk

WHERE WE BELONG
A BLACK SWAN BOOK: 9780552778039

First publication in Great Britain
Black Swan edition published 2014

A CIP catalogue record for this book
is available from the British Library.

Addresses for Random House Group Ltd companies outside the UK
can be found at: www.randomhouse.co.uk
The Random House Group Ltd Reg. No. 954009

The Random House Group Limited supports The Forest Stewardship
Council® (FSC®), the leading international forest-certification
organisation. Our books carrying the FSC label are printed on
FSC®-certified paper. FSC is the only forest-certification scheme
supported by the leading environmental organisations, including
Greenpeace. Our paper procurement policy can be found
at www.randomhouse.co.uk/environment

Typeset in 11/14½pt Giovanni Book by
Kestrel Data, Exeter, Devon.
Printed in the UK by
CPI Group (UK) Ltd, Croydon, CR0 4YY.

2 4 6 8 10 9 7 5 3 1

WHERE WE BELONG

PART ONE

The Part When i Was Only Fourteen

Chapter One

 **Hem**

By the time I was seven, I had twenty-two packs of playing cards. Twenty-two. And I never played card games with them. Not once. Card games are boring.

They were for building, not playing.

It started with the card house my dad showed me how to build when I was six, right before he stuck his hand in his shirt pocket and figured out he was out of cigarettes, and then walked out of the house to get more at the corner store and got murdered. For his watch and his wallet and his wedding ring. The watch was just a cheap Timex and the ring was only silver and thin. And he never carried a lot of cash because he never had a lot to carry.

I graduated card houses and went on to card condos, card apartment complexes, card ranches, card palaces. It's a lot of work for something that's always going to fall down at the end. But then, all of life is like that. Right?

Take my dad. He was just showing me that perfect moment when the house is getting big, when you're on the third or so level, and every card drop makes you hold your breath. You have to wait to see. You think it falls right away if it's going to, but it doesn't. There's this weird little pause, like time skipping. That pause was everything that kept me dropping those damn cards. Everything.

'I'll be honest, Angie,' my dad said. 'It brings out the gambler in me.'

But nothing needed to bring out the gambler in him. He was a gambler. It was always out.

Right after he said that, he stuck his hand in his pocket.

Now I have no packs of cards. I got rid of them all after my sister Sophie came along. Not right after. Because . . . you know. She was in a crib and all. And even when she started crawling around, it seemed like everything was OK with her. And then it wasn't. And it was hard to put our fingers on when we knew it wasn't. Probably a lot sooner than we said so out loud.

After that I knew better than to keep anything delicate and easy to ruin around the house ever again.

Anyway, what difference does it make? Now that I'm fourteen our whole life is a house of cards. Drop. Wait. Breathe. Or don't.

I liked it better with real cards. I liked how you could just sweep them all up with your hand and start over again. Everything in the world is easier to clean up after than your own actual damn life.

It was our first full day at Aunt Violet's, and I woke up wondering if it would also be our last. It can happen on any day. You think you know which ones are the most dicey, but it turns out you never do.

Besides, this one wasn't looking good.

It was a Friday, and I should have been in school, except I had to go to a new school now, and my mom said signing me up on Monday would be good enough, which really meant she needed me to babysit Sophie while she went job hunting.

We were sitting at the breakfast table eating toaster waffles, Sophie and me and Aunt Vi. This old Formica table with these glittery spots on it, like man-made stars. Those spots were holding Sophie's attention. She was eating her waffle with her left hand, and dropping the tip of her finger down on those little glittery spots over and over and over. With a little grunt on each drop.

Her hair needed brushing. Probably my job, but I was ducking it. Pretend reason, because my mom didn't really make that clear. Real reason, because it's kind of a rotten job.

Aunt Vi was watching her in a way that made it hard for me to breathe.

Aunt Violet wasn't really our aunt. First of all, she was our mom's aunt, which made her our great-aunt, and also only by marriage. Did that make her our mom's for-real aunt? I guess it did, since there's no such thing as an aunt-in-law. I didn't know, and it didn't matter. Here's what I knew, and here's what mattered: we weren't blood family. Which would make it a whole lot easier to throw us away.

'What kind of job is your mom looking for?' Aunt Vi asked. She never took her eyes off Sophie, which made it sound like she was asking Sophie. But of course that was impossible.

'She's really wanting to find a job waitressing at a dinner restaurant,' I said. Sophie's grunts were turning to little squeals that hurt my ears. I could see Aunt Vi wince on each one. The sparkle-pointing was half morphing into arm flaps. I talked through it as best I could. 'Because the tips are really good. And then I can watch Sophie while she's—'

'Can she be gotten to stop that?' Aunt Vi squeaked. Suddenly, and with her voice too high-pitched. And kind of desperate. Like she'd been just about to break that whole time.

Which I'd known. Which I'd felt. But I'd been telling myself it wasn't as bad as I thought, half believing myself and half not. Uncle Charlie had just died a couple months before, and Aunt Violet was fragile.

A weird silence followed, which wasn't a silence at all, because Sophie didn't stop her noise. It was just Aunt Vi and me holding still and saying nothing. Don't ask me how all that noise can feel like an awkward silence. But it can. And it did.

Drop.

'No, ma'am. I don't think it's possible for her to stop.'

Wait.

Aunt Vi sighed.

I breathed.

'It's just that I'm not myself since Charlie died. It's like being sick. You think you can get up and do things, but then you're still weaker than you thought. You know how when you're sick, you just can't abide anything? All you can do is be sick.'

I knew what she meant, even though I was either wrong about what the word abide meant, or she was using it wrong in the sentence.

'I'm really sorry about Uncle Charlie. He was a nice man. I liked him a lot.'

Aunt Vi's face held frozen for a split second or two. Then it twisted up into crying. And then I felt like eighteen different kinds of crap for saying exactly the wrong thing to her.

She levered up from the table. I had no idea that old woman could move so fast.

'I have to go lie down,' she said.

Of course, we'd all just gotten up for the day. I didn't say so.

'Want some earplugs?'

I dug two out of my shirt pocket and held them out in my hand. These bright, dark-blue bullets. Not foam. Foam earplugs don't do much. Well. They don't do enough. These were made out of beeswax and some kind of fiber. I held them out to her back as it hurried away.

She stopped at the kitchen doorway and turned

around. She was wearing a housecoat covered with little pink flowers. It had seen better days. The pink flowers were fading. Practically out of existence. She held on to the doorway like the house had just hit an iceberg.

She always wore make-up. Even with that horrible old housecoat. I wondered who she thought would notice or care. Well. I noticed. I mostly wondered who cared.

I just stood there with my hand out. Like an idiot. I made a gesture toward the earplugs. So comforting. So safe. Such a good solution. Couldn't she see that?

She shook her head hard. 'I'll just go lie down.'

'No, wait – don't go, Aunt Vi. We'll go outside.'

She only stood there, holding on for dear life. Probably waiting to see how I'd get Sophie to go anywhere.

I stuffed the last two bites of waffle into my mouth at the same time. Took my plate to the sink. Then I snuck up behind Sophie and grabbed the half-chewed dry waffle out of her left hand.

She shrieked.

I held it up like a carrot on a stick, just out of her reach. I knew she'd follow it right out the back door.

'I'll give it back to you when we get outside.'

I didn't know if Sophie even understood when I said stuff to her. I didn't even know if she listened. I said it mostly for Aunt Vi's sake. So she wouldn't think I was being mean to Sophie for no reason. Or maybe she wouldn't care. Maybe it was only me who cared.

I looked over at Aunt Vi as we hit the back door – almost literally. Locked eyes with her. Without really meaning to.

Wait.

'You don't know what it's like,' she said. 'How hard everything is when you've just lost someone.'

My face got hot, which it always does when I get mad. I always get mad really fast, but then I don't do anything with it. I don't let it loose. If I say I'm mad, I'll cry, which is just so incredibly unfair. It ruins everything. So I don't say.

Sophie was ramming into my side and bouncing off, over and over. Probably trying to get me to drop the waffle. It hurt, but I was only giving it half my attention.

I just thought it was a mean thing to say to me. Thoughtless. You know?

I drew Sophie out the kitchen door and on to the back porch, and slammed the door hard behind us.

And gave her the waffle back.

And didn't breathe.

Much.

I was lying on this white plastic lounge chair, with the sun beating down on me, on grass that was all marked up with yellow spots from everywhere the dog had peed. The dog was gone, too. She'd died two weeks before Uncle Charlie, which was part of Aunt Violet's extra fragile state. I used to like that dog. Her name was Beulah, and she was a fat basset hound with arthritis. She was drooly but nice.

Sophie never liked Beulah. Sophie never liked any dogs. Or cats, either. In fact, you had to watch her every minute with them because she would try to kick or punch them, even if they hadn't done anything to her. One dog she saw outside a supermarket she tried to bite, and the dog was too nice to defend himself, and I had to step in and save the day, and then it was me who got bitten.

I looked up to see why Sophie was being so quiet. She was crouched on her belly up against the chain-link fence at one end of Aunt Violet's yard. She actually looked like a dog, the way she was lying in the grass. Like the way a dog will fold up in a sphinx position. She had her chin on the backs of her hands like they were her paws. Her nose was tucked right up to the chain-link fence. On the other side of the links was just about the biggest dog ever. This all-black Great Dane with cropped ears standing up, pointy. I think they shouldn't do that to dogs, but that's beside the point for this part of things. If I had to guess I'd say he was maybe close to two hundred pounds. He was lying in exactly the same position as Sophie. His nose was about four inches from hers. It was the only part of him that wasn't black. His muzzle was gray.

I sat up. 'Hmm,' I said, out loud, even though there was nobody but me around to hear me. Then I called out, 'Sophie, you come away from him,' because I thought maybe she was lulling that poor dog into a false sense of security.

But . . . like I mentioned before, I don't even know if she heard or not. Or heard but plain didn't care. Or couldn't care, I guess I should say.

I ran things around in my head for a minute or two. She couldn't reach through the fence – anyway, not very far. That dog wasn't tied up or anything. Surely he knew how to duck? And he outweighed her three or four times over. Did I really want to take my life in my hands by going to get her? I could always have used the extreme emergency method, which was sneaking up behind and throwing a blanket over her like a net, but I tried to keep that plan in my back pocket as much as I could. Besides, I usually got kicked up just as bad.

I decided that big old dog could take care of himself. Only because of the fence, though. Without that fence I wouldn't have bet much on his chances.

Every now and then I looked up to see how it was going.

'Don't you dare hurt him,' I said. Maybe four times.

But nothing ever moved.

I thought again about brushing her hair, but I couldn't bring myself to mess up a good thing. It would've been easier if my mom had cut it short, like mine, but she loved Sophie's hair, and I didn't blame her. It was a color like mahogany, this rich brown with red highlights that came out in the sun. And in natural ringlet curls. She was a beautiful girl, more than I ever would be. My mom was always talking about her hair and those gorgeous green eyes like she didn't get it that I was here, too. She talked about those green eyes less, though, now that Sophie hadn't made eye contact with us for years.

I sighed and tried to make all that go away.

After a while I heard Sophie shrieking that special horrible siren wail of hers. Our mom calls it keening, but I've heard other people keening, and I've got to tell you, this is worse. I sat up to see that the dog had wandered away from the fence to get a drink out of his water bowl. He raised his head and looked up at me, and I looked back. He had water streaming down from the corners of his mouth.

I reached to get my earplugs out of my pocket.

I don't want to sound cold, just putting in earplugs and then letting her wail. It sounds like I don't care that she's wailing. But it's not that. I care plenty. There's just nothing I can do. Nothing. Nothing anybody can do. Except preserve their own sanity by whatever means possible.

Aunt Violet burst out the back door.

'You have to make her stop,' she said. She sounded even more desperate, like she was on her last nerve. Like she could explode at any time, and flutter down to the spotty grass in a bunch of dry bits and pieces. 'I can't take it,' she said. 'I'm not strong. I told your mom I'm not strong. I'm not myself without Charlie. I don't have a lot of . . .'

While she searched for a word for what she didn't have a lot of, I looked at her eyebrows. I was always sneaking peeks at them when I thought I could get away with it. She didn't seem to have any eyebrow hairs of her own, so she drew them on in this weird color of light brown, and too high in the middle. It made her look like everything in the world was a shock to her system. Not that her eyebrows mattered at a time like that. Just that, when things get bad, my brain goes away. Sometimes.

Just as I opened my mouth to break the bad news . . . which she damn well should have known already . . . that I can't stop Sophie once she gets going . . . that nothing can stop Sophie once she gets going . . . the dog came wandering back to the fence. I saw him out of the corner of my eye.

Sophie's cry wound down the way a siren does, getting lower and slower and then gone.

'Oh, thank goodness,' Aunt Violet said. 'Thank goodness she stopped.' Aunt Vi turned her eyes to me, her drawn-on eyebrows scrunched down as far as they could scrunch, but still looking a little too high. 'Did you take offense at something when we were talking before?'

She asked it like she'd had all this time to think and still couldn't imagine what it might have been.

My face got hot again.

'I just felt like it was a little bit thoughtless of you,' I said, and then my face burned like crazy, because it was a brave thing to say. I had to work hard not to cry.

Aunt Vi's head rocked back. 'Now what on earth did I say?' Like she already knew I was wrong and it couldn't have been anything, really.

'That I don't know how it feels when somebody dies.'

She just stared at me blank-faced for a minute. Not a real whole minute, but maybe for the count of three.

Then her eyes went wide and her hand came up to her mouth. And she charged at me. It scared the crap out of me. I thought she was about to attack me, and I wanted to run, or yell. Or something. Or anything. But it all happened too fast.

Next thing I knew she was smothering me in this bear hug, and I was all pressed up to her big belly, which was softer than I thought a person should be. She actually had hold of the back of my head and was pulling it in close, against her big bosom, and I could hardly breathe.

'Oh, honey,' she said, bending over, close to my ear. 'I'm so sorry. I forgot. I forgot about . . .'

Don't say it, I thought.

'. . . your dad. Oh, and such an awful way to go, too. And so sudden. You're right, that was very thoughtless of me. See, I told you I'm not myself.'

She pulled my head back away from her soft self, holding me by both temples. I pulled in enough air for ten breaths.

'Do you forgive me?'

'Yes, ma'am,' I said. Just parroting the words. Not forgiving and not not forgiving. Not even really thinking what that would mean.

'Oh, dear,' she said, without really telling me 'Oh dear' about what.

She swooped back into the house, slamming the door behind her with a great bang. I looked back at Sophie. She and the dog had folded up into the mirror position again.

I breathed. Even though this wasn't going to buy us much time.

See, that's always the thing. While you're breathing, and being all happy that the whole house didn't come falling down, you know there's another card drop coming right up. It's not about gaining much. It's just about gaining. It's always about not losing everything in the exact moment you're in.

I got up and wandered over to the fence, the longish grass feeling funny and tickly between my toes. I was thinking maybe I should offer to cut the grass for Aunt Violet. Make myself as useful as possible.

I stood over Sophie.

'What's up with this, Sophie?' I asked her. 'You don't even like dogs.'

'Hem,' she said.

Which is really . . . I don't know how to say it. A word from Sophie is like . . . Mark this day on your calendar.

'I'll be damned.'

Then it hit me that this was the quietest, best day I'd had with Sophie in years. Why in God's name was I trying to talk her out of it?

Whatever 'it' was.

My best day lasted until twenty-five after five, and then I had to pay double for the peace and quiet. I happened to know the time because I went into the kitchen to check, because I was thinking it was about time for my mom to be home. I didn't know if it was the good news or the bad news, that it was taking her so long.

Just as I was coming back out, the dog suddenly stood up. He stayed close to the fence, but he was looking out toward the street. Sophie stood up, too.

I couldn't hear anything, but I could definitely sense that my vacation was about to be over. I'm not sure how much vacation I'd thought I could expect, or why.

Then I heard a car door slam. It sounded far away. But the dog started wagging that huge, strong tail. He was still right up by the fence, right near Sophie, so his tail slapped the chain-link hard on every wag, and the whole fence rang like an out-of-tune bell. Sophie started jumping up and down. Which I thought was interesting. I mean, clearly she was imitating the dog, so I half expected her to wag her butt around or something, but instead she jumped up and down like she was all excited, which made me think it was the inside of the dog she was imitating. Which seemed a little bit like knowing what somebody else was feeling, which I think is like what the doctors kept calling empathy. Which I think we all thought was something Sophie couldn't do.

A minute or so later the side door opened on the house next door, and a man stood in the open doorway. He seemed shocked to see me. Which was weird, in a way, because I was in Aunt Violet's yard, not his, and I couldn't figure out why he was looking at me like he'd suddenly found me in his living room. Our eyes locked for a minute, and then I looked away.

He was an old guy. Not old like bent-over old. He was tall and kind of reedy thin, and he looked like he was in good-enough shape and all. But his hair was mostly gray, and he had just a hint of five o'clock shadow, just enough that I could see his beard would be white if he ever grew it in. He was wearing a nice gray suit, with a light-blue dress shirt and a striped dark-blue tie, but it was loosened. The top button of his shirt was undone and the tie was pulled out. To give him more room to breathe, I guess.

He stared at me for another minute, and then he looked at his dog. He got this puzzled look on his face, and I could tell, just from that look, that it was weird for his dog to still be over by the fence. The dog was slapping his tail against the fence like crazy now, but I could see that wasn't enough.

'Rigby,' the man said.

He didn't yell it, or even call it out, really. He just said it, like you'd say any word in a sentence.

That broke the dog's spell, and he ran to the man and sat in front of him, tail swinging. And he raised his face up almost pretty close to the man's face, because he was honestly big enough to do that.

And, of course, by this time, Sophie's siren had gone off.

The guy looked around, but not really at us. I don't think he'd even noticed Sophie yet. If he had, he didn't let on. I don't think he imagined that a sound like that could come out of a small person. Most people don't. He looked around some more, like he was about to see an ambulance or a fire truck coming up the street. He even looked up, like it might be something overhead, but I have no idea what. Then he looked down, and his eyes locked on Sophie.

Wait.

I could see his face twist up a little. Like he could stand the noise better if it was coming from a what, not a who. People are like that. They figure a machine or a siren doesn't know any better, can't help the sound it makes. Once they know it's Sophie, they want it to stop.

The moment dragged out. Just long enough to make my face feel cold. Then he turned on his heel and went back into the house, Rigby following with his tail still swinging. The door slammed shut.

I got up and went inside the house, leaving Sophie alone for just a minute, to get Aunt Vi ready for what we were all about to go through. It was actually pretty OK to leave Sophie, because she wasn't going to be doing anything except exactly what she was doing already. For just about . . . ever.

I found Aunt Vi in bed, a feather pillow over her ears.

I touched her shoulder and she jumped a mile. Then she sat up straight and looked at me with this look of utter misery on her face, and I felt bad for her. I did. I would have taken Sophie and gone away and left her alone if we'd had one other place in the world we could go.

I took two earplugs out of my shirt pocket and held them out to her.

'They work,' I said. 'Really. Not like there's no noise at all, but they make it sound so far away it hardly matters. You have to knead them around in your fingers till they're soft and then make them back into a bullet and press them in till it seals. You'll be surprised.'

She took them off my hand and smiled weakly.

'Thank you, darling,' she said.

Then I got up and left, because I pretty much knew she'd be happier alone with her misery. I was that same way, so I understood.

I went back outside and sat on the lounge chair near Sophie and softened up my own earplugs. I had one in place when the side door of the man's house opened again, and he looked out. Looked at me. Then at Sophie.

Just when I was wondering how long he could stand there and stare, he walked over to the fence, Rigby wagging at his heels. Sophie's siren wound down as they got closer to the fence.

He'd changed into a black sweater, but he still had his fancy suit pants on. And shiny black leather shoes.

He stood there looking down on Sophie, who was quiet now. Rigby had come right up to the fence and was sitting with his head stretched out, just inches on the other side of the fence, and Sophie had her hands wrapped in the chain-link, her face as close to the dog's as she could get it.

The man looked up at me again, and I looked away. Something about the way he stared. I didn't like it, and I couldn't hold it long. There was a harshness to it. Like he expected something and was trying to pull it right out of me.

'She stopped,' he said.

He had the voice I would have expected from him. Sharp-edged. A little hard. Almost critical.

'Yes, sir. She did.'

'Will she stay stopped?'

'Only till you go back in.'

I got up and walked over to the fence, even though I didn't really want to go closer to him. But I didn't want Aunt Vi to hear that we were having trouble with one of her neighbors. Already.

I took two more earplugs out of my pocket and held them out toward the fence. 'These help a lot,' I said.

He stared at them a long time. Like they were some kind of math equation. Maybe one that was just beyond his skills in math.

'They're earplugs,' I said, to try to break us through to a new moment.

'I know what they are.'

'You want to know why she's doing that.'

'You're getting warmer.'

'She likes your dog.' That just sat in the air for a moment, like nobody knew quite what to do with it. I guess if you didn't know Sophie, that didn't answer every question that was hanging around by then. 'She's been sitting with your dog all day, and she got upset because he went in.'

'She,' he said.

'Oh. It's a girl dog.'

'Yes. She's female.'

'My sister got upset because she – your dog – went back in the house with you.'

'And she makes that noise whenever she's upset?'

'Pretty much. Yeah.'

Then he got that look on his face that people always get. Like Sophie ought to know better. Like she ought to do better. And it makes me mad, because they don't know. They shouldn't be judging her if they don't know.

'I don't suppose your dog could stay out a while.'

He shot his gaze back up to me, and it burned. It was the same look, but this time for me. Like *I* should know better. Like *I* should do better.

'I work hard,' he said. 'Every day. And I hate every minute of it. All I want to do at the end of the day is come home and see my dog and watch the evening news in peace and quiet and have something to eat. Is that asking too much?'

'No, sir. I don't suppose it is.'

It was more than he was going to get, though. I didn't say so.

'But she'll start again the minute I do.'

'Yes, sir. I expect she will.'

'And you can't stop her.'

'No, sir. Nobody and nothing can stop her.'

'So when does she stop on her own?'

'She can generally go about two hours before she loses her voice. Then all she can do is whisper and squeak for a couple of days. That gives us all a break.'

He looked into my eyes for a minute. Like he was desperate to find the place where I was only joking. Then he looked down at Sophie with this look of total contempt. Like she was the lowest life form on earth.

My face started to burn, and I knew this time I was going to say something. Whether I humiliated myself by crying or not.

Before I could open my mouth to do it, though, he turned to go back in. And Sophie started up shrieking again.

'She's not a brat,' I said. Nice and loud, so he could hear me over the noise.

But he didn't hear. He cupped one hand behind his ear to tell me he didn't. Then he came back to the fence, and Sophie wound down. I could feel it in my gut. Or the lack of it, I guess I should say. Like something nasty had been vibrating around in there, and it felt so good when it stopped.

'What did you say to me?' he asked, which made it much harder to speak my mind.

I did anyway.

'She's not a brat.'

'Funny, because she acts like one.'

A few tears leaked out, but I couldn't let myself care. Well. I couldn't not care. But I could not stop.

I looked right into his face, tears or no.

'I'm sick and tired of people treating her like we don't raise her right or something. My mom raised me and I turned out fine. Sophie's different. Her brain is different. It's like a kind of autism. I mean, it's like autism in most ways and not like it in other ways. It's what they call the autism spectrum. The doctors still don't really understand her, but she can't help it and we can't help it, and you don't know us, so you shouldn't judge what you don't know a damn thing about.'

By now the tears had broken free, and there was no hiding them. I actually felt one slide down my cheek. Which was total humiliation, but what was I supposed to do? I wiped it off hard and fast with the back of my hand.

He just looked at me for a long time. Well. A few seconds. It felt long.

'You're right,' he said. 'Please accept my apology.'

Then he turned to go back in the house. The dog stuck for just a second, close to the fence. Close to Sophie. But then the man turned around and made eye contact with her, and then she picked him. Which I guess it was her job to do. I thought it was kind of remarkable that she hadn't all along.

The siren started up again.

The guy stopped on his front porch and gave me one long, unhappy look over his shoulder. I could see it all drain away – all his hopes for that quiet dinner in front of the news. I could just look at his eyes and see him get it. That it was never going to happen. That even that simple dream was gone.

I held the earplugs out again.

At first he just teetered there. Like the whole decision was just too pathetic. But after a time he came back to the fence to get them. And . . . this was weird, I thought . . . the dog just sat there on the steps by the door and waited. Like she was smart enough to know that going over there for just a few seconds might only make things worse.

I reached the two little dark-blue bullets through the fence on the tips of my fingers. Dropped them into his waiting hand. He had big hands, but smooth, like he'd never dug a hole or built a fence in his life. Probably he hadn't. Not in that nice suit.

'Thank you,' he said, kind of shouting to be heard over the siren.

Then he shook his head and walked back inside.

I wasn't wearing a watch, but I think it was about forty-five very screechy minutes later when the police showed up. I didn't hear them pull up and park, or knock on the door, or ring the bell, or whatever they did. Of course, I had my earplugs in, and I was still out back with Sophie, who was still keening, and if I was going to hear anything, it was only going to be that. I was daydreaming, and my head was a hundred miles away, but I don't remember where. Then I saw a movement at the corner of my eye, and it was Aunt Vi coming out into the backyard with two policemen. Well, actually one policeman and one policewoman.

I sat up very straight, this cold feeling in my gut, and I pulled out the earplugs as fast as I could.

'They got a report about the noise,' Aunt Violet said, yelling to be heard over Sophie's wail. I'd never seen Aunt Vi – or anybody else for that matter – look so completely defeated and humiliated. And I'd seen some stuff.

'I'm sorry,' I shouted. Knowing it wasn't enough, but not having much else in the way of ammunition.

The two cops looked at Sophie and then at each other.

'The neighbor who called it in thought it was an animal in distress,' the man cop yelled out.

Then I got mad, because that damn guy next door knew damn well it wasn't an animal, and he knew damn well we weren't abusing her. That was a scummy thing for him to do, I thought.

'You can see we're not hurting her in any way,' Aunt Violet shouted.

The woman cop yelled, 'What did you say her diagnosis was again?'

'ASD,' I said. And then had to repeat it, louder.

'Which is . . . ?'

'Autism spectrum disorder.'

'So she's autistic?'

'Yes, ma'am. More or less. There are a lot of different ways that can go, and she's one of them. She's upset because she likes the neighbor's dog, and he took the dog inside. I was doing my best to keep her happy, I swear.'

The cops looked at each other again. Definitely having some kind of a conversation with their eyes. I was right there watching, but I couldn't quite read it. But I didn't like the feeling.

'There's nothing you can do to stop her?' the lady cop called.

'No, ma'am. I swear I would if I could. I'm sorry. She just has to wear herself down.'

Another of those looks.

'Can you at least get her in the house? Give the neighbors that much of a break?'

I cut my eyes over to Aunt Vi. I'd purposely been staying outside with Sophie to give *her* ears a break. But she flipped her head toward the house. And that was one silent conversation I understood. Get her *in*, for God's sake, she was saying.

I stood up straight. Locked down the thoughts in my head. Braced myself.

'Can you . . . help me? By holding her feet? Otherwise she'll kick the – she'll kick me really hard. She doesn't mean to hurt me. It's just the way she's wired.'

The man cop opened his mouth to say no. He got partway through it. 'We're not supposed—'

'I'll help,' the woman said.

We stood over Sophie, and I took a deep breath and then just grabbed her up in a bear hug, pinning her arms to her sides. I kept my hands pretty low, toward her waist, in case she tried to bite. The lady cop grabbed her bare ankles, but Sophie pulled them right away again, and got me a good shot in the right thigh, and then the lady grabbed on again and held tighter this time. Now that she knew what she was up against.

I made a rookie mistake, though. And I of all people should've known better. I was holding her up too high, so her head was almost as high as mine, so that if she threw her head back . . .

Just as I had the thought, she bucked hard, trying to straighten out, and her head came back and hit me, slamming my lower lip against my teeth. Enough to really stun me.

The lady cop's head came up. 'You OK?'

I just gave her this desperate point toward the house with my head, because all I wanted was to get in, so this could be over. We moved fast across the grass and up the three little concrete steps into the kitchen. Aunt Vi slammed the door behind all of us, and I set Sophie down on the linoleum as gently as I could.

One of the cops handed me a paper towel, but I couldn't even see which one was doing the handing. It just appeared in front of me on the end of a blue-sleeved arm. At first I didn't know why a paper towel. Then I got it that my lip was bleeding.

That was when Sophie started throwing herself against the door. Hard.

See, that was bad. That was self-injury behavior. Most of the time we didn't have to worry too much about self-injury with Sophie, but we always knew things could get very bad if she ever crossed that line. It was this thing that was always out there, maybe waiting for us. And I really didn't want that to be the moment it showed up.

I grabbed her and brought us both down to the floor and just sort of lay on her, wrapping up her arms and wrapping my legs over and around hers. My earplugs were still out, and she was shrieking right in my ear, but that seemed like the least of my worries.

Her voice was still pretty strong.

I don't know much of what went on behind me after that. I heard Aunt Vi talking to the cops by the front door, but not what they said. After I thought they were gone, I felt a hand on my shoulder. I thought it was

Aunt Vi, but when I turned my head, it was the lady cop. She took my chin in her hand and wiped the blood off my lip and my neck and my shirt as best she could with some kind of damp cloth, and then she held the split together and put a little butterfly bandage on it.

She gave my shoulder a squeeze before she left. I could probably interpret it as either meaning I was doing a good job, or wishing me luck, because I'd need it. Or maybe both.

Then I didn't hear any more talking and nobody seemed to be around.

I'm guessing it was about another thirty minutes before Sophie screamed herself to sleep.

After I put her to bed, I locked myself in the bathroom. I took a long, long shower, almost until the hot water was gone. Like everything that had just happened would wash off. It did make me feel better, though. Some better.

I got out and wrapped up in a towel and wiped steam off the mirror with my hand.

My lip was swollen under the butterfly bandage, and it still looked a little bloody. I wiggled the tooth right behind it with my tongue, and then with my finger, and it scared me how loose it was. I didn't know if it would tighten up again on its own, or if I'd lose it. That would be a major disaster. It's not like we could afford cosmetic dentist visits.

I heard a light knock on the bathroom door.

'I'll be right out, Aunt Vi.'

'It's me,' my mom said.

'Oh. Hi.'

'Did you have an OK day?'

'Pretty much like most of them,' I said.

We sort of had a deal that we each wouldn't tell the other any more than they needed to know about any bad days. We'd never said such a thing out loud, but it was a deal all the same.

'I have some great news for you.'

'Good. I could use some.'

'I got hired on the spot. I'm going to be working dinners at that nice Italian restaurant on Sixth Street. It's kind of expensive. And you know what that means.'

Good tips. That's what it meant. The higher the bill, the bigger the tips.

'That's great,' I said. 'Maybe we can afford our own place.'

'Let's not get ahead of ourselves, hon. Anyway, I start next week.'

'That's good, Mom.'

'You sound—'

'I'm fine. I'll be right out, OK?'

A pause. And then I guess she must have walked away. Because I never heard another sound after that.

After I got dressed again, and dried my hair with Aunt Vi's blow-dryer, I wandered out into the kitchen to see where everybody was. I could hear Mom and Vi talking to each other in low voices.

When I stuck my head in the kitchen, they both

stopped talking and looked up at me. Like I'd caught them doing something wrong.

'Why didn't you tell me the police came?' my mom asked. Like it was my idea they should come by.

She didn't say anything about my lip, but maybe it was just the light. The light from the living room was bright behind me, and probably she just didn't see.

'You didn't ask,' I said.

I guess that was a bad-attitude thing to say. I didn't mean to have a bad attitude. I was just tired. I can live through everything or I can answer for everything, but sometimes both is just too much for one day.

Nobody said anything, and nothing happened, except it got real clear to me – real fast – that they weren't going to finish their talk with me standing right there listening. I ducked out of the kitchen again, and through the living room toward the front door.

I heard Aunt Violet say, 'I just don't think—'

And my mom cut her off and said, 'Please, Vi. Please, I'm begging you. We need a little more time. We'd literally be out on the street if—'

That was when I slammed the front door. With me on the other side. The outside. It was dusky and cool out, and I felt free somehow, being out in it. Or freer, anyway.

I looked at the house next door, pulled in a long, deep breath, drew my shoulders back, and marched over there. And knocked.

I heard big, impossibly deep woofs from Rigby. Just three.

The door opened.

The man was wearing pajamas and a nice burgundy-colored shiny bathrobe, even though it wasn't too late. Rigby was swinging her tail back and forth like she'd known me all her life. Her tail kept hitting the back of the guy's thighs, but he didn't act like he noticed.

His eyes narrowed when he looked at me. Just a little, but still . . .

'Yes?'

I almost lost my nerve.

I had to fill up with breath again. I had to re-straighten my shoulders.

Before I could speak, he asked, 'What happened to your—'

I didn't let him finish.

'That was a mean, horrible thing to do.'

He chewed on his lower lip for a moment. Just studying my face. Then he said, 'I apologized, so I thought we'd be through that.'

'That's not what I mean and you know it.'

'I don't know as much as you seem to think.'

'You know what you did.'

'I honestly don't.'

'Calling the police on us like that. When you knew I was doing my best with her. It was mean and awful.'

'I didn't call the police.'

That fell to the stoop and just lay there a minute. I wasn't sure what to do with it. I didn't really believe him. But it's pretty strong stuff to call a grown-up a liar. That's a pretty radical thing to take on.

'Well, who did, then?'

He stepped out on to the stoop, and Rigby came out with him. She sat down near my left side, and I put my hand on her back, and it made me feel better.

'Look around,' he said, pointing up and down the street. 'What do you see? The surface of the moon with just these two houses on it? Or neighbors as far as the eye can see?'

Then I felt incredibly stupid. Because it should have occurred to me that anybody could have called the cops. Just because I hadn't met any of the other neighbors didn't mean they couldn't hear the ruckus.

'You really didn't do it?'

'Let me tell you something about me. When I think something is the right thing to do, I do it. And if you ask me if I did it, I'll tell you the truth, because I thought it was the right thing. I'll tell you I did it and I'll tell you why I did it. I won't do something and then lie about it. I did not call the police. I put in your earplugs, and read the news online instead of watching the TV news, and had a roast beef frozen dinner with mashed potatoes. And that's all.'

'Oh,' I said. And, when I said it, all my tiredness caught up with me, all at once. I almost could have melted into a little puddle on his stoop. 'I'm sorry. Seriously. Very, very sorry.'

'Apology accepted.'

'This is a really nice dog,' I said, rubbing her enormous shoulder blades.

'Thank you. Now if you'll excuse me—'

'Did you name her after the song?'

'What song?'

'Everybody knows that song. About the people. Who are lonely.'

'I just like the name Rigby. Now if there's nothing else . . .'

But there was. I swear it was because I was so tired. I felt like one big raw nerve. I swear I wouldn't have said this on any other day. I would have filtered it out. That evening I was fresh out of filter.

'I wish you hadn't gotten her ears cut. I know you'll say it's none of my business. And probably you're right. She's your dog. It's just that . . . this puppy gets born, and she's exactly the way she is, and I don't get how anyone can think the way she's born is wrong somehow. And, anyway, I like the way they look with the big ears that fold over.'

I braved a look at his face. It didn't seem much different than it always had. I couldn't read anything from his eyes.

'Are you done?'

'I just feel like it's our job to take care of them. You know? And when you take care of someone, you should love them the way they are. Not try to make them different.'

Pause.

'Anything else?' he asked.

'No. Yes. Just one other thing. It's painful for them. Puppies trust people, and I don't think we should do anything that hurts them unless it's absolutely necessary.'

Another pause.

'Done?'

'Yes. Done.'

'I didn't crop her ears.'

I looked down at the dog . . . well, almost more like . . . *over* at her. Her ears came up into my line of vision. I looked at those ears like I'd suddenly see them whole again. Then I looked up at the neighbor man. Figuring he'd make some sense out of that if I only gave him time.

'I got her from a breed rescue group when she was eight months old. She was already cropped. I would have preferred an uncropped dog, but I liked this dog's temperament.'

'Oh,' I said. Feeling both very stupid and even more tired. 'I guess I owe you another apology, then.'

'I guess you do.'

'I apologize.'

'See? It can happen to the best of us.'

'What can?'

I honestly didn't understand what he meant. I thought he was still talking about ear cropping. Like ear cropping can happen to anybody at any time. Which didn't make a lot of sense.

'You don't know us. So you shouldn't have judged us over something you don't know a damn thing about.'

'Oh. Right. I did say that. And then I just turned around and did the same thing twice, didn't I?'

'You did. So maybe next time someone makes a bad assumption about your family, instead of taking it personally, maybe just reflect on the fact that anyone can jump to a wrong conclusion. Even you.'

I knew there was something important in there, but I was too tired to really think it out just then. I knew what he meant, but my brain was just in this serious shut-down mode.

I scratched my head. I don't know why. It didn't itch.

'I guess I'll have to think about that,' I said.

'Goodnight,' he said.

'I'm sorry I bothered you.'

'Goodnight,' he said again.

Then he walked back into his house, with Rigby following close by his side, and shut and locked the door. Leaving me standing there on the stoop feeling like the world's biggest and most hopeless fool.

 **Tibet**

The next day was Saturday, and I slept weirdly late.

When I got to the kitchen table, Mom and Aunt Vi were eating scrambled eggs and rye toast in absolute silence. My mom rose to her feet and met me halfway, holding me by the chin and turning my head into better light.

'Vi told me about your lip. Poor baby. That's not gonna need a stitch, is it?'

'It's fine. It'll heal fine.'

'Because you know if it needs a stitch or two, we'll find a way.'

'I know that,' I said. I did know it. I also knew she'd be awfully relieved if it didn't.

'I'm so sorry it was such a rough day yesterday, baby. And I wasn't here.'

She threw her arms around me and held me close.

And I tightened up a little. I tried not to, but then I sort of did anyway. It's not that I didn't want her to love me. I did. It's that I didn't like anybody feeling sorry for me. If I was going to get hurt, or have a hard time, I wanted to do it all alone, with nobody looking.

'I'm fine,' I said, and she took the hint and let go. 'Where's Sophie?'

My mom pointed toward the backyard.

I walked to the window and looked out. Sophie was folded into a sphinx position by the fence. Waiting. Rigby was nowhere to be seen.

'It's Saturday,' I said. To no one in particular.

'What about it, honey?' my mom asked.

I turned around, surprised to hear her so close behind me. She was at the stove, trying to light the burner under the cast-iron skillet. Blowing on it to get it to catch. Which it finally did.

In the skillet was one more helping of eggs.

'These might be a little dried-out, honey. I'm sorry. I didn't think you'd sleep so long. You must've been exhausted. What about it being Saturday?'

'The dog's owner probably doesn't work on Saturday. So he might not let the dog out.'

I was looking out the window again by then, at Sophie, even though she hadn't moved a muscle. Still, part of me thought it wasn't right to leave her too long by herself. On the other hand, she wasn't moving, and she wasn't going to move. That's one thing you can count on with Sophie. Once she locks on to something, you've got some time.

'He'll have to go out sometime, at least to pee,' my mom said, sounding a little nervous.

'She,' I said. 'The dog is a she. And then, after she pees, she'll go right back in again.'

I couldn't hear anything at all from Vi, but I heard my mother say, 'Now, Violet, I'm here to take care of it. I promise you that. Now just breathe. Please.'

I looked over my shoulder at Aunt Vi. 'What do you know about that guy next door?'

Aunt Vi seemed to mull that over. 'Not too much, honey. Why?'

Then I wondered why the question should've needed mulling. She either knew or she didn't.

'Seems kind of grumpy,' I said.

'You talked to him?'

'Yeah. Why?'

'I never talk to him. All I know is his name. Paul Inverness. And that he's a loan officer at a bank. I don't know which one. I don't know one other thing. Just name and line of work. Matter of fact, I've lived here fifteen years and haven't said more than ten sentences to that man.'

'Why not?'

'I don't know. Never got the feeling he wanted me to. He keeps to himself. You stay away from him. I don't like a man who lives alone and talks to a young girl but not his own neighbors.'

'It wasn't like that,' I said.

'You don't know.'

'I do know.'

'The world is a tough place.'

'Now *that* I *really* know.'

I opened the door to the backyard.

'Where're you going, hon?' my mom asked.

'I don't feel right with her being alone too long.'

'I'm looking out for her. Don't worry.'

I kept going.

'What about your breakfast?'

'Could you bring it out?'

I didn't really wait for an answer. I was volunteering to look after Sophie, so carrying a plate of scrambled eggs didn't seem like too much to ask.

I walked out to the fence and stood over her. She must have seen my big shadow. But she didn't seem to register I was there.

'Hem,' she said. 'Hem, hem, hem.'

So maybe she did know. Or maybe she'd been saying it all along. Her voice was scratchy. But it wasn't gone.

'What's with this "hem", Sophie?' I knew it had something to do with the dog, so I said, 'Rigby. The dog's name is Rigby.'

'Hem,' Sophie said.

Her hair was shiny and clean, and brushed. My mom had cleaned her up real nice.

'Rigby.'

'Hem.'

'Rigby.'

'Hem, hem, hem.'

I sighed, and walked back to the lounge chair, and sat.

A couple minutes later a plate of eggs was lowered in front of my nose from behind. I'd been so lost in my own head, I hadn't even seen or heard them coming. She'd put two buttered pieces of rye toast on my plate, and a tiny glass of orange juice.

'Thank you,' I said.

'Taste them. If they're not OK, I'll make you fresh.'

'They'll be fine.'

'Taste them.'

I took a bite, careful not to bump my loose tooth with the fork. They were dry.

'They're fine,' I said.

Stupid to waste them. They weren't dry enough to throw away.

'You sure you're OK out here with her? You had a rough day yesterday. It really should be my day.'

'I just want to see what happens with the dog. Then I'll take some time off.'

She sighed. Kissed me on the top of my head.

'Wish you'd let your hair grow out.'

'I like it like this. I told you.'

'It would look nice long. More feminine. Oh . . . never mind. I'm sorry. Forget I said it. I promised you I'd butt out, didn't I?'

I heard the door close after her as she went inside.

'You did,' I said quietly. 'Twice.'

I was done with the eggs and halfway through the second piece of toast when the door opened on the house next door and Rigby came bounding out. I looked up into Paul Inverness's face. He just stood there in the doorway. Like Sophie and I might only be a bad dream. He looked tired to see me there. To see us there.

'Hem!' Sophie shouted. 'Hem, hem!'

Rigby circled three times and squatted in the grass, then joined Sophie by the fence. I got up and walked over, and so did Paul. He was dressed too nicely for a day off. Not a suit, but tan pants with a crease, and brown leather shoes, and a shirt that was blinding white. He was freshly shaved, and smelled like some kind of aftershave. Like he was going on a date. Not just letting the dog out to pee.

'Thought she'd lost her voice and we'd all get a break.'

'Yeah. Sorry. She didn't really scream till her voice was gone. She sort of screamed herself to sleep instead.' Then we both just stood there, feeling awkward. Well, I'm guessing about him. But he looked awkward. 'I'm really sorry for what I said to you last night. About your dog's ears. I was tired and stressed out, and usually I'd think a thing like that but not say it. I don't know why I said it. I don't know why you even put up with all that stuff from me. And you were polite about it. I'm surprised you didn't just kick me down the steps and slam the door.'

Then I paused, finally halfway willing to hear what he would say back.

'I let you talk because I liked what you were saying.'

I made a face. It hurt my lip.

'How could you have?'

'I liked it because you were standing up for my dog. I liked that. You were championing her. Same reason I let you go on when you were reading me the riot act about your sister. That's a good quality in a person. Standing up for someone who can't stand up for herself.'

'Oh.' Which was a stupid answer, but I was embarrassed, and I didn't know what else to say. Then I had to say something, so I said, 'It's Saturday.'

'It is. Thank God.'

'You don't work on Saturday.'

'I don't. Thank God.'

'If you hate your job so much, why do you do it?'

'Because I'm seven weeks short of retirement, and I can stand anything for that long. Even my job.'

'So . . . you're . . . home all day?' Obviously, I was trying to scope out what kind of day with Sophie it was going to be. I was hoping it might be less obvious to him.

'Nope. Going to see my brother and his wife across town.'

I thought it was weird, that he would tell me that. It seemed like too much information. He didn't seem like the kind of guy who would tell you where he's going. He seemed like the kind who would just say, 'Bye.' And, if you asked, maybe would remind you it was his life. Not yours.

It seemed almost like he was really happy to be going to visit his brother, and he wanted someone to know.

'Taking Rigby?' Sooner or later I had to get to that, and we both knew it.

'Nope. You're in luck. Rigby's going to wait here.'

I breathed deeply. As though I hadn't for a long time.
I think he noticed.

'Now it's my turn to stick my nose where it doesn't
belong,' he said. 'Maybe you could just get her a dog.'

'Sophie hates dogs.'

Then we both looked down at her, pressing her face
up to the fence, trying to get closer to Rigby. I knew it
must have sounded like a weird thing to say.

'Hem,' Sophie said.

'Her,' Paul said, directly to Sophie. 'Rigby is a her.'

Most people didn't talk directly to Sophie, so that
was interesting.

'Hem,' Sophie said.

That was honestly the first moment it hit me. Sophie
was saying 'him'. Really, now that I knew, it could be
'him' or 'hem' just as easy. Her pronunciation wasn't
perfect, but it was enough like 'him' that I couldn't
imagine why I hadn't gotten that on my own. Why a
stranger had to figure it out for me. Then again, as many
words as Sophie had said in her life, Paul Inverness had
heard almost as many of them as I had.

I decided that was something I didn't want to dwell
on.

'I know it doesn't make sense, what I said about her
not liking dogs. It's true, though. She just likes *your* dog.
Not dogs in general.'

Another bit of silence, and then he shook his head.
I could tell he was done with the conversation. He
wanted out.

He turned to go.

'Have fun at your brother's,' I said.

He stopped. Turned back. Gave me the strangest look. It was actually sort of . . . suspicious. Like I must have had an ulterior motive in saying it.

'Now why would you say a thing like that?'

'I . . . Oh. Um . . . I don't know. Doesn't everybody say things like that? You seemed like you were happy to go see your brother. That's all.'

'I'm not happy to go see my brother.'

'Really? Seemed like you were.'

'I have no idea why you would say that. I don't even like my brother.'

I wanted to say, Then why are you going to see him? But . . . not really, I didn't. I wanted to think it. But the conversation had taken a weird turn, and there was no way I was saying anything brave out loud.

He looked over his shoulder at me on his way to the gate. Gave me this look. Like the sudden weirdness was all my fault, and none of his own.

I made a mental note not to get into any more conversations with Paul Inverness. Any more than I absolutely had to.

I went inside to tell my mom the good news. That things were going to be easy for a while. For a few hours at least.

A few hours of peace is a lot.

Depending on what you're used to.

*

I walked to the library, even though it was almost two miles away. It's not that I didn't have money for the bus. It's that I didn't have a lot of money, ever, and if I walked, I'd get to keep having it.

It was a smaller branch than I was used to, because we were out in the suburbs now. When I stepped inside, my eyes went straight to the computer room. It had eight computers, which wasn't even half of what I was used to. But there were only two people using them. I was used to twenty computers and a line.

I walked up to the checkout counter. The woman there was only maybe in her early twenties, with hair that was blonde but with a blue streak along one side.

I showed her my library card.

'We just moved. Can I use this same card here?'

She blinked a couple of times, like easy questions were harder to answer than hard ones. Then she said, 'It's the same library system all over the county.'

'Oh. Good. Thanks.'

Not that I wanted to check out books. I loved books. But I didn't check them out. I read them for hours, and looked at pictures in them, but I didn't take them home because I didn't want them to get ruined. But I knew I needed a library card to use the computer.

I started by sitting down at the reference computer for library books. I just sat there with my hands on my knees for a couple of minutes, trying to think. It didn't really matter, because there were three terminals and nobody was waiting to use any of them.

After a while I felt like there was somebody behind

me, so I looked up and around. There was a woman standing over me, maybe forty, with long, straight hair. She had nice eyes.

'Help you find something?'

'Oh. No, thanks. I'm pretty good at using the system. I'm just trying to decide where I want to go today.'

I watched her face for a minute. She was looking at me like that was funny.

'What?' I asked.

'Nothing. I just like that. It sounded nice. Where do you usually like to go?'

'I like travel. And travel books. And I like to look up travel photography and videos on the Internet. But my favorite are big coffee-table books that tell you all about the places but also have lots of color pictures of them. Because then I learn about the place but I feel like I can see it, too. But usually libraries don't have those, because they're so expensive. I go all kinds of places, but my favorite is Tibet. So if I can't decide, I'll usually go to Tibet. I like mountains, so I also like India and Nepal and Bhutan, because they have the Himalayas, too. But I also like the Andes in South America, and the Alps. And I like Australia because of the Great Barrier Reef. Even though that's not a mountain.'

'Hmm,' she said. 'Sounds like you know exactly what you want.'

'Yes, ma'am.'

I knew what I wanted, all right. How to get it was the problem.

She walked away, and I figured she couldn't have

cared less, and that I'd told her a lot more about what I was looking for than she needed to know. I never have much to say unless I'm in a library or a bookstore, and then I say too much. I never seem to get the talking thing right.

I was thinking maybe something new, so I started searching for Norway. Maybe someplace along the fiords or something.

A minute later she came back and said, 'We don't have too much with photos on the Himalayas, but we have the Lonely Planet books for Tibet, Nepal and Bhutan.'

She'd knocked me out of my train of thought. I felt disoriented.

'Thanks,' I said, 'but I've read the Tibet one three times. And Nepal twice. Bhutan only once.'

'Read? Or looked through? Because those books . . .'

She held her hands apart, exaggerating about how thick they were.

'Yes, ma'am, I know they're big, because I read them cover to cover and I know how much reading that is.'

'Well. Wow. We could order something else from one of the other libraries.'

'Uh. No, ma'am, that's fine. I'll just go on the computer.'

It costs money every time they send a book from another branch.

'You know there's the Global Road Warrior database—'

'Yes, ma'am. I'm good at that. If I ever go to a whole new country, I'll go back to that. But I already know all the facts it has for all the countries I just talked about.'

'Hmm,' she said. 'Can I interest you in a job as a reference librarian?'

I laughed, and it hurt my lip.

'I think I might be a little young.'

She put her hand on the top of my head for a second and then walked away. The whole time I was watching her walking, I could still feel that warm print where her hand had been.

I settled in the computer room and surfed Norway for an hour, but nothing made me feel the way I wanted to feel.

While I was out walking around I passed a bookstore. New and used, both. It was called Nellie's Books, and it looked kind of nice inside. Not like the big new modern kind of store with an espresso bar. Just books.

I went inside.

The woman behind the counter looked up at me and smiled. For some reason, that smile was almost like what I'd been looking for in Norway, except that didn't make sense, because I could never travel to somebody's smile. Then again, I'd never get to Norway, either. Who was I kidding?

'Are you Nellie?' I asked. 'Or is that just a name for the store?'

Then I stood there dwelling on what a stupid thing that had been to say. Why did I even care? I didn't, I'd just felt like I had to say something. But then I didn't even know why. I thought, 'Hi' would have been good.

'In the flesh,' she said. 'What can I help you with?'

'I was wondering if you had any of those big, nice coffee-table books that are about travel.'

'Any special place?'

'Mountains are always good.'

She looked at me a little funny when I said that. I guess because most people travel to a country, not a shape of the ground.

'I had something nice in the used section about the Himalayas,' she said. 'Let me see if I still have it.'

My heart jumped. If it was used, maybe I could even get it. But it was just one of those split-second thoughts. Those books cost big money, even used. Besides, they were way too nice to bring into my house.

I followed her down a couple of aisles, watching her, but more with the corners of my eyes. So in case she looked back at me it wouldn't look like I was staring. She had hair like Sophie's, but a little browner, and her eyes were brown. I liked her nose, but I didn't really know why. I couldn't tell you one thing that was wrong with my nose, except a few freckles, but all of a sudden I wanted to trade it in for hers.

Then she stopped and took a book off the shelf and held it with the cover out, toward me. I swear my knees turned to butter. I felt like I might fall over. It had a picture on the cover that was so much like the first picture I'd ever seen of Tibet, it made my head feel foggy and far away, like this wasn't really happening. It was like the place followed me, and found me. It had the white temple with the fancy roof, the incredibly craggy and snowy mountains behind that, the smiley children in bright clothes, the prayer flags blowing in the wind. Well. It was a still picture, of course, so the prayer flags weren't blowing. Except they were, and you could tell.

Children in Tibet are always smiling in pictures. I think that might be part of how all this started.

It had the word Himalayas really big on the cover, and in smaller letters it mentioned Tibet, Nepal, Bhutan, Northern India and Northern Pakistan.

'Can I see it?' I reached my hands out. They were shaking, and I think she noticed.

I held it in my hands for a minute. It was huge and heavy. I turned it over and looked at the price sticker. Fifty-five dollars, used. But you would really never know it was used. Except for one bumped corner, it was perfect.

'Can I sit down and look at it?'

'Of course.'

She showed me to a nice stuffed-fabric easy chair. It was pretty far away from her counter, but I could see her from there, and she could see me. I sat down and slipped off my shoes and sat cross-legged in my sock feet, because I didn't want to get her chair dirty. I opened the book between my knees.

I looked up to see she was behind the counter again, reading.

I turned one page at a time, my eyes mostly drawn to the snowy mountains. I'd never seen snow in my life. Not once. But I didn't want to see it half-plowed off a

city street. I wanted to see it like that. Blowing off the
top of a high mountain, or in cornices, or settled into
the crags on those incredible peaks. I even wanted to
see an avalanche. But only from a long, safe way away,
of course.

'Are you going to go there when you're all grown up?'
She didn't even look up from her book when she asked
it.

I looked up from mine, and stared at her for a minute.

'I don't think so.'

'That's not the answer I was expecting.'

She looked up at me. I quick looked away.

'I have to stay and help my mom.'

'For ever?'

'Pretty much, yeah.'

'I hate to be a downer, but your mom won't live for
ever.'

'Oh. Then I'd *really* have to stay. Because if my mom
wasn't around to take care of Sophie, I'd have to.'

Then I kicked myself hard, and waited for her to ask
me who Sophie was and why I had to take care of her.
She never did.

I went back to turning the pages. The next one had
monks in those orange robes.

'Maybe you'll make a lot of money and can pay someone to help your mom while you travel.'

My eyes came up again. 'I like the sound of that,' I
said.

I was hoping she'd say more, but she didn't. So I
looked through the book. It was exactly where I wanted

to go that day. It was exactly where I wanted to go every day. I was already starting to feel like I didn't want to put it down. I didn't want to leave it here. What if somebody came in and bought it? I felt like it was mine. Or meant to be, anyway. It already felt really bad to think of it being someone else's.

'What draws you to the Himalayan countries?'

Her voice made me jump.

'Well. I saw this picture when I was little. It was a lot like the one on the cover of this book. It was just so different from any place I'd ever been. And everything that was different about it seemed better. I've never been in the mountains or seen snow. I don't know. Everything was just right about it. Or maybe I just liked it because it's on the other side of the world from here.' Then I sat there for a minute, wanting to erase that last sentence. I couldn't, so I decided to add more. 'Have you ever seen a Tibetan fox? It doesn't look like any other kind of fox in the world. I swear it looks like a cartoon. It doesn't look like a real fox. It looks like a talking fox character somebody would draw wearing a smoking jacket, smoking a big pipe. Its face looks very sophisticated.'

She smiled. That was good.

I plunged on.

'Did you know that half of all the different kinds of plants you can find anywhere in China are in Tibet? Four hundred kinds of rhododendrons. Not four hundred different kinds of flowers. Four hundred different kinds of *that one* flower. Over five hundred species of wild orchids. Four thousand different plants, and over thirty per cent of all the birds you can find in the whole Indian subcontinent. And four hundred different kinds of butterflies. Did you know that?'

She was looking into my face, so I looked away.

'Are you reading that off to me?'

'No, ma'am. That's not in this book. I mean, not that I've gotten to yet. I just know it.'

'Well, to answer your question, I think the only people who know that are people who work in Tibetan travel bureaus and you. And . . . please . . . I know I'm old compared to you. But I still think of "ma'am" as somebody more like my mother. Nellie. Please.'

'Nellie. Sorry. I never know who knows stuff like that and who doesn't.'

She didn't answer for a while, but she didn't go back to her book, either. She was looking out the window. It was off to her left, and I couldn't figure out if there was something out there or if she was just thinking.

Then she said, 'You know it's not what it used to be before the Chinese invaded.'

'Yeah. I know.'

'And tourism isn't helping. Well. It helps. But it hurts, too. I heard the rivers are actually flowing with garbage.'

'It doesn't matter,' I said. 'It's just a dream. I'll never get there anyway.'

I folded the book closed and started to get up.

'I'm sorry,' she said. 'Don't go.'

'It's not your fault if there's garbage in the rivers.'

'It's my fault I brought it up while you were dreaming.'

'It doesn't matter,' I said. 'I just have to go home. I can't travel and I can't afford this book and I have to go home now.'

'You could come back again and look at the rest of it.'

'Well . . . Yeah. Maybe. Maybe I will.'

I brought it up to the counter, because I couldn't remember where it was supposed to go. You should never put a book back on a shelf unless you can remember where it's supposed to go.

'I have a big inventory coming up,' she said. 'I'd let it go for four hours of hard labor.'

I set it on her counter and looked away. Out the same window she'd been looking out. There was nothing out there.

I didn't figure she really needed the help. It felt more like charity. Which . . . I mean . . . I know she meant well and all. But I didn't like the feel of it.

'That's a nice offer, ma'am. I mean, Nellie. But I can't bring that book home anyway. It would only get ruined.'

'There's no safe place in your house to keep a book?'

'Well . . . I have this metal chest that locks. But I'd have to take it out sometime, or what's the point of having it? And I'd feel too awful if it got ruined. It's too good for that. You know?'

'Want me to put it behind the counter and you can think it over?'

'Um . . .' I thought again about the way it would feel if I came in to see it and somebody else had bought it. Somebody who had lots of money, and didn't have to think twice about fifty-five dollars, and didn't have to care about the book because what it cost wasn't too much for them to waste. 'That would actually be nice. Thanks.'

'What's your name?'

I just stood there like an idiot for a minute. Because I was trying to figure out why she would even care.

Before I could sort through that, she said, 'If I'm going to hold a book for you, I have to put your name on it.'

'Oh. Right. It's Angie. Do you need my last name, too?'

'No. Just your first name and phone number will do.'

'Oh. I don't know my phone number.' Then I winced, hearing how incredibly dumb that sounded. 'We just moved in with my aunt day before yesterday. I haven't memorized the number yet.'

'That's OK. Just bring it next time you come in.'

'I will. Thanks.'

I watched her write my name in this big, loopy handwriting on a yellow sticky note. When she stuck it to the cover of the book, I thought, See? You knew that book was meant to be yours.

Except I still didn't really believe it ever would be.

Then I walked out on to the street and blinked into the light and realized I hadn't even killed two hours yet, walking included. It wasn't really true that I needed to get home. I didn't need to and I didn't want to. It was that woman. I liked her, but she made me feel like I didn't have skin. Like there was nothing to protect me from someone seeing in. Or even getting in.

I walked around for an hour, and sat in a park for

another hour. I'd say what I was thinking, but honestly, I don't know. I don't even know that I was.

When I got home, my mom and my sister were in the closet. That was never a good sign. I found them by following the sound. I could hear Sophie, but her voice was just this raspy little leftover. It would be gone soon. Which meant she'd been at it for a long time.

I opened the closet door.

My mom looked up at me. She looked kind of startled. Then her face got soft, like she was glad it was only me.

'You got the egg cartons up,' I said.

While I was away, my mom had emptied the closet in Aunt Vi's spare room, the room we were all supposed to somehow fit into, and lined the closet walls with empty egg cartons. She'd brought them all over in a cardboard box from our old soundproof closet in our old place.

'Yeah, thank God that guy next door was gone long enough that I could do that much.'

I stepped into the closet and closed the door behind us. I'm not really sure why. There was just barely room for me to sit cross-legged on the floor. My knee was up against Sophie's side, but she didn't seem to mind.

My mom was brushing the hair back from Sophie's forehead, over and over. Stroking her forehead more than anything else, I guess. Sophie doesn't really like to be touched, but sometimes when she's really tired and worn down, it seems to hypnotize her. Her face was red and sweaty. It was a little warm in the closet, so I wasn't surprised.

Her voice was so weak that my mom and I could talk right over her without straining our throats.

'Where's Aunt Vi?'

She didn't answer for a long time. Whenever my mom waits a long time to answer a question, the answer is not going to be good.

'At a motel.'

'She went to a motel?'

'I'm afraid so.'

'We chased her out of her own house?'

'I don't know what to tell you, kiddo.'

'For how long?'

'I have no idea.'

Then we just sat there for a minute. It was getting too hot, and I was about to let myself out of there.

Then she asked, 'Where'd you go today?'

Not like I had to report in. More like she wanted me to know she was interested. She always bent over backwards to make the point that she was interested in everything I did. I guess because Sophie was such an attention sponge. But really, nothing would have made me happier than if she mostly looked at Sophie and let me do what I do with no one watching. It always made me uneasy to feel like someone was watching me do the simple, weird stuff I did every day.

'Library.'

'Emailing your friends from your old school?'

'Kind of. I guess. Computer stuff. You know. Web surfing and a little bit of social stuff.'

I didn't have any friends at the old school. Not to the

level where they'd miss me after I was gone. But I didn't want my mom to know that. And I didn't want her to ever know about the traveling, because I knew it would only make her feel bad.

'That guy next door is not a nice man at all,' she said. Just out of nowhere like that.

My head came up suddenly, but she was looking down at Sophie, brushing, and she didn't see.

'You talked to him?'

'Yeah. Why?'

'You talked to him through the fence?'

'No, I went over there.'

'To say what?'

'We've got to figure out how to get Sophie spending more time with that dog.'

'We can't. There's no way. She's his dog.'

'Yeah. That's pretty much what he said. And no chance he's going to part with the dog . . .'

'You asked him to give us the dog?' I heard my own voice come up, sharp.

'No! Not give. I would have paid him. Not right away. In installments, maybe.'

Then I was on my feet, and I didn't even know how I got there.

'I can't believe you! That's his dog! That dog is his best friend! You don't ask somebody to sell you their best friend!'

'I just asked. He can say no. And he did.'

'I can't believe you even asked. What if it calmed his

dog down to be around Sophie? Would you sell him Sophie?'

Then she was on her feet, too, nose to nose with me, and Sophie was still on the floor squeaking.

'You do *not* compare your sister to a dog!'

'I'm not comparing Sophie to a dog. You know me better than that. I'm comparing that dog to a person. That dog is the only person waiting for that guy when he gets home from work every day. You think that means nothing? That's his best friend. Not a used car.'

'We're in a bind here, in case you hadn't noticed. He could at least have been nice about it.'

'I don't blame him. I wouldn't have been nice to somebody who did that to me, either.'

I blasted out of the closet. And then I couldn't quite figure out where to go.

I ended up stomping out back and lying on the lounge chair on the back grass. The breeze was cool, and I could feel it drying the sweat on my face. I thought about that closet and got claustrophobia, but in this weird belated way. Like my whole life felt like that soundproof closet. Too close and too hot. No way to really spread your elbows or stretch out your legs.

After a while my mom stuck her head out the back door and said, 'I wish you wouldn't be mad at me.'

'Could you just give me a little time?'

That's a problem with my mom. She hates for anyone to be mad at her. Especially me. So she wants me to get over it in about a second. Or even just say I'm over it.

But I need more time. Stuff gets tangled up in me, and I have to let it unwind gradually. It doesn't help to rush it.

She must have gone in then, because I never heard another word from her after that.

I fell asleep for a while without meaning to. And that's just . . . I can't tell you how weird that is for me. I never take naps in the day. Half the time I don't even sleep much at night, and maybe that's part of the problem.

I opened my eyes.

The sun was almost down. And my mom was sitting on the lounge chair next to my hip. Watching me sleep.

'You still mad at me?'

She looked sad. And maybe even a little scared.

'How can I be? I'm asleep. I can't be mad in my sleep.'

She smiled, but without really losing the sad look. She had her long hair in one of those loose braids that looked nice on her. Little wisps had come out of the braid and were falling around her face, but even that looked nice.

She started stroking my forehead, the way she'd done with Sophie. Except I didn't have much hair to move out of the way.

'Where's Sophie? You didn't leave her in the closet by herself.'

'Of course not. You know I wouldn't do that. She's asleep. I put her to bed.'

'Awful early. I wonder if she'll sleep through the night.'

'Oh, God. Here's hoping.'

Silence for a while. I let her keep stroking because it felt nice.

Then she said, 'I hate it when you're mad at me.'

'I know you do. But sometimes people just have to get mad. I mean, that's his dog, for God's sake.'

She clapped a hand over my mouth, but gently.

'Don't get yourself started again.'

I rolled my eyes, and she took the hand back again.

'You know I meant well,' she said.

'I know. I know you're just trying to get us a place we won't get kicked right out of again.'

'It seems kind of stupid, though. What I did. Even to me. I mean, in retrospect. I swear it seemed like a good idea at the time, but now I can't remember why. For the life of me I can't remember how I talked myself into thinking it was good thinking.'

'It's only been a couple of days. How do you know Sophie won't hate the dog tomorrow?'

'Sophie? Lose interest in something? I mean, if she was ever interested in it to begin with?'

'Well. That's a point.'

'I was thinking of seeing if we can find a black Great Dane. Do you think she'd notice the difference if it had regular ears?'

'I think she'd notice the difference if it was a litter mate. I think she'd notice the difference if you had that dog cloned. It's not about what the dog looks like. It's something on the inside of the dog she likes.'

'That doesn't sound like Sophie.'

'Take my word for it. I've been watching them.'

'I feel like a complete idiot sometimes.'

'I feel like that a couple of times a day.'

'I mean around *you*, though. Sometimes I feel like you know more than I do. Like when we disagree about something, you usually turn out to be right. I feel like you're more mature than I am. And it scares me.'

'I'm not more mature than anybody,' I said.

Even though I knew it wasn't true. There might be a lot of things I hadn't figured out how to be yet, but mature wasn't one of them. I was feeling uneasy with this line of conversation. I had never said it out loud to her . . . not yet . . . but I knew exactly what she meant. And it scared me, too.

In fact, I think it scared me more.

After she went inside, I sat up on the edge of the lounge chair for a long time. It was getting near dark, but for some reason I wasn't moving. It was like I just couldn't motivate myself to do anything but that.

Finally a movement caught my eye, and I looked up to see Rigby staring at me through the fence, swinging her tail. Like if she just wagged long enough and patiently enough she could dissolve the fence and walk right over and say hi. I smiled a little, without really meaning to.

I almost wanted not to look up and see Paul standing there behind her. I felt, for a minute, like I could avoid it.

But then I heard him say, 'Oh, come on, Rig. Do what you came out here to do.'

I looked up. Locked into all that disapproval.

I sighed. Got up. Walked to the fence. Put my fingers through for Rigby to snuffle.

'I'm sorry about my mom,' I said.

It didn't get quite the reaction I was hoping for.

He stood even straighter, like his shoulders were turning into something harder than shoulder material. Concrete or granite. His brow furrowed down.

'Here's the thing about your little family,' he said. 'I don't want any part of any of it. Here's what I want: I want to be left alone. I want quiet. I want peace. I want my life to be as uncomplicated as possible. You seem like a pretty nice kid. The rest of that gang over there, I'm not so sure about. But that's not my point. My point is, it's complicated over on your side of the fence. I want simple. I want calm. If you bring me any part of your life, then my life gets complicated, too. Get what I'm saying?'

'Pretty much, yeah.'

'I just want to be left alone.'

'I get that part.'

'You, yes. I believe you do. And I believe you'll leave me alone if I ask you to. But you can't make your sister quiet.'

'No, sir. I don't think anything could make my sister quiet.'

'You can't make your mom mind her own business.'

'Well . . . I'm not sure if that's true.' I looked up from Rigby's sweet face and into Paul's not-so-sweet one. It was just barely light enough to see his expression. 'I did yell at her quite a bit for it.'

He stood there, quiet, for a minute. I watched his face change. Not a huge change. Just a little. It went from set-like-a-rock to . . . almost . . . curious.

'And she took that from you?'

'More or less. Mostly. She did get mad at one thing I said. I said, "What if he came over here and told you Sophie kept his dog nice and calm? Would you sell him Sophie?" She got mad and said I was comparing my sister to a dog. But I wasn't. I was comparing your dog to somebody's sister. Anyway, she hates it when I'm mad at her. So she really might not do it again.'

'You really said all that to her?'

'I did.'

He had this look in his eyes. Just for a second. Almost like . . . like he looked up to me or something. I know that sounds crazy. But just for a flicker of a second it was there. Then he plastered over it again.

'I actually like the way you look at things. But . . .'

'You just want to be left alone.'

'Yes.'

'Fine. I can do that.'

'I know you think I'm the grumpiest old man on the planet. Most people do. I'm really not. Or anyway, I'm not trying to be. I just . . .'

'Want to be left alone.'

'Yes.'

'Fine,' I said. 'No problem.'

He turned back toward his house. I watched him walk up on to his back stoop. It seemed like some kind of fake retreat, because he wasn't going to go back in without the dog. Or at least, I didn't think he would. I guess he could, but he was more likely to stay out until she'd done what she'd come out there to do. All she'd done so far was wag at me through the fence.

'She means well,' I said.

He turned back sharply.

'Who? Your mother or your sister?'

'Both, I guess. But I meant my mom. She's trying to be a good person. You know? She's doing her best.'

A long pause.

Then he said, 'The road to hell is paved with good intentions.'

'I don't know what that even means.'

'It means people like her do a lot of damage while they're trying to be nice.'

'And people like you do a lot of damage while you're *not* trying to be nice.'

My brain tingled, waiting to hear what he'd say. I wasn't used to insulting grown-ups. But this grown-up seemed different. I felt almost like I couldn't miss with him. The ruder I got, the more he admired me.

'Not a bad point,' he said. 'But . . .'

'You just want to be left alone.'

'Yes.'

Then he went inside. Without the dog.

That was the last conversation I had with Paul Inverness for three weeks. If anyone had asked me at the time, I'd have said it would be my last conversation with him ever. In my whole life, both before and since, I don't think I've ever fallen quite so far away from being right.

Chapter Three

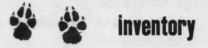 **inventory**

Three weeks later to the day – three weeks of a new school and being way behind in my schoolwork – a Saturday again, I heard someone knock on the door.

Aunt Vi was long back from her motel stay, but still in bed. My mom was out in the backyard, watching Sophie while she waited silently in the grass, by the fence, for Hem to make her appearance.

I answered it.

Standing on the porch was Paul Inverness.

He was wearing jeans and a gray sweatshirt. He hadn't shaved. His one-day growth of beard was snow white. His eyes looked exactly the same color of gray as his sweatshirt.

'Thought you wanted to be left alone,' I said.

'I knew you'd say that. But I have a business proposal for you.'

I laughed, one little short burst. It came out almost like spitting.

'You want to go into business with me? I'm fourteen.'

'I want to offer you a small job.'

I felt my eyes narrow down. 'Doing what?'

'Dog walking.'

'Oh. You want me to walk Rigby?'

'Just for a few weeks. My sciatica is flaring up again. I've been seeing the chiropractor, but it takes a while before he can offer much relief. This is the worst it's ever been. It hurts right down to my heel. Every day I've had that dog I've walked her two miles. Unless I walked her more. I never missed a day. Not one day. Not a holiday. Not a sick day. And now I missed both yesterday and the day before. It's not fair to her.'

It sounded like a speech he'd rehearsed a few times. Which, if it was true, made the inside of Paul Inverness more like the inside of me than I could bear to imagine.

'So . . . every day?'

'Yes. Just for a few weeks.'

'How much?'

'What do you think is a fair price?'

'I have no idea. I don't know what dog walkers get. Make me an offer.'

'Well. It should take you about half an hour. So how about . . . ten dollars?'

My eyes opened wider. I could feel it. I tried for more of a poker face. I don't think it worked.

'Ten dollars.'

'Yes.'

'Per . . . ?'

'Day. Per walk.'

That was twenty dollars an hour, basically.

I stuck my hand out, fast. To shake on it. Before he wised up and realized he'd bid too high. Before he changed his mind. His hand felt soft, like it looked. Like he'd never done hard labor. But kind of strong, too. And dry.

'I wouldn't let just anybody walk my dog,' he said, before he stepped down off the porch. 'I probably used to think I would never trust *anybody* with my dog. But I like your attitude toward her.'

I couldn't think what to say to that. But it didn't really matter. Before I could even open my mouth, he was halfway back to his own yard, and too far away to hear.

I found my mom out in the backyard, and told her about my new job.

'Oh, honey,' she said. 'Oh, my God. That's fabulous. We need that money so much. Seventy dollars a week! That's such a big help.'

Then we went silent, and looked at each other. And we both let that settle in. I absorbed the fact that she thought that money was for the family, while I watched her adjust to the idea that I'd thought it would be mine.

'Oh, I know, honey. It's not really fair to you, but we need it. I'll even pay you back. I swear. I'll keep a record of every cent and pay you back when things are better.'

When things are better. In my family, that was code for never. I didn't say so out loud.

'You don't have to pay me back. I'm part of this family.'

But my voice sounded heavy and sick, like I'd just bounced off a very high cliff and landed in a pile of depression. Well . . . there was no 'like' about it. That's exactly what it was.

'Oh, honey, I'm sorry. It's just that—'

'I don't get to keep any of it? Even a little?'

'That's a good point. You should keep a little.'

Then I waited, barely breathing, while she decided my little.

'You keep the money for the first walk every week. How's that?'

Wow, I thought. That's a little, all right.

'Fine,' I said. And turned to walk away.

'Angie, don't leave mad.'

I stopped and turned around. 'I'm not mad.'

'You look mad.'

'I'm not mad. I just have to go walk the dog.'

'Come in,' Paul said, and stepped back from the doorway. 'Come right in.'

That was the last thing in the world I expected him to say. I expected him to hand me out the leash with the door half closed so I couldn't even see inside.

I stepped into his living room. I tried to take in the room without being too obvious about looking around. Rigby sat by my left side, and I stroked the back of her neck, from that big bone of her skull down to her collar.

It definitely looked like a man's living room. There

were no colors. The rug was gray, the huge flat-screen TV was black, the leather couch and recliner were black. It was uncomplicated, just like he said. There was nothing lying around on any surface. No magazines. No mail. No cups or glasses.

A big bookcase covered one whole wall, but it wasn't even completely full. He used it to display vases and statues and art in frames in lots of places that weren't filled up with books. There was a picture of a woman on that bookcase. A pretty, dark-haired woman with a long, straight nose. I figured maybe he used to have a wife, but she died. Or left. Or something.

No, died. She must have died. Because Sophie's father left, and my mother took down all his pictures. But when my dad died, they stayed up.

I'd never lived in a house without clutter. It seemed almost too amazing to be true. First I wondered if he'd scraped it all off into a box, because he knew I was coming. But then I knew it hadn't happened that way. He lived like this. The house was like its owner. Just what it needed to be and no more.

'This is nice of you,' he said. 'Especially since I wasn't very pleasant the last time we talked.'

'You weren't very pleasant any of the times we talked.'

He laughed. I was surprised. Even knowing him as much as I did. Which I guess wasn't much. But still.

'Then it's even nicer of you.'

'I'm not being nice. We need the money.'

A silence fell, and I didn't know why.

'We? You don't get to keep it for yourself?'

'Well, both,' I said. But it was too late. I'd already cut my eyes away from him, so he knew I was ashamed. I'd let something get away, something I'd meant to keep. 'I'll have some for me and give some to help the family.'

'That's a lot of responsibility for a girl your age.'

'It's always been like that,' I said.

Which wasn't entirely true. It wasn't like that when my dad was alive. And before Sophie was born. But I wasn't going to say anything about that to him. And besides, that was like another life. Like I'd died and been reincarnated as this.

'It's only for four weeks, you know.'

I laughed a little. 'You already know the date your . . . whatever-you-said-you-had . . . is going to get better?'

'No. In four weeks I retire.'

'So? That gives you even more time to walk the dog.'

'No, I'll be moving,' he said. Almost like I should've known. Like he found it curious that it didn't show or something.

The news felt like a cold knife sticking between my ribs. When I tried to pull in a deep breath, I could feel the point of it, wedged in there.

'Where are you going?' I asked, trying to sound as natural as possible.

'I'm going to go live up in the mountains, in this little town in the Sierra Nevadas. Not too far from Lake Kehoe. My brother has a vacation home up there. I'm trading him this house for it.'

'Oh,' I said. Still pretty shocked. I hadn't even realized it completely, but we'd been living in a bubble of relative

silence and peace. For us, almost happiness. Not that I
hadn't known it had been silent. That was impossible
to miss. I hadn't known it was a bubble. Now I knew.
And now I knew exactly when it would burst. 'I love the
mountains. That'll be nice for you.'

'Here, let me show you how to put this on.'

He held up a leather slip-collar with a brown-leather
leash. Rigby stood up and wagged her whole body,
smacking me in the butt with her tail. It felt like getting
lashed with a bullwhip. Well, like I imagined that would
feel. Nobody had ever lashed me with a bullwhip.

'Ow!'

'Oh, and watch out for the tail.'

'Thanks for the warning.'

'She'll walk on your left. So you slip it on this way.'
He showed me the direction. With the heavy ring and
the clip of the leash coming over the top of her neck
toward me and then down. 'That way gravity will keep
it loose and open so long as she keeps the leash slack.'

'She's a big dog. What do I do if she pulls me?'

'She won't pull you.'

'Oh.'

I took hold of the leash, and took a couple of steps,
and the minute I did, she got up from her sit and caught
up with me in one step. I stopped, and she sat down by
my left heel again.

'See? She knows what to do. You know that little park
with the fountain?'

'Sure.'

I walked by it on my way to the library, every time.

'That's a mile. So just around the fountain and back.'

'OK.'

Rigby and I headed for the door.

'Your sister's been quiet,' he said.

I stopped. Rigby sat.

'Yeah. She has.'

'I thought nothing and nobody could make her do that.'

I looked over my shoulder at him. 'Nothing and nobody did. She's doing it on her own. She used to get really upset when Rigby went inside, but then the dog kept coming back out again. So it's like Sophie got it that she'll be back. So now she just sits by the fence and waits and doesn't say a word. She falls asleep out there and then we carry her in.'

'She doesn't go to any kind of school or therapy?'

'Now that's a long story.'

'Never mind, then. Forget I asked.'

'She did. In the old neighborhood. When we lived downtown. Like a special preschool program. Now we have to decide when to put her in first grade. We have to find a good school and enroll her. I think my mom might wait a year.'

'Got it.'

'She's not going to be very happy when you move.'

'No,' he said. 'I don't expect she will.'

I could tell by the way he said it that it wasn't his problem, and he knew it.

It would definitely be mine.

*

Not twenty steps out the door, I made a huge mistake.

I crossed the street.

It seemed like a simple enough thing to do. But then I heard Sophie yelling from our backyard.

'Hem!' she yelled. 'Hem, Hem, Hem! Heeeeeem!'

I whipped around, and I could see her through the fence. Which was fine. The bad news was, she could see me. And the dog. I kept walking. Quickened my step, in fact.

Three more 'Hem's, and then the third one morphed into the siren scream.

I walked back to the fence. What else could I do?

Except now I was totally stuck.

By the time I got there, both my mom and Aunt Vi were out in the yard, bickering.

I heard Aunt Vi say, 'I thought she was done with this. You told me she was done with this.'

And my mom said, 'She stopped, OK? She stopped. Please. Just go back in the house, Vi. I'll take care of it.'

I waited by the gate until I heard the kitchen door slam. Then my mom came out to where Sophie and Rigby and I stood on opposite sides of the fence.

She looked scared. It's always scary when even your mom is scared.

'She saw you.'

'Guess so.'

'Why doesn't she do that every morning when that man walks him?'

'Her. No idea. I guess maybe they don't cross the street. I think she only saw us because I crossed the street.'

Her eyes came up to mine again, and again I caught that panic, and it jolted me right down to my gut.

'What are we going to do now?' she asked.

'I don't know, Mom. I have to take the dog for a walk. It's my job.'

She sighed. 'I guess I'll just scoop her up and we'll go in the closet. And by the time you get back, Vi'll be at a motel again. But there's nothing else we can do. Oh, dear God, don't let this be the day she asks us to leave.'

'No. Open the gate.'

Silence.

'Open the gate?'

'Yeah. Try it. Open the gate.'

'And then what?'

'Then I walk away down the street, and we'll see what she does.'

'She'll follow you.'

'That's what I'm thinking. Right.'

'You sure you can handle her on the street?'

'No. You sure you can handle her here?'

Another long, panicky silence.

'What if she runs out into traffic or something?'

'I'm thinking she'll stay close to Rigby, but anyway, let's just try it. You know. In the driveway. Or right in front of the house.'

I swear I could hear her next breath. She opened the gate.

Sophie trotted around to my left side, to the outside of where Rigby was sitting politely by my heel. She dropped to her knees, folded her legs under her, and propped up on straight arms. Made herself into the same sort of triangle as the dog.

I took a few steps down the driveway, Rigby heeling. It seemed to surprise Sophie, and she got off to a late start. She had to stumble to her feet and run to catch up. By the time she did, I'd stopped again, and she dropped into the same sit, in the same position, to the left of the dog.

I looked over my shoulder at my mom.

'We're going,' I said. 'Wish me luck.'

She didn't. She didn't say a word. She had this look on her face like she couldn't have said a word if she tried.

'Mom. Do something. Go inside and tell Aunt Vi everything's OK.'

She stood frozen for another moment. Then she raised two crossed fingers and hurried away. Like she couldn't bear to see what came next.

Sophie scuttled along to keep up, looking bizarrely un-coordinated. I guess I wasn't used to it, because I wasn't used to seeing her walk any distance in a semi-straight line, with purpose.

I found myself looking at her a lot. Part of the time because I was worried about her, but part of the time because she was fun to look at. She was wearing a tee-shirt, her pink skirt over thick black tights, and sneakers that were blinding white except for the grass stains on the toes. My mom had put her hair into two big curly pigtails. Her legs were long and skinny and cute.

Whenever I passed somebody, they'd either give me

a little nod, or not look at me at all. Or sometimes they smiled at me. Then their eyes would go down to Rigby, and usually they'd jump a little. Like she was a grizzly bear or something. Or sometimes they smiled at her. But every single person I passed broke into a smile when they looked at Sophie.

I started thinking maybe I should take her every day.

Then I realized this was about five times more exercise than she was used to, and I got worried for the long run. What if she got tired, and couldn't walk home? Could I carry her that far? Would she even let me?

Then again, if she could go the distance . . . man, would she ever be nice and tired for the rest of the day. Maybe for every day. That could only be good. Right?

If. And if not, I was out there alone.

I tried to pull myself back into the moment. Because the short run was going fine.

I stopped at each corner and waited for the light to turn, or, if it was just a four-way stop, for cars to go through and leave us a big space to cross. Rigby sat and patiently waited. Sophie sat and patiently waited. Then Rigby and I stepped into the street, and Sophie came scrambling after. She never did get the hang of taking off when we did. Just of catching up pretty fast.

Of course, I looked over my shoulder for her constantly. But she was always doing the same thing. And if there was one thing I could always tell you about my sister Sophie . . . once she fell into a rut of doing the same thing, she just kept doing that same thing.

After a while my mind even drifted off a bit. Then

I'd jerk it back, thinking I'd already caused some kind of major disaster by letting my attention slip. I'd quick look back. And there she'd be, just rambling along, slightly behind us. It was kind of nice. I mean, not nice as in, it wasn't a total freaking disaster. Nice, as in . . . nicer than it would have been without her along.

All of a sudden I looked forward again, and realized I was almost at Nellie's Book Store. It made my heart pound to see it there in the middle of the block, but I wasn't sure why. I hadn't been back there to look at the book. Not even to give Nellie my phone number. Probably she'd put the book back in stock by now. Maybe she'd even sold it. Thinking that made the bottom of my stomach feel kind of sick and disgusting. But it was probably true. It was probably gone.

I had to decide if I was going to hurry by and hope she wouldn't notice, or if I'd stick my head in and ask if she still had it. I could give her a ten-dollar deposit on it later in the day. If she still had it.

That decided me.

I stuck my head in the door, my heart pounding so hard I could hear and feel it in my ears, both. It was making me a little dizzy.

It took her a minute to look up. She was looking down at the counter – probably reading – and chewing on a long twist of black licorice. I stared at the side of her face for a while, and then when she saw I was there, I quick looked away.

'There you are,' she said.

'Yes. Here I am.'

'I thought you might not come back.'

Me, too. I didn't say so.

'Well. I've been busy. You know. Starting in the new school and all. Trying to catch up. Anyway, later today I'll have ten dollars and I'll come back and put a deposit on that book. If you still have it. Do you still have it?'

Her face just completely fell. That made me feel like crap. For two reasons. Because it meant she'd probably sold it. And because I liked to make her smile. Not . . . whatever she was doing right then.

'You don't want to do the inventory, huh? I guess I don't blame you.'

I checked on Sophie. She was right where she was supposed to be.

'Oh. I didn't think you really wanted me to.'

'What gave you that idea?'

'I don't know. I figured you just felt sorry for me because I couldn't afford it.'

'Is there a reason why only your head is inside?'

'Yes, ma'am. Nellie. I have a big dog with me.'

'You see any signs that say "No Dogs Allowed"?'

'No, ma'am. Nellie. Are they? Allowed?'

'If they're polite dogs.'

'She's the most polite dog ever.'

'Bring her in, then.'

I took about ten steps, and then all three of us were standing on the rug in front of her counter. Well, actually, that's not right. I was standing. Sophie and Rigby sat.

Nellie stood up and leaned over the counter. I could

smell her hair. It smelled like fruit. Like some kind of shampoo with coconut or mangoes or both.

'And who's this?'

'This is Sophie.'

'Oh, *this* is the Sophie you were telling me about. Is Sophie your little sister?'

'Yes, ma'am. I mean, yes, Nellie. Or, actually . . . I guess . . . just yes. I don't know why I keep doing that.'

'Me, neither. Hello, Sophie.'

'Um. Don't take this personally. But she won't say anything. She doesn't even say hello to *me*.'

'Does she say *anything*? Ever?'

'She says "him". But it sounds sort of like she's saying "Hem". It's what she calls the dog. She really loves the dog.'

'That makes sense.'

'Not really. It's a girl dog.'

'And that's the only word? Ever?'

'Well, not ever. When she was little, she started to talk. Kind of late. Like three. And not much. Just a few words. And then we kept waiting for her to talk more, but instead she started talking less. And then she stopped making eye contact. And then she didn't want to be touched . . .'

I trailed off, suddenly wondering what the hell I was doing. I'd been so grateful that Nellie hadn't asked me about Sophie. And now here she was pulling the truth out of me when I wasn't even looking. Or maybe I was doing it to myself.

I think she could tell I wanted to change the subject.

'Licorice?' she asked.

She held out a big plastic tub of black licorice twists. I was happy for the distraction.

'Sure. Thanks.'

'Does Sophie like licorice?'

'Sophie loves licorice.'

I took a piece for Sophie first. Sophie reached her arm up, wanting, impatient, but she didn't move out of her sit. Because Rigby didn't.

I handed her the licorice, and she immediately handed it off to the dog.

'No! Don't give it to . . .'

I tried to dive for it, but it was too late. I even opened Rigby's mouth and looked in. It was already gone. She must've practically swallowed it whole. And then there I was sticking my face in the mouth of this dog I barely knew, and her teeth were unbelievably huge, and I felt like a lion tamer, but with a lot less experience. But she just wagged her tail at me.

'Damn it, Sophie. I don't know if the dog is supposed to have that.'

'I don't think it'll hurt her,' Nellie said.

Which was perfectly good thinking if it had been my dog. But Rigby wasn't my dog. I was responsible for her. But there was nothing I could do now. Except tell Paul the truth.

I changed the subject fast.

'So, you seriously have this inventory you want somebody to help you with? What do you need to do?'

Nellie put her face into her hands and sighed.

'I'm embarrassed to tell you. Because I don't want you to know how stupid I am. I want you to think I'm a better businesswoman than this.'

That seemed weird but also incredibly cool. That she would want to put her best foot forward for me. Not just the other way around. But I didn't say so. I didn't say anything.

'You know I sell both new and used. And when I buy from a distributor, I have a record of that. And when I send returns, I have a record. But then I started offering a twenty per cent discount for customers who sell back their books. But, like an idiot, I didn't set up a record-keeping system for those books. So now it's hard to find if I have a book or not.'

'But you keep them in alphabetical order by author, right?'

'I do. And then the customers come in and browse and put them back *out* of alphabetical order. And by now I've probably spent a hundred hours re-alphabetizing, trying to save myself maybe ten hours of inventory work. Thing is, I need two people. I need somebody to read me off the titles while I sit at the computer. Cathy says she will, but she doesn't really have the hours. If you could at least get me started . . .'

'If you really need the help. I didn't think you really needed the help.'

'I really need the help. You have no idea.'

'When?'

'Tomorrow?'

'Aren't you closed on Sundays?'

'Yes, and that's the point. No customers. No ringing phones. How about eleven? Eleven to three.'

'OK.'

'Oh, my God,' she said. 'I'm saved.' She looked down at Rigby. 'I love your dog. What a sweetheart.'

'She's actually not mine. I'm just walking her for my neighbor.'

'Oh. I thought . . . Because you said Sophie was so attached to her . . .'

We both looked down at Sophie, waiting in absolute silence, with absolute patience, on the rug.

'Yeah. It's weird. It's kind of a weird situation. Sophie is in love with the dog next door.'

'Hmm,' she said. 'How does that work?'

I thought again about Paul Inverness and his news.

'That's what we're waiting to find out,' I said.

Sophie made it all the way to the park and back on her own steam. But then, when we got home, I realized this was the tricky bit, right at the end. I couldn't put her in the yard and then walk away with the dog. She'd bring down the whole neighborhood again. I'd have to take her to Paul's door with me. Even though I wasn't sure if she would scream when he took the dog back inside. She hadn't been screaming any more when Rigby went into the house, but that was from across the fence. Now that she was used to being right beside the dog . . .

It was time to see how much of a monster I'd just created.

We all three stepped up on to his porch, and I knocked.

The door swung wide, and Paul looked down at all three of us. Rigby wagged hard, whipping Sophie with her tail, but Sophie didn't make a sound. Didn't even flinch.

Without a word, he reached into his back pocket and took out his wallet. Peered in and pulled out two five-dollar bills.

'I have to tell you something,' I said.

His head came up fast.

'Rigby got a piece of licorice. I really hope that's not bad for her. It was an accident. I promise I'll be more careful next time. If you let there be a next time. But I understand if you don't trust me with her now.'

I waited. It felt like a long wait. I wanted to look at his face, but I couldn't bring myself to do it.

'Actually . . . I trust you more now.'

My eyes came up to his and then I quick looked away again.

'How? Why?'

'Because you told me. You didn't have to tell me. Now I know you'll tell me the truth even if you don't have to. Even if I would never know.'

'I hope it's not bad for her. Is it bad for her?'

'She'll be fine.'

He handed me the two bills, took the leash back, and led his dog inside. Then he closed the door.

I winced, and waited.

Nothing.

I looked down at Sophie. She was still in the same sit. In the same spot.

What would she do when I walked home? Would she try to stay on the neighbor's porch for ever? Would we have to wrap her up and drag her kicking and screaming home?

I took three or four steps, then looked over my shoulder. Sophie was rambling after me. Not quite as fast as she had when Rigby was with me. Not quite as anxious to catch up. But she was following.

I opened Aunt Vi's gate, and she tumbled past me into the yard and took her usual spot by the fence. Crouched down in the grass and waited for the next time she'd see Hem.

My mom was in the kitchen, her face over a steaming cup of tea. Like it was a facial, not a drink. Her head snapped up when she saw me there.

'It's fine,' I said. 'It went fine.'

'Where is she?'

'Right where she always is.'

I watched all the tension drain out of her face. Well, not all of it. The extra tension. I watched her slip all the way back down to baseline tension. Which was bad enough.

Instead of looking relieved without it, she just looked tired.

'So . . . tomorrow . . .' she began. Like a question, when you don't dare ask it.

'She can come with me again tomorrow.'

'Really?'

'Sure. She was fine. She was good.'

'Oh, my God. That would be great.'

She took a big gulp of tea, and then seemed to drift away in her head. Like she was following that great thing to Great Thing Land.

'Where's Aunt Vi?'

'Napping.'

'She does that a lot.'

'Well . . .' she said. And then her face twisted into something like a smile. 'She hasn't been the same since Charlie died.'

This little snort of a laugh burst out of me. My mom quick put a finger to her lips to stop me. I sat down at the table, and we looked at each other, and then the laugh burst out again – out of both of us – and we had to swallow the noise of it.

Oh, I know. It sounds terrible. It wasn't funny that Charlie died. We didn't mean it like that. It was just that Vi said that so much. It was just funny to hear somebody else say it. Well, no it wasn't. It probably wasn't funny at all. I think it was just our way of letting off a little of that tension.

My mom looked up at me, and she had a look on her face I hadn't seen for a long time.

'I feel hopeful,' she said. 'I don't even remember the last time I felt hopeful.'

I thought, I can't tell her. I just can't. I have to let her have the hope for a little while longer.

I got up from the table and went into my room. Well.

Everybody's room. And I sat on the bed. And I thought, No, that's wrong. That doesn't work. Then she's just stuck in that place she calls a fool's paradise. And that's not the same as hope. That's pathetic.

I went back to the kitchen, my heart feeling like it was down somewhere in my large intestine. I sat down at the table with her, and she picked up the bad news right away.

'What? What is it? Just say it. Hurry.'

'He's moving.'

I could hear her swallow.

'The guy with the dog?'

'Yes.'

'He's moving?'

'Yes.'

'When?'

'In four weeks.'

A long silence. Long, long, long. And ugly. Like if you took our whole lives for the past few years and strained out everything we wished had never happened, what you'd get left behind in the strainer would feel just like that silence. Really that bad.

'What are we going to do?' she asked.

I said, 'You ask me that a lot.'

I didn't say, I wish you would stop. I didn't say, You're forty. I'm fourteen. If you can't figure it out, it's hardly fair to hand it off to me. But I'm sure a little of what I didn't say came through all the same.

*

'*The Bell Jar,*' I called out. 'Sylvia Plath.'

'I have a copy of *The Bell Jar*?'

Nellie's voice sounded soft and far away. I peeked around the end of the shelf for about the hundredth time. She wasn't smiling, and I was trying to figure out how to get her to. But it's hard to make book titles sound funny.

'You do.'

'Are you sure?'

'I have my hand on it.'

'I honestly didn't know that.'

'I honestly think that's why we're doing this.'

Bingo. She smiled. And looked up and caught me looking. I disappeared my head again.

'You know we're never going to make it through four hours of this,' she said.

'I'll make it.'

'I won't. I'll die of boredom.'

'How long have we been doing it?'

'An hour and fifty minutes.'

'I don't think that's long enough.'

'I'm dying of boredom.'

'Well,' I said. 'I don't want you to die.'

'I'm ordering a pizza.'

I stepped out from behind the stacks and looked at her straight on. She already had the phone at her ear.

'And then we finish?'

'How about two more hours next Sunday? Wait . . .' She held one finger up in my direction. 'Hi. A large . . . Yes, delivered . . . Nellie's Books . . . Wait. I know what

I want on it, but I have to see what my friend wants . . . Yes, I'll hold. Angie. What do you like on your pizza?'

'Um. I don't know. Anything, I guess.'

'OK. Anchovies, pineapple and jalapeño peppers it is.'

Then she looked at my face and burst out laughing. I wondered what she'd just seen there. I could only imagine.

'I'm kidding. I'm a vegetarian. So I'm having mushrooms, green peppers and olives. You want pepperoni on your half?'

'No, I'll have it the way you're having it. But if we finish next Sunday, won't they be back out of order by then?'

'We can't finish today, anyway. It's a lot more than four hours' work. I'll just have to put them . . . hello? Yes. Mushroom, bell pepper and olive. Large, yeah. And make it double cheese. OK, thanks.' She flipped the phone closed. 'Twenty minutes.'

'Should we work till it gets here?'

'No way.'

'You'll die of boredom.'

'Correct.'

Then I knew why Nellie hadn't done the inventory in all this time. Why I saved her by saying I'd show up and call out the titles. Because, left on her own, she would never do it. She would just keep knowing she should. She didn't want to do the inventory at all. She just wanted it to be done. And those are two very different things.

I started feeling like, if it was ever going to get done, I had to be the one pushing it. And suddenly it seemed very important that it get done.

She reached under the counter and pulled out my big book on the Himalayas. Held it out with the cover facing me, like she had the first time. It melted me. Just like before.

'Sit,' she said. 'Read.'

I took it in my hands. And yes, my hands shook a little this time, too. But it wasn't just the book, or the picture on the book. Well, I don't know what it was. A lot of different things, I think.

I slipped off my shoes and sat cross-legged, like last time. But I left the book closed, and just stared at the cover. All of a sudden I was in Tibet, but not by myself. All of a sudden it was Nellie, too, walking alongside the row of prayer wheels, and reaching her hand out to spin them around. Always spinning to the left, never to the right. And I was walking behind her. Also spinning. And it was like a different country than it had been before, when I was alone. Alone is a whole different thing. And every time I'd traveled in my head, I'd always been alone.

This time, when I saw Annapurna rising up in the distance, spindrifts of snow blowing off its peak, I put my hand on her shoulder to get her attention, and pointed. Like, to say, You have to see this, too, Nellie, but I'm too overcome with the sight to speak. And then she squeezed my hand . . . which was still on her shoulder . . . because Annapurna was so beautiful. Because it was too beautiful for words.

'Can I ask you a personal question?'

It jolted me so hard, the book almost ended up on the floor. I'd forgotten she was there. Well, there in the bookstore. I'd been so busy thinking of her there in Tibet.

My heart pounded until it felt like it was about to break loose. I wanted to ask, How personal?

'Um. I don't know. I guess.'

'Are you being abused at home?'

'Abused? What do you mean? Abused how?'

'Hit?'

'No. I don't get hit. Why did you ask that?'

'It didn't escape my eagle-like powers of observation that the first time you came in here you had a fat lip. With just a butterfly bandage on it. When it probably could have used a couple of stitches.'

My heart slowed down. Some.

'It healed, though,' I said. I touched the scar. It wasn't really healed healed. Just scabbed over. 'And my tooth was loose, but now it's tightening up on its own. No, I'm not being abused at home. Sophie did that. But not on purpose.'

'Oh. Sophie.'

'Yeah. And that's completely different. Right?'

'Well. It is and it isn't. It's still just as bad a situation for you. It still hurts.'

I looked back down at the book. Opened it up. Turned pages I hadn't read. Looked at pages I didn't see.

'I didn't mean to make you uncomfortable.'

'It's OK.'

But it wasn't, really. I hated moments like this. And

yet, underneath all that hating, I liked the fact that she wanted to protect me. It was almost like . . . it was almost as good as Nellie giving my hand a squeeze.

'How are things at the new school?' she asked.

I had moved the book off on to the rug, pretty far away. So I wouldn't get any grease from the melted cheese on it. I was still staring at the cover.

'Mff,' I said, because my mouth was full.

'Sorry.'

I chewed and swallowed as fast as I could, but it was hot.

'Sort of surprisingly OK.'

'Kids aren't giving you a hard time?'

'No. Why would they?'

'I don't know. They always did with me. My dad was in the military, and we moved around a lot, so I was always the new kid. And the other kids were hard on me. Maybe it was just me.'

'Maybe they were smaller schools,' I said. 'This is such a big school. I swear to God nobody even knows I'm there. I mean, the teachers have me on their attendance sheets and all. But it's like . . . it's like everybody looks right through me.'

Then I went quiet, and decided Nellie had made me do that thing again, where I tell her more than I meant to say. I bit off about a quarter of my slice of pizza in one bite.

'You know, kiddo . . . you don't really always have to stay and help your mom.'

I didn't answer, because my mouth was too full.

'When you have a kid, there's this huge responsibility. There's not much getting out of it. If it goes wrong, you're in it all the same. But you didn't have a kid.'

I swallowed hard. Twice. That still left some pizza to talk around.

'Who would help her if I didn't?'

'I know this sounds terrible . . . and it may be hard for you to understand from where you're sitting . . . but I don't think that's your problem.'

'I can't just leave. Sophie's father just left. He just sort of wandered off when he figured out it was going to be hard.'

'I don't think that's your problem, either. I'm not sure you can make up for other people's letdowns with other people.'

'She couldn't take care of Sophie alone. Nobody could.'

'Well, then how will you do it? When you're both much older? Like, after your mom's gone?'

I took another huge bite of pizza. The edge of the crust scratched the roof of my mouth while I chewed.

She said, 'You want to talk about something else, don't you?'

I nodded. Hard.

'OK. Sorry. What?'

I swallowed with great effort.

'I want to talk about how pathetic you are about just buckling down and doing this damn inventory. And how I'm ever going to get you to get it done.'

'Hmm. That is a problem. I can do two hours at a time. Maybe.'

'Try an hour and fifty minutes.'

'Close enough.'

'So, next week at the same time?'

'Yeah. That's fine. But after you're not here to help, no promises.'

'I'll be here to help. I'll be here to help every Sunday till it's done. Otherwise it'll never get done.'

'In return for what? You've only got two hours due on the book.'

'I don't know. Pizza. Anything. We'll figure it out.'

I levered to my feet.

'No, I'll pay you. You have to let me pay you. You want to take this leftover half a pizza home?'

'Yeah. Sure. Thanks.'

When I went up to the counter to get it, I found her staring right into my face. I knew she was going to ask something important. And that I wouldn't like it.

'If you were ever really needing help, Angie . . . if you were ever in over your head . . . would you tell me? Or somebody?'

I picked up the pizza box and shifted back and forth on my feet a couple of times.

'No,' I said.

'No,' she said. 'I didn't think so.'

Chapter Four

 **Crushed**

On moving day – Paul's, not ours – I woke up and stumbled into the living room to see my mom peeking out through the curtains.

I ignored her and plowed into the kitchen.

Aunt Vi was nowhere around. Sophie wasn't there, either, but I knew where to find her if I wanted to. I wasn't looking for Sophie or Aunt Vi. I was looking for breakfast.

Nothing looked like breakfast in that kitchen. I seemed to have been the first person to have even had the thought.

I grabbed some cold cereal. I rummaged around in the fridge for milk. There was none.

I just sighed. What else could I do?

I looked out at my mom, who was still peeking through a mostly closed curtain. I wanted to tell her it was making me nervous. But I didn't. What would've been the point of that?

When I couldn't stand it any more, I carried my cold cereal over to the window and yanked the curtain back, which made my mom jump back out of the way. I wanted to tell her she missed her true calling as a private detective, but then I decided that would have been mean.

There was a huge moving truck in Paul's driveway, with the name of a rental company on the side. And a painting of a mountain. Like they already knew where he wanted to go, before he even rented it. It had a tow bar on the back for his car.

'He sure didn't waste any time,' my mom said.

'I never thought he would. He can't wait to get out of here.'

I stared down into my cereal bowl. My stomach was growly, so I ate a handful dry.

'Oh, my God,' she whispered. 'He's coming this way!'

I looked up to see Paul crossing the lawns.

'So?'

'He's coming to the door. What do we do?'

'Um . . . Open it?'

'I don't want to see that man. I don't want to talk to him.'

'Fine. I'll open it.'

I walked over to the door, and, while I did, I looked once over my shoulder and watched my mother disappear. I wondered what she was so afraid of. But not for long. It really doesn't pay to spend too much time wondering what other people are afraid of. Everybody's always afraid of something, it never makes much sense, and wondering never gets you anywhere.

I opened the door while Paul was still coming up the walk.

'Good morning,' he said, and I thought he sounded unusually cheerful.

Also, he was dressed nicely again. With a new-looking light-blue shirt and navy slacks with a crease. And when he got closer, he smelled nice. Like that one other time. He never smelled nice on a day off, or on his way to work. Only on his way to his brother's house, that one other Saturday.

I said, 'Thought you'd be gone before the sun was up.'

'So did I,' he said. 'I'm four hours behind schedule.'

'You need some help packing or something?'

By that time he'd gotten up to the door, and, when I said that, he actually took one step back. Like he was that surprised.

'Well, that's a very nice thing to offer. But no, we can handle the packing.'

I was curious who 'we' was, but I didn't ask. Just waited.

'I just wondered if I could talk you into one last dog walk. I thought I'd have time to take her myself, but it's not going well. I don't want to skip it, because it's such a long drive. She'll be cooped up in the cab of that truck for six or seven hours.'

'Sure. No problem.'

He looked down at my cereal bowl.

'Wait until you're done with breakfast, though.'

'No, I can come now.'

'Your cereal will get soggy.'

I held the bowl out farther for him to see.

'Not with no milk on it, it won't. That's the only nice part about being out of milk.'

He laughed, but just a little bit.

'Bring it over. I've got milk.'

I shrugged and stepped outside, pulling the door closed behind me. Just as I did, I looked back into the house. My mom was peeking out at us from the hall. She'd wedged herself into a spot where I could see her but Paul couldn't.

I gave her a little frown as I shut the door.

While we were cutting across the lawns, I wondered if it seemed weird to her that Paul and I talked like we were friends. Like any two regular adult friends. That's when I realized it seemed weird to me. And that I'd never noticed it before. Or at least, I'd never stopped to think about it.

'Last ten bucks for the road,' he said, knocking me out of my train of thought.

'No, it's OK. This one's on me.'

'You don't have to do that.'

'It's fine. I don't mind. I'm going to miss that big old girl when you go.'

'Not half as much as your sister will, I'll bet.'

I frowned without meaning to. 'We don't talk about that at my house.'

'Oh. Sorry.'

'You don't need to be. There's plenty to be sorry about at my house, but none of it is your fault.'

He smiled a little as he opened his front door for me. But it was a sad smile. And I wondered if he really knew me enough to be sad for me, or if I just reminded him of something he was sad about on his own. That's what it is with most people. More about them and less about you.

If it was really for me, it made me uncomfortable.

Rigby greeted me with kisses. Actual face kisses. Which she had never done before. I wondered if she was smart enough to know she was leaving.

When I looked up from that, there was a woman standing there. In Paul's house. A woman.

'Oh,' I said. Lame, but I was surprised.

I knew her, but I didn't know from where.

'Hello,' she said.

Just that. Just hello.

I thought she had the tiniest trace of an accent, but unless she talked more, I'd never figure out what it was.

'This is Rachel,' Paul said. 'My sister-in-law. Rachel, this is Angie. From next door. She's going to walk the dog while we pack.'

'I'm very happy to meet you,' Rachel said.

She was about Paul's age, but pretty. Thin, with dark hair and eyes and a long, straight nose. And I'd seen her before.

'I know you,' I said. 'We met already. Right? I mean . . . didn't we?'

That's when it hit me. Just kind of all at once like that.

I turned my head to the bookcase. But the picture was gone. But that's who it was. It was the woman from the picture on Paul's bookcase. The one I'd figured must be dead. But I'd figured wrong, because she was standing right in front of me.

The weird thing was, nothing else on the bookcase was packed yet. But that picture, the only picture of an actual human being, was gone.

Paul stepped into my line of sight, and his face looked tight. It almost seemed like he was trying to catch my eye. I couldn't make any sense of any of it, but it made me want to shut up. Fast.

'I guess I'm wrong,' I said. 'I guess you must just remind me of somebody.'

I looked back at Paul, who looked relieved.

I had no idea what to do with any of that. It made me curious. But it was like a ball of tangled rope, and I couldn't begin untangling it until I could find the ends. So I just gave up and put the whole mess away for later.

'Where's Dan?' Paul asked her.

'In the bedroom closet. Packing your suits.'

'He's wasting his time. I'm going to burn my suits.'

'No, save them,' she said. 'In case somebody dies.'

Paul smiled, like that was funny. Only it was too much smile for not enough funny. And I decided her accent was European, probably German or something like that, but faded. Just a dull leftover.

I was about to grab for Rigby's leash when Paul said, 'Milk.'

'Oh. Right. Milk.'

He sat me down at the kitchen table and put a carton of milk in front of me. And got me a spoon from a kitchen drawer.

And I thought, Boy, he really is behind in his packing if the spoons are still in the kitchen drawer.

Then I just sat there and ate my cereal, with Rigby's head on my knee. Which involved a lot of leaning down on her part, which made her look like a vulture.

I looked out in the living room, and watched Paul and Rachel walk back and forth in front of the doorway. And I knew there was something there to know, but I didn't know it. That bothered me some. But like just about everything that bothered me, there wasn't a damn thing I could do to sort it out.

I didn't take Sophie. I kept pushing myself to, but I just couldn't be pushed. There was this giant pushback in my gut that I couldn't quite explain. I finally decided it would be best for Sophie not to let her anywhere near Paul's house to see the packing.

I didn't really know what Sophie did and didn't understand, like I said. But she'd sure had a lot of experience with the people around her packing.

I think that was probably a bullshit excuse, though. I think I was being selfish. I really was going to miss that great big angel of a dog, and I think I wanted her all to myself this one last time.

So I stayed close to the houses on our side of the street, where Sophie wouldn't see us go.

I walked along with my hand on Rigby's huge

shoulder blades, feeling them shift and then shift back as she took her slow giant steps. I felt sadder than seemed reasonable.

'Wish you didn't have to go,' I told her.

She looked into my face like she wanted to answer. Funny, but for a split second I almost thought she would.

Then she looked where she was going again.

'And not just because of Sophie,' I added.

It's always best to like people for more than just what they can do for you. I guess I was counting Rigby as people by then.

I was pretty sure anybody who knew that dog would do the same.

When I took her back, Paul stepped out on to the stoop and took the end of the leash from me. He seemed to be a little awkward and sad in the goodbye, too, even though I knew he was really happy to leave that city and his job for ever.

'Could you do me a favor?' I asked him. 'When you back your moving truck out of the driveway, could you go that way?' I pointed down the street away from Aunt Vi's house. 'I'm not sure what's going to happen if Sophie sees you and Rigby go by. I know it's going to hit the fan sooner or later. It's just . . .'

Then I ran out of words for what it just was.

'Of course,' he said. 'That's no problem. Are you sure you don't want that last ten dollars?'

'No, it's OK. This one was my going-away present.

Just be happy in the new place, OK? I'm jealous, you know. Going up to the mountains. I'd love to live up there so much. Anyway, you probably don't care about that. Just be happy, OK?'

I really meant that sincerely, and I think he could tell. I didn't know Paul very well back then. But I knew he wasn't happy. It really didn't take much knowing him to figure that out. Here he was turning sixty-five and retiring, and if he didn't find happy now, when was he going to find it? This was like his final season.

He put one hand down right on the crown of my head and just left it there. It surprised me. It was almost like something affectionate. Like your mom or dad would do.

'You're a good kid,' he said. 'Don't let anyone tell you otherwise.' Then he looked at his hand on my head like he'd only just noticed where it was. He took it back again. 'Well, that's a stupid thing to say, I guess. Nobody's going to tell you you're not. I guess what I mean is, be careful not to tell *yourself* otherwise.'

I could see his point, how that was trickier. But I didn't quite know how to put it into words. So I just stood there like an idiot and said nothing at all.

Rigby was still sitting by my left heel. Even though Paul had her leash, she hadn't gone to him yet. I think she knew this was an ending. I know dogs aren't supposed to know stuff like that. But it seemed like she did.

After too much quiet, Paul said, 'You may see us again. If we come back here for a visit.' On the word 'here' he pointed over his shoulder into the house.

Which now belonged to his brother and the woman in the picture.

'You don't even like your brother,' I said. But I said it quietly, so no one in the house could hear. Maybe his brother didn't know Paul didn't like him. Paul wouldn't be the first person to ever keep a thing like that to himself.

He cracked just a little bit of a smile. On one side of his mouth only. 'Too true,' he said. 'But . . .'

Then he just trailed off.

And I wanted to finish the 'but' for him. I swear I almost did. I almost said, But you like Rachel a lot. I stopped myself just in time. What the hell kind of thing is that to say to someone who's practically a stranger?

But then I thought, If we're strangers, why are we saying goodbye like we're friends?

I stepped away, and when I was on the last stone stair, I said, 'Drive safe.'

As I was crossing his lawn, I looked over my shoulder at him. He was still just standing there on the porch.

He raised one hand. Just held it still in a wave that didn't move.

I waved back. With actual waving.

'You can't go,' my mom said. 'How can you go?'

It was the following morning, and I was on my way out the door to help Nellie with the inventory. Might've been the last inventory day. Then again, with Nellie you could never tell.

I was going. That bookstore was the only thing in my

whole miserable life that I actually looked forward to. I didn't say so, of course.

What I did say was, 'I'm going.'

'This might be the day your sister falls apart.'

'Yeah. It might be. Or it might be a week from Tuesday.'

'I might need help with her.'

'Help how? Help to do what? If she screams, two of us can't stop her any better than one of us. You just want me to stay here and help you worry. You've got to stop hovering over her, worrying. She's going to pick up on your stress, and that's only going to make it worse.'

'See? That's exactly why I need you.'

'Oh, my God!' I said. Actually raising my voice. 'You're *my* mother, not the other way around!'

That fell hard. Nobody said a thing for an uncomfortable time. Actually, my mom never did.

'Look. I love that damn bookstore, and I'm going. Good luck with her here. I'll help when I get back. If you need any.'

I tried not to look at her on my way out the door, because that pouty lip thing was damned irritating. Even *I* didn't do that. I mean, not even when I was six.

Then again, it all just sort of stressed my point.

I was working with a bookshelf between me and Nellie, which made things easier. I loved talking to her. But face to face it was a little too . . . intense. Or something. So this was easier.

'What would you think about a guy who only has

one picture of a person in his whole house, and it turns out it's a picture of his brother's wife?'

I was holding a hardcover novel in my hand, but not reading off the title yet. Nellie didn't care. The less we inventoried, the happier she was.

'What would I think of it?'

'Yeah. What would you think?'

'I'd think it was a little weird.'

'But what would you think it meant?'

'Was it a picture of a bunch of people doing something interesting?'

'Nope. Just a posed picture of this woman.'

'I'd think his own wife or girlfriend or whatever would be right pissed.'

'He's not married. He lives alone except for a dog.'

'Then I'd think he was having an affair with his brother's wife.'

'I don't think so. Because when she came to visit, he took the picture down. So if they were having an affair, she'd know how he feels. He wouldn't have to hide it.'

'The very fact that she'd come to visit him without her husband seems to bolster my theory.'

'Oh, no. Her husband – this guy's brother – he came, too.'

'Then maybe that's who he was hiding the picture from.'

'Maybe,' I said.

But I didn't believe it. I didn't think that's how it was. Paul's life seemed too sad and empty for that. He seemed more like the kind of guy who would just sit in a corner by himself and feel what he felt and not act on it. Then again, what did I know? There could have been all kinds of things I didn't know about those two. I'm just saying how it felt.

I read off the title of the novel, and she read it back to me, which was sort of her way of saying, 'Check.'

'It just seems weird to me. How there are these people who are alone, and they act like they're alone by choice, like all they want is to be alone. And I believe them, because why wouldn't I believe them? And then it turns out they don't want it that way at all. Nobody tells the truth. Haven't you noticed that?'

'Yeah, I might've noticed that,' she said. Then there was a pause, like she was waiting for me to read off another title. When I didn't, she said, 'Is this an actual person, or are you doing that "my friend has a problem" thing?'

'No, he's real. Not exactly a friend. Well. Sort of a friend. I guess. Do you think it's weird that I only have two people who are even sort of like friends, who I even talk to at all like you'd talk to a friend, and they're not kids? One is sixty-five and the other is your age.'

'You don't know how old I am, so how do you know?'

'Well. She's you. You're your age. Right?'

'I never talk about my age, so I'm not saying.'

Nobody said anything for a time, so I stuck my head out, and she was looking right at me. I took my head back again. I always felt like a turtle when I was doing inventory with Nellie.

'Don't joke your way out of answering my question, though. Is it weird?'

I heard her sigh. 'You must know you're bizarrely mature for your age. Very little about your brain seems even remotely fourteen. You know that, right?'

I walked out from behind the shelves and sat in the big stuffed chair. Picked at a frayed spot on the cuff of my jeans.

'I think it's because my mom acts sort of younger than me in some ways. But I'm not really sure it's true, what you said. I mean, I feel fourteen enough. But I don't have anything in common with anyone my age, and everybody says what you're saying, so it must be true.'

I just sat there picking for another minute or so. Then I looked up suddenly and wondered what I was doing.

'What the hell? I didn't even mean to sit down. We have inventory to do.'

I scrambled up again.

Nellie said, 'It'll hold. You want to talk, talk.'

'No. I don't want to talk. I hate talking. I want to get this done for you.'

I found my way back to the spot where I'd left off. I always left the last book sticking out a little, so I wouldn't lose my place. I pulled out the next book and held it in my hand.

It was *The Tibetan Book of the Dead*.

My heart nearly stopped.

'Oh, shit,' I might've said. Or maybe I just thought it.

'What's wrong?'

'Oh. Nothing.' So I hadn't just thought it. 'Nothing. *The Tibetan Book of the Dead*. This one doesn't exactly have an author. Just a translator. Can you use that as an author?'

She never answered the question. She just asked, 'Have you read that one?'

I let out a little laugh that sounded more like a fast sigh. 'No. I haven't read that one. I know what it's about, but I haven't read it.'

'Is it about what it sounds like it's about?'

'Pretty much, yeah. Understanding what happens when somebody dies.'

'Since it's part of Tibetan culture, I'm surprised you didn't read it cover to cover seven times at the library.'

'Not sure I want to read this one.'

'Want to take it home and decide? I owe you lots of books and money for all this work. It's yours if you want it.'

I couldn't answer the question. I literally couldn't. I just stood there with the book in my hand and couldn't say a word.

Finally I walked out from between the shelves. Still carrying the *Dead* book. Walked right up to her counter without ever looking at her. I was still looking at the cover.

'Have you lost someone you were close to?' she asked.

I was trying to decide whether or not to tell her when her head snapped up and she smiled.

'Oh, look,' she said. 'Cathy's here.'

I looked, too.

She'd mentioned somebody named Cathy once, and I'd filed it away in there somewhere, but I hadn't thought too much about who it was. I actually thought she had an employee I hadn't met yet.

Cathy walked in, grinning. I didn't think she was an employee. It was Sunday. And besides, no one's that happy about getting to work.

She looked Asian, or maybe half-Asian, and her hair was no longer than mine. She was a little bit older than Nellie. Old enough to have laugh lines at the corner of her mouth and eyes.

Meanwhile Nellie was introducing us, but all I was doing was staring.

Cathy walked right around behind the counter, like she owned the place just as much as Nellie, and slid one arm around Nellie's waist. Then she kissed her on the cheek.

I took one long step back.

Then they both looked at me, I guess because I stepped back. I accidentally dropped *The Tibetan Book of the Dead*. I reached down fast to pick it up and banged my head hard on Nellie's counter. Hard enough that I saw these little bursts of light. It was the first time I ever understood that thing about seeing stars.

I heard Nellie say, 'Ow. You OK, kiddo?' But it sounded far away.

I tried again for the book, and when I had it, I set it on the counter. But I shouldn't have straightened up so fast, because it made me dizzy.

'You OK?' Cathy asked. She looked kind of . . . puzzled.

'I need to use your bathroom,' I said.

Then I just dove off in that direction as fast as I could go.

I was just opening the door to the back room when I heard Cathy say, 'That was weird. What was that all about?'

I couldn't hear what Nellie said back. It was a mumble.

'Young homophobe-in-training?' Cathy asked. She had a loudish voice. It carried.

But then Nellie spoke up more, and said, 'That's just about the dumbest thing you ever said to me. Is your gaydar in the repair shop or something? She has a little crush on me, that's what that was about. Use your head.'

By that time I was hanging on to one of the book-shelves. Like I would fall over if I didn't. Which wasn't out of the question. I could feel my heart hammering. And I hated it. I was so tired of it. I would have traded my life away in one of those heartbeats, because I was so tired of feeling.

Cathy said, 'If I'd known that, I wouldn't have been leaving you two alone so much.'

Nellie sounded mad then. She said, 'Don't even joke about it, Cathy. It's not funny at all. She's fourteen.'

'Oh. I'm sorry,' Cathy said. 'I didn't know she was that young. She seems older.'

'Yeah, we were just talking about that. You know, we shouldn't be . . . I have to check. We shouldn't be talking about her like this. I have to make sure she's where she can't hear us.'

The deeper she got into that thought, the more I could hear she was coming closer. But I couldn't move. I was completely frozen. I didn't have time to get into the back room, and I couldn't have anyway. Even if I'd had time. I didn't even have time to will myself to die on the spot. Which I definitely would have. If she hadn't shown up when she did.

I looked up, and there she was at the end of the shelves. Looking right at me.

'Angie,' she said.

I let go of the shelf. Stood on my own. I wouldn't look at her. I looked down at the pattern on the carpet.

She didn't move and neither did I.

Then all of a sudden I got unstuck. I walked right at her. Like I was going to bowl her down. I couldn't even open my mouth to say, Excuse me, or Get the hell out of my way. But she seemed to get the idea that she'd better.

I could feel my shoulder slam into her as I passed her in that small space. I could tell it knocked her off balance. But I just kept going. Didn't look back. Didn't look up at Cathy as I walked by. I'd rather have jumped into a pit of scorpions. I just kept looking at the carpet until I was free.

When I got out on the sidewalk, the light was too bright. It cut through my eyes and my brain like a knife.

I heard her call my name again one more time.

'Angie!'

I broke into a run.

'Angie, wait up!'
I didn't.
I ran all the way home.

I could see Aunt Vi's house at the end of the block, and I was still running. I had a stitch in my chest, and my lungs ached. I could have stopped. There was no real reason not to. I told myself that. But I wasn't stopping.

Maybe I wanted to hurt.

That was when I heard Sophie. Her siren wail. And just for a second I thought, Oh, shit. If I can hear her from the end of the block, that's bad. That's worse than bad. That's a freaking disaster.

Then it hit me that the sound was coming from behind me.

I stopped, and turned around, crouching a little to lean the heels of my hands on my knees. So I wouldn't fall right over. Just trying to halfway get my breath back. I lifted my head as much as I could.

My mom pulled up behind me in our old station wagon, Sophie screaming in the back seat. And . . . get this . . . pulling a trailer. It wasn't one of those open trailers that people usually rent when they're moving. It was the kind that looked like a horse trailer, except no open places for a horse to look out, and barely big enough for a pony. It spelled moving all right. There was nothing else it could mean.

I squeezed my eyes closed.

At first I tried to resist it. Like, No, this can't be happening. Not everything at once like this. Then I hit that place where things are so bad that you don't fight any more. Where you just go belly up and sink to the bottom. Where you're beyond even trying to save yourself.

I just folded up.

'Get in,' my mom said.

She'd leaned over and rolled down the passenger-side window. The car was so old it didn't even have power windows. The shrieking got way louder.

I didn't move. Couldn't, I think.

But then a neighbor we didn't know came out on the porch to see what the awful noise was.

'Hurry,' my mom said.

So I got myself to move.

I plunked into the seat, still trying to breathe. Rolled up the window as she pulled away.

I thought we were going back to Aunt Vi's, which was only a few houses down from where she picked me up. But she drove right by.

'Where are we going?' I asked.

'What happened to your head?' she asked, almost at the same time.

We were both shouting to be heard over the Sophie siren.

Then we both just waited. Like the other one would answer.

'Where are we going?' I asked again.

'You first.'

I'm not sure why I let her win that one. I just had no fight left at all.

'Does it look bad? It's probably not as bad as it looks. I just hit my head reaching down for a book.'

'Why were you running?'

'I just felt like running. It's your turn. Where are we going?'

'We're moving.'

'I sensed that. But why aren't we going to Aunt Vi's for our stuff?'

'I've got our stuff.'

'How could you possibly? I was only gone for . . .'

'Two and a half hours.'

'How could you get a trailer and pack up all our stuff so fast?'

It was making my throat scratchy to have to talk so loud.

'Because, in case you hadn't noticed, it's not much stuff.'

'I can't stand this. I need my earplugs.'

'I'm sorry. They're packed.'

'I need to find them.'

'Kiddo, they're packed. I threw everything in boxes and trash bags and threw them all in the trailer. How are you ever going to find something that small?'

Something snapped in me. Something that was stretched way too tight in the first place. I put my hands over my ears and dropped my head down and pressed my knees in against both hands, and just held my head as tight as I could.

It was still loud.

I could feel us making right turns. One after the

other after the other. It took a good five or ten minutes before I could know for a fact that all we were doing was driving around in a circle.

Then it took me another fifteen or twenty minutes to be completely worn down by the pointlessness of the whole thing.

I picked up my head.

'If you're just going to circle the block, could you let me out at Aunt Vi's? I gave her a pair of earplugs. Maybe she still has them.'

'I don't know if we're welcome there, kiddo.'

'I'm only talking about me. Not all of us. Besides, I want to check and make sure you didn't forget any of my stuff.'

'There's not a damn thing left in that bedroom.'

'Did you get my best jacket out of the hall closet?'

'Um . . .'

'Great. Good job, Mom.'

'OK. Fine. I'll drop you back.'

A few minutes later she pulled up in front of Aunt Vi's, and I jumped out, and she took off again. I barely had time to close the door.

I stood on the curb and watched her drive away, and realized I had no idea when she was coming back for me. But that wasn't the scary part. The scary part was, I didn't care. It flashed through my mind what it would be like not to be tied down by either one of them. Sounds terrible, but I thought it. Sure, I was only fourteen. It would be hard to make it on my own. But . . . harder than this? How could anything be harder than this? I felt like I put more into the arrangement than I got out of it. But I pushed the thought away again.

They were my family, like it or not.

I knocked on Aunt Vi's door. Just in case I really wasn't welcome there. When nobody answered, I let myself in with my key.

I found Aunt Vi in the bedroom, in bed, in her faded housecoat. Under the covers, but not asleep. She looked up at me like everything that had ever broken her heart was right in front of her eyes.

'I'm really sorry for all this,' I said.

She smiled that sad smile. 'I'm sorrier for you. You can never get away from it like I can. You can't just say, "That's all I can take."'

That sank in hard. Because I was right there. Right at that point. It really was all I could take. But she was right. I couldn't just say it. She could draw a line. I couldn't.

'What happened? How did she find out the dog was gone?'

'The door opened next door, and somebody she'd never seen came out. A woman. And no dog. It was right after you left. She just fell apart. I've never seen her like that. And I thought I'd seen her at her worst.'

'I'm not sure any of us have seen her at her worst,' I said.

Then I wished I hadn't said it. It was one of those things that was right there to say all along. But it took a really bad day to put me so far off my game that I forgot to avoid it.

'You just missed your friend.'

'What friend?'

'That nice lady from the bookstore. She left a little package for you.'

That hit me like a baseball bat made of ice. So I guess I was kidding myself, thinking I was all the way at the bottom and not even trying to save myself.

'How did she know where I lived?'

'She called, and I told her. We thought you'd be home by the time she got here, but you just missed her. The package is by the door. Where will you all go, dear?'

I made an exasperated sound. It was a wild question to ask me at a time like that. Why did people ask me questions like that, like I was the brains of the outfit? Why didn't I just get to be a kid?

'I have no . . . freaking idea.' I almost said something stronger. Not out of anger at her. More as a way of insulting the situation itself. But I reined it in just in time. 'OK. Look, I'm sorry for everything. I'm just going to look around and see if my mom forgot any of my stuff. And . . . remember those earplugs I gave you? Do you still have them?'

She half sat up. Like she could only think when her brain was upright. 'I think they're in the bathroom cabinet. But you wouldn't want them once I'd had them in my ears. Would you?'

'I'm kind of desperate.'

'Well . . . go look.'

I made my way into her bathroom. My own reflection in the mirror floored me. I had a huge purple knot on my forehead, and my eyes looked like I'd just been through a war. I quick opened the cupboard door. Found the earplugs immediately. I knew that color of blue anywhere.

'Thanks,' I said on my way back through her room. I dropped the key on her bedside table.

Then I went into our old bedroom.

I felt around under the bed. Sure enough, my little locked trunk was still under there. So . . . only the most important things I owned. A doll and two books my dad had given me. One of his old shirts. My Himalayas coffee-table book. A ring that used to belong to Grandma.

I stuck my hand under the mattress and felt around until I got my fingers on the key. Stuffed it deep in my pocket.

'Great job of packing me, Mom,' I said out loud, to no one.

I carried the trunk out to the front door. Grabbed my best jacket out of the hall closet.

On the little wood table by the door was the bag. It was a plain paper bag stamped with the Nellie's Books logo and address. I threw the jacket over my arm and carried it all outside.

My mom was nowhere to be seen.

I sat on the stoop, feeling exposed. Like Nellie was about to swoop back down and want to talk to me or something. I hated talking. Hated it so much. Why did everybody always want to talk about stuff that was better left alone?

I unlocked the trunk. I was going to throw the bag in without opening it and lock it all up again. But I just had to peek into the bag. I couldn't stop myself.

Inside was *The Tibetan Book of the Dead*. Which made me even more nervous. Now that it was mine. And a sealed envelope.

I got this weird, dizzy feeling, like I was in some kind of time warp. How had so many people gotten so much done so fast? How could we go from living here to not living here while I was at Nellie's? How could she put all this together and get my address and drop it by while I was running home? Or . . . well . . . while we were driving around in circles, I guess.

It's like we weren't all traveling at the same speed.

I couldn't decide if I could bear to open the note or not. I felt equally strongly about seeing and not seeing what was inside. Then I decided I'd better look now, before my mom showed up again. It would be too late to change my mind for God only knows how long.

I tore it open. Inside was a hundred-dollar bill, with a printed receipt wrapped around it that said, 'Back pay for inventory work.' And then there was a long hand-written note. Which – now that I was looking at it – I was absolutely sure I didn't want to read.

I just looked at the first line. Kind of squinted at it. I swear I'm not making this up – I read it with my eyes half shut. Like I could see it and not see it at the same time. I just saw, 'Angie, I'm so sorry. I never meant to embarrass—'

I quick shoved it back in the envelope. Before I died

of embarrassment. The only thing more embarrassing than what I'd just been through would be somebody pointing out how embarrassing it was.

For a minute I wondered if there was something wrong with everybody else in the whole world. Or if it was me.

My mom turned the corner at the end of the block, and I shoved the money deep down into my jeans pocket. Then I threw the book and the note in my little trunk and locked it again.

I could hear, as they pulled up, that Sophie's voice was getting broken and scratched. But she was still giving it all she had.

I softened up the earplugs and got them in just in time.

I put the jacket and the trunk in the back section of the wagon and got in beside my mom.

She said something, but I didn't make it out.

'What? I have my earplugs in.'

'I said, "Oh, the trunk."' Much louder.

'Yeah. Oh, the trunk. Just the most important things I own.'

'Sorry.'

'You shouldn't have packed me. I should have been able to pack my own stuff.'

'I told you not to go.'

It hit me then that she was right. I shouldn't have gone. I'd known it all along. But it was something I hadn't been willing to give up.

'You're right. I'm sorry.'

We drove without talking for a while. Sophie's voice

was beginning to crack. Everybody only has just so much voice. Even my sister.

My mom was still going around in a circle. Which seemed so insane that I barely felt able to speak to it.

Finally, when I couldn't stand any more, I said, 'Where are we going?'

'No idea.'

'Can't we just park somewhere?'

'I can't think of any place far enough away from people that no one will call the police. I'm just going to keep moving till she stops.'

'Then what?'

'You're asking too many questions. I need time to think.'

'Sorry.'

It was the middle of the afternoon. But all of a sudden I woke up, even though I had no idea I'd fallen asleep. The car was parked in front of Aunt Vi's house. Sophie was fast asleep in the back seat. My mother was nowhere around.

I closed my eyes again.

I felt a little better, because I figured she'd gone in to talk to Aunt Vi. Maybe they'd even work it out. Maybe we could stay here, at least for the night.

I don't know how long my eyes were closed, but when I opened them, I saw my mom in the side-view mirror. She was standing on the porch of what used to be Paul Inverness's house.

She was talking to Rachel.

'What the hell?' I said. But quietly, so I wouldn't wake up Sophie. That was hard to do once she'd worn herself down. But I wasn't taking any chances.

I jumped when the car door slammed. I looked over at my mom.

'What was that all about?'

She didn't answer. Just started up the car and drove. I had to think how much I wanted to push for answers. On a day like that one, did I really want to keep hurrying the bad news?

We didn't go in a circle this time. We got on the freeway.

'So . . .' I said, kind of testing. 'Now can I ask where we're going?'

'Yes,' she said. 'Now you may ask. We're going to a lovely little town in the mountains. And we'll start over there. If it's as small as I think it is, maybe we can even rent a place that's out of earshot from the neighbors.'

'The mountains,' I said. Hardly daring to believe it.

'It'll be nice up there. You'll see.'

That's when it hit me that my mother had no idea how much I loved the mountains. I'd really kept my inside life that much of a secret.

'What mountains? Where?'

'The Sierra Nevada mountains. Up near Lake Kehoe.'

It took a minute to settle in. It fell into my brain like the pieces of a puzzle. Some assembly required.

When it hit me, I yelled so loud it's a miracle Sophie didn't wake up.

'Oh, my God!'

'Keep your voice down!'

'You wouldn't! You can't! You can't be serious! He worked his whole life so he could have some peace and quiet up there!'

'He doesn't own the town.'

'How can you think this'll work? You think you'll just happen to find a place for rent on the other side of a fence from his dog? This is crazy!'

'We can at least try.'

'I can't believe you would do this. He'll die when he sees us.'

'You got a better idea?'

It always boiled down to that. Accept my mom's very bad ideas or think of better ones on my own. Always those two terrible choices.

Neither one is any way to grow up.

At least, not in my opinion.

I kept my eyes closed for most of the ride out of town. I would have bet money I'd never manage to sleep, but then all of a sudden my eyes opened, and we were out in the middle of nowhere. It was dark, and raining hard. And we weren't moving.

My mom had her arms draped over the steering wheel, her forehead down on her arms.

I watched her for a minute, trying to shake myself awake. I watched the rain battering the windshield, huge drops that exploded into smaller drops on contact. The sky lit up with lightning, and I could see the actual webs of lightning on the horizon, the way they arced down through the sky.

I looked over the seat at Sophie, but she was still asleep.

When the thunder came, it made my mom jump.

'Oh, you're awake,' she said.

'Yeah. What are we doing?'

'Not much.'

'Couldn't you see to drive?'

'I could see. It's not that.'

I could have asked, What is it, then? But that's a pretty obvious question. Once you've told somebody, 'It's not that,' you should be prepared to cough up the second half of the story. They shouldn't have to ask.

After a time, she said, 'Maybe this is insane.'

'Oh, it's definitely insane.'

Then she didn't say anything for a long time and neither did I.

Finally I got tired of waiting. So I said, 'What else could we do? If we didn't do that?'

She laughed in a way that had nothing to do with any kind of funny.

'Well, there you have the problem. That's how I always get to insane decisions and irrational behavior. No backup plans.'

'How far did we drive already?'

'More than halfway.'

The lightning electrified everything again, and my mom winced, bracing for the thunder. But it was a dud compared to that last time.

'Maybe . . .' she said.

And I already knew something bad was coming. And what it most likely was.

I felt like maybe the Earth really was flat, and I'd sailed right off the edge without knowing it. It felt like falling. Like nothing was going to stop this fall. I'd been feeling that way since the bookstore. No bottom yet.

'Maybe what?'

'Maybe we have to think about some things we took off the table a long time ago. And . . . you know. Maybe . . . put them back on the table again.'

I couldn't feel much of a reaction inside my gut because there wasn't much room for things to get worse.

'I can't believe you would do that. I can't believe you would even say it. You promised. We both promised.'

'We've got our backs up against the wall here, kiddo. In case you hadn't noticed.'

'It doesn't matter. It's a promise. You keep a promise no matter what. You don't keep a promise until it gets hard. What about me? What about if I make your life hard? Am I out the door, too?'

'That is *so* not fair,' she said, her voice seething with this hurt anger. 'This is not the same and you know it.'

'Why isn't it? We're both your daughters. That's either for ever or it's not. That's either no-matter-what or it's not.'

Another flash of lightning.

She wouldn't answer me. Sometimes when my mom was really upset she'd lose her words completely. I never knew if she couldn't find them at all, or if she just didn't like the ones she could find.

'OK,' I said. 'It's not completely the same. I'm sorry. But we did make a promise.'

'So what's your plan?'

I hated to think that way, but I had a flash of a thought that she'd done that whole thing on purpose. That the talk of sending Sophie away was just a ruse to dump the next move off on to me. I pushed it down again. It might have been true. But it wasn't helping.

I said, 'Maybe we could go to that little town where Paul lives. But there would have to be some rules. I don't want you or Sophie going near him at all, because I don't think he'd want that. But I get along with him pretty well. Maybe I could just tell him the situation we're in. Maybe offer to walk the dog for free. And Sophie could come along on the walks, because he wouldn't be there, anyway. And maybe she'll just settle down and figure she'll see Rigby again the next day. You know. The way she did at Aunt Vi's. Do we have money for a place to stay?'

'Yes and no.'

'Meaning what?'

'We could stay someplace for a little while. Or feed ourselves. Not so much both.'

The heel of my hand was resting on the slightly crackly lump of Nellie's hundred-dollar bill, still stuffed deep in my jeans pocket. I didn't mention it. Not that I planned on withholding it. I mean, we had to eat. I just wanted it to be all mine for a little while longer. Before I gave it all up for the good of the family. Like I always did.

Chapter Five

 **Gone**

In my sleep, I was replaying a moment of the Horrible Bookstore Fiasco. Just one endless, disgusting moment. I was standing behind the bookcase, knowing Nellie was about to find me. To find out I was listening. Except, in the dream, the aisle was about as wide as a football field, and angled out into infinity. When I saw her face, there'd be room to pass her by a mile.

Except I was frozen, and couldn't move.

Then she was there, at the end of the aisle, but she wasn't exactly Nellie. More like Sophie, but grown up. And not ASD. Don't ask me how I knew it was Sophie. I just did. She looked right at me and her eyes took in everything. They were perfectly clear.

A sound startled me awake.

I sat up fast.

Now for the bad news. There was no room to sit

up. Turns out I was sleeping in the back of the station wagon, where I had no memory of ever going to sleep. I didn't even remember climbing back there. My forehead hit the headliner, which was old and not very tight, and didn't protect me from the actual metal of the roof of the car. The spot I hit was the same spot I'd hit on Nellie's counter.

I fell back down again.

'Ow,' I said under my breath. And then, 'Shit.' Even more quietly.

The sound startled me again. It was a knock. Someone was knocking lightly on the back window of the station wagon.

My first thought: It's a cop. We shouldn't be sleeping here. We're in trouble.

It was light out, and I could see the knocking person, but it was sheeting rain, and he had a slicker and hood on, so I could only see just so much. I could tell he was an older guy, maybe Paul's age, but with a softer face and eyes.

I sat up again, careful to slouch over and not hit my head. I looked around to the front of the car. Sophie was still fast asleep strapped into her car seat on the passenger side in the back. My mom was asleep in the driver's seat, which was leaned back almost flat.

I opened the back window. It flipped up, like a hatchback. Well. I guess it *was* sort of a hatchback. It felt weird to sit up all hunched over like that. But I didn't have too many choices.

'Good morning,' he said.

'Did we do something wrong?'

'Not at all. I just saw you sleeping in your car, and I wondered if you had a tent. Sorry I woke you.'

'Tent?'

'You don't have one?'

I looked around. It was hard to see in the downpour, but we were in some sort of campground. I saw a couple of tents and a lot of trailers and motor homes.

'Um. No. We don't have one.'

'Thought that might be the case. We have three in Lost and Found that were never claimed. You'd be amazed how often people break 'em down and then drive off without 'em. You can borrow one if you want.'

'Oh. Thank you. That's nice. Only . . . I don't really know how long we're staying. When my mom wakes up, I'll find out. I'm not sure if she's going to wake up and get right back on the road again.'

'Well, you let me know. See that big trailer with the picket fence around it? My wife and I are the campground hosts. So if you need anything, come by.'

'Thanks,' I said.

I probably should have said more. He was being nice. But I couldn't shake the sleep, and I couldn't shake the dream. And I didn't even know where we were.

He walked off in the rain, holding the edge of his hood out to protect his face.

'What was that about?' my mom asked.

'So you *are* awake.'

'Yeah.'

'But you still made me handle it.'

'What did he say?'

'Just that he'll loan us a tent if we want one.'

'Good. Run catch him. Tell him we want it.'

'I don't have to run. I know where to find him. We're staying here? Why are we staying here? Where are we?'

'We're right outside that little town.'

'So why are we staying *here*?'

'Where do you suggest we stay?'

'In a . . . you know . . . place. With a roof. It's pouring rain. Not exactly camping weather.'

I leaned over the seat to see if Sophie was sleeping through all this. She was.

'Roofs cost money. You got money?'

I chose not to let on, right in that moment, that I did. 'You said we had some money.'

'I said we had enough to stay someplace for a little while, or to eat, but not both. I'm thinking eating would be good. And I have to return the trailer. I'll probably have to drive all the way down to Fresno to return it.'

'You can't return it. It has all our stuff in it.'

'We'll just have to move everything out. I'm paying for it by the day, kiddo.'

'So you want to put all our stuff out in the pouring rain and live in a tent. And when the money runs out . . . then what?'

'You know . . . I could work anywhere, any shift . . . we could live anywhere . . . if it wasn't for . . .'

'Stop. Do *not* bring that up again.'

'I have to, kiddo. I'm sorry. I can't help it. I'm just sort of at the end of my . . .' Then she started to cry. Not just little tremors on the words, with maybe a tear or two. Full-on sobbing. 'We're homeless. Do you get that?'

I could barely make out the words. But I got it. And all I felt was numb.

I also got that if anyone was going to solve things, it would have to be me.

I climbed out the back window into the rain. Ran to the trailer of the campground host. It was raining so hard I couldn't see much. But we were in a thick forest of evergreen trees. That much I could see. By the time I ducked under his awning I was already soaked to the skin. And cold.

The door was wide open, so I just stuck my head in and said, 'Hello?'

'Oh,' the old guy said. 'That didn't take long.'

'My mom says we're staying. So I'm going to take you up on the tent thing. But I have to ask a big favor. I have to ask if I can borrow two. Because we have to get all our stuff out of that trailer so my mom can take it back.'

He scratched his chin, which was bristly with short gray beard hairs. 'I don't see why not. They're not doing anybody any good in the lost and found.'

He ducked out the door, grabbing his slicker on the way out. Then he disappeared into the rain, slipping it on as he ran. When he got back, he was carrying two mismatched green stuff-sacks. One was maybe two feet long, the other closer to three feet. They weren't so thick that I couldn't just tuck them both under my arms.

'You know how to set these up?'

'Not really.'

'Well, this one has a diagram. But they all work pretty much the same way. The poles are in sections, and you put them together. They fit together. And then you slide them through these loops on the outside of the tent. And then when you put the ends of the poles into these grommet holes, it stands up like a dome.'

I followed along on the diagram, and it looked easy.

'Thanks. I think I can manage that.'

'This one has a footprint. Like a tarp you can put down underneath to keep the bottom dry in the rain. So my advice is, sleep in that one. Put your stuff in the other one, but put things on the bottom that won't get ruined if they get wet. If you have boxes, maybe stack them on top of more waterproof things.'

'OK.'

It sounded complicated, and hard. Like something a parent should take charge of. It made me wish I had a parent who took charge.

'If you have any trouble, come back.'

'OK.' I started to turn. To go back out into the downpour. But I stopped. 'How did you know we didn't have a tent?' I asked him. I could hear my teeth chattering a little while I asked it.

'I didn't, for sure. But you're not the first family to ever show up in a campground with everything they own, and not quite prepared for camping.'

'Oh. I thought it was just us. I thought everybody else had it together.'

He laughed, one quick little snort. 'Hardly.'

I turned to duck out into the rain again, but he stopped me with a word.

'Wait.'

I waited.

'I have to ask you something. I'm sorry, but I just have to. Are you safe? Or are you being hurt?'

I swear I didn't know what he meant. I didn't feel safe, no. And I got hurt every time I turned around. But it didn't feel like he could be talking about any of that.

'Not sure I understand the question.'

He lifted one hand and pointed to his own forehead. My hand immediately went up to mine. It hurt to touch it.

'Oh. That.'

'That and the fact that you have that old scar from a split lip.'

'I'm safe. I'm not being hurt.'

'I *want* to believe you.'

'This,' I said, pointing to my forehead, 'was my own stupidity. I reached down to get something I dropped and banged it on a counter. The lip was my little sister. But not exactly on purpose. I do get hurt sometimes trying to take care of her. But she can't help it. She's got ASD. That's—'

'I know exactly what that is,' he said. I watched his eyes change. All the warm open stuff flew away. What got left behind looked lost and sad. 'My wife and I have a son who's autistic.'

'How old?'

'Thirty-six.'

'He live with you in there?'

'No.'

'You're lucky. You're lucky he can live on his own.'

Even less warm and open. Even more lost and sad. 'He doesn't live on his own. He's severely autistic. He lives in a facility where they know how to take care of people who have his problems.'

Just in that moment I realized something. Two things, really. That for a minute I'd liked this guy. And that I didn't any more.

'We're not doing that,' I said.

'I wish you the best. My wife still has a little white line of scar on her chin. Nearly thirty years later you can still see it.'

'I have to go,' I said. 'Thanks for the tents.'

I ran all the way back in the rain. But . . . back to what? It wasn't like this rented patch of dirt was any kind of shelter. It wasn't really much of anything. But just at the moment, it was all we had. I had no choice but to think of it as home.

'You're going to have to back up more,' I told my mom.

My teeth were chattering. I was soaked to the skin from putting up both tents in the pouring rain. But then again, I'd been soaked to the skin before I'd started on the tents. So I kept telling myself, Once you're soaked, you can't get any more soaked. But it was only around forty degrees out. Which meant when night came, I might be seeing my first snow. Which would have been great through a window. Or in dry clothes. Neither of which seemed likely.

I wondered how many blankets we had.

My mom got into the car to try again to back the trailer right up to the flap of the big tent. The one with no footprint to keep it dry on the bottom.

I heard her shift the station wagon into gear. I could hear Sophie, awake now and still strapped into her car seat. But I think my mom and I were the only ones who would have known what that sound was. She'd lost her voice completely. It sounded like a steady whisper. Like wind blowing hard in dry grass, but a little louder.

The trailer came back toward me, but not straight. It jackknifed a bit, heading off in the wrong direction.

'Stop!' I yelled.

She did.

'Just leave it right there.'

I decided it would be easier to move the tent into the right position than to try to get my mom to move the trailer into the right position.

I pulled up the tent stakes. Then I threw the trailer doors open wide. And I slid the tent so the open flap was right up against the back of the trailer. It didn't help much. There was still a steady sheet of water pouring off the tent, and we'd still have to hand everything right through it. I didn't stake it down again, because it struck me that we'd be filling it with lots of heavy stuff.

My mom climbed into the back of the trailer and grabbed a box.

'No,' I said. 'Boxes last. I told you.'

'Oh. Right.'

She handed me my metal trunk. Apparently she'd thrown it into the very back of the trailer so I'd have more room to sleep in the car. I placed it off to the side of the tent where it wouldn't get buried.

'I'm getting soaked,' she said.

'Join the club. I hope we have a lot of blankets.'

'Some. I'm not sure what you mean by a lot.'

She handed me a plastic bin full of towels. I put those off to the side, too. It was dawning on me that almost everything would need to be where we could reach it easily. Which was sort of impossible.

'We'll need a lot of blankets,' I said.

'There were always enough before.'

'It's going to be cold tonight.'

'It's practically summer.'

'We're at a higher elevation. Do you really not get it that it's colder in the mountains?'

'Oh. Right.' She handed me a cardboard carton. 'I'm sorry. There's really nothing much that isn't a cardboard box. So I'm just giving you the ones with dishes and pots and pans and stuff first. The boxes'll get soaked, but at least the stuff won't get ruined. There's some stuff in trash bags. That can go on the floor. But we can't really stack much on them.'

I dropped the box right in the middle of the tent, which was already wet. I didn't know if it was coming up through the tent floor, or blowing and splashing in through the open flap. Or pouring off me. I couldn't believe we were supposed to live like this for as long as anybody could imagine.

'Take Sophie with you when you go to take the trailer back,' I said.

'You're not coming?'

'No.'

'Why aren't you coming?'

'I need to get dry.'

'We'll wait.'

'I don't want all our stuff left alone. What if it gets stolen?'

'It's not worth much.'

'It's all our stuff.'

'Sooner or later it'll have to be here without us.'

'I'm not going. OK? I'm not. I'm upset, and I want to be by myself. I need alone time. Usually I'd just go out if I needed alone time. But we're not in walking distance of anything and it's pouring rain and freezing. So take her and go take the damn trailer back and at least leave me in the sleeping tent by myself. You have any idea how hard it's going to be living like this? All three of us, in that tent? In the pouring rain?'

'Can't rain for ever.'

She handed me another box. It felt light.

'Are we on to clothes already?'

'I don't know,' she said. 'I can't tell what all's in here. Just put it on top of the kitchen stuff. I don't know what I packed in what. I was in a hurry.'

'And what if it stops raining? There's no fence. We

don't have a yard. How are we supposed to handle her if we're not fenced in?'

'Your complaints aren't helping, Angie.'

'Well, I'm sorry. They're all I've got right now.'

'Just go in the other tent and be alone. I'll finish this. And then I'll take Sophie and we'll take the trailer back.'

I ducked out into the rain fast, before she changed her mind.

'You have to let her out first, though,' I said. Even though it meant I had to stand there in the rain to say it.

'Why? You just said there's no fence.'

'You can't keep her strapped into that seat for a whole day. Which it will've been by the time you get back. It's cruel. It's like abuse.'

I could feel the rain running into my eyes and ears.

She didn't answer. So I just ducked into shelter.

It wasn't much shelter. It was out of the rain – there was that to be said for it. But there was nothing inside the empty tent but me. And I was soaked through, so the more I sat there, hugging my knees and shivering, the more a pool of rainwater formed under my butt.

But at least I was alone.

It was probably an hour later when I unzipped the tent flap and stuck my head out. Rain blew in, adding to the lake I'd created.

I'd begun to wonder what was taking my mom so long.

I was pretty desperate to go into the big tent and find

towels and dry clothes, and maybe a blanket. But I'd been trying to wait until they were gone. They should have been gone by then. I was starting to wonder what the hell was going on. I knew I would have heard the car start up and drive away. If it had.

The car and trailer sat right where they'd been all along. No Mom, no Sophie.

I climbed out into the downpour.

I looked for them in the storage tent.

Nobody in there. Just what looked to be maybe two-thirds of our stuff. Like she hadn't even finished un-loading.

I looked into the trailer. It was empty.

She hadn't been kidding when she'd said all our stuff wasn't much.

I looked again at the stacks of boxes, trying to adjust to the idea that this really was everything we owned. It seemed impossible. Pathetic.

I sighed a couple of times and then grabbed the plastic bin of towels. I saw a tied-up garbage bag that looked like blankets. I took it sight unseen.

I ran back to the sleeping tent, forgetting about dry clothes. When I got zipped back in, and remembered, it was more than I could take on. It was too much trouble.

Everything was just too much.

I opened the lid on the bin of towels, and took out the rattiest one. I used it to soak up most of the water on the tent floor. But it soaked through immediately, and the floor was still plenty wet. I pulled out another towel.

Underneath it, I saw my mom's old jewelry box. Which seemed weird, because she'd sold all her jewelry a long time ago. I wondered why she even kept it. Then I wondered what she kept in it if she had no more jewelry.

I opened the lid.

Inside was a wallet, a Timex watch, and a plain silver ring.

I opened the wallet. My dad's face smiled back at me from the driver's license. Which was a shock I can't quite describe. I quick shut the wallet, threw it back in the box, and shut the box. I covered it up with a clean towel and put the lid back on the bin.

First I thought, I know what this means. It means the police returned that stuff to her.

Except, she never told me they returned it. Why would she not tell me that? Besides, they could only get it back to us if they caught the guy. Which they never did.

Then I thought, It means they caught the guy. Whether I know it or not.

Except, then there would have been a trial. And besides, how could I not know? It would have been on the news, and in the paper. The other kids at school would have seen it. The neighbors would have seen it.

I tore open the plastic blanket bag, even though I knew I should have carefully untied the knot. I wrapped myself in a blanket, and sat there wondering where Sophie and my mom had gone, without the car, in the pouring rain.

But I couldn't keep my mind off the watch and the wallet and the ring.

I thought, I have no idea what it means.

Except . . . I knew it meant that everything I'd always believed was not necessarily true.

It was probably another hour before my mom stuck her head into the tent. Rainwater poured from her long hair, pooling on the floor I'd worked so hard to get dry.

'We've got a problem,' she said.

I thought, Are you a liar? Do you lie to me? Because that would be a problem.

I said, 'Where's Sophie?'

'That's the problem. I have no idea. I let her out to move around, and she ran. I tried to catch her, but I slipped in the mud. By the time I got back up, I couldn't see where she'd gone. I've been looking for her for hours. She must be hiding. I have no idea what to do.'

Which was my mom's way of saying, Now *you* do something. When my mom said she was out of ideas, it meant I had to step up.

I just sat a minute, not sure what to say. It seemed to make her nervous.

'You think I should ask the campground host for help?' she asked. 'He seemed nice.'

'No,' I said. I thought he'd just use it as proof that we couldn't handle Sophie. That he and his wife were right and my mom and I were wrong. But I kept that part to myself. 'What's he supposed to do, anyway? If *you* can't find her, how's *he* supposed to find her?'

More silence. I was feeling frozen, like in that dream. No part of me wanted to move. Or even felt like it could.

'Kiddo,' she said, 'we have to do something.'

I opened my mouth to say, 'I can't do this. You can't keep asking me to take care of things.' I was overwhelmed, out of ideas, almost at the edge of tears. I was cold, I was wet, I was homeless. I was fourteen. I wasn't anybody's mother. I hadn't lost Sophie. It wasn't fair that I had to be the one to find her.

I closed my mouth on all of those things.

When I opened it again, I heard myself say, 'Do you have Paul's phone number?'

'No, but I have his address.'

'I'd want to call first. It's going to really freak him out if I just show up at the door.'

'OK. I'll go to the pay phone and see if I can get a listing.'

Her head disappeared.

I sat a while longer, wondering why I hadn't heard her calling for Sophie. I could only guess that she hadn't called. Maybe she'd thought it went without saying that Sophie wouldn't come.

But I wondered if it was more my mom Sophie was hiding from. Less me.

I stuck my head out through the tent flap and yelled her name. I didn't mean to scream it. But it came out as a scream. It came out with all the panic, all the confusion . . . everything I'd been holding in.

Another tent flap opened next door, and someone peeked out. I saw the curtain shift aside in the window of a motor home. Then nothing moved. Wherever Sophie was, she couldn't hear me. Either that or she heard me fine, and just decided to stay put.

I looked up to see my mom standing over me. 'No listing,' she said.

'All right. Take me there.'

'Take you there?'

'Did you really not hear me?'

'What if she comes back while we're gone?'

'I don't know. I just know I have to try this. We have to do something that might work. She's soaking wet. If it gets down below freezing tonight . . . which it might . . . she'll freeze. She won't survive a night out.'

A long pause, during which my mom stood in the pouring rain. Not trying to stay dry in any way.

'I think we need to call the police,' she said.

'Let me try this first.'

'We're burning daylight, kiddo.'

'It might work, though. And then we wouldn't have to tell anybody. What if the police find her and don't give her back?'

'Why wouldn't they give her back?'

I didn't answer.

After a while I guess she got tired of standing in the rain, because she came inside the tent and sat close to me. I could feel a whole new lake pouring off her wet clothes and pooling underneath my butt.

'Why wouldn't they give her back?'

'I don't know. Because we can't handle her. How many times are they supposed to come out and find her if we can't keep her from running off?'

'Look. Kiddo. They might charge us for her rescue the

second or third time. They might even stop responding to our calls. But they can't just keep her.'

'They take kids away from parents when the parents can't keep them safe.'

'I think the parent has to be unfit for that to happen.'

'You sure?'

Long silence.

Then she said, 'What's Paul supposed to do?'

'Nothing. I'm not going to ask him to do anything. It's his dog I think could help. What if I could yell to Sophie that Rigby was here? She'd come running when she heard that.'

A sigh from her. 'And if she doesn't?'

'Let me try it. It's our best bet. She'll hide from the police or a search and rescue team, too. This is the only thing I can think of that might really work.'

'I'll have to tell the campground host to watch for her while we're gone.'

'Fine. Whatever.'

She ducked out of the tent again, leaving rain blowing into my face. I zipped up the flap again.

I wondered what time it was. If it was already afternoon. I wondered how much time we had. If it would ever stop raining. If it would snow. If the whole soaked forest scene would ice over. If the ground would be slick, and the branches would fall under the weight of the icicles.

I wondered if it was my fault, for telling my mom she had to let Sophie out of the car.

I wondered if we would ever see my sister again.

I grabbed my mom's jewelry box out of the towel bin, and ran it next door to the storage tent. I wedged it in the middle of a carton, between some fitted sheets. She wouldn't remember where she'd packed it. At least, I hoped she wouldn't. And I didn't want her to know I'd seen.

'Leave me around the corner.'

'Aren't you tired of being soaked?'

'I don't care. I don't want him to see you. If he sees your car outside his new house . . . it's too stalker-ish. He'll freak. It has to just be me.'

I stepped out into the rain, which had lightened to more of a steady mist.

I looked around. I couldn't even see houses. Just mailboxes. And the streets weren't paved. I mean, in town they were. But out here in the residential part of things, it was just muddy gravel roads, dense stands of trees, and mailboxes.

I turned the corner in the rain and found the mailbox with the right number on it. It had flowers hand-painted on. It didn't look much like Paul's style. I wondered if Rachel had painted the flowers. And if Paul would leave them there. Because Rachel had painted them.

I still couldn't see his house. Just a very long three flights of stairs straight up the side of a hill, completely surrounded by flowering trees. They covered the staircase like a tunnel. I could see the way they'd been trimmed so they didn't completely block the path to the front door.

I was halfway up the third flight of stairs before I saw the house. It was a wooden A-frame, blue with white shutters and trim. It looked like something out of a fairy tale.

I realized I wasn't breathing.

Then I started thinking he wasn't really there. Somehow my mom had made a huge mistake. It just didn't seem real that he could be behind the door of this fairy-tale cottage.

Rigby knocked me out of that thought. She barked. Twice. She must have heard me, or smelled me, on the stairs.

So it wasn't all a mistake or a dream.

I saw Paul's face in the window, looking out. Just for a moment, I almost ran away. I was that scared of what he would think. I tried to calm myself. I told myself it didn't matter what he thought. It did, though. I just wasn't sure why. Or at least, why so much.

The door opened. He stood there in the doorway. Just staring.

'I know,' I said. 'This is weird. I know.'

Rigby leaned out toward me, wagging her whole body. But she was too polite to step out unless Paul did.

'How did you find me here?'

'Your sister-in-law told us where you were.'

'*Why* did you find me here?'

'That's a little harder to explain.'

'You look upset. Is everything OK?'

'No. Nothing is OK. Can I come in?'

A long pause. He must have been considering it. It

must have been a temptation to say no. It was weird that we followed him to his new home, barely two days later. Undeniably weird. And it went without saying that my life was more complicated than ever, and I was asking his permission to carry the mess into his living room. Just for a flash of a second I thought I wouldn't blame him one bit for slamming the door again.

'Sure,' he said, and stepped back out of the doorway.

I stepped inside.

It was small, but wonderful. Hardwood floors. Everything wood paneled. The windows had shutters on the inside, too. Nothing was unpacked yet. It was all sitting in a neatly arranged mountain of boxes in the middle of his new living-room floor.

Rigby was so glad to see me that she actually jumped up. Which was weird, because then her head was higher than mine, and she couldn't lick my face.

'Get down, Rig,' he said.

She did.

He moved a couple of cartons off the leather couch and indicated that I should sit. I sat down, self-conscious about my clothes being wet. I wondered if that would hurt his nice couch.

I wondered if we really were friends in some strange kind of way.

I figured I was about to find out.

'What's this all about, then?' he asked, sitting on the other end of the sofa.

Rigby wiggled up close to me and licked my neck. I

put my arms around her huge head. I was so happy to see her, I could have cried. I almost did.

'I'm not sure where to start. We got kicked out of my aunt's house right after you left. So now we're homeless. So my mom had this insane idea to come here. First I told her it was just crazy. Just completely crazy. That you'd freak, and you'd hate us for ever. But then I thought, What if they never came near you? What if you never saw either one of them? Only me. What if I just came by once a day and took Rigby for her walk, no charge? You'd never see Sophie. Or hear her. And you'd never have to deal with my mom. Sophie would just see Rigby while we were walking. And then maybe she'd just settle down like she did at Aunt Vi's, and wait to see her again the next day. And then we'd be saved.'

'How would you be saved? You'd still be homeless.'

'No. We wouldn't. We could live anywhere if Sophie was quiet and good like she was at Aunt Vi's.'

I waited. Watched lines wrinkle up into his forehead.

'Your family would be living here. *Here*. That *is* weird. I won't lie to you. That's very weird that I move hours away and then here you all are again.'

'I know. I agree. I'm sorry.'

Silence.

I was about to get up and walk out in complete defeat.

'I'm back to walking her myself now,' he said. 'My back is better.'

'Wouldn't she love two walks a day? Wouldn't that be twice as good?'

'Not necessarily. She's an old girl.'

'She is? How old is she?'

'Six and a half.'

'That's not old.'

But I'd always noticed that her muzzle was gray.

'It is for a great Dane. They don't live long. Seven, eight years usually.'

'That's terrible.'

'It's just how it is.'

'Why do people even have them, then?'

'Because they're great dogs.'

'But it's terrible to lose a great dog when they're only seven.'

'Or eight. Or maybe nine or ten. Who knows? Look, maybe I could walk her a mile a day and you could walk her a mile a day. As she gets older, I think two short walks might actually be better for her than one long one.'

I tried to answer, but I had no idea what to say. Even though I hadn't really known it, I'd never expected this to work. I'd fully expected him to throw me out on my ass, with a few unkind words to go with the boot down the stairs. You could have knocked me over with a feather.

'You're saying yes?'

'Didn't you want me to say yes?'

'Yeah. But I didn't think you would. In fact, I was sure you wouldn't.'

'You want to just keep telling me how out of character it is for me? Or you want to tell me when you want to start?'

'Today. I really, really want to start today. Oh. But is it bad for her to go out in the rain? If it's cold? And she's kind of older?'

'It's not raining any more.'

'It's not?'

I followed him to the window. Rigby walked with us. The clouds were parting and blowing around between us and the bluest sky imaginable.

'So, where are you going to take her? Do you even know the town at all?'

I was still busy being knocked over by the fact that the rain had stopped in time to save me. I'd thought it was going to rain for ever. If not longer.

I said, 'Remember how you liked when I told you the truth even when I didn't have to?'

'The licorice.'

'Right. I need to drive her back to the campground where we're staying and take her for a walk there. Sophie ran off, and I think she'll come out of hiding if Rigby is with me.'

He looked at me with a curious look on his face. It looked like it meant no.

'You're not even old enough to drive.'

'No, I'm not driving. My mother's driving.' Then I quickly added, 'I made her wait around the corner. So she wouldn't even be coming near your house.'

He smiled just a little bit at one corner of his mouth, the way I'd seen him do before. At the old place. That seemed so long ago. Like a different life.

Then he walked out of the room.

When he came back, he had Rigby's leash.

All the tension and fear melted down in the middle of me, like it was on its way to pool at my feet and then maybe even be gone.

'One condition,' he said. 'That you set a reasonable time limit. Two hours, maybe. If she hasn't come out after that, then it just isn't working. And then I'd like my dog back anyway.'

I held my hand out to shake, and he shook it.

'You have no idea how much I appreciate this.'

'Just go. It gets dark fast in the mountains. It's a cold storm.'

'I know.'

'Good luck.'

'Thanks.'

I felt like there was a whole lot more I should say. And wanted to say. But I couldn't wrap my head around it yet. Besides, he was right. We didn't have a lot of time.

'Sophie? Sophie, guess who I have with me? Rigby. Rigby's here. Hem! Come see. It's true, I wouldn't lie to you. It's *Hem*!'

It was a variation on something I'd called out at least thirty times.

Still nothing. Then again, she could be a mile out of earshot. I could have gone in the wrong direction entirely.

I looked down at Rigby.

'Rigby, do you know where Sophie is?'

She raised her nose to the wind. I didn't get the sense that she latched on to any scent right away. But I did get the idea that she understood the question. But maybe that was just me and my hope.

We slipped and slid up a steep ridge, and I looked out and saw beyond the trees for the first time. I sucked in my breath. We were really in the mountains. I hadn't gotten much of a sense of my surroundings until just that moment. I looked out over a canyon and saw higher Sierra Nevadas all the way out to the horizon, some with snow on their caps. I saw a little lake, and trees growing out of what looked like solid rock. And the sky was a steely blue high overhead, a deeper blue closer to the mountains, with billowy white clouds sliding through.

Just for a moment, I got that same feeling as standing in front of Paul's house. Like this was something I'd imagine. Not someplace real.

'Sophie?' I called out again. 'I have *Hem*!'

I didn't hear anything like a reply. But suddenly Rigby was pulling me down the steep slope, my heels sliding in the loose mud and shifting stones. Rigby never pulled, so I knew she must have heard or smelled something. I slipped a few times and managed to get my balance before I went down. Then I slipped and landed on the heel of my free hand, but she pulled me right back up again, and we kept going.

The ground leveled off, and she led me up to a tumble of boulders, each about the size of a small car.

In between them, I saw my kid sister lying in the mud,

wet and shivering. She opened her eyes and looked up. Not at me. At the dog. She had mud in her hair.

'Hem,' she said. But it sounded weak.

Rigby licked her face and neck. Not so much like kisses. More the way a mother dog cleans her puppies.

Sophie laughed out loud.

I squatted down and put my hand on her shoulder. She didn't shake it off again. I could feel her deep trembling. For the first time I really let it hit me how bad it would have been if I hadn't found her by nearly dusk. It was there all along, but I hadn't let myself think it.

'Why did you run from us?' I asked her. Even though I knew she wouldn't answer. Even though I wasn't sure she'd even know.

I hauled her up on to my shoulder, and she let her face fall into the crook of my neck. She felt as limp as a sack of wet clothes.

I looked around.

'Oh, shit,' I said out loud.

I didn't know where we were any more. I didn't know which direction to go to get back to camp. I looked around three-hundred-sixty degrees, and it could have been any one of them.

'Rigby,' I said. 'Let's go back.'

She started off, and I followed her. We climbed back up to the top of the ridge, climbed down its spine, then crossed a muddy ravine and started up another hill. It was hard carrying all the extra weight uphill, but I didn't have any choice.

But if we were going the wrong way, and had to wander out here for hours . . .

I puffed my way to the top of the second ridge. Just following Rigby. There was the campground spread out below us.

All the air rushed out of me at once.

'Good dog!' I said.

'So . . . I'm starting to think your dog is magic.'

I was standing just inside the door, in Paul's living room. I knew my mom was waiting around the corner, but I figured the least she could do was wait.

'She's a great dog,' he said. 'Nobody's a bigger fan of Rigby than I am. But she's not magic. She just has hearing that's ten times better than ours, and a sense of smell that's dozens of times better. She can just do things you can't.'

'But when I said, "Let's go back . . ."'

'I do that with her all the time. When we've gone as far away from home as we're going, I say to her, "Let's go back now." And we retrace our steps.'

'Oh. Well, OK. She's not magic. But she's a hero. We should get her on the local news or something.'

'No!' he said, too loud, and I wasn't sure if he was half joking or genuinely yelling at me. 'I don't want news crews at my door.'

'You just want to be left alone.'

'Right.'

I turned to go. 'What time tomorrow?' I asked over my shoulder.

'Anytime. Doesn't matter.' Then he said, 'Maybe not completely alone. It's different here. No working with people whether I like it or not. I haven't even seen the new neighbors. I like it, don't get me wrong, but it's not so bad to think about one person coming by every day. I mean, if it's someone I can deal with.' He didn't say, Like you. But I knew that's what he meant. 'So maybe that's why I didn't take it too hard when I saw you.'

I almost said, So we *are* friends. I was thinking it.

But then my eyes drifted to his new bookcase. It was completely empty except for that picture of Rachel. It must have been the first thing he unpacked.

He saw me see it.

'Then again,' he said, 'when you let people in, they start to know things about you. That's not my favorite part of the whole people business.'

'Tell you what,' I said. 'Next time I see you, I'll tell you something about me, too. Something I'd just as soon nobody else knew. Then we'll be even.'

I didn't know what it would be yet. But that gave me time to think. I knew Paul wouldn't tell anybody, whatever it was, because he never talked to anybody anyway. Except Rigby.

And now me.

I trotted down all three flights of stairs, feeling weirdly happy. My sister was back. And at least I had one sort-of friend.

You have to have gotten down pretty low before something as small as that starts to look like happy to you.

 **Truth**

When I woke up in the tent, the three of us were all huddled together. My mom was in the middle, on her back, with her arms around both of us. She was stroking my hair.

I think we were all mostly trying to stay warm.

I lifted my head and looked over my mom at Sophie.

Sophie was awake, but not making a sound. Just playing in the air with her own hands. She looked perfectly relaxed. Which could only mean one thing. She already trusted she'd see Hem again. I'd told her so the night before, and she must have believed me.

Which put us back in a bubble of peace.

She had a scrape on her cheek, and her hair was still packed with dried mud. But I was so happy to see her, it just filled me up. I was so happy she wasn't gone for ever that I almost felt good. Like it didn't matter that the ground was hard and we had no way to pad it. It didn't matter that I had no idea how we were supposed to get clean. Or that we'd gone to bed without dinner in all the confusion.

We were all still here. That was the only thing that felt like it mattered.

'So, you're awake,' my mom said.

I didn't answer. Because the minute I heard her voice, something started scratching at the back of my mind. I couldn't quite pin down what it was yet, but it was not a good or happy something. I could feel the nuisance of it, like a tag that irritates the back of your neck, or a little burr in your sock.

'Well?' she said. Like I was supposed to talk.

Then I remembered.

I let it sit inside me for a minute, feeling the size and weight of it. Feeling it like a bruise you purposely poke to see how sore it is. God knows I'd had enough experience with bruises.

Then it came up, all on its own. I couldn't have held it down if I'd tried. Also, I didn't try.

'Did they ever catch the guy who killed Dad?'

She sat up so fast that I fell off her shoulder and hit my head on the hard ground. The bottom of the tent was hardly a cushion.

Sophie let out a little noise of surprise.

'What the hell kind of question is that?'

'It's just a question. Don't get all freaked out.'

'How can I not get freaked out? I wake up in the morning and you start asking about a thing like that.

How am I supposed to feel? What made you even think about that?'

I sat up, rubbing my head. Then I wrapped myself in my own arms to try to stay warm. It didn't work.

'I think about it all the time. Every day.'

'*Every day?* I had no idea you thought about it every day. It was like eight years ago.'

'It was a pretty big deal, you know.'

'Of course I know. How dare you talk to me like I need to be taught that?' Every now and then when I hit a special sore nerve in her, she suddenly got very mother-like. 'He was my husband, and I adored him. It was a big deal for me, too, kiddo. More than you know.'

'But you don't think about it every day?'

'I hate this line of questioning. Hate it. I have no idea why we have to discuss this.'

'You're still ducking my question. Did they catch the guy?'

'Or guys. Might have been two or three guys.'

'Still ducking.'

'No! No, all right? No. They didn't catch him. Or them. Now can we talk about something else?'

'Sure,' I said.

And I meant it. Because if someone's going to lie to your face, there's really no point talking to them any more. It gets you exactly nowhere.

Apparently I'd spent the last eight years of my life getting exactly nowhere. I just hadn't known it until that moment.

*

'We're all going to take a nice shower, and then I have to go take the trailer back. It sucks that we couldn't take it back yesterday. I'm really upset about that. That's a big bite out of our food money.'

I didn't answer. Because I was officially not speaking to my mom.

I got the feeling she hadn't noticed.

I wanted to ask where we were supposed to find a place to take a nice shower. I definitely would have, if I'd been speaking to her. I didn't know yet that the campground had public showers for the campers.

I found out soon enough, though, because I tagged after my mom and Sophie and that's where we ended up.

The showers ran on quarters.

My mom took Sophie in with the quarters we had, and gave me a dollar. If I wanted a shower, I had to go to the campground host and get change.

It was early, and I was afraid I'd wake them up. But then I saw his wife go by the window inside their trailer.

I ducked under their awning and knocked.

The door opened with a light creak, and she peeked out. She had deep wrinkles at the corners of her eyes and mouth, but I could tell she used to be pretty. Or . . . actually, she sort of still was. Just old pretty instead of young pretty. I saw that scar on her chin right away. It was small, but it was hard for me to look away.

'Good morning,' I said. 'You must be Mrs Campground Host.'

She laughed. 'Geralynne,' she said.

'I was wondering if you could give me change for the showers.'

'Of course.'

She took my dollar and disappeared. When she came back with the quarters, I knew they weren't even half of what I wanted. I stared at my palm as she dropped them into my hand without touching me.

'I also wondered if your husband was around.'

She gave me a curious look.

'No, he's out checking tags.'

I didn't know what tags were, and I didn't ask. It didn't really matter.

'Oh. I wanted to thank him for yesterday.'

'Are you the girl who lost her sister?'

'Yes, ma'am.'

'We didn't do much. Just kept an eye on your campsite in case she wandered back.'

'Well, I appreciate it.'

'We're just so glad she's safe.'

I was beginning to realize that this conversation had something in common with the quarters. Turns out *it* wasn't really what I was after, either.

'I wanted to tell him I was sorry for something, too.'

'Oh?'

'Yeah. He was telling me about your son, and I—'

The look on her face stopped me cold. She turned to stone. Right before my eyes. Fast, too.

Then she looked over my head, and said, 'Here he comes back, so you can tell him yourself.'

She disappeared into the trailer, leaving the door hanging partway open.

'Good morning,' the man whose name I didn't know said.

'Hi. I came by to get change for the showers. But your wife helped me with that. And to thank you for yesterday. And also to say I was sorry for something, but I think I upset your wife just now, so I guess I have to be sorry twice.'

I waited, in case he wanted to say something. But he just looked a little confused. So I kept going.

'When you told me about your son, I think I was kind of rude. I didn't mean to be. But I shouldn't have said, "We're not doing that." Because I don't know what we're doing. I can't really know. I just know what I want. If she starts hurting herself, or even if she gets big and we can't handle her and we're just getting too hurt . . . or if she starts running off all the time . . . maybe we won't have any choice. I shouldn't have said it like you were wrong. You probably did what you needed to do. I *hope* we don't have to do that. That's all I should have said.'

I watched him take in a big, deep breath. I thought, He's like my mom. Doesn't like to get hit with heavy stuff first thing in the morning. Then I felt like it was my fault and I was doing life all wrong, always in everybody's face about stuff that's better left alone. Me, of all people. The one who hates to talk about everything. Or at least, who always did before.

'Don't think of it like it's the worst thing in the world,' he said. 'There are some nice places. They're like group homes. They could teach your sister to do as much on her own as she's able to do.'

'She's six,' I said. 'She's barely old enough for school.'

'But later . . .'

'Oh. Later. Yeah. Actually . . . I hadn't thought of that. Maybe when she's eighteen or something. Maybe I'll grow up and go off on my own and get a job and she'll grow up and go to one of those homes and learn stuff. That might be OK. Thing is, if we had to do it now, it would be like we didn't even raise her. Like we had her and then just sort of changed our minds. Anyway, you don't need to know all that. I just wanted to say I was sorry.'

'Don't worry about it.'

He went back into his trailer, and just as I stepped through the gate in their picket fence, I heard Geralynne say, 'Why on earth did you tell her about Gary?'

Then I felt bad again, like I was always upsetting people. Always remembering things they wanted to forget. I think I had a broken forgetter.

While I was walking back, I also thought about how I'd said, '*We* had her.' We. Like I had Sophie just as much as my mom did. Then I remembered when Nellie said just the opposite. That my mom had her, but I didn't. That Sophie wasn't really my problem. But I didn't like thinking about Nellie, so I put the whole thing out of my head as best I could. Which – between that and the situation with my dad – didn't turn out to be a very good job.

*

My mom stood by the car with her hands on her hips, glaring at me. She was still mad at me for asking what I asked about Dad. But she wasn't admitting it.

'You're going? After all you said about not wanting to go?'

'I'm not going. You're going to drop me at Paul's.'

'We'll be hours.'

'So? I'll sit and talk to him. Or I'll help him unpack. Or if he doesn't want me around, I'll just walk the dog and then sit at the bottom of his stairs and wait for you.'

She came in my direction fast, moved in really close, and it startled me.

'And Sophie?' she asked, too quietly for Sophie – who was already strapped into her car seat – to hear. 'The whole point is to take her on the walks with you.'

Amazingly, I'd forgotten that. I'd been thinking of going to Paul's as sort of its own reward. I didn't admit it.

There was lots of not admitting going on that morning. Lots.

'I'll bring Rigby out to the car when you come back to get me. And Sophie can see her then. She'll come with us the next day. Otherwise what am I supposed to do? Just sit in the tent for hours? I'd rather visit with Paul.'

She took a step back, looked at me strangely, then got in. She started the car before I could even scramble into the passenger seat. Slammed it into gear before I had my seat belt on.

Fortunately our camping space was the kind you

can drive all the way through. My mom wasn't good at backing up that trailer.

We drove halfway into town without either one of us saying a word.

Then she said, 'You *sure* this guy's not a perv?'

'Positive.'

'And . . . if he hates everybody . . . how did you two get to be so buddy-buddy?'

This was starting to feel too much like speaking to my mom, who I wasn't. Speaking to. So I just shrugged.

Besides, it was a question I really had no answer for. I'd been wondering about it a lot myself. I hadn't even coughed up so much as an educated guess.

'Is it OK that I'm still here?'

I had my head half into a huge cardboard barrel in his kitchen. I was handing him up dishes and he was arranging his cupboards whatever way he wanted them to be.

'It's fine. Why?'

'I don't know. I don't want to be somebody who just invites myself in. I promised I'd walk the dog and then get out of your hair.'

'It's fine. People who are willing to help unpack are always welcome, wherever they go.'

We worked in silence for a few minutes. I kept looking at Rigby, who was stretched out across the kitchen floor. From the front of her front paws to the back of her back paws was just about the whole width of the kitchen.

'I sure love that dog,' I said.

I hadn't meant to say it out loud. It came out too emotional. More love than I'd meant to admit. It's strange to love somebody else's dog that much. It's hard.

'Me, too,' he said. 'She's a good girl.'

If he thought I was being weird, he didn't say so. So I jumped in even deeper.

'When you told me yesterday that she was old, I didn't think about it that much, because I couldn't. Sophie was gone and I was supposed to find her, and I wasn't sure if we'd ever see her alive again. But then when I was trying to get to sleep last night, I started to think about Rigby being old. And it was sad. It really bothered me. But, then, everything is sad right now. I've got so many things bothering me, half the time I can barely tell where the sad is coming from.'

I looked up, and he was looking right into my face. It made me nervous. Even though he seemed interested, and he was obviously being nice. I thought about the time when we didn't used to get along. When he'd been grumpy and told me to go away. For the second time in as many days, it felt like another lifetime completely.

Why is it that years can go by and it feels like nothing moves, and then the whole world changes three or four times in a couple of weeks? I can never figure that out.

'When I was six,' I said, still halfway wondering if I was really going to do this, 'my dad died.'

'Oh. I'm sorry. Of . . . ?'

'A gun.'

'Suicide? Or did someone kill him?'

'Someone killed him. I was too young to really understand what was going on at the time. So I've always just gone by what my mom told me. She said it was a robbery. She said they knew it was a robbery because when they found him, his wallet and watch and wedding ring were missing. It seemed kind of weirdly random, you know? Like he just went out for a pack of cigarettes and then all of a sudden the whole world fell apart.'

'I can imagine how it must have made you feel. But it happens.'

'Yeah. I know it does. But I'm not sure now if that's how it happened with my dad. You know I told you we got kicked out of my aunt's? So my mom threw all our stuff in boxes and bags and bins and threw it all in the trailer. Really fast, you know? No special order of things. And then yesterday I was looking for towels, and guess what I found?'

'Can't imagine.'

Rigby stretched, her front paws pressed up against the wall on one side of the kitchen. It seemed strange that she should be so relaxed. I was so tense it was making me sick.

'His watch and wallet and wedding ring. She had them stashed away in an old jewelry box.'

'The police must have given them back to her.'

'But they were supposed to be missing.'

'Maybe they found the killer and he had the items on him.'

'Right. That's what I thought. So I asked her this

morning if they ever found the killer. She said no. She really didn't want to talk about it at all.'

'Hmm.' He scratched at one of his sideburns. 'So, two things I can think of. Either the police found the items without finding the killer. Like maybe somebody sold them illegally, and they came into police custody. Or they were on him when he was found. Despite what she told you.'

'And what would that mean? If they were on him when he was found?'

'Well. I don't know. It means it probably wasn't a robbery. But I don't know what it means it was, then. I'd need more information. Why don't you ask your mom?'

'Because I think she's lying to me about it. And it does no good at all to ask somebody questions if you're pretty sure they won't tell you the truth.'

'Hmm,' he said again.

I tried to hand him another stack of pottery soup bowls, but he didn't take them from me.

He just asked, 'Are you online?'

'Me? No. We're camping. We not only don't have a computer, we don't even have an outlet to plug one in.'

'You want me to look into it for you?'

'How could you do that?'

We still weren't putting dishes away, and it was making it harder to talk to him, because I didn't want to look at the person I was talking to at a time like that, and I didn't know where else to look.

'Shouldn't be hard. It was a crime, so it must have been in the papers.'

'Oh. Right.'

'Write down his name before you go today. And where you lived at the time. And the date as close as you can figure it. Only thing is . . .'

The pause made me nervous.

'What? The only thing is what?'

'Are you sure you want to know? Might be that your mom lied to you because the truth is hard to take. Sure you want to know the truth?'

'Um. No. Not positive. Depends on how hard a truth. Maybe you could find out and then tell me how bad it is.'

'Sounds like a tough judgment call.'

'It doesn't matter,' I said. 'You won't have to judge. Once I know there's a truth that's different from what I thought, I have to know what it is. Right?'

'That's how it would be for me.'

'Maybe you could just give me the details one at a time if it's really bad. And I could say, "That's enough," when I didn't want to hear any more.'

'That might work.'

He took the bowls out of my hands. Which surprised me. I'd forgotten they were even there. He put them up in the cupboard while I dove in for some drinking glasses individually wrapped in newspaper.

'That's not exactly something to be ashamed of,' he said.

I had no idea what he meant.

'Who said it was?'

'What I mean is, even if your mother lied, that's a

bad thing about *her*. Not you. Although . . . I guess you wouldn't want me to tell anybody . . .'

'Oh. That. The thing. I forgot I was going to tell you something about me. That wasn't the thing. It was just on my mind. And I couldn't talk about it with my mom.'

'You don't have to tell me anything about you.'

'No. I will. I don't mind. I just forgot to think of anything.'

'It's OK. I trust you. I know you won't say anything to anybody about . . . my situation. Just don't tell your mom, whatever you do. She has a way of sticking her foot in it. I wouldn't want it getting back to Rachel.'

'She doesn't even know how you feel?'

'Hey. I didn't say I was willing to go into detail.'

'Oh. Sorry.'

We worked without talking for a while longer. We emptied that whole huge barrel and then started in on a box of silverware and cooking utensils.

'I think I might be gay,' I said.

I halfway knew it was about to come out a second before it did, but I didn't plan it, and there wasn't much I could do to change it by then anyway. And I guess maybe part of me thought it was better off out.

He stopped putting silverware away and looked at me, but I didn't look back.

'Is that the thing?'

'I don't know. Maybe. It's *a* thing.'

'It's still not something to be ashamed of.'

'Neither is being in love with somebody. It's just one of those things I wouldn't want you to tell anybody.'

'Would your mom be upset?'

'I think she would, actually. She wouldn't be hateful about it. But she really wants me to be a girly girl, because she was. Is. She wants me to grow my hair long. She says pretty soon it'll matter, because I'll be getting interested in boys. I mean, duh, Mom. I'm fourteen. How old do I have to get before she figures out it's not happening like that? God knows she's watching close enough.'

'You don't seem fourteen. You seem more like twenty. Just maybe a little shorter.'

'Everybody tells me that.'

'So . . . not to be nosy. And not to make you go into detail if you don't want. But . . . you think you might be? Or you are?'

'I am. That was just an easier way to say it the first time.'

'Right. I thought so.'

'Why did you think so? How did you know?'

'I didn't mean that. I didn't know. I never thought about it. I just meant, when you said it, I thought, When somebody thinks they might be something, it's usually because they are.'

Then we didn't talk for a while, and it felt strangely OK. Not like we were afraid to say more. And it wasn't awkward. We just put pots and pans and stuff away and that was enough.

When I heard my mom honking, I said to him, 'That was fast.'

'Not really. You got back from walking Rigby almost two hours ago.'

'Are you kidding me?'

He showed me his watch.

It was a nice watch.

'Time flies when you're spilling your guts,' he said.

I knew then that my father died for some other reason than a robbery. Because his watch wasn't a nice watch like Paul's. I knew it wasn't good enough to sell.

I ran down the steps with Rigby at my side, and when we got down to the gravel road, I heard Sophie squeal with joy. That was a big squeal, too, because my mom was parked a pretty good long way down the road.

I opened the back door and encouraged Rigby to get in with Sophie. She barely fit. She had to crouch with her head down, right across Sophie's car seat, which of course Sophie loved. I had to move her tail carefully before I closed the door.

I got in up front beside my mom, who was grinning. It made so little sense that she should be happy that I really didn't even take it in.

'I need a pen and paper,' I said. 'Do we have one?'

'I got a job.'

'You're kidding. How did you get a job already?'

'I stopped on the way out of town at this little diner to get some muffins to go. And guess what I found in the window? A "Help Wanted" sign! They hired me on the spot. How's that for luck? I start tomorrow!'

I couldn't get my brain to make the sharp turn. I

really only wanted a pen and paper. That was all I could think about for the moment. My brain flopped around and landed on neither.

'Muffins? You had muffins? I'm starving to death. I didn't get muffins.'

She grabbed a white paper bag off the floor near my feet and threw it in my lap. 'I saved you one.'

'Oh. Good. Thanks. Do we have a pen and paper?'

'You don't sound very excited about my news.'

'No, it's good. Really. Tomorrow? What time? What shift?'

The smile stayed on her mouth, but it faded a little from her eyes and the rest of her face. 'I'll be working a morning shift. Through the lunch rush.'

Silence. For a minute I even forgot about the pen.

Until she said, 'There should be a pencil in the glove compartment.'

I opened the glove compartment. Found the pencil in the amazing mess. I tore a piece of white paper off the bag. Then I decided not to write anything on it until I was all the way back up at Paul's door. She'd freak if she saw me writing something about my dad.

I looked right into her face. She shifted her eyes away.

'So,' I said. 'I'm babysitting days now. Have you thought about how I'm supposed to go to school?'

'Of course I thought about it. I just figured . . . there's only a few weeks left in the school year anyway. It hardly pays to start in a new school now. Better to start in the fall. I'll find something better by then.'

'I'll have an awful lot of catching up to do.'

'You're so smart, though.'

I looked over into the back seat. Rigby was licking Sophie's closed eyelids – and most of the rest of her face by default – and Sophie was cooing with happiness. Everybody was happy that day. Except me.

'If I do well for tips tomorrow, we can get a cheap motel room tomorrow night. This could be our last night outdoors.'

'Well,' I said. 'That would be nice.'

There was no point arguing the school thing. I didn't get a vote. And the election was over, anyway.

It bothered me that I was supposed to be happy with my mom while I was still not speaking to her. She did that a lot. Always found a way to take away my time to get through what I was feeling. Not that I thought this one was on purpose. But on purpose or not, she always managed it.

'I don't get it,' I said. 'How did you even go in for muffins and an interview? You had Sophie. Did you bring her in with you?'

I knew the answer by the way she cut her eyes away. The more she didn't answer, the more I knew I was right.

'You left her in the car.'

'It was only a few minutes.'

'Unbelievable.'

'It was locked. And the windows were cracked. And besides, I was parked where I could see her. Look. Kiddo. You want to bust my chops for that when nothing went wrong? Or you want to be happy that I got a job and we can live under a roof again?'

I sighed big. 'I just want to bring Paul his dog back and then go . . .' I had no idea how to finish that sentence. There was no home.

I climbed out, and took Rigby out of the back seat. It reminded me of all the tall clowns coming out of the tiny clown car at the circus. Yes, my dad took me to the circus.

'You'll see her again tomorrow, Sophie, I promise.'

But I needn't have bothered, from the look of things. Sophie didn't seem the least bit upset.

We trotted up the stairs until I got too winded to trot.

The door was hanging open, so I just rapped on the door frame and walked in. Paul was putting books in the bookcase, on either side of Rachel's picture.

'I'm going to write down the stuff about my dad,' I said.

I sat down and wrote his name, and the Los Feliz section of Los Angeles, and that I didn't know the date exactly, but it was eight years ago and it was summer.

When I handed it to him, he said, 'Dan. Like my brother.'

'Who you don't even like.'

We both laughed a little at that.

But I definitely understood more by then. Like why he didn't like his brother. And why he used to be happy about going over to see him anyway. Well, I didn't know, really. Maybe he had lots of other reasons not to like his brother. But even just that one seemed like enough.

I thought about Cathy. Then I quick stopped thinking about her again.

It was cold in camp that night. I wanted to think at least it was the last night out. But I wasn't really sure. My mom just said 'if'. If the tips were good enough her first day. Besides, last was kind of a relative thing. That was the first time we'd found ourselves homeless. I wasn't entirely sure it would be the last.

I didn't sleep as much as I would have liked.

'OK, just wait here,' I told my mom. 'I'll come out with the dog.' I looked over my shoulder at Sophie. 'I'll bring Hem, Sophie. And you can go with us.'

I ran down the road to Paul's house and all the way up all three flights of stairs.

Rigby heard me coming, and barked, and Paul opened the door before I even got there.

'So, what did you find out?' I asked him, pretty out of breath.

It was nearly four in the afternoon, and it was all I'd been thinking about, and all I'd been able to do all day was sit around in the campground with Sophie while my mom worked. And wait. And wonder.

I could tell by his face that he knew something.

'It wasn't a robbery,' he said.

'I didn't think so.'

I heard myself say it, but my lips felt numb. Like whoever was speaking wasn't really me. And, also, whoever was speaking was saying she knew it would turn out like this. When the truth was, I'd really expected him to say he couldn't find out anything.

'I bookmarked a couple of articles. Come back into my office.'

I followed him down the hall like I was on the way to my own public execution. Rigby wagged along beside me, whipping my butt with her lethal tail. I didn't say, Ouch, because I was too busy with the inside ouches.

His office was – so far – just a high wooden table with an open laptop on it, and a neat pyramid of boxes in the middle of the floor.

The computer was making me nervous, and my brain was starting to tingle, like the way your foot does when it's falling asleep. So I walked to the back window and looked out. You could see the mountains with snow on them.

'Nice view,' I said.

'Thanks.'

He was clicking around on the laptop, I guess to find again whatever he'd found before.

'So, you didn't have much trouble finding stuff about him?'

'Not at all. I just did a search on his name and it came right up.'

'You have a garage.'

I'd finally pulled my eyes away from the mountains and looked down at the back of his property. I knew it was his garage, because it was blue with white trim, like his house. But it was two levels, like somebody could live or work in the room on top.

'Does that seem strange?'

'Yeah, a little. Because you don't have a driveway. I mean, that I could see. How do you get your car up there?'

'I have a driveway. It's just so far from the house you probably thought it was somebody else's driveway. It's a big property. You're not ready for this, are you?'

'I might be. Maybe I might be ready to do this in a minute. Can I take a minute?'

'Of course. Take all the time you need.'

He came over to the back windows and stood with me, and all three of us looked out at the view together.

'So what are you going to do with that room over the garage?'

'No,' he said.

'No what? It wasn't a yes or no question.'

'I was saying no to what you were thinking.'

'What was I thinking?'

'Sorry. Maybe I was wrong. I thought you were going to ask me if I was renting it out. But I'm not ready for the full force of the whole family, Angie. I'm sorry. I need more space than that.'

'Oh. Yeah, I wouldn't ask that.'

'That wasn't what you meant, was it?'

'No. I hadn't thought of it.'

'Sorry.'

We looked out over the view in silence for a while. Maybe some seconds or some minutes. I'm not sure I was in any kind of mood to tell one from the other.

'You know,' he said, 'I could just delete the bookmarks for those articles and pretend I never found them.'

I breathed a couple of times, wondering why I could hear myself breathe when I never could before. That I know of.

'I don't think *I* could pretend you never found them.'

'If it helps any to know, they don't really say all that much. They don't say why he was killed, because the police didn't know. Either that or they thought too many details would compromise the investigation. But nothing was taken. And they're pretty sure it wasn't random. They think he knew his assailant. But they didn't say why they think that.'

'I bet my mother knows more.'

'Maybe.'

'I can't ask her, though.'

'I think sooner or later you will.'

'Is that really all there is to know?'

A silence I didn't like.

'Just that he wasn't killed with a gun.'

'My mom said he was.'

'She also said it was a robbery.'

All of a sudden I couldn't swallow. Like I'd flat-out forgotten how.

'How was he killed? It was some bad way, wasn't it?' In my head, I heard Aunt Vi say, 'Oh, and such an awful way to go.' 'No, never mind. I don't want to hear that part. Don't tell me about it.'

'OK. I won't. I'll never bring it up again.'

We just kept standing there for a while. I felt like I'd

turned into a statue. I was still looking out the window, but I wasn't even seeing what I was looking at.

I pulled my eyes back down to his blue-and-white two-floor garage.

'So what *are* you going to do with that room?'

'Not sure yet. I could use it as an office. But I have this back bedroom for that. Besides, I'm retired. Why do I even need an office? Just force of habit, I guess. I could rent it out if I needed the money. But I don't. At least, not right now. It would make a nice guest room.'

'Maybe Dan and Rachel will come visit.'

'I doubt it. They got pretty tired of this place. Or, anyway, Dan did. That's how I was able to get it away from him.'

'So . . . if you don't have to work, what are you going to do? How will you fill up all the hours in the day?'

'Well, let's see,' he said. 'First Rig and I will get up in the morning and walk into town and buy a newspaper. And a double espresso. And a muffin or a scone, unless I start gaining too much weight. And then I'll read the paper for half the morning. And then sometimes I'll go fishing in a cold stream, or one of those mountain lakes. Catch some fresh trout for dinner. And I'll read the rest of the books in my library. The ones I've had for twenty years and never read. And maybe I'll put my woodshop back together and make bookcases and tables, like the old days. And if I get bored, Rig and I can go for a hike on one of the mountain trails. There are only about a billion that start within a five-mile radius of here.'

'That sounds like heaven,' I said.

'Doesn't it? And I only had to work at a job I hated for forty-five solid years to make it happen.'

I think I was supposed to laugh. But somehow it didn't feel funny. It felt like something that wasn't right about life the way it was.

So I said nothing at all.

'You doing OK?' he asked.

'Um. Yeah. I guess. I feel like I'm asleep. But I'm OK. Sort of. I think I need to sit down before I go for a walk. My legs are kind of shaky.' That's when it hit me. 'Oh, crap. I can't sit down. My mom is waiting in the car with Sophie, so she can go on the walk with us. I forgot all about her. She must be getting pretty impatient. I better just put the leash on Rigby and go.'

The story of my life in two sentences:

I need time to sort all this out.

I'm not going to get it.

It was one of those patterns that just kept cropping up. Every time it showed its ugly face, it won. I never had any more power over it than I'd had the time before.

My mom took Sophie to the public restrooms at the campground when we went back to get our stuff.

I didn't get my big idea right away. At first I just stood there, leaning on our car. Like I had time to kill and I didn't even know what to do with it.

I wasn't thinking much, but I remember being glad we really could afford a motel for the night. I'd never been particularly grateful for stuff as simple as a bed and a roof, but I swore to myself in that moment that I always would be again. Then I wondered if that was really possible, or if I'd just get used to it right away, and forget.

Next thing I knew I was rushing for the storage tent. And I knew what I was after, too. But I swear I didn't form it as a series of thoughts in my head first. It just sort of did itself.

I ducked inside and found the box with the sheets.

My heart thrummed while I stuck my hand around and under different sheets, and then I bumped the jewelry box. I closed my eyes and breathed for a second. But only a second. I got worried about how long my mom and Sophie would be gone, and if my mom would come looking for me and catch me doing this.

I was going to take the whole box, but then I decided against it. Because, if I did, she would just think she lost it in the packing. She'd just wait for ever for it to turn up. But if she found the box, and it was empty . . .

I stuck my hand into the wood box, blind, without even taking it out. I grabbed the wallet and the watch and the ring all in one hand, all on one grab. I pulled them out and stuck them in my jacket pocket.

I leaned out of the storage tent and looked for my mom, but they weren't on their way back yet.

So I finished the job.

I stashed my dad's things away in my locked trunk.

I looked in one more time before I locked it all up.

Counted all the things I wasn't ready to deal with. The note from Nellie. *The Tibetan Book of the Dead*. The truth about my dad. I took the hundred-dollar bill out of my jeans pocket. My mom had a job, so she could take care of us. I could keep my little nest egg.

I threw the money in the trunk and slammed the lid and locked it.

I wasn't stealing my dad's stuff. Just to be clear. Those things rightfully belonged to my mom. And I would give them back to her. Just as soon as she noticed they were gone. Just as soon as she looked me in the eye and told me she knew I had them.

Then she could tell me why they were there. She'd have to. I wouldn't even need to ask. The very fact of my knowing we had them was a question all in itself.

Yeah, I know it's not as good as being able to just open your damn mouth. But I just couldn't. I couldn't bring myself to do it. So I set the question up to ask itself. Pathetic, in hindsight. But that's how I played it at the time.

The weeks we lived in the motel were quiet, and sort of a blur. I guess because every day during that part of my life was just like every other one. There's only one time that stood out. And even it wasn't much of anything. I'm not telling it because it's a big deal. Just because I remember it.

One evening I was hanging out at Paul's, and I saw a deck of cards lying out on the coffee table. Hard to imagine why, because there was nobody around for him to play cards with. Solitaire was the only answer that made any sense.

He was off in the kitchen making us each a sandwich.

The bad thing about the motel was that it used up just about every cent my mom made. So she brought us home food from the restaurant, enough for one meal a day. And I usually ate another meal at Paul's, and saved some for my sister. The good news was that it was less than a mile from Paul's house. So I could walk over anytime, so long as my mom was home to take care of Sophie. I didn't always have her waiting for me out in the car.

I walked over to Paul's a lot. It was a small motel room. Even for one person. For three it was torture.

I hadn't seen a pack of cards for a really long time.

It was weird to see them there, and a hard feeling to describe. Like an old friend you had a fight with, and don't see any more. And then suddenly there they are, and you think, What's *she* doing here? Like being mad, but kind of hurt, too. And maybe not wanting to admit it.

I stared at them for what seemed like a long time.

Then I slipped them out of the box, and started building.

Just a basic house at first, but pretty soon I decided to give it three levels.

Then I got really into it and sort of lost track of my surroundings, like I'd always used to.

Then I was almost out of cards, and I didn't want to stop. I mean, I *really* didn't want to stop. It was like it had gotten into my blood again, under my skin, and I needed more decks of cards. And I needed them fast.

I was so caught up in the feeling that I didn't realize Paul was standing over me with two sandwiches on plates. I could smell the smoked turkey, and I hadn't had any breakfast. But still, all I wanted was more cards. More risky drops.

'Wow,' he said. 'You're good at that.'

'I haven't done it for years.'

'Must be something like riding a bicycle.'

'This is nothing. I used to build ranches with a ranch house and a barn and sheds and corrals . . .'

'Why?'

'Just to kill the time, I guess.' I dropped the last card, and the whole thing held. But there was nowhere left to go with it. 'My dad had just died, and I guess I was needing something to be compulsive about.'

'Sorry. I think that sounded rude. I just always wondered why people do things like that. You know. Things that . . .'

Rigby trotted in, her tail going. Paul and I both saw it about to happen. But he still had a plate in each hand, and I didn't dare reach across the card house. Even the wind of a sudden movement could bring it crashing down.

'Rigby, no!' he said.

She froze in place, her wind-producing nose not two feet from my construction project, and looked up at his face with what I swear was the most wounded look. I guess she wasn't used to being yelled at. Since she never did a damn thing wrong.

'Good girl,' Paul said. 'Stay.'

She did.

But she didn't sit. Because nobody told her to. She stood there swinging that massive tail, and on about the fourth swing it worked up just enough of a wind.

I saw a card in the second story collapse, and then there was that moment. That frozen split second of time. It's so short you could convince yourself you imagined it, but I'd decided a long time ago to go the other way and convince myself I didn't.

Cards fluttered everywhere, some off on to the hardwood floor.

'I'm sorry,' he said.

'It doesn't matter. It's nothing. Don't make her feel bad. It was coming down sooner or later anyway. They all do.'

I scooped up the cards on the table, then went after the ones that had landed farther away.

'I think that's what I was about to say a minute ago,' Paul said. 'But I'm not sure, because it wasn't a very clear thought. But I think I've always wondered about things like card houses and sand castles. And ice sculptures. So much time to put into something that's destined to undo itself.'

I sat down on the couch, and counted the cards out really fast. Fifty-one.

I got down on my hands and knees and fished the last one out from under the couch. The Queen of Hearts.

That felt meaningful, but I was probably being dumb.

'Here's how I look at it, though,' I said, sliding the deck back into the box. 'I figure that's true of everything. You get born, you build all this stuff. Buy houses and cars and save money. Then you die, and it's all right back down to the ground again.'

'Not always. What about if you build a bridge? That stays up.'

'Maybe for a while after you die. But not for ever. Sooner or later they'll decide it's unsafe and they'll tear it down and build a newer one. Build a real house, eventually it comes down. May take hundreds of years, but it'll go back to the ground again. Card houses are just faster, is all.'

He sat down on the couch and set our sandwiches on the coffee table. I took a huge bite of mine. My stomach was so empty that it turned a little when the food hit it. But it was a good sandwich. It was always hard to save half for Sophie, because I was always hungry for all of it and more. But I always did.

'That's a depressing theory,' he said.

'Not really. I mean, not in my head. In my head it's just the opposite. Some people never do anything, because they're so afraid it'll get undone again. They get overwhelmed by the fact that nothing lasts. Then there are the brave people who do all kinds of stuff anyway. Even though none of it is for ever. I want to be one of those people. That's why I build card houses. Or why I used to. Before Sophie came along. Or maybe it was partly because it was the very last thing I did with my dad before he got killed. But that's only part of it. The other part of it was what I said before.'

We ate in silence for a few minutes. I finished my half of the sandwich in only about three more bites. It was good while it lasted.

Like everything, I guess.

Then he said, 'You sure you're not a forty-year-old midget?'

'Believe me. There are parts of me that are completely fourteen.'

'They don't show.'

'Good,' I said. 'Then it's still working.'

I saw that deck of cards on his coffee table maybe ten more times that year. But I never opened the box again.

PART TWO

The Part When I Was Fifteen

Chapter One

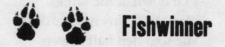 **Fishwinner**

For reasons I can't explain after the fact, I expected a little hoopla.

It was my first day of summer vacation. One full school year in the new place. Which, frankly, was a lot harder than the old place. Because it was a tiny school. I thrived in huge schools. There was no way to get lost in a high school with a grand total of three hundred students in all four grade levels.

It was pretty unavoidable, at close range, that they'd find me a bit weird for their tastes.

I found Sophie and my mom at the breakfast table. My mom was shoveling in rice and beans left over from dinner the night before. Sophie was sitting in front of hers and focusing on something else entirely. I have no idea what. Something in the air. Something I would never find.

We were in a new place. A real place. It was something like a guest house. One bedroom, but incredibly small. But my mom was thoughtful enough to share the bedroom with Sophie, leaving me the fold-out couch. Doesn't sound like much. And it wasn't. But at least she didn't ask me to share the living room with my sister.

I really don't care much about the size or fanciness of my living space. I'm not picky at all. Just so long as I have something that's mine.

I sat down at the table.

'Breakfast?' my mom asked.

She sounded half asleep.

I knew it was self-defeating to hope for too much, but I thought she should be happy for me. She knew it was my first day of summer vacation. I felt the way I figured Paul did when he told me what he was going to do with his retirement, after paying the price for forty-five years.

I wanted a little fanfare. Hell, I wanted a freaking parade.

'Leftover beans and rice is hardly breakfast,' I said.

'I'm afraid it's that or nothing.'

'Nothing.'

No reply. No interest.

I looked up at Sophie, who seemed to be communicating non-verbally with something hovering over the empty place at the breakfast table.

'I see Sophie chose nothing, too.'

Still no reply.

After my mom paid the rent on that place, we were left

with almost no money. She walked to work and back, because gas was out of our price range. She'd bought a huge bag of rice and five pounds of dried beans, and that just about strapped us till the next payday. I was getting pretty tired of rice and beans. The paycheck before that, it'd been pasta. I'd gotten pretty tired of pasta.

'At least she gets school lunch,' I said. 'She does still get lunch in the summer-school program. Right?'

'What?'

'School lunch. For Sophie. She still gets it in the summer. Right?'

'Well, of course. What do you think, they just starve the Special Ed kids all summer?'

'Pardon me for caring,' I said under my breath. Then I glanced over at the clock on the microwave. 'She's going to be late. The van'll be here any minute.'

My mom's head shot up. She looked at the clock, too. 'Oh, shit!'

Then she clapped a hand over her mouth, and looked at Sophie. Why she should worry about Sophie picking up bad words, I couldn't imagine. Sophie had never picked up any words at all, in seven years. Except 'Hem'. And that had something to do with extreme motivation. It wasn't likely to repeat itself anytime soon.

My mom stormed into the bedroom and came out a minute later with Sophie's socks and shoes.

'I'm going for a walk,' I said.

No reply.

I stopped at the door and looked back. My mom was on her knees on the rug, putting on Sophie's sneakers.

'Happy summer vacation to me,' I said. Wondering, even as I said it, what the point might be.

'You seem happy enough for yourself,' she said. 'I guess you don't need any help from me. Which is good, because I'm having a crappy morning.'

I sighed, and walked out. I hadn't even gotten the door closed behind me when I saw Mr Maribal pull into the long driveway. Mr Maribal was the Special Education van driver for the school district. He seemed like a patient man, but sometimes I wondered if that was more on the outside.

Usually he honked. But, since he saw me, he just waved.

I stuck my head back in.

'Van's here.'

'Then why didn't he honk?'

'Because he saw me see him.'

She came thundering over to the door, practically knocking me out of the way. Looked down the driveway.

'Way to take my word for it,' I said.

She waved to Mr Maribal. Then she said to me, 'Walk her down there if you're going for a walk, OK? I have to get ready for work.'

'Sophie,' I said. 'Come on. Van's here. Let's go.'

Nothing.

Not that I expected much. I mean, it was Sophie. She seemed OK on the concept of getting into the van and going to school. But that didn't mean she was ready to go on nothing but requests.

I walked back to the breakfast table and took her hand.

In the old days, she would have yanked it away again. But she'd been calm ever since we came to town. And she particularly clung to me, because I was the one connected in her mind to Hem.

I led her out of the house and down the driveway. I heard the door slam behind us.

'*She's* in a mood,' I said to Sophie, who of course paid no mind.

Mr Maribal was out in the driveway by the time we got there, opening the side door. It was just a normal-size van, like the kind a soccer mom would drive. There were only seven Special Ed kids in the whole district.

I lifted Sophie into her seat, then stuck my head in the back while Mr Maribal buckled her in. He liked to do the seat belts himself. He had a strong sense of responsibility. Or fear. Or something.

'Morning, Reggie,' I said. 'Morning, Ellen.'

We were the third stop.

'Morning!' Reggie said. 'Morning. Morning. Morning. Know what I saw? It was . . . Um. Know what it was? I saw it. This morning. Just now. It was . . .'

'What, Reggie?' I tried to sound encouraging.

I was never sure about his situation. I thought he was ASD, but he might've been developmentally disabled. All I knew is that he was exactly the opposite of Sophie when it came to words.

'I forgot now,' he said.

Mr Maribal slid the van door closed with that satisfying thunk.

'Bye, Sophie,' I said.

Nothing. Then again, as much as I expected.

Reggie launched into a string of, 'Bye, Sophie's sister. Bye! We're going to school now! See you tomorrow, Sophie's sister.'

I waved until they were gone, then walked the rest of the way down the driveway and started puffing up the hill into town. It was hard, because I was hungry. As usual. That made it hard to put out much energy.

I was thinking it might be nice if Sophie were more talkative like Reggie, because I would feel more connected to her. Then I decided it was one of those things that would be nice for an hour or two and then hell for the rest of eternity.

I wasn't really sure why I was walking into town. I knew in my head I was looking for that stuff Paul described. Walking into town and reading the paper, and drinking a double espresso and maybe getting a scone or something. But Paul had money in his pocket.

Still, I was determined to find some of what he'd described. Maybe I could go to the coffee house and read one of the communal papers, at least.

A car pulled up beside me and slowed almost to a stop.

I heard, 'Happy first day of vacation.' I recognized his voice immediately.

Rigby's head was sticking out the back window. I

walked to the car and wrapped my arms around her huge head and kissed her good morning. Then I stuck my head through the passenger window in front, which he'd powered down.

'I kept waiting for my mom to say that this morning. Seemed like a simple enough thing.'

'Never happened, huh?'

'Never happened.'

'Where're you going?'

I sighed. 'I have no idea, really. I wanted to have a vacation sort of a day, so I was walking into town. Like you do in the morning. But I don't have the money for pastry and espresso, so it's all kind of a joke. I'm just trying to make this morning different and good, I guess. What about you? I thought you *walked* into town in the morning. Where are *you* going?'

'We're coming back. Rigby and I went fishing at dawn.'

'Ooh. Nice. Catch anything?'

He reached down for an oddly shaped wicker basket with a lid. It was sitting on a blue tarp on the passenger-side floor. It had a leather shoulder strap, and a leather strap to latch it closed. But it wasn't latched. He lifted the lid. Inside were five beautiful fish, silver, with shiny bellies and a rainbow of color glinting along their sides, lying side by side and on top of each other in perfect stillness.

'Trout?'

'Yes. Rainbows.'

'What are you going to do with them?'

'That's an odd question. I'm going to eat them. Pretty much right now.'

'For breakfast?'

'You're not much of a camper, are you?'

'Not much of one, no.'

'It's a classic camper's breakfast. Freshly caught trout cooked over an open fire. Because dawn and dusk are the best times to fish for trout, anyway. I'd invite you to see what I mean, but you probably already had breakfast.'

'Actually, no.'

'You weren't hungry?'

'I'm starved. I'm always starved. Breakfast was just so horrible I couldn't bring myself to eat it.'

'Jump in. You're in for a treat. Careful not to step on the fish.'

I held the basket of fish on my lap while he drove, just to be safe.

I lifted the lid once, and looked in. Their wide, glassy eyes stared into nothing. I thought it was sad how just this morning they were swimming free in a lake or a stream, thinking everything was fine. That it was going to be a great day, just like every other day. And then this happened.

Then again, everybody has to eat. And I was part of everybody.

The fish were still whole when he carefully lifted one on to my plate with a spatula. He'd only gutted them, cleaned the insides under running water, then dried them with a paper towel and brushed them with olive oil before broiling.

'Is he going to be staring at me like that the whole time I'm eating him?'

Actually, his eye had gone milky white under the broiler. But it was still an eye. On my plate. Aimed at me.

'I forgot you're new at this. Tell you what . . .'

He picked up a fork and a steak knife, and made one quick move that separated the whole top filet from the rest of the trout and slid it down on to the plate. Then he grabbed the tail in his fingers, holding down the bottom filet with the fork in just the right place. The whole fish skeleton lifted up, taking the head with it. Leaving the two perfect filets steaming on my plate.

It was a big fish, maybe thirteen or fourteen inches long when the head and tail were still on. It was more food than I'd seen waiting for me – and only me – on a plate in a long time.

'Thank you. It's weird when something watches you eat it.'

He had a kitchen trash can that opened when he stepped on a pedal, and I watched as he dropped the fish skeleton in. It reminded me of cartoons I saw as a kid. Just like what the cartoon alley cats always pulled out of the trash.

'Under the broiler is not the same,' he said. 'I'm thinking about getting an outdoor grill. But even with a gas grill, it's not the same as a wood fire. I miss camping.

Part of me wants to go again, but I'm too old to sleep on the ground.'

He crossed back to the stove to serve up his own breakfast.

The smell was heavenly. It was making my stomach cramp and growl.

'What about one of those camp cots?'

'Yeah. Maybe. Still, I think Rigby's too old to sleep on the ground, too. She's already getting a little arthritic. I've had to put her on medication for it.'

'I didn't know that.'

'Yeah. Well. I didn't make a big point of it. I know neither one of us wants her to be old. What are you waiting for? Dig in.'

'I didn't want to be rude.'

'Nonsense. Eat it before it gets cold. Watch out for small bones. Oh. Here's some salt and pepper.'

I pressed the side of my fork down on a filet, but it was clear that it would fall apart at the slightest touch. That I could just flake off a bite. I did. I popped it into my mouth. Half excited, half nervous.

The flavor exploded on my tongue. And yet it wasn't too fishy. It was fluffy, like a cloud. It was the best thing I'd ever tasted in my life. I swear. That's not just one of those things you say. I thought of pizza, and the steak my mom used to bring from her old job at the restaurant. And the shrimp I had once at a party. They were nothing. Next to this trout, they were cardboard.

I grabbed the salt and pepper and sprinkled lightly. Took another bite.

Even better than perfect.

Paul sat down with his breakfast. 'What do you think?'

'I think I died and went to heaven.'

'Hate to say I told you so.'

'Where's Rigby? I'm surprised she's not interested in the smells.'

He pointed.

Rigby was in the corner, daintily eating from her enormous food dish.

'She gets her own fish. It's sort of a tradition with us. If I catch more than one, she gets one of her own.'

I wanted to say something about that, but I didn't want to stop eating.

We ate in silence for what felt like a long time. I tried to remind myself to slow down. The food was making me feel real. Like I was here in the room in a way I couldn't be when I was hungry. Like I was fully in my body and that was a fine place to be. For a change.

Paul spoke first. 'Is Sophie on vacation, too?'

'No, there's a summer-school program for the Special Ed kids. Thank God. Otherwise the parents wouldn't be able to work a regular job all year. Or, in my case, I wouldn't get much of a vacation.'

'She still doing well there?'

I bit down on my first small bone. I separated it from the good stuff with my tongue and pulled it out with my fingers.

'So far as we can tell. She doesn't mind going. I think it's a much better program than the old preschool. She hated going to the old preschool. Then again, that was before Rigby came along.'

Speaking of Rigby, she set her head on my thigh. Which was always funny, because it involved leaning down. I guess she'd finished her fish.

'Not fair, Rigby,' Paul said. 'You had yours.'

She shuffled into the living room, looking a little ashamed. Even from behind.

'Will you teach me to fish?'

It surprised us both. I really hadn't known I was about to ask.

'I'm surprised,' he said. 'You don't seem like the fishing type.'

'Yeah. I'm a little surprised, too. Because I'm *not* the fishing type. But I'm the eating type. And this is the best thing I've eaten for a long time. Well. Ever. And you didn't have to buy it. You just went out and cast a line into a lake or a stream, and there was breakfast. And it was free.'

He laughed, a sort of snorting laugh. I wasn't sure why.

'Free. Let's see. Forty-five dollars a year for the license. Probably close to a thousand on a half-dozen rod-and-reel combos. Sinkers. Live bait. Hooks. Spinners. Salmon eggs. Floats. Line. Divide that by the number of fish I've caught, and it probably comes out to about fifty dollars a breakfast. Then again, I'll catch more in the years to come. Maybe I can get it down to ten a fish.'

'Oh. I knew that was too good to be true. Everything that's this good has to have a catch. No pun intended.'

'Well, not necessarily. Maybe not for you. You wouldn't need a license.'

'Why wouldn't I?'

'Sixteen and older.'

'Ooh. I have a year of free fishing left. Except for . . .'

'And the fact that I have half-a-dozen rods means I could loan you one. I'll give you a couple of hooks and some line, and when you've lost that, those are the cheap parts.'

'So you *will* teach me?'

'Sure.'

'When?'

'What are you doing today?'

'Today? You've already been fishing today.'

'So? You forget I'm retired.'

'Yeah, but won't you be sick of it twice in one day? Besides, you said dawn is best.'

'In the creeks, yes. The water's very shallow, and it's best when it's nearly dark. Just enough light for them to see your bait. Not enough for them to catch your movement on shore. Or for the sun to glint off the line in the water. But we could drive to one of those little stream-fed mountain lakes. They're just jumping with brookies. In the warm part of the day, they go into deep water, but the lakes are so small you can wade in up to your waist and cast into the deepest part of the lake.'

I started getting excited then, because standing in a lake up to my waist catching dinner sounded like a genuine summer vacation. Almost as good as Paul's retirement.

I'd not only have a great summer, I might even eat regularly. My whole family might even eat regularly.

On me.

In my mind, I watched rice and beans fade into the distant past.

'I could actually buy some fishing stuff,' I said. 'I have a little stash of money that nobody knows about.'

He pulled a rod out of the trunk and handed it to me. I swished it back and forth, and it was surprisingly flexible. Like you could almost bend it in half. I touched the line. Held it between my fingers. It was clear, and so thin it was almost like a human hair. Well, not quite. But really thin. I thought of the fish on my plate an hour earlier. The size of him. I wondered why he couldn't have broken it. His life depended on it, after all.

'That took some willpower,' he said.

He slammed the trunk.

We stood there by the lake, Paul in waterproof waders, me in just my tee-shirt, sneakers and cut-off shorts. He had a plastic tackle box in one hand, a rod and a net in the other. The basket, which I'd since found out was called a creel, was strapped over his shoulder.

'What took some willpower?'

I'd forgotten what we were talking about.

'Having money but not spending it. When I know you could have used more and better food.'

'I hope it didn't seem wrong to eat at your house when I had money stashed.'

'Not at all. It wouldn't have lasted long if you'd used it. Right?'

'Exactly. That's exactly why I didn't. Because it would've just been gone, and our problems would still be our problems. I used to give my mother most of the money I had, like when you paid me to walk Rigby. But it never solved our problem. The way to solve our problem is for my mom to make more money, or to figure out a place we can live for less money. If I gave her my hundred dollars, we'd eat well for a couple weeks and then it would be gone. And if anything I'd just have helped her not solve the problem for real. I keep thinking if things get tight enough she'll figure something out. But nothing so far. But this might be worth the money.'

'Save your hundred dollars. I'll give you what you need to start. I have enough tackle to last me as long as I live. If you run out of hooks or need a new spool of line, by then you will have put a dozen meals on the table. Tell her to invest a couple of dollars in the breadwinner.'

'Fishwinner,' I said.

'Fishwinner. Yes. But don't get cocky. You haven't caught anything yet. And you have a lot to learn.'

Paul leaned over closer and whispered, 'I'm finally getting nibbles. Are you?'

It was important to be quiet around fish. Well, trout. Otherwise they'd get spooked and go someplace else. We'd been standing in the lake being quiet for what seemed like about an hour.

'No,' I whispered.

I felt a little jealous, because he was getting nibbles. I was beginning to think this whole fishing thing wasn't all it was cracked up to be.

I was standing in water about to the tops of my cut-off jeans, which were pretty short. I was wearing my sneakers, because the lake bed was slippery and slimy. They'd dry out eventually.

I looked over my shoulder at Rigby, who was curled up in the shade on the shore. She hadn't moved. She wasn't the least bit concerned that we were someplace she didn't want to go. I would have known just to look at her that she'd done this before.

Then I felt something. Like someone gave my line a tiny tug.

'Yes!' I whispered.

'Remember what I told you?'

I nodded.

I was supposed to wait until I'd gotten another tug or two, then give the line a good jerk. That way, if the hook was in the fish's mouth, that would set it nice and deep.

I felt a flurry of little tugs. Almost like a stutter.

I jerked.

Nothing.

I waited. No more tugs.

'I don't think I got him,' I whispered.

'Reel in. Make sure he didn't steal your bait.'

I reeled in until I saw the hook break the surface of the water. It was bare. No salmon eggs.

'Now how did he manage to do that?'

'They'll do that to you all the time,' he said. 'Just because they want what's on the hook doesn't mean they'll take the whole hook to get it. Sometimes they just kind of poke at the bait. Or grab it and pull.'

'You think they know?'

'Probably not. But it's hard to say. Since I've never been a fish. Here, take a few more salmon eggs.'

He held the jar out to me. They were bright red, and about the size of baby peas. I put four on my hook. So all the fish would see was salmon eggs. So he wouldn't see the hook.

'I'm sorry if I gave you the wrong impression by coming home with five beautiful big rainbows. Sometimes you come home empty-handed. It's not as easy as just casting your hook into the water and reeling them in. Sometimes you get your bait stolen and nothing else. Other times you'll swear there's not a single living thing lurking under that water. But they're there. They're just either biting or they're not.'

'How do you know if they're biting?'

'By casting a baited hook into the water and seeing if they bite it. If there was a way of knowing before you left the house, and I knew it, I wouldn't have had to work in a bank all my life. I'd have bottled the secret and sold it to fishermen all over the world. I'd be a rich man indeed. Whoops.'

I didn't know what 'Whoops' meant until he set the hook and started reeling in. I could tell he had something, because I could see his rod bending under the pressure. I watched what he did, so I'd know what to do when it happened to me. If it happened to me.

'Get the net ready,' he said. 'Help me land him.'

'How do I do that?'

'Just hold the net out. I'll do the rest.'

I slipped the net off his shoulder – it was hanging by a loop of green rope. I held the net out with both hands, holding my fishing rod between my knees. I watched the fish break the surface of the water three times. Like he thought he could fly away. But he couldn't.

A couple seconds later he was in the net, and Paul was taking the hook out of his mouth. He didn't even need to put fresh salmon eggs on the hook. He only had to slightly rearrange the ones that were there.

The fish wasn't a rainbow. He was a darker color, a mottled brown with a long flash of dark red under his belly.

I watched Paul hold the fish by the bottom half of its mouth and move him to the creel basket, which was hanging down into the water. I felt bad for the little guy. He wanted so badly to get free. I could see his whole body twist into spasms, every ounce of his energy spent to save his own life. But his life was over.

'Too bad for him,' I said.

'Yeah, but good for us.'

'Ever feel bad for them?'

'Yes and no. When they die in the wild, it's usually by being eaten alive. This has to be better than that.'

I was going to say something, but I got a nibble.

I waited. Felt two more. But they were stronger. Like big tugs.

I yanked hard. The fish yanked back.

'I got one!' I said, forgetting to whisper.

'Nice and steady. Don't hurry. But don't give him any slack, either.'

The whole time I was pulling him in, I could feel him pulling back. Then, sooner than I expected it, I saw him under the water. He was less than a foot from my right leg. He was bigger than the one Paul had just caught. He was a beauty.

Then I was looking down at nothing. He was gone.

'What just happened?' I asked.

'Your fish swam away.'

'How did he get off the hook?'

'You stopped reeling. When you take the pressure off the line, that helps them wiggle off the hook if they're ever going to.'

'But it has a barb. So it'll stay in.'

'So it'll usually stay in. If you're lucky. Almost any trout can twist off almost any hook if you give him too many chances. Think of it as a gamble between you and the fish. There are odds on both sides. Be glad you're not the one betting your life.'

It made me uneasy to think of this as gambling. Because things that had gambles involved seem to hook me. I swear I didn't mean that like a pun.

I put on four more salmon eggs and cast again.

Paul said, 'You're getting good at that.'

A split second later, there was something on my line again, and I was reeling it in.

'Just keep reeling until it's out of the water and then see if you can drop it in the net.'

I watched this beautiful living thing come up out of his lake, and I jerked him up higher, trying to wait until Paul had the net under him. I could see sunlight blinking off his wet, dark-red belly, and then he twisted and flipped hard, both at the same time, and came off the hook. And dropped right into the net.

'You just caught a fish,' Paul said.

'Wow.'

I stared at him while Paul was putting him in the creel. And I thought, I killed him. I'm killing him. But I needed to eat. And it did occur to me that when we ate fish filets from the grocery store, somebody killed those, too. But this wasn't somebody killing a fish for me. This was me, doing it directly.

But I didn't back down. Because my family needed more food to eat. Yeah, it was tough that his life was over, but that was the way it was. If a lion or a wolf ever needed to eat, my life might be over. I would just have to deal with killing a fish. And the fish . . . well, he had no choice. Did he?

In my head, I told him I was sorry. But also that I was not putting him back.

'What if I came out here to fish by myself? How would I get him in the net?'

'Here's what I do. I come out into the lake, and cast into deep water. Then I open the bail and let out line as I walk back to shore. And I fish from shore. If I catch something, I reel it in and then turn and throw it on to the ground as far from the lake as I can. He can flop around all he wants, but you've still got him. Even if he comes off the hook, you've still got him. But if he can flop back into the water, he'll be—'

Then he had to stop talking, because he'd hooked another one.

It didn't matter, because I knew the end of the sentence anyway. I knew, if he flopped back into the water, what he'd be.

Then I caught another one.

Then Paul caught a third.

I didn't catch a third.

Then no more nibbles. No more tugs.

We stood there for another half an hour or so. I didn't mind the time going by. I wasn't bored. I just watched the way the mountains reflected in the surface of the water, and the way that reflection rippled when a wind gust came up. I watched long-legged birds wading around near the shore.

I was on vacation. And I was happy.

Paul said, 'Funny how they won't be biting. And then all of a sudden they are. And then all of a sudden they're not again. We might just as well call it a day.'

While we were driving home, Paul asked, 'You want me to gut those for you?'

'I will. I mean, I think I can. I mean, I just will. Maybe you could teach me.'

'You take three of the five.'

'That's not fair.'

'It's fine. You have three mouths to feed at your house. I have two still left from this morning. So I'll take two and that'll be two meals each for Rigby and me.'

'OK. If you're sure.'

'I'm sure,' he said.

When we got inside his house, something was beeping.

Paul was in the kitchen, dumping the fish into his stainless-steel sink. It didn't seem like he heard it.

'What's that beeping?'

'It's my message machine. Let me wash my hands and I'll come see what it is.'

I leaned on the table instead of sitting. Because my cut-offs were still wet. The beeping made me nervous, but I wasn't even sure why.

A minute later he came out, drying his hands on a dish towel, and hit a button on the machine.

'Paul,' a voice said. A woman. With a trace of accent. 'Call me. OK?' Pause. 'Call me.'

We looked at each other.

'Rachel?' I asked.

'Yes.' Long silence. Then he said, 'Is it just me, or did that sound . . . not good?'

'It definitely sounded not good.'

'OK, I have to call her.'

'Want me to go?'

'I haven't given you your fish yet. I have to show you how to gut them.'

'I could wait outside.'

'It doesn't matter. I don't care. You don't have to go. I just have to call her right now.'

He picked up the phone and punched the number in by heart. Which made sense, since it had been his number for decades.

She must've been close to the phone.

'Rachel. Yeah. Are you OK? You sounded—'

Then it must have been her talking. For a long time.

I watched him. I just stood there and watched him listen. What else could I do? The more he listened, the older he looked.

After a while, he said, 'I'll come down.'

Silence on our end.

'No, I can put her in a kennel.'

Silence.

'Well, no. You're right. Not if it was that long. But I can work it out. I might even have a dog sitter for her. Right here.'

More silence.

'Rachel, are you sure?'

Silence. The silences were starting to hurt. I felt like someone was sitting on my chest. And I didn't even know what the hell was going on.

'But what about *you*, though?'

More hurt.

'OK. I don't know what to say. Will you call me if you

change your mind? And if you don't change your mind, will you call me the minute you know more?'

Quick silence.

'OK. Can I call you every day?'

Medium silence.

'OK. I'll call your cell. Bye. Take care, OK?'

He clicked the off button on the phone. But he didn't put it down. He just stood there, not moving, not talking. Not looking at Rigby or me. Just looking at the phone like it must have something more to tell him. Even though there was nobody left on the line.

I wanted to ask, 'What is it? What's wrong?' But I didn't want to burst him out of this delicate moment. It felt like that thing about never waking a sleepwalker. It felt like it might be dangerous.

I had time to think, He does have all the same feelings everybody else has. When he acts like he doesn't, that's a lie.

He looked at me. His eyes bored right in.

'Something wrong with Rachel?' I asked.

'No. Dan. Something's wrong with Dan.'

He didn't say what. Not right away. I just waited.

Then, finally, 'He has stage four stomach cancer.'

'And they just now told you about it?'

'They just now found out.'

'What's going to happen to him?'

'They're not sure yet. He's going in for surgery day after tomorrow. They're pretty sure it's metastasized. But they'll know more when they get in there. I wanted to go down, but she insisted I stay. That I stay and enjoy my retirement. I should be down there, though.'

We stood in that painful silence for another space of time. Minutes, from the feel of it. But the feel of things can be a lie.

Then he said, 'Come on. Let's get you those fish.'

I followed him into the kitchen, my legs wobbling a little.

'I would take care of Rigby if you wanted to go down there.'

'I know. I tried to tell her that. Do you mind if I don't teach you this today? How to clean them? Do you mind if I just do it?'

'Fine. I don't mind.'

I sat at the table, and watched his back. He was working with his hands down in the sink, so I didn't have to see any blood or guts.

'Can I ask you a question?' I said, kind of quietly.

'I guess so,' he said. Without turning around.

'I know you don't like your brother, but . . . do you love him?'

He didn't answer for a long time. Long enough that I thought he never would.

Then he said, 'Yes.'

That's all. Just yes. Nothing fancier than that.

It got quiet in that kitchen again.

A minute later he spoke up, and it was loud. Too loud. It startled me.

'I'm going down there.'

He wiped his hands off on a white dish towel, leaving it smeared with bright-red fish blood. He hurried into the living room. I got up and stood in the doorway and watched him punch buttons into the phone.

'Rachel, listen. Please. Just listen. I'm the only living blood family he's got. And it's going to be a big job to take care of him after surgery. And you don't have family close by. Please. Don't argue. Just let me come. If you won't let me come for you, or for Dan, let me come for me.'

The first silence of the second phone call. It didn't hurt quite as much as the earlier ones.

'Angie will take care of her. Won't you, Angie?'

He looked up at me, his eyes different. Deeper than before. Like a cave you can suddenly walk further into.

'Yeah. Sure I will.'

'For as long as she needs to. Right, Angie?'

'Yeah. Doesn't matter how long. All summer if I need to.'

'She could stay here with Rig all summer if she needed to.'

'Oh, wait,' I said, and motioned for him to cover the phone.

'Rachel, hang on just a minute.' He pressed the heel of his hand on the mouthpiece. 'Problem?'

'I couldn't take her to my house. They don't allow pets.'

'You could stay here.'

'OK.'

He put the phone back to his ear, then thought better of it and covered the mouthpiece again. 'Would your mom let you stay alone?'

'I think so. I'm not positive, though.'

'Are *you* OK staying alone?'

'Are you kidding me? When am I not alone? And in charge of my sister to boot.'

'I'll pay you.'

'You don't have to pay me.'

'Of course I'll pay you. Don't be silly.'

'Paul. We're friends. You don't have to pay me.'

He stared at a spot around my chin for a second or two, and I had no idea what he was thinking.

'We'll work something out,' he said. Then he put the phone to his ear again. 'I'll leave in the morning,' he told her.

'Right,' he said.

'See you then,' he said.

'Rachel?' he asked.

Silence. I had a funny feeling it was silent on both ends of the line.

'Never mind. I'll see you tomorrow.'

I watched Sophie wolfing down her trout. Eating the usual way. With her fingers.

'Did you check hers really carefully for small bones?' I asked my mom.

'Stop changing the subject. Back up. Why are you not getting paid for this?'

'He offered to pay me. But I said no. Now, if you don't mind, I'm going to eat my fish while it's still hot.'

We ate in silence for a long time. The only sound was Sophie making a little noise on every chew. She always ate with her mouth wide open. It was kind of gross, but I figured she couldn't help it. So I just didn't look in. My mom was smoldering, and I was trying to ignore it. I was also trying not to let it affect my appetite or upset my stomach. It was my second high-protein meal in one day. I swear all that protein was going to my head. My brain felt clearer than it had in months.

When I finally swallowed the last bite, my mom broke her vow of silence.

'OK. You're done. Why did you say no to money, again?'

'Because he's my friend. You don't charge your friend for doing a favor. Especially at a time like this.'

'You do if you need the money. If he was really your friend he'd know you needed it. And he'd insist.'

'He did insist. Or anyway, he tried. I turned him down. He does stuff for me all the time. I ate there almost every day from the time we moved here to the time Sophie and I went on the school-lunch program. What did you think we were eating all day? You never even paid attention. He taught me how to fish. He's loaning me a fishing pole and enough tackle to get me started. Which is how I brought home this great dinner. Which you haven't even bothered to thank me for. You've been in such a rotten mood lately, I hardly even know how to deal with you any more.'

The room went quiet for a bit. Except for the Sophie noises.

My mom took a bite of her fish. It must have been really cold by then.

'It's very good. Thank you. It's just that we could really use some extra cash.'

'We can always use extra cash. And you always try to solve the problem by looking at me. There are child-labor laws, you know. If we're not eating enough, you're supposed to get a better job or something. Or a second job. Or a cheaper place to live. You're not supposed to look at me like it's my job to feed us. I learned to fish so I can bring home food. And you don't even appreciate it.'

'I don't see how fish will solve our problem.'

'*I* do! We can *eat* it!'

I was starting to get mad. Sophie's little noises got bigger, because we were making her nervous. She didn't like it when we yelled.

'Don't you think we'll get sick of fish after a while?'

'Unlike rice and beans, or pasta. Which of course we never get sick of!'

'Don't raise your voice to me.'

'You want that fish, or don't you? Because I'd be really happy to eat it if you don't even care.'

First she didn't answer. But when I dove for the plate, she defended it. She wrapped her arms around it and boxed me out.

'Look, I'm sorry,' she said. 'Yes. I want it. I'm worried about money is all.'

'Is that why you've been in such a bad mood?'

'I haven't been in a bad mood.'

I snorted louder than I meant to.

'Right. Of course not. I'm going for a walk.'

She didn't say a word. She didn't even try to stop me. I looked back to see her scarfing down the fish. I shook my head and kept going.

Paul's porch light was off, so I stood in the dark by his door until he had time to come open it. Then he snapped the porch light on, and it stabbed into my eyes like twin daggers. I shielded my eyes with my hand.

When he opened the door, I just stood there for another second. Not sure what to say.

'I had a fight with my mom. Can I come in?'

He stepped away from the door, and I walked in, and leaned over Rigby and hugged her and hugged her and hugged her. I thought, Don't you ever die, Rigby. Don't you dare ever die. Between that and my mom, I felt a little close to crying, so I hugged her even longer, until I got it under control.

Then I straightened up and had no idea what to say to Paul.

I wanted to ask if I could sleep there for the night. But I knew I couldn't. I knew there was nothing perverted about Paul and me, and he knew it, but there was that place where you have to bow to what other people are bound to think. I couldn't stay at his house until he wasn't there any more.

So I said, 'Maybe I could just stay here until I'm sure she's in bed.'

'Sure.'

'I sleep in the living room, so until she goes to bed I get no privacy.'

'You'll get plenty of privacy in the next couple of weeks.'

'Yeah, that'll be really nice.'

I looked around the place and started to think how great it would be to have it all to myself, all day long, day after day. It made me want to go home even less.

'I won't get in your hair, I promise.'

'You never get in my hair. You know how to play gin rummy?'

'No. But I could learn. If you're willing to teach me.'

We played more than twenty hands before I finally went home.

I started to like it too much. Like maybe everything having to do with cards was bad for me. But it wasn't the cards, really. It was the gambling. We didn't play for money, but I could see how easy it would be to cross that line.

What if I was a gambler at heart? Just like my dad?

I'd have to be careful about that.

Chapter Two

 **Because**

'Kibble is in this cupboard,' he said. He opened the pantry to show me a plastic bin that was almost as big as a garbage can, but with a tighter lid. 'There's a measuring scoop inside. So one scoop, and one can of the wet food. Twice a day. You can put the arthritis pills right into her food. I left them by the microwave.'

'Does it matter exactly what time?'

'Not to the minute. I feed her when I get up and then again around five. She'll bug you if she's hungry. An hour here or there doesn't bother her much.'

I counted the dog-food cans on the shelf.

'Two a day. So what if you're gone for more than eighteen days?'

'Well, I doubt that. But just to be on the safe side . . .' He pulled out his wallet and took out a twenty. Stuck it under the last can on the shelf. 'They sell it at the local market, so just save the last can so you know you're getting the right stuff.'

'OK. How do I know if she has to go out?'

'You don't have to worry about that. I had a doggie door installed in the back door. She'll let herself out.'

'Is it all fenced?'

'Not completely. But she won't go away. She's too well-trained for that.'

'What if she gets worried because you're gone?'

'I go away and leave her all the time. She'll just wait for me at the house. She's a good dog. Trust her.'

'I do,' I said.

But it was a big responsibility.

'Here's the number of her vet. And my cell-phone number. If you have any questions, just call me.'

'OK.'

'You sure I can't pay you for this?'

'Positive.'

That seemed to stop him for a minute. I wondered what he was thinking. I couldn't tell from his face.

'Eat everything. I expect to find not one scrap of food in this house when I get back. And the fishing stuff is all in the garage. Take it out. There are lots of places you can walk to. I'll leave you a map of the town, and you'll be able to see where the streams run through. Unless you've already figured that out since you've been here.'

'Not really. The map would be good. Should I take her?'

'Sure. If you want.'

'What if it's too much walking for her?'

'Try taking her everywhere. If she comes up limping, or stiff, that's too much. Cut back a bit. If you're not sure, call.'

'OK.'

'Nervous about it?'

'A little.'

'Don't be. You love her. That's all the skills you really need for the job.'

We stood on the back porch and watched him drive away. I waved, but, because of the way we were looking down on his car, I doubt he could even see me.

'He'll come back,' I told Rigby. 'And I'll take good care of you while he's gone.'

I'm not sure why I bothered, though. She didn't seem the least bit nervous. The only nervous in the place was coming from me.

I opened his refrigerator door. Because of course I hadn't had breakfast. I found orange juice. Two dozen eggs. Bacon. Cheddar cheese and cream cheese. Milk. Salad makings in the vegetable drawer. An opened package of smoked salmon. A shrink-wrapped package of lean ground beef. Half-a-dozen peaches.

'Holy crap!' I said out loud.

Rigby came over to see what the fuss was about. She looked where I was looking, into the fridge. Like she expected to see something unusual. Then she looked at me, like she wanted to know what all the excitement was about.

I guess it looked normal to her. I guess she was used to the fact that lots of people lived like this, with their refrigerators full of food. I'd completely forgotten.

I decided if there was cream cheese and smoked salmon, there must be bagels. So I looked on the counter. In the bread box.

I finally found them in the freezer.

I toasted up both halves of one and slathered them with cream cheese and mounded them up with half the smoked salmon, which was twice what any normal person would have used.

Paul had said he didn't want to see one scrap of food left when he got back. And he would never know what I ate when. Only I would know that.

The idea of eating more than I really needed was so foreign by then. I'd had no idea how much I missed it.

Then I got this sudden impulse to cut it in half and save half for Sophie. But it hit me that there was more. Lots more. I could make her a whole other bagel just like the one I was about to scarf down.

I took my first big bite and sighed. Literally just sat there at his kitchen table, not even chewing. Just tasting what I'd already bitten down on.

'This is the life, Rig,' I said, my mouth still full.

I found a trail down to the creek following Paul's map. Rigby followed so close behind me that if I stopped for even a second her nose bumped into my back.

The trees got closer in, and I kept catching the end of the fishing pole on the branches. Then I'd have to stop and make sure the line wasn't tangled in the pine needles.

When we got to the creek, I looked down into the water. It was only maybe a foot deep, running clear with a wonderful sound. But if there had been fish in there, I would have seen them.

There were no fish.

I wished there'd been time to take *two* fishing lessons before Paul had to go away. Like maybe one lesson in stream fishing. So far I only knew how to fish in a lake. And the lakes were too far away to walk to.

I looked down to see Rigby staring up into my face. I could tell she wanted to know what my problem was. Why didn't I just go fishing? Maybe there were certain spots where the fish liked to hang out. Maybe Rigby came down here all the time with Paul. Maybe she knew where he usually liked to go.

'Which way, Rigby?'

It might have just been me, but she seemed happy I asked. She headed off right away, upstream. I followed her, puffing up the hill. Trying to look down, so as not to trip on the brush poking out on to the trail. And to look up so I wouldn't snag a tree with the pole. Both at the same time.

'Wait up, Rig,' I called.

She did.

About five minutes of brush-popping later we came out into a clearing, dappled with sunlight through overhanging trees. The stream gave way to a flat, level pool, much deeper than the rest of the water, and about five times wider. I set down the tackle box and rod, stepped out on to some huge, smooth rocks. Got down on all fours. There was a bare downed tree half under the water, and I steadied myself on one of the branches as I leaned out over the pool.

More than a dozen rainbow trout skittered by, the ripples of the pool bending their images.

I made my way back to Rigby.

'Good dog,' I said.

I spent probably ten minutes just getting a hook on to the end of the line. Because I'd forgotten how Paul had taught me to tie the knot. I kept doing it the way I thought was right, but then I'd pull hard on the hook to make sure it would hold. And it would pull right off again.

I looked over at Rigby, who was lying beside me, front legs outstretched, eyes half closed in the dappled sun. Her eyebrows were gray now, too, her muzzle grayer.

I started the knot over.

'So you put the end of the line through . . .'

For one insane moment, I swear I held it out for her to see. Like she would show me which loop to put the end of the line through. The way she knew where Sophie was, where the campground was. Where to find Paul's best fishing spot.

I caught myself, and hit myself in the forehead with the heel of my hand.

'Right,' I said. '*That* magic you're not.'

But just by holding the half-done knot out to her, it

made more slack in the knot. And I saw the other place the end of the line could go through. I watched it open up.

'Of course. I remember now. First twist it a few times. Then through *here*. Then through the loop it makes. I think that's it, Rig!'

I pulled it tight, and pulled hard on the hook. Careful not to stab myself. I pulled almost hard enough to break the line, but the knot held.

I pressed two split-shot sinkers on to the line the way Paul had shown me, biting them to get them to clamp down tightly.

I threaded four salmon eggs on to the hook, then walked carefully out on to the slick boulders. I swished the rod back behind my shoulder, ready to give it a good snap. A nice, long cast like I'd done at the lake. When I jerked the rod forward again, it hung up. I'd snagged on something before I even finished my first cast.

I climbed back down off the rocks and followed the line until I could see it was hung up in a tree. I couldn't reach up high enough to untangle it. I tried pulling the limb down, but the line snapped.

I sighed, and walked back to Rigby. And sat.

'Great,' I said. 'Lost a hook before I even got it wet the first time.'

I tied another hook on the line, added two more sinkers, and threaded on four more salmon eggs. The tiny jar was more than half empty. A handful more mistakes like that and I'd have to figure out how to use some other kind of bait.

I crawled out on to the boulders again. Looked down into the water, and felt a little thrill when two trout slid by underneath me. I wondered if this was how a lion felt watching a herd of zebras trot along the plain.

I opened the bail on the reel and let the line drop straight down.

At first, nothing. All those trout, and not one seemed to notice. A ray of sun lit the pool where my baited hook had landed, and the salmon eggs looked illuminated, like tiny bright-red light bulbs.

I looked over my shoulder to be sure Rigby wasn't going anywhere. Even though I knew that was the sort of thing she would never do.

I could hear Paul's voice saying, 'Trust her.'

I took a deep breath and tried.

When I looked back, a rainbow trout was just inches from my bait. Holding perfectly still. Looking at it pretty much the way I was looking at him. Then he swished his body and came closer. Stopped. Waited.

He reached out and pulled at a salmon egg, then spooked away when the hook moved. I swear I wasn't breathing at all. A mosquito bit the back of my leg, and I couldn't even slap it.

The trout came in again and swallowed the bait, hook and all.

I tightened the line and he took off, bending my rod forward. He disappeared under the fallen tree. My rod stayed bent but I couldn't feel him pulling. I tried to reel in, but the line was stuck. He must've wrapped it around a branch.

I pulled. I waited.

Finally I knew I was sunk, so I just gave up and broke the line.

I slouched back off the rocks to start all over again. I stared into the salmon egg jar and knew I needed to get away from that downed tree. I got the hook all baited and ready, and then closed and latched the tackle box.

'Come on, Rigby. Let's see if we can figure out how to get to the other side of this stream.'

It wasn't hard. At the bottom of the pool the stream narrowed. It was only a foot or two deep. So I waded right through it, careful not to slip on the wet stones. Rigby splashed along behind me.

We hiked back up to the deep pool and stood on the other side, where the slickrock sloped right down into the water. I wouldn't be able to hide as well there. But I wouldn't get my line caught. If I hooked one, there would be nothing to snag on as I pulled him out.

This time I looked behind me before I cast. It was a long way back to the closest tree. So I gave it a good backward swing and cast it nice and far. Right out into the deep center of the pool.

I took up the slack in the line, and looked down at Rigby, who was sitting on the slanted stone.

'I feel optimistic again,' I said.

I made a mental note to see if I could find a flashlight in Paul's house. So we could leave much earlier in the morning next time. He struck me as the kind of guy who would have a flashlight, in case the power went out. He probably carried emergency road flares in his car trunk, too. Not like anybody in my family. We just hoped for no disasters. We didn't actually prepare or anything.

I lay back on the rock with my head on Rigby's side and tried not to fall asleep. Maybe I did, though. Or maybe no time went by at all.

It wasn't a tug I got on the line. It was a full-fledged fight, right from the start. I sat up fast, and my pole bent nearly in half, and I wondered if it was possible for a fish to break it. But then I decided the line would break first.

I remembered what Paul taught me. Don't hurry, but go steady. No slack on the line. I just kept reeling when he came up out of the water, and dropped him on to the slickrock a good ten feet from the edge of the pool. He didn't come off the hook.

Rigby reached her nose out to sniff him, to get the measure of him. But she didn't try to touch him or get in my way.

I took him by the bottom half of his mouth, the way Paul showed me. But I couldn't get the hook out. And I felt bad, like I was hurting him by trying. So I just held the hook, so it wouldn't pull on his mouth, and broke the line. And put him in the creel, in shallow water. Later, before I cooked him, I could take the hook back. It wouldn't hurt him by then.

I used the same artificial worm, because the fish hadn't swallowed it, and cast again into the deep part of the pool. But this time I sat up, and forward. Staring.

Ready. Because this time I believed something would happen.

I swear it wasn't ten minutes later when I reeled in another one.

I thought, This fishing thing is great. It's like magic. I'll just keep dropping the hook in, and pulling them out. Every ten minutes. All morning. Or, anyway, until I caught the daily limit, which was five. And then I'd feel bad that I had to stop. Almost like I couldn't stop. Kind of the way I felt when I was building that last card house and I got to the fifty-second card.

I thought, Damn that limit thing, anyway. I thought, I wonder if anyone would notice. I wondered how often anybody even checked. Even though I knew I'd probably decide to do it right.

I needn't have gone to all the bother of wrestling with myself about it. I didn't catch another thing all morning.

I was napping when the phone rang.

It was about 4.30 in the afternoon. The phone startled me out of a dream, and I woke up on my feet, panting. Still scared, even though I knew by then it was only the phone. I tried to remember the dream, but it was gone.

I didn't know if I should answer it. I'd forgotten to ask Paul if I should answer his phone if it rang.

I moved closer, watching it, startled by every ring.

On the fourth, I picked it up.

'Hello? This is . . . the Inverness residence.'

'It's Paul.'

I let out a boatload of breath I hadn't even known I'd been holding.

'Oh, thank God. Because I didn't know if I was supposed to answer your phone.'

'That was fine,' he said. 'Just what you did.'

'How's your brother? Did they do the surgery?'

'Yeah. He's out. He's in recovery.'

'How does it look?'

He didn't answer right away. In fact, he didn't answer for quite a while. So that's how I knew.

Finally, finally, he said, 'Bad.'

But it didn't even need saying by then.

'I'm sorry.'

A chunk of quiet. On both ends of the phone.

Then he said, 'Remember when you said you could stay all summer if you needed to?'

'Yeah. I still can.'

'Good. Because I want to stay down here. Until . . .'

But then he didn't want to say until what. But I pretty much knew. There was really only one 'until' it could be.

'How long, do you think? I don't mind. I like it here. A lot. I just wondered. You know. My mom'll ask. So . . . just so I can tell her.'

'They're saying two to four months. But probably more like two and less like four. I'll come back a couple of times, so Rigby doesn't think I forgot her completely. And, look . . . I know she's OK. I mean, she's healthy. She's seven and a half, but she's in good shape. But if anything happens, call me right away. I'll come back up. If you have to take her to the vet, or she's acting funny, call me so I can get back. The last thing I want to do is miss the last days with my dog.'

It bothered me that he would say that. I mean, I knew why he said it, and I knew he had to. I just wished it hadn't been like that. I wished it hadn't been there to need saying.

'She's fine. She's in great shape.'

'I know she is. I'm just a little gun-shy right now. Life seems very impermanent.'

'She's fine.'

His tone changed, like he'd shaken himself out of a dream. 'You have to let me pay you now. If it's going to be a couple of months.'

'No. No way. Don't even bring it up again. We're friends.' A long pause. Then I said, 'I'm sorry you're having to go through all this.'

'Thanks.'

'You can call. You know. If you ever just want to talk about . . . things.'

Another long pause.

'You know, I just might take you up on that. It's not the usual me. But it's not impossible. I'll keep you posted. I'll call again soon.'

I could tell he'd done all the talking about heavy stuff he could manage for the time being. So we just wrapped it up quick and got off the phone.

I looked around his house, and got hit by this rush of relief that I didn't have to leave the place anytime soon. It was the kind of place you could get used to.

I fetched the two fish out of the refrigerator and put them back in the creel basket, and then at the last minute decided to cover them up with ice cubes for the walk.

I put on my sneakers, even though they were still wet.

'Come on, Rigby,' I said. 'Let's go see Sophie and my mom and bring them some dinner.'

The phone rang again.

I picked it up faster this time.

'Hello?'

Then I remembered I didn't say it right, like last time. All polite and fancy.

'Me again.'

'Hi.'

'I've been thinking.'

He sounded pretty serious. And I got scared. I thought it was all about to come out from under me again.

'About what?'

'I was thinking you should move your family into the apartment over the garage while I'm gone.'

I didn't say anything. Because I couldn't. My mouth was out of order.

'I don't just mean only while I'm gone. But I also have to be honest and say I don't promise it's permanent. When I get back, I think we should make some really solid ground rules for my privacy. If they work, great. If not, I know it'll take you a while to find a new place, but you can stay until you do. But even if it doesn't work out, wouldn't it help to have free rent for a few months?'

'Yeah. A lot. We'll follow the rules.'

'I know *you* will. We'll see how it goes, OK? No promises.'

'OK.'

'Just you in the main house, though. Please. Even while I'm gone. Just you, OK? Even though I'd never know.'

'You know I always tell you the truth. Even though you'd never know.'

'I do. Yes. I know that about you. Will this really help? Or am I just pretending it helps?'

'It really helps. A lot.'

Silence.

Then I asked the pressing question. 'Why? Why did you decide that all of a sudden?'

'I thought that would be obvious,' he said.

'Sorry,' I said.

'Because we're friends.'

'Oh. Right. Because we're friends.'

I walked down the back stairs and up the steep dirt driveway. I could hear and feel Rigby padding along close behind me. I'd never gone out to the garage before. It was bigger than it looked from the house. Two cars wide, and deeper than usual, with a workshop and firewood storage place. I puffed up the stairs and tried the door, but it was locked.

I thought I'd have to go back to the house and start over, but I felt my shorts pockets and found the keys Paul had given me. It was a huge relief. Not because it was so miserable to walk a few yards uphill. Because I couldn't wait to see the place.

I opened the door and sucked in my breath so hard that Rigby jumped a little. It was half-again bigger than the place we were spending all our money on. And it was just as nice as the main house, with the same hardwood floors and wood paneling and shutters on the inside. About two-thirds of the floor was covered with this beautiful old antique Persian rug in soft blues, and one whole wall was a built-in bookcase.

There was no bedroom, though. It was all one big room. But it did have a screen, kind of a room divider, wrapped around a bed. I figured we'd need to get another bed, unless the huge brown suede couch folded out. But I didn't feel like I had to worry about that just then. One corner was set up like a little kitchen, with a two-burner stove and a sink and refrigerator about the size of the ones they make for mobile homes. And a round wood kitchen table with two chairs. We'd need another chair. Which also didn't matter yet.

At the back of the place, facing the snowy mountains, most of the wall was a sliding-glass patio door. So you could walk over and look out at the world like you were standing right out there, right in it. Not like you were inside at all. Or you could slide it open and step out on to a wooden deck with a rail. Which I did, just for a minute. Just to get the feel of it. There were wooden chairs out there, to sit on and watch the view. I didn't sit. I wasn't done looking around.

But that wasn't even the best part yet.

The ceiling was built like an A-frame. I guess to match the house. I don't think it was constructed as a genuine A-frame, but it had that high, slanty ceiling. The middle just went up for ever. It had open beams, with baskets and dried flowers hanging on them. And on each sloping side, a skylight.

I looked up and thought every place I'd lived, right up until that moment, had given me claustrophobia. All of a sudden I got free of this sickness I'd never even known I had.

I walked around for a minute like I was walking in a dream. Which I think I felt like I was. I ran my hand along the edges of book shelves. I bounced once on the couch to see how it felt.

It felt just the way it looked. Rich. Like I was suddenly rich.

I walked in a circle for a minute, because I couldn't think what else to do. Then I sat down in the middle of the rug and cried. Rigby sat with me.

At first I tried to explain to her that I wasn't unhappy. It was more that I'd always been unhappy before. That things had been so terrible right up to that moment that it was almost like I didn't dare cry until it was over.

But maybe it was myself I was explaining it to, because Rigby is the last one in the world who wouldn't get a thing like that on her own.

I just know I cried for a long time.

I put fresh ice on the fish before we left the house, and it melted as we walked, and dripped all down my leg. It smelled a little fishy. I kept expecting to be followed by a herd of cats or something. At least, it would have gone like that in a cartoon.

It didn't happen.

'I hope you're not disappointed,' I said to Rigby. 'I know when Paul catches two fish, you get one. But the first two are for Sophie and my mom, because they don't eat as well as we do. If I ever catch an extra two instead of just the two for them, I'll give you one. In fact, I'll take it a step further. If I ever catch two for them and then one more, I'll split it with you.'

By this time we were walking up the driveway of the old place. Funny how fast I'd started to look at it that way. It sure didn't take me long to throw that tiny, expensive place away. I checked to make sure the ice wasn't completely melted, but there was plenty to keep the fish cold. More than half what I'd started with.

My mom must've seen me out the window, because she threw the door wide.

'You can't bring her in here. We'll get in trouble with the Magnussons.'

The Magnussons were the people who lived in the big house. Our landlords.

'Fine. Come out.'

Sophie heard my voice and came blasting out shouting, 'Hem, Hem, Hem!'

I held the creel out to my mom.

'I caught you two fish. But I need the basket back.'

'OK. I'll put them in the fridge and bring it back to you.'

'Wait. I have news first.'

'It'll only take a minute.'

She disappeared.

'You need to gut them,' I called after her. 'Do you know how?'

'I'll manage,' she called back.

'Teach me how, then, OK? And save the hook in that one's mouth. I need all the hooks I can get.'

But I couldn't tell if she heard me or not.

I looked down at Sophie, who was sitting in the dirt beside Rig. I wondered if she thought we were going for a walk. It surprised me a little to realize I'd missed her. Even though it hadn't even been a full two days.

My mom popped back out and handed me the empty creel basket.

'What's the news? Good or bad?'

'Good.'

'Thank God. Tell me, then.'

'Paul's going to be away much longer than he thought—'

'How long?'

'Like, months.'

'Ah. Great,' she said. Like it wasn't great at all. 'So he must be paying you a lot. Because nothing else makes this good news. You come over here and tell me I'm on my own to work and pay bills and take care of Sophie for months, and you tell me it's good news. So it must be a lot of money. It'd better be.'

'It's not money. I'm not letting him pay me.'

'Get to the good part, Angie, and get to it fast, because my head is about to explode here. If you think I'm going to—'

'He's letting us live in the apartment over his garage.'

Her eyes narrowed a little.

'How big is it?'

'Bigger than this.'

'Is it nice?'

'It's incredible. Nicer than any place we've ever lived.'

'Then we can't afford it.'

'Oh, yes we can.'

'What does he want for it?'

'Nothing.'

We just stood there in the warm sun for a minute while she let that sink in. Rigby was snuffling Sophie's hair.

'He's letting us move in for free?'

'Yes.'

'Why?'

'Because I wouldn't let him pay me for taking care of his dog. Which you thought was such a terrible idea.'

She just stood there blinking for a while longer. I could tell the idea of the thing just couldn't quite break through.

'Just while he's gone?'

'Not necessarily. He says when he gets back he'll make some ground rules so he can still have his privacy. And if you can stick with them, we can stay. If it doesn't work out, we can stay till we find someplace else.'

I waited. But she still just blinked.

'I'm waiting for the moment you get it and start being happy,' I said.

That seemed to be the ticket. Her face changed, like somebody had stopped electrocuting her with cattle prods all of a sudden. She rushed in and picked me right up off my feet in a hug.

'Oh, my God,' she said. 'No rent?'

'No rent.'

'So the money I make . . .'

'We can buy food with it. And put gas in the car. And stuff like that.'

'Oh, my God, we'll have so much money!' Her voice came up to a shriek on the word money, and it hurt my ear. But I really didn't mind. She put me down and let me go. Held me out at arms' length by my shoulders. 'Can we go see it?'

'Sure. Do we have any gas at all?'

'None. I'm not even sure it would start. We'll have to walk.'

'Fine. We'll walk.'

As we massed down the driveway together, all four of us, she stroked my hair and said, 'Honey, I'm sorry I've been such a mess lately. I know I haven't been very nice to be around. I was under so much pressure and I was just so scared.'

'I know,' I said. 'I knew that.'

But she'd denied it, right up until that moment. So it was nice to hear it from her own mouth. Not like I always needed to be right, exactly. More that it felt good to be told I wasn't imagining things, and I wasn't crazy.

*

'Oh. My. God,' my mom said.

She was looking straight up when she said it. Right up into the middle of the ceiling. Up at the rafters with the baskets and the dried flowers. And, between us and them, all that room. All that space. Almost like freedom. Like not having to live with your elbows in, even though I knew that wasn't really right, because that's horizontal space and this was vertical. But that was how it felt.

'This is so much bigger than it looks from the outside. So you're telling me we can stay here for ever and not pay rent? I can't quite wrap my head around that.'

'For ever is kind of a long time,' I said. 'But if it works out, we won't have to move when he comes home.'

'I'll follow the rules. I promise.'

'Told you it was good news.'

'You did.'

Rigby was lying stretched out on the rug like a sphinx, the way she used to do on the other side of the fence at the old place. Sophie was lying right beside her in the same position.

'How's his brother?'

'Dying. That's why he's not coming back right away.'

'Oh. I'm sorry. That must be hard. What's his brother's name?'

'What difference does *that* make?'

'I just asked. What's wrong with wanting to know the guy's name?'

'Dan,' I said.

First no answer. Then she said, 'Ouch.' And, a minute later, 'Does this couch fold out?'

'I don't know. I didn't look.'

'Well, let's find out.'

She pulled all the couch cushions off and threw them on the rug. I wanted to tell her to be more gentle with everything, even though I didn't really suppose it hurt a cushion to get thrown on a rug.

'It does,' she said. 'It even looks like it has sheets on it. Oooh. Flannel. How about if Sophie and I take this and you sleep in that corner behind the screen? Since you like your privacy and all.'

'Well, later. After Paul comes back. Till then I'll be in the big house and you and Sophie can have this all to yourself.'

She didn't answer right away. Instead she walked to the big sliding-glass door and looked out over the mountains. I walked over and looked with her.

'If you'd told me a year or two ago we'd be here,' she said, 'I'd have told you you were nuts. We could barely afford a city apartment in an iffy neighborhood. And now here we are in this gorgeous little place in this tiny town where the schools are great and the air is clean . . .'

'And Sophie is quiet.'

'And I'll get some alone time for a change, because Sophie will want to be in the big house with the dog.'

'No,' I said, and she looked at me strangely. 'Only me in the house. Not Sophie and not you. I made him a promise.'

'He'll never know the difference.'

'Oh, my God! I don't believe you! You just stood here not two minutes ago and said you'd follow the rules. Do you want us to get to stay here or don't you?'

She cut her eyes away, like she always did when she didn't respect herself compared to me. After a few seconds she walked back to the couch and flopped down with a sigh. Like all the air had leaked out of her.

I pretended I wouldn't have to do it for a minute. Then I went over and sat with her. First neither one of us said anything at all. The silence got heavy and weird.

So I said, 'Penny for your thoughts.'

It's something she used to say to me all the time when I was a kid. Especially after Dad died. This was the first time I'd said it to her. Usually I was all too happy not to know.

'I was thinking about how you got us this place to live. And how I kept telling you to charge money for taking care of the dog. And how I'm supposed to be teaching you stuff like "Do good for others and it'll come back to you". Instead of you teaching me.'

'Yeah, well, don't put too much faith in me as a teacher,' I said, trying to find my way back into the daughter role. 'Half the time I feel like I have no idea what I'm doing.'

'I feel that way *all* the time,' she said.

Reminding me in one sentence that I could squeeze into the daughter role all I wanted, but getting her to stay in the mother role was another matter altogether.

*

Paul called at eleven o'clock the next night. The phone blasted me out of sleep. I'd been dreaming, and I had a weird sensation that Nellie had been in there somewhere. But she was gone as of that first ring.

Fortunately, there was a phone by the bed.

I picked it up and said hello. I turned on the light, but I don't know why. Because the moon was full, and I'd seen the phone just fine. And it hurt my eyes and made me squint.

'I know I woke you,' he said. 'I knew I would. I'm sorry. But you said I could call.'

I turned the light off again. Then it seemed really dark until my eyes adjusted.

'It doesn't make any difference. I'm on vacation. I can sleep till noon if I want.'

'I keep thinking how you said we were friends. And I said we were friends. And you're supposed to call and talk to a friend at a time like this. And . . . well . . . I hate to admit this. It's pathetic. But I really couldn't think of anybody else I could talk to.'

I wanted to tell him I was honored – no, actually moved in a way I could feel in my gut – that he called me to talk. I didn't think he ever would. It made me feel like I mattered. Like somebody thought I was good for something. Besides watching my sister.

He still hadn't said anything more, and I didn't know what to say. Rigby was up on the bed with me, lying flat out on her side with her back up against my hip, her legs hanging off into nothingness. I scratched behind her ear and she stretched.

'Nobody talks to anybody down here,' he said. 'It's very strange.'

'You can't talk to Rachel?'

'Yes and no. We say things. But it's like nothing is real. I think we're both in shock. So we're walking around like we're wrapped in cotton batting or something. We say words to each other, but they're nothing like the kind of things we'd say at any other time. They don't seem like they mean anything. They don't feel real.'

I waited a minute, to be sure he was done.

'I was kind of hoping you'd get to talk to Dan more. You know how they say . . . sometimes . . . well, I don't know. I don't really know, so maybe I shouldn't say. But they say people are different when they know they're near the end, and sometimes old grudges and stuff just sort of . . . actually, I don't know what they do. I was just hoping you two could talk.'

'He's out of his mind,' Paul said. A weird pause. Then he said, 'I didn't mean that the way it sounded. I didn't mean it like an insult. I mean literally. He's literally out of his mind. He's on so many drugs and painkillers he's someone else entirely. He doesn't know who he is half the time. Or where he is, or what's happening. He keeps asking me for a pad of paper so he can write down all these notes.'

Nothing more seemed to come out of him, so I said, 'What kind of notes?'

'Just all this stuff he thinks he's forgetting. He still thinks he has stuff to do. I spend five or ten minutes settling him down. Convincing him he doesn't have to be responsible for anything any more. Then he'll put the pad down and drift off, but when he wakes up it starts all over again. A few minutes ago I brought him a fresh legal pad that I'd just bought, because he'd filled up the only one he had. I'd just taken it out of the plastic. He calls me over a minute later and tells me there's something written on every single sheet. It's a brand-new pad. I go and look, and it's blank. "Dan," I say, "it's blank." We look at this pad together, page after page, and every page I say, "Nothing. There's nothing there." And every page he says, "You're kidding."'

My eyes were completely adjusted to the light by then, and it felt good to be in that room, and to be in the half-dark. And to be there on my own with Rig but not feel alone. I watched the way the wind bent the tree outside the bedroom window. Through the window I could see the branches sway, and out of the corner of my eye I could see the shadows sway on the wall.

'That must be awful,' I said.

'That's not really the hard part.'

'Right. I guess not.'

'I can't wrap words around the hard part. But maybe you know.'

'I think so. I think maybe it's Rachel and how she's about to be by herself and not married. But not for any reason you would have wanted. You must be wondering what that means. You know. For you. But then you probably feel bad for even wondering. And I know you could never ask her or talk to her about a thing like that while her husband is . . .'

I stopped because I heard a little noise on his end of the line. Just a sniff. Maybe he was allergic to something down there. Or had a cold. But probably not. Because I would have heard that right from the start.

'You OK?' I asked.

'Yeah.'

And even just in that one word, I heard it. I'd made him cry. Or, anyway, something had. Life, I guess. I didn't think people like Paul cried. I thought people like me cried. I thought people like Paul handled themselves.

'Well. Not OK. But OK. I mean, this sucks. But I'm OK in that I'm not falling apart at the seams. I'm OK because I will be.'

'I'm sorry if I shouldn't have said all that.'

'No, it was good that you did. That way I didn't have to.'

Silence on both ends of the line for a long time. But it didn't feel too uncomfortable.

Then Paul said, 'Did your family move in?'

'Not yet.'

'What am I thinking? That was just yesterday. My God. Feels like a week ago. The days feel so long.'

'They came and looked at the place. My mom gets paid in three days. Right now she doesn't have money to put gas in the car to move all our stuff over. So that's when we'll move. Because she doesn't have to take most of that paycheck and put it away for next month's rent. For a change. We actually have money for stuff now. Or, I mean . . . we will. In three days.'

'I thought she worked on tips.'

'Oh, no. She hasn't had that job for a long time. She works at the pharmacy while Sophie's in school.'

'Take that twenty I put under the dog-food can. You can put it back when she gets paid.'

'Oh. OK. If you're sure.'

'Of course I'm sure. I'm surprised you didn't think of it.'

'Well. I knew it was there. But it's yours. It's for dog food.'

'Even though I never would have known. Listen. I called the grocery store and set up a line of credit. So when you need more dog food, just go in and charge it. And if you need to get more food in the house, go ahead, but do me a favor and don't feed the whole family on it.'

'I won't buy anything but dog food with it. We can afford food now. Thanks to you.'

'I should let you get back to sleep.'

'You know you can call anytime if things are weird down there.'

'Yeah,' he said. 'I do know that.'

After we got off the phone, I wondered where he was staying. Probably in his old house right across the fence from Aunt Vi.

I should have asked him to tell her where we were, and that we were OK. She must have felt guilty. Putting us out like that. She must've wondered how we were. Where we landed. I wondered if my mother ever bothered to tell her.

Then I laughed a little snort out loud, and Rigby woke up and looked over her shoulder at me.

'Nothing,' I said. 'It's fine, girl. Go back to sleep.'

She did.

I made a mental note to ask Paul to do that next time we talked. It just wasn't one of those things you want to leave to my mom.

Chapter Three

 **Break**

The place hardly looked different with our stuff in it.
After all those moves, the beds and coffee tables and
couches, and all those other big, hard-to-move items
had peeled away. I tried to think back on where they'd
gone, and when, but I swear I couldn't remember. The
time between when we first got thrown out of our house
– the one we used to live in with my dad – and this
place was all muddy and thick with fog. Like maybe I'd
only dreamed the whole thing.

Now we just had stuff like sheets to put on the beds
and eating utensils to put in the drawers and towels
to hang in the bathroom and clothes to hang in the
closets. And not too much more.

So once we'd put it all away, the place looked a lot
like it did before we started.

In other words, it still looked wonderful.

My mom was in the bathroom, and I heard her shriek. I thought she'd seen a mouse or a cockroach or something. But I was so happy in the new place. Nothing could ruin it. I just thought, Whatever. We'll buy a mouse trap or some bug spray and still be happy.

But when she stuck her head out, she was beaming.

'It has a bathtub!'

'Most bathrooms do.'

'But the one at the Magnussons' didn't. And the one at the motel before that didn't. I'm so tired of stall showers. I haven't taken a hot bath in a year. And it's huge. And deep. Looks like I can get every part of me under hot water that I don't need for breathing.'

'Well, this is your big night, then.'

'I think we should order a pizza,' she said.

'We can afford a pizza?'

'Of course we can. We have . . .'

I braced myself for loudness. Literally winced.

'. . . *no rent!*'

She never said those two words in a normal voice, only screamed them. I was nearly used to it by then.

'Tell me what you want on it,' I said, 'and I'll call from the big house.'

'I think we should get pepperoni and mushrooms and double cheese. After all, this is a major celebration.'

'Sounds good to me. Come on, Rig.'

I walked to the door, opened it, stepped out on to the landing, and waited for Rigby to come through the door with me. She didn't. I looked back and found her lying on the rug next to Sophie, giving me a look

I could only call apologetic. Like she needed to stay with Sophie because Sophie needed her to, and maybe I would understand.

'Never mind,' I said. 'I'll go by myself.'

When I got back up to the apartment, my mom threw her arms around me. And not just for a quick second, either. She got me wrapped up and didn't let go.

It was kind of disturbing.

'You really saved our collective ass,' she said.

Then I felt even more weirded out.

I wiggled loose. 'Don't say that.'

'Why not? I'm giving credit where credit is due.'

'I don't know. It just makes me uncomfortable. I don't know why.'

She sighed.

I knew why. It was because every time I solved a problem that should really have been hers to solve, I figured she was that much more likely to dump the next one on me. That situation with her was like a stray cat. I really wanted that cat to go away. Fixing it a nice fish dinner and a bowl of milk was not the way to get what I wanted.

Then again, I'd tried leaving things unfixed. And that only left things unfixed.

'I can't believe we killed that whole pizza,' my mom said.

'I believe it.'

'Sophie had two slices. Now that's hard to believe.'

'We've all been hungry. She just didn't have the words to say it.'

That stopped the conversation dead.

Actually, I hadn't been hungry for days. I'd been gorging myself out of Paul's refrigerator. But I hadn't gotten used to having plenty to eat yet. I was still over-compensating. So the point still held.

'I guess Rigby and I are going back to the house. You take your hot bath. I'll see you tomorrow.'

I got up and crossed over to the door, suddenly wondering if Rigby would try to stick with Sophie again. I looked over my shoulder at her. She was in that same position on the rug, giving me that same look.

I made a mental note to bring her padded floor bed to the apartment. It might be bad for her arthritis not to have the padding. And she never used it in the house anyway. She always used half of Paul's bed.

'Rigby. Seriously this time. We sleep in the big house. We've got to go.'

She rose to her feet, all long legs and a little bit of stiffness. I wondered if I should tell Paul about the stiffness. Or maybe just cut back on our walk mileage a little and see if that was enough.

She ambled over to the door, and me, in about four steps.

I opened the door.

Sophie opened her mouth. And screamed.

It was the first time we'd heard that horrible sound since leaving the city to come here. Since she lost her voice on the drive.

I looked at my mom and she looked at me.

'Why is she doing that?' I asked, all panicked, shouting to be heard.

'I don't know!'

'She can't do that here! We're not that far from the neighbors!'

A wild shrug. That was the only answer my mom seemed to have.

I walked back to where Sophie sat on the rug, and Rigby followed me. And, of course, Sophie quieted right down.

I frowned, and sat cross-legged on the rug beside them. Purposely not looking at my mom.

So this was one more stray cat I'd just fed, even though I never wanted it to come around again. I'd just taught Sophie that if I took Rigby away, and she shrieked, I'd bring the dog back. But what was I supposed to do? I couldn't have Paul's neighbors calling the police.

I sat there for a couple of minutes, nursing this heavy, sick feeling in my gut. For a few hours there I'd been totally relaxed and thinking everything was going to be OK. And it obviously wasn't going to be OK at all.

I wondered if the hoping was where I'd gone wrong.

I finally braved a look at my mom, who looked like she was having a hard time holding down all that pizza.

She put words to the sick thing in my gut. She said, 'Shortest vacation in the history of the world.'

'Thought you were going to take a bath.'

'Maybe you'll have to live here with the dog. Not in the big house.'

I didn't say what I wanted to say.

What I wanted to say was, That's the stupidest, most short-sighted idea you've ever had. Which is a tough contest to win. Because then when Paul gets home and wants his dog back, the whole thing will be over. We'll be out looking for a new place again.

What I actually said was, 'I can't. Paul might call, and then he won't know where I am. Or how his dog is.'

Somehow I'd have to train Sophie to wait patiently for the next time she'd see Rigby. Like she'd been doing nearly all along. But I had no idea why she'd done it so well for so long. Or why she'd stopped. So I had no idea where to start.

'So what are we going to do?' my mom asked.

Something inside me . . . sort of . . . snapped.

'And there it is again,' I said. My voice sounded hard. Even to me.

'Meaning what?'

'Every time things get bad, you ask me what *we're* going to do. Which is like . . . in case you don't get it – how that comes through – the message in there is real clear. You don't know what to do, so you're hoping I do.' Fortunately, I was not raising my voice. I was wondering if I could keep it that way. 'I can't take the pressure any more. Look at all I've done to fix our situation. And then something goes wrong with Sophie, and I'm your go-to fixer again. I get it that sometimes you feel like I'm better at this than you are, but could you at least try? Could you . . . I don't know . . . practice? Or something?'

A long silence, during which I didn't brave a look at her face.

Then I did.

She was leaning with her back against the sliding-glass door. Arms crossed over her chest. Looking away from me, down at the hardwood floor at the edge of the big rug. Her face looked heavy and dark, like a storm cloud right before the thunder and lightning starts. But nothing happened. She just brooded there.

'Take your bath,' I said. 'I'll stay till Sophie goes to sleep.'

She just stayed frozen there for a long time. Like she hadn't even heard. Then she broke loose suddenly and marched into the bathroom. Slammed the door. Hard.

I jumped. All three of us jumped.

I looked at Rigby and Sophie. Rigby looked back.

'Well, that was a major disaster,' I told her.

She reached out and snuffled my ear. It sounded funny, so I laughed. It felt good to laugh at a time like that, but weird, too. I guess I'd thought maybe I never would again.

It was after ten when I finally got inside the big house. The message machine was beeping.

I'd never learned how to play messages.

I squinted at the buttons for a while. It was probably Paul, but I was afraid I might accidentally erase it, and then it might turn out to be from someone else, and be important. So instead I got Paul's number from the list on the side of the fridge, and called him.

'Did you call?' I asked.

'I did,' he said.

'I'm sorry. I was in the apartment with my mom and Sophie.'

'You don't have to be sorry.'

'I thought maybe you'd be worried if I wasn't home at night.'

'It occurred to me that you might be with your family.'

'Are you OK?'

A long silence.

'I probably shouldn't call you and tell you my problems,' he said.

'I really don't mind.'

I took the phone over to the couch, and sat. Rigby lay down so close that one of her front paws draped over my foot.

'But you have a life. And problems of your own.'

'So? Everybody has a life. And problems. But then they also have friends, and sometimes they listen to their friends' problems. It's normal. Well. Listen to me talk like I know what normal is. I'm not saying I've done it that way all my life or anything. But I'm pretty sure lots of people do.'

A little sound from him that could have been a laugh, but came out as more of a light breath.

'What's going on down there?' I asked.

'It's just moving really fast.'

I got a clutch in my chest and gut, thinking I didn't have much time to solve the Sophie problem. Then I felt guilty for only thinking of myself. But it wasn't thinking, really, anyway. It was my gut. I guess my gut only knows me.

'How fast?'

'Kind of hard to say. Hard to know how much is the pain medication. Maybe part of it is that he's still not fully recovered from the surgery.'

'Is he at home?'

'Yeah. He's back. And we have Hospice coming in to help us.'

Weird, maybe, but I wondered how it felt to him to use the word 'us' for himself and Rachel. But it didn't seem right to ask.

I looked out the window and saw lights of houses clustered at the foot of the mountains, and it felt comforting somehow. Like life is always going on somewhere. No matter what.

I said, 'Can I ask a little favor?'

'Sure. I guess.'

'You're staying right next door to my Aunt Violet's house, right?'

'Yeah. Right where you met me.'

'When you get a chance, would you tell her where we are, and that we're OK?'

'Sure. I could do that.'

'I think she probably feels guilty for putting us out.'

'Probably.'

'But . . . I'm sorry. You were talking about Dan. And I sort of changed the subject. You were saying it all seems to be going so fast.'

First nothing.

Then, 'I keep thinking about a week or two back. He hadn't been to the doctor's yet, and nobody knew anything was wrong. Well, that's not right. He must have known something. Or he wouldn't have gone in. I guess he'd been having trouble for a while, but he probably thought it was excess stomach acid or an ulcer or something. And then he gets the news. Bang. He's in for surgery, and then everything's falling apart. It must be really fast-growing. Plus it was late stage and spreading to his lungs when they found it. But still, I expected things to go slower. It just seems strange that everything is falling apart so fast. It's hard to understand.'

Silence. I focused on the little lights out the window.

'How's Rachel doing with all this?'

For probably a full ten seconds all I heard was his breathing. It seemed weird that I could hear it so clearly. Like he was breathing purposely and carefully instead of naturally.

'She's beside herself,' he said. Then a long pause. Then, 'And it's really hard. You know. To . . .'

I waited. For a long time. Wondering if I'd ever hear the end of that sentence. It wasn't one I could just guess.

'. . . watch her loving him so much.'

His voice kind of broke up on the last words. But not really into crying, exactly. He just sort of crumbled.

He didn't say anything for a long time and neither did I. I had no idea what to say to him, and he seemed like maybe he was never going to talk again.

'It was so much easier when I only saw them for

a few hours once or twice a month. I think I was in this insane denial. Like, yeah, they'd been married for decades, but it wasn't all that serious. Like they just sort of existed in the same house, but . . . I don't know. I don't know what I'm saying. What was I thinking, coming down here? Watching her with him, day in and day out? Watching how hard it is for her to lose him? What was I thinking?'

'I think you wanted to be there for both of them. I think you knew it would be hard, but you knew you'd regret it if you didn't.'

'I didn't know it would be *this* hard.'

In some small way, it broke part of my heart. I guess I let my heart be close to his for a split second. And I felt the break. It was weird. Like nothing that had ever happened to me before. Then again, I usually kept plenty of distance between me and everybody else.

I had no idea what to say.

'I should go,' he said.

'You don't have to.'

'That was a lot more than I meant to say.'

'It's OK, though. I mean, it's OK with me.'

'I just need to go sit by myself and process this.'

'You can call again.'

'I think I have to now. It's like when you don't let yourself cry, but then you do. It's one thing to open that floodgate. It's another thing to get it shut again.'

'Call anytime.'

'Goodnight, Angie.'

'Goodnight.'

I went to bed. But I didn't get to sleep until the wee small hours of the morning. And even then I didn't manage to sleep much.

I woke up when I heard the clear, flexible plastic flap of the doggie door clatter open, then fall closed again. I thought it was Rigby going out to pee. So I just rolled over to see if I could go back to sleep. But I rolled right into Rigby. She was up on the bed with me. Her head was up, and she was looking toward the back room. She'd heard the flap, too.

I told myself to get up and go see what it was. But I was frozen. I wondered if wild animals would come in through that thing. It was a big doggie door. It had to be. Or it would be of no use to Rigby. I'd worried about that, once, when I first came here to stay. But I'd figured Rigby would defend the place.

Now I wondered if it was fair to make her try.

Before I could think it out any better than that, Sophie stuck her head into the bedroom.

'Hem!' she squealed.

I was on my feet before I even knew I was about to get up.

'Sophie! No! You can't be in here!'

I grabbed her up, almost without thinking, and she gave my thigh a vicious kick. I half dropped her, half set her down. I grabbed her hand and tried to pull her toward the back door. She started that ear-splitting keen, sliding along the wood floor on her bare, braced feet.

'Rigby,' I shouted. 'Come on. Let's go out.'

Rigby jumped down off the bed, and the three of us walked down the hall to the back door together. Suddenly all calm again. And Sophie quieted right down and walked right along. Of course. Of course she'd stop shrieking if I gave her what she wanted. Access to the dog. Which I'd just done a second time.

I still felt half asleep, and I couldn't get my brain to function. I knew I had a problem, and I was only making it worse. But I couldn't think it out any more clearly than that. I had no idea how to solve it. That is, without letting her scream till she lost her voice. Which I couldn't do while we were here at Paul's house.

She'd been so good about trusting she'd see Rigby again soon. I had no idea where that had gone. Or why. Or what to do about it.

We stepped out the back door and on to the landing, and I looked up to the apartment and saw the door hanging wide open.

'Come on,' I said. To both of them. 'Let's go have a talk with Mom.'

My mom was fast asleep on the fold-out couch.

'What was that all about?' I asked. Nice and loud. It didn't seem right for her to go back to sleep after causing a problem like that.

She sat up. Looked around. Looked at me. Rubbed her eyes.

'Close that door,' she said. 'It's cold.'

I felt my jaw drop open.

'Close the door? *Close the door?*'

'What part of "Close the door" don't you understand?'

'I didn't *open* the door. You did. And I just woke up with Sophie in the big house. Where she's not allowed to be. Did she wake up fussing and you just decided to sic her on me?'

'Kiddo, you woke me up just now. I've been asleep all night.'

'Well, then who let Sophie out?'

'I have no idea.'

I didn't entirely believe her. I couldn't. Maybe she'd been half asleep.

'I wonder if Sophie learned to open the door,' she said.

'Impossible.'

But it wasn't impossible at all. That was just the problem. Sophie wasn't stupid. She was different. But the differences didn't involve lack of brain power. I wanted it to be impossible. That's why I said it was. But that didn't make it so.

'Even if she did,' my mom said, 'how did she get into the big house? Don't you lock the doors when you go to sleep?'

'She came in through the doggie door.'

'Oh.'

'Now I don't know what to do. I want to go back in the house, but now she's awake. So now she'll scream.'

'Leave the dog here.'

'I can't keep doing that. It's just training her to scream.'

'Fine. Don't keep doing it. But do it now. Then the van'll come and she'll go off to school. And next time she sees the dog, it'll be something different. Like you come get her and take her for a walk. Like the old days. And you can tell her she'll see Rigby tomorrow. Like the old days. And then maybe we can get back into some kind of a normal pattern here.'

I wasn't the least bit sure that would work. But it felt good to hear a plan come from my mom. Whether it was a good plan or not, at least she was practicing.

So I said, 'Rigby, stay here with Sophie, OK?'

And I walked out and left them there. And went back up the back stairs, and went back to bed.

But I was too worried to get any sleep.

Sophie got home at about a quarter after four. I was braced for just about anything. What I didn't expect was to hear my mom yelling. All the way up the driveway.

'Sophie, wait! Sophie, come back!'

I winced, thinking of Paul's neighbors. I wondered how long it would be before they complained to him. And how he would take it when they did.

Then my mom's yelling morphed into yelling to me.

'Angie, look out! Block the doggie door or something!'

I was sitting at the kitchen table, and I looked down at Rigby, who was already looking up into my face. Like she was wondering whether I had any explanations or instructions.

'You want to go for a walk?' I asked her.

She stood up and started wagging. Of course. What else would she do? That's not a yes or no question for a dog. It's a yes question.

I stayed clear of her lethal tail on the way down the hall to the back bedroom. I grabbed her leash off the peg by the door. We stepped out on to the landing together just as Sophie hit the bottom of the stairs.

'Wait there,' I told Sophie. 'We're coming down. We're going for our walk.'

She didn't wait. She started up the stairs.

I didn't like my odds if I tried to reason with her, so instead I just led Rigby down, and when Sophie bumped into us, she had no choice but to turn and walk back down again.

We all three walked down the driveway past my mom, who looked like a limp dish towel somebody needed to wring out.

'We're fine,' I said. 'We're going for a walk.'

She let out a deep breath, but didn't say anything. And, also, she didn't look much happier or more settled.

That was the problem with being the one who solved everything. I tried to take the stress off my mom, but then it was more like we both had it.

Sometimes I wasn't sure if I was solving anything at all.

We walked all the way into town. I was hoping it would tire Sophie out. I was hoping it wouldn't make Rigby stiff or sore. It was always a balancing act. My whole life was one big act of skating on a frozen pond not long enough before the spring thaw.

Everybody seemed to know us.

It wasn't a total surprise. But there was something . . . *more* about it that day, and it surprised me. It was a very small town. Just a village, really, and we'd been walking those streets for a year. And it's hard to miss a teenage girl with a dog the size of a small pony and an autistic kid. We didn't look like every other person or group walking down the street.

Mostly I didn't know them except for their faces. Sometimes I knew how I knew them, like the woman who worked at the Post Office or the guy who was a checker at the supermarket. I saw three girls I knew from school. Two pretended not to see me back. Or maybe they really didn't. It's always hard to tell about a thing like that.

One woman knew Sophie's name. I passed this woman, and she smiled at us. And she said, 'Hi, Sophie.'

I stopped. 'How do you know Sophie's name?' I asked.

'My daughter is in the Special Ed program,' she said. 'Sophie's already in the van when Mr Maribal stops every morning.'

'Oh. Nice to meet you.'

Then we just kept walking. But it was a strange feeling. And it took me a while to put my finger on why. Something about people noticing us. Knowing they knew us. Knowing we lived around here. Which meant, if we were about to not live around here any more, somebody would actually notice we were gone. It was like existing in a way I'd never been totally convinced I existed before.

I liked it and I didn't like it. Both at the same time.

When we got home, Rigby and I walked Sophie upstairs to the apartment. Opened the door.

'Sophie's back,' I called to my mom. 'So you might want to keep an eye on the door for a while. Sophie,' I said, looking right down at her. She didn't look back, of course. 'You'll see Rigby tomorrow, OK? Just like always.'

I handed her off to my mom, and Rigby and I turned and walked down the stairs. Without looking back.

We were halfway across the gravel driveway to the house when I heard it. The famous Sophie shriek. I stopped. Squeezed my eyes closed. Opened them again, and looked down at Rigby, who looked back up at me for instructions.

'Come on,' I said.

We turned around and walked back to the apartment.

'Don't look at me like that, Rigby. We don't have any other choice.'

But, really, she wasn't looking at me any special way at all. I was the one watching myself from the outside, criticizing. But if there was a better way to handle things, I couldn't reach it. I couldn't even see anything better from where I stood.

*

'So, this is not working out at all,' I said to my mom. 'And I really thought it would.'

We were on the back patio of the apartment, looking out at the mountains. Most of their peaks still had snow in June. Sophie was inside with Rigby. It was really just an excuse to have a hard talk.

'I'm thinking it's because the dog is with you,' she said. 'So she thinks she should get to go along. You know. All the time. When the dog was with a stranger, she didn't feel that way.'

'What do you think'll happen when Paul gets back?'

'No idea.'

'What if she goes right in through the doggie door after Paul gets home?'

'We could always lock the apartment door from the inside or something.'

'And then she'll shriek.'

She didn't say anything. Neither one of us said anything. For quite a long time.

After a while I sat down on one of the wooden chairs. My mom called them Adirondack chairs, but I wasn't sure why. She stood at the railing for a couple of minutes more. Then she came and sat down, too.

She looked over her shoulder, through the sliding-glass door. So I did the same. But nothing had changed. Just Sophie and Rigby, lying on the rug.

'I'm going to say some things,' she said. 'And I'd really appreciate it if you wouldn't yell at me while I'm saying them. At least let me get the whole thing out before you start to yell.'

I pulled in a long breath. Let it out again. My way of getting prepared, I guess.

'I don't think I have enough energy to yell, anyway.'

'Good.'

Too long a pause.

So I said, 'Please just go ahead and get this over with.'

'I think we're trying to do something that can't reasonably be done.'

I sat a moment, letting that roll through me. It didn't make me want to yell. I hated it, but there was nothing in me that wanted to fight with it. In fact, I felt around and found this place that would be incredibly relieved to admit it was true. Not happy. Just relieved. When something is true, it takes a lot of energy to pretend it's not. It pretty much uses up all the life energy a person's got, and doesn't leave much energy over for anything else. After years of that, you just get so exhausted. Almost everything sounds OK if it comes with a rest.

'You're not saying anything,' she said.

'I was just thinking.'

'This feels like progress for us.'

'I still don't want it to end like that.'

'It wouldn't be the end, Angie. We could go see her all the time. Whenever we wanted to.'

I just sighed. Didn't answer.

'I don't want to leave this place,' she said. 'I need rest. And peace. Need. Not want. Need. I can't go through getting thrown out on the street again with two daughters, one with special needs. This place feels like a home, and we need a home. Sophie needs a home, too. It's not good for her to be living in a tent. Running off into the woods.'

I didn't say anything for a long time.

We looked over our shoulders again. Nothing had changed inside the apartment. Just Sophie and Rigby lying on the rug together. Sophie was a perfect angel, so long as I gave her something that wasn't mine to give.

'Penny for your thoughts,' she said.

'I was thinking you're talking like you're the one in charge.'

'Is that a good thing or a bad thing?'

'Well, it's both. Since I don't like what you're saying much. But it's sort of a relief for me when you act like the mom. Then I get to step down and be the kid and have no idea what I'm doing.'

A long silence. Maybe three or four minutes. Or more. It was still only about seven, but the sun was on a long slant, nearly ready to go behind the mountains. Even though it was one of the longest days of the year. The sun sets behind the mountains quite a while before it sets on the horizon. Especially when the mountains are tall. And close.

'If we placed her somewhere, could we ever get her back? You know. If we stayed here and saved up money for a place? Maybe someplace a long way from the closest neighbors? I could even get a weekend job and help.'

'Oh, now you want to make money and help.'

'If it would get Sophie back.'

'She's not gone yet, kiddo.'

'You didn't answer my question.'

'Because I don't know. I would think so. But I really don't know. I could look into some options. How 'bout if we just take this one step at a time? First thing is to see what happens when he gets back.'

'Right,' I said.

'When do you think that'll be?'

'Probably soon. He said things are falling apart really fast.'

'You talked to him?'

'Yeah. He calls.' Then the silence felt a little strange, so I said, 'You know. To see how Rigby is. And to keep me posted on when he'll be back. I mean, as much as he can know a thing like that.'

'So . . . best guess.'

'I don't know. A couple or three weeks, maybe.'

'*Weeks*? You said he'd be gone *months*!'

Then we both looked over our shoulders again. To see if either Sophie or the dog had caught the upset. But they both looked asleep on the rug.

'I meant he'd be gone till his brother died. Which the doctors thought would be two to four months. But Paul always thought it would be more like two and less like four. And now he says it's going really fast.'

'I better start doing some research into places.'

All of a sudden I didn't feel like I could be there any more. I got up and went inside. Didn't say goodbye to my mom. Didn't say anything.

Sophie was indeed asleep on the rug next to Rigby.

But not actually touching any part of the dog. I put my hand on Rigby's head, and she woke up and looked into my face to see what would come next.

'Let's go back to the house,' I told her.

So that's what we did.

For the second night in a row, I had a hard time sleeping. So I was pretty groggy when Sophie flapped through the doggie door in the morning.

I raised my head, and Rigby raised her head. But this time we both knew exactly who to expect.

When I saw her face in the doorway, I said, 'Game over, Sophie. And we all lose.'

I don't know why I said a thing like that to her. I just did.

Then I got up, and walked Sophie and Rigby out the back door and up to the apartment. And asked Rigby to stay there while I went back in the house. Not that she had much choice. The door was about to be closed again. But the least I could do was talk to her. Tell her what was expected of her. What was about to happen.

Then I went back to bed.

I never got back to sleep.

I just lay there nursing this strange feeling that we wouldn't be a family any more. Just my mom and me didn't feel like a family at all. I thought about what it would be like with just us. It pretty much felt like two people who sometimes almost got along but mostly didn't. Two people who didn't feel all that related, considering they were. It was Sophie who tied it all together into something that felt like a family.

At least, for a couple more weeks, she did.

Paul called later that night. Nearly midnight.

I'd been asleep for a change, and it was hard to pull myself awake. But I was still glad to hear from him.

'I just had to tell you this,' he said. 'Dan and I had that moment. The one you were talking about.'

'What one was I talking about?'

'The one you wished for us. You said when someone is near the end, sometimes you can be close to them in a different way.'

'Oh. Right. That. I remember that. What happened?'

'He had this moment. He's been nearly unconscious. Most of the time. Almost all day and night. But all of a sudden, a few minutes ago, he had this lucid moment. Just out of nowhere he opened his eyes and looked right into my face. And he said . . .' An awkward pause. 'He said . . . "I'm sorry we broke your heart."'

'Whoa.'

'That's what *I* thought. He never would have said anything like that to me before this. Ever. He never acknowledged that. I wasn't even sure if he knew.'

'How long have you felt this way? You know. I mean . . . about her?'

Then I immediately thought I'd been wrong to ask. And that he'd say something sharp. Like, 'Hey. I didn't say I was up for twenty questions.'

He didn't.

He said, 'Forty-nine years. Since I was seventeen.'

'You've known her since you were seventeen?'

'Yes. Since before she met Dan. She was an exchange student studying over here. But the thing is, she was nineteen and a half. She's two and a half years older than I am. I know it doesn't sound like much now. But she was in college. She was a sophomore in college and I was a junior in high school. At the time, it felt huge. Like she was a grown woman and I was a kid. I was friends with her before she even met Dan. Turns out she was hoping for an introduction to him. And I was hoping she'd see beyond the difference in our ages.'

Silence for a moment, filled with shadows moving on the bedroom wall. I was stunned that he would tell me so much. But I was afraid if I pointed it out, he might stop.

So all I said was, 'Ouch.'

'I don't mean to give you the wrong impression. It's not like she was just using me to get to him. She's not like that. She was a good friend. Always has been. It's just that he was the one she had the romantic feelings for.'

I wanted to say, Maybe that could change now. Or sometime. Maybe when she gets over this huge loss.

I didn't. I still felt like his life was none of my business. If he wanted to tell me about it, that was fine. That was up to him. But I didn't feel like I had the right to comment much.

I said, 'I'm glad you had a good moment with your brother.'

'Well,' he said. 'A tough moment. I guess it was good, though.'

'What did you say? When he said that?'

'Not much. Just what I tell him a million times a day. That he doesn't have to worry about anything any more.'

Long, fairly comfortable silence. I knew that was all he'd called to tell me. And I wasn't sure where that left us.

After a while, when he didn't rush off the phone, I said, 'Would it be OK if I told you something that's going on with me?'

'Of course. I'd like that.'

'I'm not sure it feels right, though. When you're down there going through all the stuff you're going through.'

'Please do. It would be good to get out of my own head for a change.'

'I think we're going to have to put Sophie in some kind of a home.'

A beat of silence. I wondered who was more shocked to hear me say those words out loud.

'Oh, dear. That's too bad. I thought it would solve everything if you could live in the apartment.'

'Yeah, we all did. I'm not sure what went wrong with that. It's like she knows Rigby is with me, so she thinks she should be allowed to be with us all the time. I've had to be in the apartment with Rigby, or leave her in the apartment with them, until Sophie goes to school in the morning, and from after our walk till she goes to sleep. And in the morning, Sophie opens the apartment door and comes up the back stairs and lets herself in through the doggie door. I don't let her stay, of course. I walk her right back out again. But she was in your house twice, for about a minute each. No, not even that long. Seconds. But still. Sooner or later I had to tell you.'

'Even though I never would have known.'

'Even though you never would have known.'

'Maybe when I get back, it'll be more like it was when we were on the other side of the fence.'

'Maybe. That's what we're hoping for, of course. But my mom's already made up her mind that she doesn't want to leave this place. Which I sort of don't blame her for. Whatever place we found, we'd probably just get thrown out of it again. That being homeless thing was scary.'

'Maybe it really would be the best thing for all. Including Sophie.'

'I don't know. Wouldn't it be hard for any seven-year-old kid to get taken away from everything they've ever known?'

'I guess it would.'

'And Sophie's even worse with change than most kids.'

'I guess I'm sorry I ever said that.'

'You don't have to be. Maybe it *is* the best thing. Not because it's good, but maybe because all the other things are even worse. I don't know. I just know I was hoping we could wait until she was old enough that it would be more like a normal time to leave your family.

And I keep getting this feeling that without her there's no family. Just me and my mom. That doesn't feel like a family, exactly. That just feels like two people.'

Long silence. I realized I was done. I'd said all I had in me to say. The same feeling I'd got when he was done talking earlier. I watched shadows on the wall and wondered how to wrap this up.

'Well, if nothing else,' he said, 'you reminded me that I'm not the only one who's got it hard right now.'

I didn't say anything. I didn't know what to say.

'You know I'll work with you as best I can when I get back.'

'I do. I do know that. But I also know it's your life. It's your retirement. And you worked hard for it, for a long time. And you have a right to it. You have a right to have it the way you want it.'

First, nothing.

Then he said, 'I might have been wrong about the alone thing. It's not what I had it made out to be.'

'I still like it, myself. Besides, you also wanted uncomplicated. You still want uncomplicated, don't you?'

'I'm on the fence about that. Other people always bring complications. That's just the nature of human relationships. You can't separate people from their complications. Uncomplicated and alone are more or less the same thing. I don't know. I'm still thinking about that. And my thinking is probably skewed right now anyway. I should let you get some sleep. We should both get some sleep. Maybe things will look a little better in the morning.'

'Maybe,' I said.

But I didn't think they would.

'I'm sorry you're having a hard time,' he said.

'I'm sorry *you're* having a hard time,' I said.

'Sleep well,' he said.

'Goodnight,' I said.

Then I hung up the phone and hardly slept at all.

After a couple of hours of not sleeping, I dragged my little trunk out from under Paul's bed. I opened it with the key, which by that time I was keeping on the ring with Paul's house keys. I was careful not to look at the note from Nellie, or *The Tibetan Book of the Dead*, or the hundred-dollar bill. Or my dad's watch and wallet and ring. I couldn't exactly not see those things, but I was careful not to let my eyes rest there long.

I took out my Himalayas book, and locked the trunk again and slid it back under the bed. Then I sat propped up with pillows for a couple of hours and traveled to Tibet and Nepal. Where I hadn't been for a long time.

Only one bit of trouble. It was hard not to think about Nellie. She kept coming in through the back door in my head. I kept pushing her out and locking up again. But it was never a very good lock job. Because she always found her way back.

One thing I can say for sure. She did not travel to Tibet with me that night. I was a solo traveler on that trip. Just like the old days.

When my eyes got too tired and grainy and sore, I closed the book. Rigby was lying with her back up against my hip, her legs dangling off the bed. I petted her, and she woke up and stretched those impossibly long legs even farther over the edge.

'Wish I could travel with *you*,' I said. 'You're like the perfect person to be with. Except you're not a person. Well. In some ways you sort of are.'

I left the book out on the bedside table. Because I could do that at Paul's. I had no idea how long I'd get to live that wonderful way. I just knew that, whatever happened, someday my life would be like that again. Someday I would live in a place where everything was safe sitting out. Somehow I would get there.

I just didn't know where 'there' was. Or how long I had to wait.

Paul didn't call again for weeks. And nothing else happened that was really worth reporting. Just some fishing trips, and this one tiny moment.

It was after six in the evening, and we were all in the apartment. Rigby was lying on the rug with Sophie right beside her. The late afternoon sun was glaring through the sliding-glass door, and it fell over both of them, and made them look the way a manger decoration looks at Christmas. That spooky, almost supernatural, amount of light. A halo for a whole scene.

My mother was staring at them.

After a minute of staring, she said, 'How old is that dog?'

Truthfully, I'd wondered when she was going to wonder.

'Old,' I said.

And that was the end of that conversation. It was never brought up again after that.

Chapter Four

 **Calm**

Next time I heard from Paul, it was almost three weeks later. And it wasn't the same as the other times at all. It wasn't late. He didn't call to tell me what hurt most in what was happening to him. He sounded closed-up. Far away. I don't mean his voice sounded like it was coming from far away. It was the same volume as always. I mean he sounded like he was somewhere else.

'I'm coming home tomorrow,' he said.

I was hoping he meant for a visit. So Rigby wouldn't think he forgot her. I wanted a lot more notice when he was coming home for real. Not that notice would have helped much. There wasn't a lot I could've done to prepare. But I felt like it would help me prepare on the inside. But maybe that's just a story I told myself.

'For a visit? Or did Dan . . .'

'Dan's gone,' he said. Just like that. Flat.

It reminded me of something. Or somebody. But I didn't have enough time to think what. Or who.

'Oh. I'm sorry. When did that happen?'

'Last night while we were all asleep.'

'Oh. What about Rachel, though? Doesn't she need somebody with her?'

'Apparently not. She just told me she needs some alone time.'

I started to say, Ouch. At the last minute, I changed it to, 'Oh.'

That couldn't have been a fun thing to hear. I mean, in addition to the fact that his brother just died. But I knew if somebody had said something to hurt me, the last thing I'd want is somebody pointing out the obvious. As in, That must have hurt. So I left it alone.

'Rigby will be so thrilled to see you,' I said.

'Yeah. That'll be nice.' His voice sounded softer. 'I'll probably get in around late afternoon. Want me to call from the road? Tell you more about what time?'

'No, it's fine. It'll be good to see you whenever you get here.'

I could tell from the silence that he was a little surprised to hear me say that. But I wasn't sure why. It's like we'd lost all that friendship progress we'd made while he was away.

'See you tomorrow, then,' he said.

We said our goodbyes and I hung up the phone. And it hit me. What he'd reminded me of. The old Paul. From before.

Paul from the other side of the fence.

*

When I heard the tires of his car crunching on the driveway, I ran to the apartment and got Sophie and Rigby and brought them down to meet him. I knew he wouldn't want to see my mom. And I knew he wouldn't want to come home to screaming. Which he would have, if I hadn't let Sophie come down the stairs with us.

Rigby smacked me with her tail a few times, no matter how hard I tried to stay clear of it, because she just couldn't hold still. She kept lifting her front legs off the ground, rearing up. As long as I'd known her, I was still amazed by how tall she could be.

Sophie jumped up and down like a kid on a pogo stick, because she always picked up on what Rigby was feeling. Something struck me. Not for the first time, but in a different way. At a different level. That's why she was almost always calm when Rigby was around. She was imitating the inside of the dog by calming down.

Paul came out of the garage looking tired and old. Like he hadn't shaved that day. Like he hadn't slept for a week. He was carrying two bags of groceries.

His face lit up when he saw Rigby.

She sat in front of him, barely able to hold the position, looking like she might explode into more dancing at any moment.

'Well, don't you look wonderful?' he told her. 'Looks like your dog sitter took very good care of you.'

I wondered if her muzzle and eyebrows were any grayer than when he'd last seen her. It's hard to tell about these things when you see somebody every day.

Then he looked up at us.

'Hello, Angie,' he said. 'Hello, Sophie.'

'I hope it's OK for Sophie to be here,' I said. 'I wanted her to see you and see that you're taking the dog back. I thought it might help.'

'And if not? What's our Plan B?'

'Well. We soundproofed the closet with egg cartons. That won't do everything you might want it to, but it'll help some. And I still have a couple fresh pairs of those good earplugs.'

'Sophie,' Paul said, looking right at her. She did not look back at him. 'Rigby has to come in the house with me now. Just wait until tomorrow and Angie will take you both for a walk again. Sound OK?'

Then we waited a minute, but I had no idea for what. I wondered if he had any idea, either. Or if it's just one of those things you do because you're not thinking things through very well.

'I'll go upstairs with her now,' I said. 'Because there might be trouble if she thinks I'm with Rigby. But after she goes to sleep I could come up and visit.'

'Don't take this wrong,' he said. But I already knew I would. 'I know how Rachel feels now. I just need some time by myself. Just me and my dog.'

'OK. I can understand that.'

And I could. And it hurt me. Both at the same time. I wondered where that guy was, the one who used to call me at midnight. If I'd ever see him again. Why I'd been so sure that would be a permanent change.

I gave him his keys back. Watched him walk up the stairs to the back door, Rigby wagging behind.

I realized two things.

One, I'd forgotten to get the key to my trunk back from his key ring. But there would be time for that later.

More importantly, that Rigby was the only friend I had who'd never once said anything that hurt my feelings.

I looked down at Sophie.

'Let's go upstairs, Sophie. We'll see Rigby again tomorrow.'

We walked up the stairs together, and she followed me in. And I closed the door behind us.

I looked at my mom, who was sitting on the couch, and my mom looked at me. I crossed my fingers on both hands. Held them up for her to see. Then she crossed her fingers, too. Then she crossed her feet. Then she crossed her eyes, and I laughed. Probably too hard and too long, because I was nervous.

Sophie settled in front of the door in a sphinx position, the way she used to do by the fence at Aunt Vi's. My mom and I watched her for a few minutes. Then after a while there was nothing much to watch.

She fell asleep that way, and my mom unfolded the couch and put her to bed.

'I guess we can uncross everything now,' she said.

In the morning I woke up early, maybe six. It was light, and very cold. And drafty. But I wasn't sure why.

I was sleeping on the single bed behind the room

partition. It was the first time I'd ever slept in the apartment, so, in my half-asleep state, I just assumed it was cold and drafty every morning.

There was a gas fireplace to keep things warm, but it seemed weird to turn it on in the summer. But then I got shivery and decided I didn't care.

I got up and walked around the partition.

My mom was fast asleep on the fold-out couch. The door was hanging wide open. Sophie was nowhere around.

I got dressed as fast as I could. Pulled on jeans and a sweatshirt, and ran down the stairs with my feet still bare. I trotted up the back steps as quietly as I could. But then I had no idea what to do.

If I knocked, I'd wake Paul up. He was probably sleeping, and didn't even know Sophie was in his house. I sat on the back landing for a few minutes, trying to think of a way to get her out of there without his ever knowing she'd been. But I was still half asleep, and not exactly flowing over with brain power.

The only thing I could think to do was open the bottom of the doggie door flap and call for Rigby. If Rigby came out, Sophie would come out, too.

'Rigby,' I hissed.

I wasn't sure about the volume. She had to be able to hear me. But I had to not wake up Paul. I remembered when Paul told me Rigby's hearing was ten times better than ours. I was thinking that could save the day now. But I waited, and nothing happened.

'Rigby,' I said again, a little louder.

'You don't have to whisper,' Paul called out to me. 'I'm awake.'

'Oh. Sorry.'

I sat there for a minute, because I didn't know what else to do. Then the back door opened in, and Paul stood over me in his pajamas and that nice burgundy robe.

'Looking for your sister, I assume.'

'Right.'

'She's in here.'

'Yeah. Sorry about that.'

'Well. She's being nice and quiet. She just wants to lie down next to Rig. Have you had your breakfast?'

'Um. No.'

'Come on in.'

So I did. I just sort of put away my amazement and did as I was told. Sophie was lying on the kitchen floor next to Rigby. I sat down at the table.

'Are you a coffee drinker?' Paul asked.

'Sure. I'll have some coffee.'

'Cream and sugar?'

'How did you know?'

'Most beginner coffee drinkers do it that way. Look, I'm sorry if I was in a bad mood last night.'

'No, it's OK. You weren't. You just wanted to be left alone. I get that.'

'I was going to make myself a bagel with cream cheese and smoked salmon.'

'Oh, my God, that sounds like heaven.'

I watched him rummage around in the fridge.

'There was still a little bit of food in the house when I got back. In the freezer. And some canned stuff. You know what I told you about that.'

'I did my best.'

'I guess you did OK. Considering I wasn't gone as long as I said I'd be. Is that your key on the table? It was on my key ring.'

'Oh, yeah, thanks,' I said, shoving it in my pocket.

Then it was silent for a long time while he poured the coffee and toasted the bagels. And put cream cheese on the table, and a knife. He mounded up a little plate with what looked like enough smoked salmon for four people. Even four people who heaped it on like I did.

Then he sat, and we ate. And didn't talk. I remember thinking that whatever we would say next was almost guaranteed to take us into some kind of dicey area or another. So we just ate.

After maybe five minutes of that, he took the first step.

'It's not so much that I regret the way I shared my thoughts with you in those late-night calls . . .' he said.

Then he didn't go on right away. And I didn't know what to say. Except that they were less thoughts and more feelings. But I didn't want to say that. So I said nothing at all.

Then, after a while, 'It's more like I got tired. I felt like there was nothing covering my nerves. They were getting sandpapered. I had to close up just to get some rest.'

'That makes sense.'

We ate in silence for another few minutes.

Suddenly I surprised myself by saying, 'Did you . . . ?'

But then I couldn't finish. I never should've started the sentence, and I couldn't keep going.

'Did I what?'

'Never mind. None of my business.'

'No. I didn't talk to her. How could I? At a time like that?'

'Yeah. I guess I see your point.'

We ate in silence until there was nothing left on the table to eat.

I looked down at Sophie and wondered how I would get her back to the house to get her dressed and ready for school.

'Sophie,' I said. 'The van will be here soon. Let's go get you dressed. When you get home from school, I'll take you for a walk with Rigby. But right now she needs to stay here with Paul. Thanks for breakfast, Paul.'

I stood up from the table, not sure whether I should try to take hold of any part of my sister. I decided to first try walking to the back door. With great assurance. Like I was sure she would follow.

She followed. In absolute silence. And calm.

When we got up to the apartment, my mom was awake. Sitting up. Looking panicky.

'Oh, God,' she said 'Oh, God. Was that a total disaster?'

'Strangely . . . no.'

'Why? Why was it not a total disaster? How was it not?'

'I really have no idea. It just wasn't. I'm not going to look too closely at why it wasn't. Because I'm just so glad it wasn't. And I suggest you try it my way for now.'

I was the one who went down the driveway to meet Sophie's van after school. We stood on the dirt and gravel for a minute, waving as Mr Maribal drove off. Well, anyway, I was waving. Then we turned to go up the driveway, and Sophie took off. Sprinted, in her awkward way, for Paul's back stairs.

I handled it differently than I'd been handling things all along.

I caught up with her and flying-tackled her on to the driveway. I landed on top of her, and heard and felt all the breath come out of her. It tore a hole in the knee of my jeans and scraped up my hands, and I could tell right away that she had a scrape on her chin that was going to bleed some. But it all seemed minor compared to being sent away to live in an institution.

'Now, you listen here,' I hissed, straight into her ear. 'You want to see Hem? Then you work with me. You play by the rules. You mess this up and you're going to lose. We all are. You take things in your own hands, it's going to ruin everything. I don't know how much of what I say you understand, but if you only get one thing I ever say to you, this should be it. I will get you in to see that dog as much as Paul will let us. So you follow my lead. You walk up there with me, nice and calm. Otherwise you're going to end up getting just the opposite of what you want.'

I lifted up off her, and sat her up, and watched her struggle to get her breath back. I felt bad. But I had to remind myself how much worse things could still get.

'You OK? You ready to go see Rigby?'

I reached a hand out, but she didn't take it. I wasn't sure why I'd ever thought she would. I took her by both elbows and helped her to her feet. A little blood from her chin dribbled on to her tee-shirt.

I wondered if I should have led with the tough stuff. Back when we first moved in. But there wasn't much point hashing over the past.

We walked up the rest of the driveway together, nice and slow. Up Paul's back stairs. But I wasn't really fooling myself into thinking she'd understood me and was doing what I asked. It might just have been that I'd knocked the wind out of her, both literally and figuratively.

I rapped on the back door. Rigby said, 'Woof.' Twice. The door opened, and Paul looked us both up and down, Rigby wagging behind him.

'Oh, dear. What happened to you two?'

'We had a little tumble in the driveway.'

'Both of you?'

'It's kind of a long story.'

'How about an adhesive bandage? And something to clean up that chin?'

'That would be nice. Thanks.'

We came inside, and Sophie shadowed the dog while Paul got me a plastic bottle of something to spray on her chin. Some kind of disinfectant for wounds.

'This shouldn't sting too much. What about your hands? Do they need anything?'

I looked down at my scrapes. Held them out for both of us to see.

'They're fine. They're not even bleeding.'

'You should go wash them, though. Looks like you ground a little dirt in.'

While I was in the bathroom washing my hands, I noticed my knee was bleeding some. But the jeans more or less covered that up. So I was hoping Paul wouldn't notice. I didn't want to complicate things any more. I just wanted to get out on that walk.

Paul was waiting for me with a cotton ball and the spray stuff and an adhesive bandage, and I was grateful that he'd known better than to try to do anything to Sophie himself.

She didn't give me a hard time, though. She was lying on the dog bed in Paul's bedroom, with Rigby. Rigby was relaxed and so was she.

I got her chin cleaned up and covered, and Paul held out his hands to take the paper wrapper and the cotton and the spray stuff back from me.

'Want to go fishing in the morning?' he asked me.

'Love to,' I said.

Then I took Rigby's leash down from the peg by the door, and we set off on our walk. I was thinking, after the fact, that it would be complicated to go fishing in the morning, because if the three of us – Paul and Rig and me – took off fishing before her school van came, Sophie might scream.

And, of course, the best fishing was always before the school van came.

We didn't make it all the way into town. Rigby came up sore. She started favoring her right front. I stopped, and she sat, and Sophie sat, and I picked up her paw and looked between the pads, thinking she might have a burr or something. But there was nothing wrong that I could see. We probably hadn't gone more than a quarter of a mile. I wasn't sure if we should go on.

We walked another minute or so in the direction of town, but she was really limping by then.

A woman jogger passed us going the other way, and looked down at Rigby with this sad smile. 'Poor guy's getting old,' she said.

'Girl.'

'Oh.'

I don't know why I said that. I don't know why it mattered. It didn't matter if Rigby was a boy or a girl. It mattered that she was getting old.

I stopped, and we just stood – and sat – there for a time. Probably a full minute. Then I decided we'd better turn around and call it a day.

'You were right to come back,' Paul said. 'Here. Walk her toward me so I can see.'

I led Rigby through the back bedroom while Paul watched. Sophie ambled along behind.

'That's not her paw. That's her shoulder. She's having trouble with her right shoulder.'

'You think it was all that jumping around when you came home?'

'Maybe. It's definitely tied in with her arthritis.'

'But she takes medication for that.'

'The medication doesn't cure it. Just helps her handle it.'

'Oh. Well, I guess we'll go and leave you alone now. Sophie. Come on back and see Mom with me. We'll see Rigby again tomorrow. Oh. And, Paul. About that fishing. I'm wondering how we're going to get out of here in the morning without Sophie wanting to come along.'

'Under the circumstances,' he said, 'I think it might be best to leave Rigby here. I'm not sure how good it would be for her to lie on the hard ground for hours if she's having a flare-up.'

'Could she stay in the apartment while we go?'

'Sure. That would be fine. If we bring her bed up there. I'll come knock on your door when it's almost time to go. It'll be early.'

'I don't mind.'

'It'll be dark.'

'I don't care. I can't wait.'

Then Sophie and I walked out of his house. She came along quietly, and stayed calm.

In the morning, Paul's knock woke me up. It was dark, just like he'd said it would be. I stuck my head out from behind the room divider to see the door open. He was standing in the wide-open doorway, knocking lightly.

I went to the door, a little embarrassed because my

pajamas were raggedy. But I didn't want to call over and wake my mom.

'I have my clothes all laid out,' I whispered. 'So I'll just be a minute. Where's Sophie?'

'In the house with Rig.'

'I thought we'd be up before her this morning. How long's she been there?'

'She was there at two in the morning when I got up to go to the bathroom. That's all I know for sure.'

It was still nearly pitch dark when Paul handed me a fishing rod from the trunk. I looked at it closely, and felt along the length of it. It seemed short, but then I realized it was in two pieces.

'What's this?'

'Your fishing pole.'

'Not like any other fishing pole I've ever used.'

'That's because we're not fishing for trout.'

'What are we fishing for?'

He shone the flashlight around in the trunk to be sure we had everything, then slammed the trunk and locked up the car.

'Not sure if I should tell you or let you be surprised.'

We set out walking together, following the thin beam of flashlight on a dirt trail. I could hear flowing water already. It sounded like a lot more water than I was used to.

'If they're that much bigger than what we always caught before, maybe you better tell me.'

'They are.'

'You better tell me.'

'Channel cats.'

I stopped dead, which plunged me into total darkness when he kept going.

'Cats? We're fishing for *cats*?'

'Catfish,' he said, stopping and shining the light at my feet.

I caught up with him.

'Catfish. Right. I knew that.'

A thin layer of light was just starting to glow over the eastern mountains when we got to the water.

'Is this a river?'

'Not really. Technically it's a creek. But it's as big as a small river. And there are channel cats in the deeper pools.'

'What do channel cats bite on?'

'All manner of things. The stinkier and more horrible, the better. They're kind of like the goats of the water. But chicken livers are their favorite.'

'You brought chicken livers?'

'I did. Here. Hold out your hand. Careful. I'm going to set a hook on it. It's a treble, so you have three chances to impale yourself. So be careful how you handle it in the dark.'

'How am I supposed to see to tie it on the line?'

'Let me do mine and then I'll shine the flashlight on it for you.'

'This hook is huge. And the line feels so thick. I feel like we're fishing for giants.'

'They get big. Twenty pounds or more sometimes, around here. Though it's not likely we'll catch one that big.'

'I didn't even know they made hooks this big.'

'They make hooks the size of my hand. People go out in the ocean and catch marlin and tuna and halibut that are bigger than you are. Bigger than I am. Hundreds of pounds.'

'Weird,' I said.

'What's weird about it?'

'I don't know. I was just thinking about life, and how you never really know as much as you think you do. You think there's one thing you know so much about, and then it turns out you haven't even scratched the surface. Like Tibet.'

He shined the flashlight on my face and I winced, and covered my eyes.

'I give up. How is it like Tibet?'

'Because . . . I know more about Tibet than anyone I know. I had a bookstore person tell me once that only somebody from a Tibetan travel bureau knows what I know. I had a woman in a library offer me a job as a reference librarian, I know so much. Well. She was joking. But she was joking about it because I know so much. But I've never even been to Tibet. What if I got there and it was nothing like what I thought? Or what if it turned out that what I know isn't one per cent of one per cent of all there is to know?'

'If you've never been to a place before, I can just about

guarantee you that what you know isn't one per cent of one per cent of all there is to know.'

'See what I mean? That's what I think is weird.'

The sun was up over the mountain, shining into my eyes, before we talked again. Our lines were in the water, in that deep pool, weighted down with chicken livers and those huge hooks. We were sitting with our backs up against the trunks of two evergreen trees. The sound of the water was like music. I didn't care if we ever caught anything or not. Except I did want to see what a channel cat looked like.

I was the one who opened my mouth.

'Seems weird, fishing without Rigby.'

No answer for a long time.

Then he said, 'I don't know what I'm going to do without that dog.'

'Don't even say that. She'll still be around a while. Won't she?'

'I certainly hope so.'

We sat in silence for another few minutes before I said, 'You should ask Rachel to come up for a visit.'

'Where did that come from?'

'I don't know. I was just thinking. You said Dan was sick of it up here. Which made it sound like Rachel still likes it. Maybe she misses the place.'

'Might be too soon for her.'

'Do you talk to her?'

'Yeah. She calls, or I call. Just about every day. It hasn't been long enough yet, if that's what you're thinking. It's only been a few days. She needs time to get over losing him. I'm not saying anything until the time is right.'

'How long, do you think?'

'I don't know. Probably a year at least.'

'A year. Wow.'

'She was married for a long time. Forty-seven years. It takes time to get over a loss like that.'

I decided my line was too slack, so I reeled in a little. But I hit the end of the slack in a weird way. It just stopped reeling. I couldn't move it any more.

'Crap,' I said. 'I think I'm hung up on something.'

'Give it a steady pull. See if you can work your hook loose.'

I gave the line a good solid pull. It pulled back, bending that huge rod over into an arch shape.

'Ah, yes,' Paul said. 'You're hung up on something. A large fish.'

'What do I do?'

'Bring him in.'

I reeled. Or, at least . . . I tried. But I felt like I was trying to haul in the trunk of a tree. And it hurt the scraped-up heels of my hands. A lot.

'Loosen your drag a little. Remember how I showed you that?'

'Yeah, but it's different on this rod.'

'Here, just hold steady. I'll do it for you.'

He reached over me, and twisted a knob on the reel, and then when the fish yanked, I heard a zipping sound as he pulled some line free.

'Why are we doing that?'

'Makes it harder for him to break the line.'

It also made it easier for me to reel in. Less like I was hooked on a brick wall. I reeled him in closer, and he zipped off a little line and got farther away again. And we did that for a long time. I have no idea how long. I wouldn't even try to say. I'm sure time was playing tricks. I just know my arm muscles were screaming, and I thought they might give out. I wasn't sure what I'd do if they let me down. My hands hurt so bad it was hard not to yell out loud. But I didn't. I kept my pain to myself.

Then, just when I thought I was getting nowhere, I saw him come up on the muddy bank. When he tried to pull again, he couldn't do much. Mired up in all that mud like he was. So I got up and walked straight backwards, pulling, until he was well out of the water. I ran to him, taking up the slack in the line as I went.

'Good job!' Paul said.

We stood there and looked at him for a second or two. Just in that brief moment, he held still. Like he knew it was over.

He was thick-bodied. Greenish brown, with weird eyes. And these long things like whiskers sticking out from both sides of his mouth, but made of the same stuff as the rest of him, not hair. I started to say that out loud, how they looked like whiskers. Then I realized how stupid it would sound. Of course they looked like whiskers. That's probably why they call them catfish.

'Careful how you handle him,' Paul said. 'Do *not* put

your fingers in his mouth. They can really hurt you. Want me to put him on the stringer for you?'

'Yeah, would you?'

I didn't even know what a stringer was. We'd always put fish in that creel basket. But this guy was about twice as long as the basket, which Paul hadn't even bothered to bring.

I watched Paul take a yellow cord, like thin nylon rope, out of the tackle box. It had a metal ring on one end, and a metal tip on the other. I watched him thread the metal tip through the cat's gills on one side. He kept feeding it through until it came out the fish's mouth, which was open and gasping. Then he threaded that end through the ring and pulled it snug, and he had the thing roped, the line looped right through the gills. He took my hook out of the fish's mouth, and I reeled it back in.

He carried the catfish to the edge of the creek, a little downstream of where we were fishing, and set him in shallow water. Tied the end of the stringer around a sapling, so he couldn't swim away.

I put another disgusting chicken liver on the hook and cast in again.

'You're getting really good at casting,' Paul said.

I hadn't known he was watching.

He sat down at the next tree again, and picked up his pole.

'Well,' he said. 'That was exciting.'

'I never thought I'd catch a fish that big in my life. How much do you think he weighs?'

'Seven, eight pounds maybe.'

'How much do the trout usually weigh?'

'A pound. Or less.'

'Wow. That's going to make some good eating.'

We settled into quiet fishing for a while. Fifteen, twenty minutes with nothing said. Now and then I'd pull gently on my line to see if it pulled back. But I could always feel the hook move.

Then I said, 'What if you wait a year, and talk to her, and it turns out she's already seeing somebody?'

'Well. I talk to her almost every day.'

'Yeah. But what if it's a year from now, and you're talking to her, and she tells you she just started dating some new guy? Then it's the wrong time to tell her again, and you waited too long.'

Speaking of waiting too long, I sat a long time thinking he was about to answer. But he never did.

'Sorry. I guess maybe you don't want to talk about that. I was just thinking. Yeah, it's a weird thing for me to say to you. I know. And I know you didn't really like hearing it. But isn't hearing me say it an awful lot better than having it happen?'

First nothing.

Then, 'Look, I know you have my best interests at heart, but . . .'

'Fine. I'm sorry. It's really none of my business. We'll talk about something else. Where was Sophie when you woke up the last two mornings? She wasn't right up on the bed with you, was she?'

'On the bed? No. Why would she be on the bed? She wants to be with Rig.'

'Doesn't Rig sleep on the bed with you?'

'No. Rig sleeps on her dog bed on the floor.'

'Oops. I think I made a mistake. I thought she was allowed up on the bed. She got up there with me, and I figured she wouldn't do it if she wasn't allowed.'

'I don't mind if she gets up there. I just don't want her up there while I'm sleeping, because I won't have any room.'

'She was really nice about only taking up half.'

'How is that possible? She's bigger than the bed.'

'She slept with her legs hanging off.'

'That dog is so smart it scares me sometimes.'

'Sorry if I did that wrong.'

'It really doesn't matter. I don't mind if *you* didn't mind.'

'I was thinking maybe we could get one of those chain locks. For the inside of the apartment door. And put it up high, where Sophie couldn't reach.'

'OK. We'll stop and get one on the way back through town. I'll put it up while your mom's at work.'

And I thought, Fine. Maybe that solves the problem. Maybe it's just all good from here on out. But the part of me that was supposed to relax and be happy said, Right. Like I haven't heard that a hundred times before.

'Tell me the story of what happened in the driveway,' he said. 'Since we have all this time.'

He looked over at the ripped knee of my jeans. With

my knees bent, you could see the dried blood pretty clearly through the hole in the denim.

'She decided to break away from me and run up to your house. So I flying-tackled her. I was trying to get her attention. I was trying to get some control back. I didn't mean to hurt her. I have no idea if it was a right or a wrong thing to do. I just don't know. Do you think it was right?'

'No idea at all,' he said. 'But I applaud you for trying something new.'

We stayed out for nearly another two hours. Till the sun was up pretty high, and it was getting too warm. We never caught another channel cat.

The next morning, Paul's third full day back, I woke up in my bed in the apartment. It was cold. And drafty.

'Not possible,' I said. Out loud. To myself.

I got up and peeked around the divider. The door was hanging wide open. Paul's new chain lock was dangling, undone.

I woke up my mom. My arms were sore, but I shook her by the shoulder until she sat up. She looked pissed. I didn't care. I was pissed, too.

'The lock doesn't work if you don't put it on at night.'

'I did put it on.'

'Apparently not. Or Sophie wouldn't be gone.'

She craned her neck around to see.

'I'll be damned,' she said. 'I wonder how she did that.'

'You must've forgotten to lock it.'

'I locked it.'

'I doubt that. She can't reach it.'

'Hmm. I have no idea, kiddo. But I did lock it.'

'Fine. Whatever. I'll just apologize to Paul one more time. But you won't mind if tonight I lock it myself.'

That night before bed, after Sophie was long asleep, I reached up on my toes and locked the chain. It was high up, even for me. And my arms still felt like they were about to fall off.

'I swear I really did lock it,' my mom said.

I figured she was wrong, but I didn't feel like arguing.

The next morning, Paul's fourth full day back, I woke up and it was drafty and cold.

'Shit,' I said. Before I even got up and looked.

I woke my mom again, and we stared at it. And shook our heads.

'Maybe she dragged one of those kitchen chairs over,' she said.

'I can believe Sophie would figure that out. But I think after she got the lock off, she'd just go. I can't picture her moving the chair back first. I can see her figuring out how to get what she wants, but I can't see her covering her tracks.'

'Hmm. You think this couch is too close to the door? You think she climbed up on the back of it and braced herself on the wall and leaned way over?'

'I have no idea. But let's move it farther away. Just to be safe. And I'll just have to apologize to Paul one more time.'

*

The next morning, Paul's fifth day home, I woke up to find the door wide open, and one of the kitchen chairs dragged over by the door.

I woke my mom again.

'Well, I was right about one thing. She doesn't bother to cover her tracks.'

'I'll move the table and chairs down to the garage before I go to work. You go apologize to Paul one more time.'

'Right. Like we don't say that every morning. Like we should be so lucky that it's only this one more time.'

On Paul's sixth day home, the door was hanging open. In front of it was my locked trunk and a rickety stack of books.

I woke my mom.

'I think we're screwed,' I said. 'Pardon my language.'

'It's more polite than what I would have said.'

'It's just not going to work.'

'I did some research.'

'Did you find any place decent?'

'Not close. Not someplace we could go visit anytime.'

'I better go talk to Paul.'

I paused a long time at the back door, my hands and my ear against the wood. I wanted some evidence he was awake. I thought I heard water from a faucet, so I knocked.

Paul opened the door, all dressed and shaved.

'Good morning,' he said. 'She's right where she always is.'

'You're being incredibly patient about this. But it feels like time to talk about the fact that it isn't going to work.'

'Come in.'

I followed him into his kitchen, and sat at the table. He poured me a cup of coffee and put sugar and milk in front of me.

'Thanks,' I said.

I wasn't sure what I was supposed to say or when I was supposed to say it. It seemed like the whole thing had already said itself. So I sat there like a lump and watched him get Rigby's food ready. He put it down in the corner, and called her, and she came in, looking stiff and limpy, Sophie tagging right behind.

Then he sat at the table with me, with his own cup of coffee, and we stared at them and didn't say anything for a long time.

Just as I was gathering up to talk, he beat me to it.

'It just doesn't seem like such a terrible situation,' he said. 'I thought it would be. But it isn't. Don't ever quote me on this. Don't tell anyone I said it. I wouldn't say this to anyone but you, and I'm trusting you not to take it the wrong way. But it's a little like having another dog. A very well-behaved one. I know she's not a dog. I totally give her credit for being a human girl. But she's doing a dog impression. So that's what it's like for me. It's not like having another person in the house. Not in any way. Another person would be looking at me. And trying to talk to me. I'd have to be careful what I said and did in my own home. Sophie never looks at me. She pays no attention to me at all. She doesn't even seem to know I'm here. Or maybe she doesn't care. Either way. She just really doesn't take up any space at all.'

'So . . . I'm not sure what you're saying. Or maybe I know what you're saying but I can't believe you're saying it. You're saying it's OK?'

'I'm saying . . . I wake up, and she's sleeping quietly on Rigby's bed, and then you come get her and take her out to meet her ride to school. And it just doesn't seem like a thing she should be confined to an institution for doing. It just doesn't feel like such a terrible thing.'

My mom was up and dressed when I got back, and looking plenty stressed out. In fact, she looked like she might be about to throw up.

'What did he say?'

'You're absolutely, positively not going to believe it.'

I made a mental note that I had until winter to teach Sophie to close the door behind her after letting herself out.

PART THREE

When i Was Sixteen, and Now That i'm Seventeen

 **Smile**

My mom was sitting at our little kitchen table in the corner of the apartment when I came out from behind the room divider, first thing in the morning. She was drinking tea and eating buttered toast.

It was a year and a half later, and we still didn't have a third chair. We didn't need one. Sophie was never home. She was at school, or she was at Paul's with the dog.

'It snowed buckets in the night,' she said. 'Put on your boots before you go.'

'OK.'

'You might need snowshoes or cross-country skis to get to the house.'

'Is that a joke?'

'I'm half joking. But it's deep. Try to get Sophie back a little early, so I can get her all suited up. And we'll have to climb over that big snowdrift the plows leave behind. If the plows have even been through. You think the plows have been through? Did you hear them? Maybe the schools are closed.'

'I guarantee you the schools are closed. It's Christmas vacation.'

'No, that starts tomorrow.'

'No, that starts today.'

'Not for Sophie.'

'Yes, for Sophie. I asked twice. Everybody goes out on the same day.'

'Oh. I wonder how I got that wrong.'

'No idea.'

I was anxious to get going. Paul needed help first thing in the morning. The sooner the better. I wondered if my impatience showed.

'How's the dog? Any better?'

'Mom. It's not something she's going to get better from.'

Her forehead wrinkled up. I waited for her to say something, but she never did.

'Now . . . Paul needs help with her. I have to go.'

I held on to the railing on the way down the stairs, kicking snow off as best I could before stepping down. When I was sure I was off the last stair and on to the ground, I took a long step and sank in up to my knees. But I just kept going, even though my boots were filling up with snow.

Paul had his back steps shoveled off. He must have been up awfully early.

I rapped on his back door.

'It's open,' he called. 'Come in.'

I did. And headed straight for Rig.

Rigby was lying flat out on her side on Paul's bedroom floor, on the heated bed Paul had bought her. She was covered with a heavy handmade quilt, and Sophie. When she saw me, she lifted her head about halfway, and thumped her tail, bouncing part of the quilt up and down.

'Think we can get through this again?' Paul asked me.

At the exact moment he asked, he handed me a cup of coffee with sugar and milk.

'We just will,' I said.

I looked down at Sophie, who, bizarrely, did not look calm. I hadn't seen her not look calm since the first few days we moved in here. Her face was twisted, like something invisible was poking into her side. And she was making fussy little complaining noises.

'Let me just set this coffee down,' I said.

'You can drink it first. She can wait.'

'That doesn't feel right. I think what Rigby wants should come first.'

'Fair enough,' he said.

I set my coffee on his bedside table.

'Come on, Sophie,' I said. 'Come on, Rigby. Let's move. Let's go out.'

Sophie didn't get up. Usually she got up. She just lay there. Fussing and frowning.

'How long has Sophie been like this?' I asked Paul.

'Just since Rigby woke up this morning. When Rigby slept, she slept.'

I had a theory. But I didn't like it. So I didn't share it. I shoved it down and hoped it would go away. I lifted Sophie by both elbows. She complained bitterly, but she didn't fight being lifted.

'Ready?' Paul asked me.

'As I'll ever be.'

We worked together, the two of us, to help Rigby get on her feet. It had been a major production for nearly a week. That morning it was closer to an impossibility. I had to keep stopping and getting her legs back under her. And Paul had to keep her from falling down while I did. My back had been seriously sore for as long as I could remember. I didn't even want to think how Paul's must feel.

When she was standing, and fairly balanced, we got on both sides of her. We each had to take a side and stay close, because she could unbalance to either side at any time. If we gave her enough room, she'd go down.

We led her carefully to the front door. No more back door for Rigby. The back door was nothing but a landing, with stairs. Rigby didn't do stairs. Rigby hadn't done stairs for months. Outside the front door was a little patch of fairly level ground. Just one step down on her way out, one step up on her way back in.

Every step we helped Rigby take, Sophie complained. Like someone stuck a pin in her each time Rigby put her weight down. It wasn't helping me bury my theory at all.

When we got out front, I saw that Paul had done a little shoveling there, too. So Rigby could walk around without stepping in deep snow.

'You got a lot done for so early in the morning,' I said.

'I haven't been sleeping well.'

'Oh. Sorry to hear that.'

We steadied Rigby carefully as she stepped off that one concrete stair. Then she half squatted immediately into a peeing position. Without even sniffing around first. And almost fell over. Paul caught her, but then he slid and went down on one knee himself, and a big explosion of sound came out of him. I knew he'd hurt himself. I just didn't know how badly. But he stayed there, and braced her, until I could get her centered again.

She couldn't really stop peeing once she started, so she peed all over her own back legs as we stood her up again.

'We can take her in now,' he said. 'She won't need to do anything more.'

'She's still not eating?'

'She hasn't eaten for almost three days.'

We walked her back inside, Sophie following behind and fussing. We got her centered over the bed, and tried to help her down easy, but it came out more like falling. The bed protected her from being injured. But I knew it must have hurt her poor arthritic bones. She winced, but made no sound.

Sophie shrieked once on impact and then curled up against Rigby's side.

I sat cross-legged on the floor by Rigby's head, and stroked her ears, and she set her gigantic gray muzzle on my knee and sighed.

Paul came back with a bowl of warm water and a rag, and cleaned off her back legs, and dried them with a towel, and we covered her up again.

'How bad did you hurt yourself?' I asked him.

'I probably won't know the whole story until I try to get out of bed tomorrow. But, anyway, bad enough.'

'Your back?'

'Unfortunately, yes.'

I wanted to ask how I'd get Rigby out in the morning if he was injured. Without bringing my mom into his house. If he'd liked that idea one bit, I'm sure he would have suggested it a long time ago.

I didn't ask. Because there was no good answer. If we couldn't do it, the two of us, I couldn't do it alone.

'I have a theory about Sophie,' I said. 'The way she's acting.'

'Will I like it?'

'No.'

First I thought he really didn't want to hear it. And never would. Then he tugged at my sleeve and flipped his head toward the kitchen.

Before I left Rigby, I said the same thing I'd said to her every day for the past three months. But not out loud. I never said it out loud. And yet I trusted the message to get delivered all the same. I said, silently, If I don't see you again, Rigby, I love you and goodbye, and thanks for everything.

I picked up my coffee and joined Paul in the kitchen. And just sat. At first we just sat.

'I think the pain medication isn't working any more,' I said.

'It's nearly enough drugs to kill her. I can't believe it wouldn't kill her pain.'

'I think the pain's breaking through.'

'I thought this was a theory about Sophie.'

'It is.'

I could tell he didn't get how, but he didn't ask. Probably because he didn't want to know.

'Sophie imitates the inside of Rigby. Which has mostly been calm. But when Rigby was all excited to see you, Sophie imitated that.'

'So you're saying she's fussing because Rigby is in pain.'

'It's possible.'

'You know if I can't keep her relatively pain free I'll have to take her to the vet and call this.'

'I know. I'm sorry. I just thought I should tell you.'

'Yeah. You're right. I guess. How sure are you? Maybe she's fussing because she knows she's going to lose Rigby soon. Maybe she can sense that.'

'Maybe.'

'But you think it's the pain.'

'You heard her when we were walking Rigby to the door. Every step. Every time Rigby put her weight down. And when Rigby hit the bed, she shrieked. Rigby didn't make a sound, but Sophie shrieked.'

He closed his eyes. At first he didn't look like he was

breathing at all. Then he sighed. Long, and strangely slow. The silence was starting to scare me.

He got up and walked back into the bedroom. I didn't follow. I'd grown roots, and they were tangled up with the chair legs.

He came back out again in about an hour. Or two or three minutes. It was hard to tell.

'I'm not even sure how I'd get her to the vet. We'd need another person or two just for that.'

'Or maybe the vet would come here.'

'Maybe.'

We finished our coffee in silence. And it was so heavy, that silence. It was so heavy it felt like the heaviness of it was sitting in my stomach, pulling it down. Like it might tear right through the bottom of my stomach and keep going.

'It's a hard decision to make,' he said. 'If she still wants to be here, I don't want to cut her short. If she's in pain, I don't want to prolong it. I don't know what to do. What should I do, Angie?'

I didn't answer. Because I didn't know.

I tried to answer. I tried to at least say I didn't know. But the words were too huge. They got stuck coming out.

After a few minutes I said, 'I think you should call Rachel.'

'And tell her what?'

'Ask her to come up.'

'For what?'

'For support. You were there for her when she was losing Dan.'

'She didn't ask me to be, though. She said I should stay up here and enjoy my retirement.'

'That was when he was going in for surgery. Not when she found out he was going to die. She wouldn't have wanted to go through that alone. Would she?'

'Maybe. She wanted to be alone the minute he died.'

'Do you want to be alone? Or do you want her here with you?'

A couple of breaths, both of which I could hear. Then he said, 'It would be nice to have her here. But . . . that's . . . I don't know how to say what it is. To tell her that out of all the people I've ever had in my life, she's the one person I want with me at a time like this . . . it says an awful lot. It almost tells her all there is to tell.'

'Paul. It's been a year and a half. Don't you think it's time?'

He shook his head. Almost violently.

'It's too much. I can't do it now. It's too much all at once.'

'Fine. Then ask her to come up because you need another pair of hands to get Rigby to the vet.'

He said nothing. For a bizarre length of time. Like he hadn't heard, or had no opinion on what I said.

Then he jumped up suddenly. 'That's good,' he said.

Which made me proud I'd thought of it.

He called Rachel, who agreed to come up the following day.

When I woke up the next morning, my very first thought was that I might not be able to be with Rigby on her last days. Because maybe when Rachel got here, Paul would want me to make myself scarce. And Sophie. I hadn't even asked if Sophie could be there. And yet, after all this time, I wasn't sure how anyone could get her to be anywhere else.

It felt bad. Really bad. I could feel it in my chest, and I remember thinking I knew why they call it getting your heart broken. That was exactly how it felt.

But then I thought, If I had it to do over again, would I do the same?

I would have. I knew I would have. Because she was Paul's dog, so Paul was more important.

So I just got up and faced the day and got ready to find out.

What else was I supposed to do?

The back door was unlocked, which usually meant Paul was up. But when I went in, I couldn't hear him, and he didn't seem to be around. I stuck my head into the bedroom to check on Sophie and Rig. Paul blinked back at me from the bed. He was awake, but not up.

'I was up till three,' he said. 'But it's OK. You can come in and check on them.'

Rigby was fast asleep on her side. She didn't wake up and thump at me. Sophie was lying on her back, not touching the dog in any way. Staring off into space. Smiling.

'Sophie is smiling,' I said.

'That's odd,' he said. 'I'm not sure I've ever seen Sophie smiling. What do you think it means?'

'I don't know.'

'You think it means Rigby's not in pain this morning?'

That's when it hit me. And I think it may have hit him at the same time. Because he got over to us fast.

I watched him put his hand on Rigby's chest. Then on the side of her neck.

'She's not in pain,' he said.

He covered her up with the quilt. All of her. Even her beautiful black and gray head.

We sat in the kitchen and waited for Rachel to get there. We didn't talk much while we were waiting.

Except I remember at one point I said, 'She saved you from the decision. Because she knew it would be hard for you. That was nice of her.'

'That's the kind of dog she was.'

'Want me to shovel the driveway so Rachel can get in?'

'Good idea,' he said. 'Thanks.'

Then at least I had something to do.

'We never had any breakfast,' he said. 'Do you want lunch?'

'No. Do you?'

'No.'

We sat a while longer.

Then I said, 'When Rachel gets here, should we leave? And, if so, leave how? Leave the house and stay in the apartment? Or leave completely?'

In the last year and a half, I'd told him maybe ten times that he should invite Rachel up for a visit. He finally invited her once. And she came. She stayed four days. My mom and Sophie and I went camping. At the same place we camped before. But in Paul's tent, and in nice weather. We arranged it all in advance, so he'd be able to talk to her.

He didn't talk to her. Not about the big stuff, anyway.

He never really explained why not, and it never felt right to ask.

'Is it OK if I don't really know yet?' he said, finally.

'Sure.'

'It would be nice if you could get ready to take off if Sophie gets noisy. But, I don't know. If she's like this . . . I don't know if it matters.'

'You don't have to figure it out now.'

'Good. Because I can't really think.'

'Is that her?' I asked, because I thought I heard a car in the driveway.

'Yes,' he said. 'It is.'

But he didn't move.

'You going to get up and go meet her?'

'I don't know,' he said. And continued to sit. 'It's not looking that way.'

'OK. I'll go.'

I ran, carefully, down the back steps and opened the garage door so she could pull her car in next to Paul's. And when she took her two suitcases out of the trunk, I took one. To be helpful.

'Thank you, Angie,' she said. 'Where's Paul?'

She looked so young. Not younger than usual or anything. It just hit me again, the way it did both other times I'd seen her. Except, the first time I saw her I hadn't known she was a little older than Paul. It was hard to believe she was seventy. I couldn't see that when I looked at her. She looked like an actress who's about fifty now but still looks like an actress and still looks good.

'He's in the kitchen,' I said.

I set the suitcase down, and closed the garage door behind us. And we walked toward the back stairs together. Side by side. Careful not to slip.

'Rigby died in her sleep last night,' I said.

'Oh, dear. Is Paul all right?'

'I don't know. He isn't crying.'

'I'm not sure that's a good thing.'

'I never meant it was. He seems kind of frozen.'

Then I let her go up the stairs ahead of me, because it was only wide enough for two people if they weren't both carrying suitcases. When we met up on the back landing, I said, 'Can I ask you a favor?'

'I don't see why not.'

'It's not for me. It's for Paul.'

'Then definitely yes.'

'If he acts like it's OK for you to go soon, because he doesn't need help lifting the dog, could you please not believe him?'

She looked into my face for what felt like a long time, and it made me squirmy. But I held still. I watched the way her frozen clouds of breath and my frozen clouds of breath came together into one big cloud. Then she put her hand on my cheek. Kind of cupped it in her palm. And I thought, This is how a mother should touch you. Like the touch is really for you, not for her. But I figured it was too late for my mother to learn.

'I'll stay a few days,' she said. 'Until we're sure he's doing all right.'

'Thank you.'

Then I opened the back door, and let her in, and closed it after us. We walked through the back bedroom together. It still had a single bed in it, that Paul had gotten for her first visit.

'Did you ever have kids?' I asked her.

She looked at me in an odd way, and I wondered if it had been a rude question. If I'd been wrong to ask.

'I have no children. No. Why do you ask?'

'I don't know. I just thought you'd be a good mother.'

Before she could even answer, we were in the kitchen, with Paul, and then Rachel and I didn't get to talk any more, because then it wasn't about the two of us in any way.

My mom got home from work at the usual time. About two thirty. I made sure I was there to meet her and talk to her.

'What?' she said. 'The dog died. Didn't he?'

'She. She, Mom. You knew that dog for years. How can you not get that she was a she?'

'I'm sorry. Where's Sophie?'

'Right where she always is. On the dog bed at Paul's. And right now Rigby is there, too. But in an hour or so, a place that does cremation is going to send two big guys over to pick her up.'

'And then Sophie's going to freak.'

'That's what I'm thinking. And Rachel is here, so if Sophie freaks we're going to have to clear out.'

'And go where?'

'Anywhere that isn't here.'

'Not exactly camping weather.'

'We could go to a motel. You said we had a lot of money saved.'

'The money is not the issue, kiddo. How can we go to a motel if Sophie is freaking out?'

'I don't know, Mom. I don't know what we're going to do. But brace yourself. Because we're about to have to figure it out.'

My mom kept looking out the window. Peering around the edge of the curtain, the way she'd done the day Paul moved away from the old place.

It made me nervous this time, too.

'They're here,' she said.

I went to the window and looked out on the snowy scene. The snow had started up in flurries again. There was a gray van parked near the bottom of the back stairs, but I couldn't read what it said because it was too covered with snow, and that dirty sleet that gets thrown up from your tires when you drive on a barely plowed road.

I realized I didn't want to see what came next. So I sat down on the couch.

It bothered me that my mom didn't. So after a minute, I said, 'Come away from the window!' But it came out harsh. So I followed it up with, 'Please.'

She came and sat on the couch with me, looking like a puppy who's just been smacked on the rump.

'Sorry,' I said. 'I'm just nervous.'

'You're not crossing anything.'

'I think it's going to take more than crossed fingers to save us now.'

I heard the thunk of the van door slamming, and then the engine started up. I ran to the window and watched it inch down the driveway, back wheels losing traction and spinning now and then.

Then I paced for a minute or two.

Until my mom said, 'Now who's driving who crazy?'

'Sorry.'

I sat back down on the couch.

'She's not freaking out,' my mom said.

'She's not.'

'Why do you think she's not?'

'I have no idea.'

'I would think she'd have freaked out when the dog died,' she said.

'She was happy when the dog died.'

'How is that possible?'

'My theory? It's just a theory. I could totally be wrong. But I've decided to believe it means wherever Rigby is now, she's happy. Even if I'm wrong, and it's not true,

I'm going to keep believing that. Because that's what I choose to think.'

I waited for close to two hours. Because I really didn't want to go knock on their door. Maybe he was talking to her, right then. Telling her how he felt. Or maybe he was crying, and she was holding him. I had no idea what was going on in there. I only knew I didn't want to interrupt it.

But there was an obvious loose thread hanging, because they still had Sophie. And I had no idea if that was OK.

'I better go see what's what,' I said to my mom.

I bundled up warm and walked all the way down the slippery, snowy driveway, because I didn't want to knock on the back door, because the back room was Rachel's guest room. I slipped twice and fell on my butt on the steep part of the driveway, but I kept going.

I walked up the front stairs, which was easy, because the tree tunnel had kept them pretty much free of snow.

I paused. Wished like hell I didn't have to knock.

Knocked.

Rachel answered the door.

'I'm so sorry to bother you,' I said.

'It's all right.'

'I didn't know about Sophie. I didn't know if I should . . . What about Sophie? What's she doing? Should I be trying to get her back?'

'I'm not sure. Let me ask Paul. Come in.'

I waited in the living room, dripping snow on to the mat by the door. They had a fire going strong in the woodstove, and it was warm. In my big jacket, I felt like I was suffocating, but I didn't figure I'd be there long.

Then she came back, and said, 'She's just lying on the dog bed. She's not causing any trouble. Paul says she can stay until she has to go to school.'

'It's Christmas vacation. She doesn't have to go to school until January.'

'Oh. Hold on.'

I sweated by the fire for another minute or two. I wasn't sure why Paul wasn't coming out and talking to me himself. If I had to guess, I think he might have been more OK with crying in front of her than me. Which I guess seemed right to me, since they'd been friends for more than fifty years and he loved her.

She came back and said, 'Paul says fine.'

'OK.'

'She's being very well-behaved.'

'I'm not sure why, but good.'

'She's acting like the dog is still here.'

'Pretending, maybe.'

'Or maybe the dog is still here in some way she can feel.'

I didn't answer, because I couldn't. Because I had no idea what I thought about that.

'Well, you know where to find me if there's a problem.'

I turned to go.

'Don't you want to go out the back way in this bad weather?'

'OK.'

'Why didn't you come to the back door?'

'Because it's your guest room. I didn't want to disturb your privacy.'

She smiled with only one corner of her mouth. A lot like the way Paul sometimes did.

'No wonder he likes you so much,' she said.

In the morning I woke up, and started to jump up. Force of habit. I was going to go help Paul get Rigby out to pee. I was already half sitting up, swinging the blankets off, when I remembered.

I laid back down and covered up, and tried to understand the idea that there was no Rigby any more, not anywhere in the world. That she'd gone from existing to not existing. I knew all about it in my head. But, in my gut, it didn't make a damn bit of sense.

When my father died, I'd spent months doing the same thing.

Now here's the weird part. It had been ten years since my father got killed, and I realized I still hadn't made any progress with that. Oh, I was used to it. It didn't surprise me or anything, and I accepted that it would always be that way. But in my gut, going from existing to not existing still didn't make a damn bit of sense.

I just didn't get the whole dying thing. I wondered if that was everybody or just me.

On the second full night after Rigby died, we heard a little rustling noise on the landing outside the apartment door. I was in bed, and so was my mom. I wasn't asleep, though. I didn't know about her.

Until she said, 'Did you hear that? What is that?'

'I don't know. Wild animal, maybe?'

I waited, but she didn't answer.

So I said, 'I should go look.'

'No, don't. It could be dangerous.'

'I'll put the chain on and peek out.'

I got up, a little cold in just my pajamas and bare feet, and locked the safety chain, and opened the door just a crack. Sophie was waiting on all fours on the landing, her teeth chattering. Wearing the clothes I'd put her in that morning, but no coat. She must have gone out the doggie door, and Paul and Rachel must not have known she was gone.

I closed the door and undid the chain, then opened up wide, letting a blast of cold air in. Sophie wandered in and took up a spot on the rug, right where she used to lie with Rigby.

'Huh,' my mom said.

I sort of expected her to say more. But, really, I'm not sure what more there was to say.

I rubbed Sophie's little hands between mine until they warmed up, took off her sneakers and her pink socks, and rubbed her feet. Then I covered her up with a spare blanket and left her there to sleep.

A few days after that, at about ten o'clock in the morning, Rachel came to the door of our apartment to tell me she was leaving, and to say goodbye. Fortunately, my mom was at work. It was just Sophie, lying on the rug, and me.

'I could have stayed longer,' she said. 'But it's been six days, and I think he's all right. I think he just needs time to process. You know. Alone. Besides. I'm pretty sure he's getting sick of me.'

'Oh, I doubt that,' I said.

'You know how he is. A bit of a loner.'

'I'm not sure.'

She looked at me strangely. 'You don't agree?'

'I think he might be changing. Some, anyway. So . . . six days. That's a nice long visit. You must have had plenty of time to talk.'

I watched her face for a moment. But she didn't know what I was talking about. It was a disappointment I could feel all down through my chest. Like I was a sword swallower. I thought, Why can't he just tell her?

Not that I thought it was easy or anything. But I would have done it by then, and I'm the world's worst spaz about things like that. Well. About everything.

'We talked, yes,' she said. 'Mostly about the dog. But different things. Nothing special. Why? Was there something else?'

'No. Not really. I just . . . I know what good friends you two are. And how much it meant to him to have you here. Do you want to come in? It's cold and I didn't mean to be rude.'

'No, I really should go,' she said. 'I don't have the best night vision, so I want to get home before dark. But before I go, I want to tell you how much it means to *me* to have *you* here. I feel so much better leaving him here knowing you're here to help.'

'How's his back?'

'Getting a little better.'

She shifted her weight from one foot to the other on the landing, and I knew she was ready to go.

So, nice and fast, before she could get away, I said, 'You should come visit more often.'

'I'd like that. But I can only come up as often as Paul invites me.'

'I think he wants to invite you more. But I think he feels like maybe it's imposing . . . to ask you. So if you ever wanted to suggest it . . .'

She looked into my face for a long moment, like she'd lost something there. I looked down at the snowy landing. I was worried I'd said too much. Given too much away.

'I just might do that,' she said. 'Maybe I will. Happy New Year.'

Then she kissed me on the forehead and headed out down the stairs, being careful not to slip.

I watched her and thought it was no wonder Paul was in love with her. If I was in my sixties, I figured I'd probably be in love with her, too. She was one of those women who just almost made it too easy to fall.

'Happy New Year,' I called after her.

At first, I left Paul alone. I wasn't entirely sure if he wanted me to. But we had a phone by then. And he didn't exactly live far away. So I figured he'd let me know if he wanted company.

He called me in the early evening, about three or four days after Rachel left. Asked me if I wanted to play a few hands of gin.

'Anytime,' I said. 'Always. I just didn't want to bug you.'

'Thank you,' he said. 'But now would be good.'

'I'd have to bring Sophie. My mom is out with her friend Jenna from work.'

'Not a problem. Back door's open. Just come in.'

So I picked my way down the snowy, icy driveway and up his back stairs. Holding Sophie's hand so she wouldn't fall. I led her through the back door and the back bedroom, and then she pulled her hand out of mine and ran to Rigby's old dog bed and curled up tight.

Paul showed up in the bedroom doorway with me, and we watched her for a minute.

'I'm glad you didn't get rid of it,' I said.

'Sophie was a good excuse, but really, I think it would have broken my heart if I'd had to throw it away.'

'Maybe you'll get another dog sometime.'

'Maybe.' We watched her in silence for a minute. Then he said, 'What do you think Sophie would think of a new dog?'

'Pretty sure she'd hate him. And that we'd have to protect him from her.'

'Oh. Well. Cross that bridge when we get to it.'

We wandered into his kitchen and sat down at the

table. He'd set a glass of iced tea by my plate, which was my favorite. He made good iced tea.

He shuffled the cards.

'So,' I said. 'You got lonely.'

He looked up from the shuffling like it required a lot of concentration and I'd distracted him.

'Did I? I thought I just got bored.'

'You never got bored when Rigby was around.'

'Oh. Good point, I guess.'

He dealt the cards, and I reached out and put my hand on his arm before he could pick up his hand.

'Wait, don't look at your cards yet.'

'Why not?'

'How about if we play for money?'

He looked into my face, his eyes dancing with this weird amusement that might have been partly critical. 'Money? Since when do you have money to burn?'

'I don't. I only get ten dollars allowance a week.'

'Then why do you want to play for money?'

'I don't know. Just because I never did before, I guess. I just want to see how it feels. I'm not talking about a lot of money. Maybe, like . . . a quarter a round or something?'

He was still looking at me that way. So I looked down at the backs of my cards. Like I had something to hide, though I wasn't sure if I did or not. I didn't want us to look at our hands yet, because it seemed fairer to decide if you're going to bet before you see what you're betting with. Otherwise it's sort of a biased decision.

'On one condition. Ten dollars is the limit. I don't want you losing more than a whole week's allowance.'

'What makes you think I'm going to lose?'

He broke into a twisted half smile, and we picked up our hands. I had two queens and an eight and nine of clubs, so that got me off to a pretty good start.

'I had a feeling there was a little gambler in you,' he said.

'Probably. My father was a gambler.'

He looked up from his cards. Into my face. A little too suddenly, I thought.

'You didn't tell me that.'

'Well. Didn't come up, I guess. I mean, when would I have told you?'

'I would think you'd have mentioned it when we were trying to figure out how he died.'

'Why? What does one thing have to do with the other?'

'Oh. Never mind. Forget it.'

'No, what? Tell me.'

He didn't, at first. But after a while he did.

'If someone is pretty deep into compulsive gambling, that can get dangerous. They usually end up owing huge amounts of money to the wrong people.'

'Well. Yeah. I guess. But a loan guy wouldn't kill you, would he? If he did, then you could never pay him back.'

'Unless he wanted to make an example of someone. Or unless . . . No. You know what? Never mind. I'm sorry I ever started with this. Let's drop it. This was your father, and we don't know, so why am I speculating?'

'It's OK. Maybe you know more than I do about it.'

He laughed a big, snorty laugh, but I wasn't sure why.

'Angie,' he said. 'Do I *look* like an expert on gambling? I worked forty-five years at a job I hated for the retirement benefits. I've been in love with the same woman for more than fifty years, but haven't bothered to share that information with her. Where do you see big risk-taking on this side of the table? You're the gambler here, not me.'

We played in silence for a while, and then I called gin and won a quarter. He actually paid me right then and there. Took a quarter out of his pocket and pushed it across the table at me. It was exhilarating, but by then I knew it shouldn't be, so I felt bad that it was.

While we were looking at our next hand, I said, 'She told me she might come up and visit more often. That would be good. Right?'

I could see him looking at me, but I refused to look up from my cards.

'I didn't tell her,' he said.

'I figured you didn't.'

I threw my worst card down and picked up a new one. And tried not to say it. But I had to. I had to say it. I'd been not saying it for so long.

'You're not going to . . . You're going to tell her eventually, right? You're not just never going to tell her. Are you?'

'I might be never going to tell her.'

I dropped my cards on the table face-down. Then it was his turn to avoid my eyes.

'How can you do that? I don't get that at all.'

'I already told you. I'm not a gambler. I don't take risks well.'

'What risk? You're not with her now. The worst that can happen is that you still won't be.'

'That's not entirely true. I have a good friendship with her now. We talk nearly every day. If I tell her, and she doesn't feel the same, she might feel terrible about hurting my feelings. Or it might be too hard for me to talk to her after that. It might drive a wedge between us. This way I have half of what I want. I don't want to wager with it and end up with nothing.'

'Or everything.'

'I don't think she feels the same. She would have said so.'

'*You* didn't.'

'Or I'd be able to tell.'

'*She* can't.'

'Look. Angie. I know if you were me, you'd go for it.'

'I would. Definitely.'

'But I'm not you. OK? I'm me. Now how about if we just play cards?'

We played about twenty more rounds, and I left two dollars and twenty-five cents richer than before. Which wasn't much, I know. But it was still a win.

Sophie was asleep, so I threw her over my shoulder in the fireman's carry.

Paul put the outside back light on for me, so I could

pick my way through the snow and ice and get home.

I knocked, but my mom was still out. So I opened the door with my key.

After I got Sophie down in bed, I was about to shove the ring of keys into my pocket again. But first I looked at them. I think I might have known why. I might have done it on purpose.

I stared at the key to my locked trunk for a minute. Swallowing too much and too hard.

Then I pulled the trunk out from under the bed, and opened it up.

I took out *The Tibetan Book of the Dead*, and put it on my bedside table. Sophie hadn't been doing much shredding for a long time anyway. And I didn't have any books going.

Then I took out the note from Nellie. The two-and-a-half-year-old note that I still hadn't gotten up the nerve to read.

I sat on the edge of the bed and I read it. With my heart pounding, and my hands shaking, and my mouth so dry I could hardly swallow.

I read it three or four times. And I've read it so many times since then, I could almost recite the whole thing by heart. But I won't. Because not all of it matters to anybody else except me. And because it's a little private. Not for any special reason, but . . . just in general, it sort of is.

I'll share the gist of it.

She was completely sorry, and felt stupid and bad for carelessly hurting and embarrassing me.

She wanted me to know that even though I was hurt and embarrassed, and she could understand that – because she remembered being a teenager and how incredibly mortifying everything was – I really shouldn't be, because I hadn't done a damn thing wrong.

And, probably most important, she said that liking her the way I did was more like a compliment, like a gift to her, not like an inconvenience.

I wished I'd known that last part all along.

I called Paul on the phone, because his lights were still on.

'I'm a terrible phony,' I said.

'I doubt it,' he said. 'But tell me why you think so.'

'Because I'm no better than you are. There was somebody I liked, and I didn't tell her. And when she figured it out on her own, I was so humiliated I ran away and never said another word to her again. She wrote me a note about it, and I stuck it away and never even read it. So . . . some risk-taker.'

'Well,' he said. 'Now that you've figured that out, are you going to read it?'

'I just did.'

'Then you're *not* a terrible phony. And you *are* better than me.'

Looking back, I guess I sort of got it in my head somehow that he'd follow my example. That if I could get a little braver, so could he. But six months and two Rachel visits went by. And he still didn't take the risk.

Chapter Two

 **Risk**

It was June again, and it was four o'clock in the morning.

I left a note on the table for my mom.

It said,

> You need to trust me. I know I'm technically
> a minor, and I know you'll be pissed, but I'm
> almost seventeen now and I think I'm grown up
> enough to do things by myself. I have to go talk to
> somebody (actually a couple of somebodies), and
> the phone just won't do it. Sometimes you have
> to look at somebody face to face and say what you
> need to say to them. I should be back tomorrow
> (but it might even be the next day, so please don't
> freak), and then you can be as mad as you want.

I thought about signing it, but then I decided that was stupid, because there was only one person it could possibly be from.

I slipped out of the house and walked by flashlight into town. All the way to the bus station.

Then I pulled Nellie's hundred-dollar bill out of my jeans pocket, the one she gave me after the fact for my inventory labor all that time ago, and bought a round-trip ticket to go home. Except that wasn't a good way to say it, because that didn't feel like home any more. This did.

I got the window seat. And I got that view of the mountains I really never got on the way up. When we'd driven up three years before it had been sheeting rain, and I'd mostly either been asleep or hiding my head.

The bus was full, so I didn't get to spread out over both seats the way I was hoping. A woman sat next to me who reminded me a little bit of Nellie. I'm not really sure why, though. She didn't look much like her. But she was about the same age, and seemed smart in all the same places. I knew because we'd chatted a little about this and that, and then she'd taken out her book and started to read.

I took out *The Tibetan Book of the Dead*, even though I knew I wouldn't be able to read much of it, because I get sick if I try to read for long on a moving bus. I figured I'd read a page, then look at the view for a while.

Just as well, because it wasn't what you might call light reading.

'I tried to get through that once,' the woman said. 'It was too dense for me.'

Her voice startled me. I wasn't expecting it.

'I think it's too hard for me, too,' I said.

'Did you know that *The Tibetan Book of the Dead* is just an informal title for the English translation? The real translation from the Tibetan would be something more like *The Great Liberation Upon Hearing in the Intermediate States.*'

'I did *not* know that. What does it mean?'

'I don't have the first clue. I told you, it was over my head. And I'm a librarian. And you're . . . what? Sixteen or seventeen? So it's a little intimidating for me to watch you stick with it.'

'The fact that I'm still reading doesn't mean I understand it. I don't. I don't understand about dying at all. That's why I'm reading it. I thought maybe it would help explain it. Not so far.'

'Did somebody in your life die?'

'Yes,' I said.

But then I didn't say more. After a while she went back to her book.

'My dad,' I said. Because by then I knew I didn't really have to. I wasn't feeling trapped once she started reading again. 'But that was more than ten years ago. And one of my best friends at the end of last year.'

'Oh, dear. I'm sorry. Someone your age?'

'No. She was old.'

Actually, she was much younger and much older than me, both at the same time. Which is a riddle, like one of those Zen koans. The answer is dog. I didn't say any of that.

'Do you believe what that book is teaching?' she asked me. Like my opinion mattered. 'That part of us goes on, and there are choices when we leave our body?'

'I want to,' I said. 'I'm trying to decide.'

I had to take two city buses from downtown. I had to transfer.

Eventually I got off the bus right across from the park with the fountain. The one that used to be the end point of my walks with Rigby and Sophie, back before we all moved. Back when Paul used to pay me to walk her. Because we weren't exactly friends yet.

I set off on foot for the old neighborhood, Aunt Vi's neighborhood, my backpack slung over one shoulder. I realized right away that the walk would take me right past Nellie's bookstore. Which I hadn't really thought out in advance. I wondered if it was on purpose that I hadn't thought it out. Oh, I knew I'd be sticking my head in the bookstore and saying something to Nellie. At some point. She was part of the plan. Maybe thirty or forty per cent of the important stuff I had to do on this trip. Just, somehow, I didn't have it down in my head as the first thing. More tacked on as an afterthought for the end of the day.

First I wanted to put it back in that old position. After all, I'd walk by her store again on the way back to the bus. But then I thought, What if she looks out the window and sees me walk by? Without sticking my head in and saying a word?

She'd think I hated her.

I got hit with a thought so sudden and so strong, it stopped me. Literally. I stopped walking and stood still on the sidewalk. And just thought it.

She might already think I hated her. That was the thought. She'd had nothing to go on but her own imagination, all this time. I'd put her in a position where she had to guess how that whole thing was left. Make it up in her head. You know. That place where things can get out of hand. Get blown all out of proportion.

At least, in my head things do.

That really was the first moment it dawned on me how big an apology I owed her.

I started walking again, then had another thought that stopped me cold.

Maybe the bookstore wasn't even there any more, three years later. Little bookstores closed all the time. Maybe Nellie was out of business. Then the apology would never get delivered, because I'd never find her. I didn't even know her last name.

I started to walk again, and my steps got fast, because I was anxious to find out.

The bookstore was still there.

I slowed down, but I kept walking. Closer and closer. I expected my heart to pound and my hands to get shaky, but it didn't happen. I just felt numb. Like my body and my brain were made of petrified wood. I just felt heavy and numb.

When I got to her door, I paused a minute. With my hand on the door pull. Just froze there, looking at my own hand. Just seeing and feeling what I was doing. I knew it was a being-alive thing, but I still just felt numb.

I opened the door and stuck my head in.

'Hey,' I said. Quiet. Like a breath.

'Good afternoon,' she said. Flat and regular. Nothing special at all.

My heart dropped into my gut. And I felt it. Where was all that numb when I needed it most? It had never occurred to me that maybe *she* hated *me*. She liked me in the letter, and that's how I'd expected things to stay.

I almost turned and walked right back out again.

Then I heard, '*Angie?*'

That's when I realized she hadn't even known it was me.

'Yeah. It's me.'

'Oh, my God. Angie! I didn't even recognize you! You're all grown up.'

'It's been a long time,' I said.

'Is there a reason just your head is inside?'

'Yes.'

'Do you have Sophie and that huge dog with you?'

'No.'

'Then what's the reason?'

'I'm a big coward.'

She laughed. It turned out I liked to make her laugh just as much as I'd always used to.

I opened the door the rest of the way and went in. I stood in front of her counter, shifting back and forth from one foot to the other. Trying to feel if I was still numb or not. I had this thing in my stomach that felt like a little buzz of electricity. So probably not.

'I have to be honest,' she said. 'I figured you were gone for ever. I never thought I'd see you or hear from you again.'

I nodded. A little too much, in fact. 'It was looking that way for a while.'

'What changed?'

'Me. I guess.'

'Duh,' she said.

I got hit hard with how much I'd missed her, without even knowing it.

'I meant, what changed in *you*?' she added.

'Hmm. Well. I watched a friend of mine being a big coward. And I thought he shouldn't be. And then I realized I was, too, more than I'd been admitting. And I didn't want to be any more. And, also, I sort of felt like I owed you a big apology.'

'Want to know how you can totally make it up to me?'

'Yes.'

'You can sit down. That thing you're doing is making me nervous. You look like a racehorse fidgeting in the starting gate. That in combination with our shared history makes me think you're about to bolt out of here.'

'Sorry.' I sat down in her big stuffed chair. Slipped off my shoes and crossed my sock feet. Set the backpack on the rug. 'Better?'

'Much. So. I was wondering if you were even still in town.'

'I'm not. We got thrown out of my aunt's house that same day. That last day I saw you. We moved out of town that same day.'

'Oh. Well. That explains a lot.'

'Not really. I still could have called you.'

She laughed out loud, but I had no idea why.

'That's such classic Angie. I'm trying to let you off easy, but you have to turn yourself in. I don't think you owe me an apology. I think it was all me. I think I could have handled things better. I should have told you who Cathy was right at the beginning. I should have said right up front that she was my girlfriend. No surprises, you know? Hey. Are you hungry? I'm thinking pizza.'

Part of me didn't want to stay. Or at least, commit to staying. But I hadn't eaten all day, and I was pretty damn hungry.

'I could eat some pizza.'

She picked up the phone, and ordered it. And I got a chance to watch her while she wasn't watching me watch her. It was a weird experience, because I was bowled over by how big and strong denial can be. I couldn't grasp how I ever looked at her and didn't completely know how much I wanted to get closer to her, and why. That's a pretty damned big secret to be keeping, especially from yourself.

When she got off the phone, she said, 'So . . .'

And I said, 'So . . . is Cathy still your girlfriend?'

Which, the minute it came out of my mouth, I knew

was a stupid question. Because what difference did it make? If Cathy wasn't, somebody else was. Or would be. Because Nellie was still in her thirties and I was still in my teens. It was a brick wall I knew damn well we'd never get around. So I don't even know why I asked.

'Yes and no,' she said. 'More like my wife now.'

'Ah. Well, that's good. If you're happy.'

It was. It was good. And it hurt to hear it. Both at the same time. I only told her the half of it, but I had a funny feeling she knew both halves all the same.

'Wow,' I said. 'This is even better than the pizza we used to get.'

'Yeah, that old place went out of business. I think this is better, too. More expensive but better.'

'So, do you remember the first question you ever asked me?'

'Um. Let me think. I asked if you were getting beaten up at home.'

'No, that was the second one. Or the third.'

'I give up. What was it?'

'You asked me if I was going to go to Tibet when I grew up.'

'And you said no. Which surprised me.'

'Can I get a do-over on that?'

'Absolutely.'

'I think I'm going to go to Tibet.'

'Wow. You've made progress. What about your mom and Sophie?'

I stretched my legs out in front of me, and stared at

my socks for a second, and thought about my mom, at home, plenty pissed at me. I hoped she wasn't having a bad day with Sophie, who'd been more Sophie-like lately.

'I think maybe Sophie won't live at home for ever. I mean, I won't live at home for ever, so why should she? I think I'll go off and get a job and a life and go on a trip to Tibet. And I think Sophie will grow up and live someplace different. Like maybe a group home with other people who have problems like hers. And where they can teach her to do stuff on her own. However much she can learn.'

'That's a pretty sane decision. What does your mom think about that?'

'She wanted to find a place for her a long time ago. Around the time we got thrown out of Aunt Vi's. She got totally overwhelmed, and just wanted to give up. I was the one who wouldn't let us give up. I feel like if we're going to do a thing like that, it should be because the timing is right. And because it's really best for all of us. Not just because we got to the end of our rope. You know? But, things aren't as good with Sophie as they were before Rigby died, so—'

'Rigby?'

'The dog.'

'Right. The dog.'

'So that's assuming we can even wait that long. We'll just have to see.'

She shook her head a few times. I wasn't sure why.

'What?' I asked.

'I just forgot. I forgot how you're, like, twenty years older than you are.'

'I'm sorry I went running out of here and never talked to you again. The weird thing is, I can't even exactly say why. I mean, I know how it felt and all, but I don't really know why it needed to feel *that* bad. Sometimes I think the way I handled what happened didn't quite match what happened.'

We ate in silence for a minute or two. I was glad for the silence, because I was starting to feel scraped out inside. I remembered what Paul said about opening up to me, and then feeling like his nerves were being sandpapered. And having to withdraw just to get some rest.

I was starting to need some rest.

'Try this on for size,' she said. 'You overheard two people telling each other your secret, out loud, and it was a secret you hadn't even told yourself in the privacy of your own head yet.'

'Wow. I think you actually get it.'

'Been there, done that. So where are you living now?'

Like she knew I needed to talk about something easier than all that.

I took a deep breath, and swallowed another bite of pizza, and told her all about living in the mountains. Which took a while. Because, believe me, when you finally get to live in the mountains, there's a lot to tell.

Just as I was leaving, she said, 'You didn't come back just for this, did you?'

'No. I have to talk to somebody else.'

It made me feel tired. I'd barely even started.

She handed me one of her business cards.

'You don't have to call or write all the time,' she said. 'But every now and then it would be nice to know where you are. And how you are.'

'Tell you what. Make you a deal. I'll send you a letter from Tibet. I mean, I'll try to say hello sooner than that, but whatever else happens, I promise I'll send you a letter from Tibet.'

We shook on that deal.

I stepped out on the sidewalk, and let out a big breath. Like the first good exhale in a long time. And I thought, Oh, my God. I did it. It's over. I got it behind me.

Then I remembered, again, that it wasn't even the main thing I'd come here to do. It wasn't even the hard one. Because the thing with Nellie, if I'd done it all wrong, probably nobody would have gotten hurt except me. It's always easier to take a risk when it's your own stuff you're risking. Nothing is harder than risking something that belongs to somebody else.

I looked at Aunt Vi's house, and then I looked at Rachel's house. And then back at Aunt Vi's. I tried to decide.

It would have been a lot easier to go sit with Aunt Vi for a while. Rest my sandpapered nerves. But it was weighing heavy on me, this thing I had to do, and I knew I wasn't going to be even a little bit OK until I got it done.

I marched up the walkway to Rachel's door, raised

my hand to knock, and froze solid. This jolt of panic cramped up in my stomach. I thought I might be about to be sick. I thought, Don't do this. This might be incredibly wrong. You're breaking a huge confidence. You're risking your friendship with Paul, that apartment your family needs. The happiness of two other people. Well, five. If you count Sophie and my mom and me.

I thought, How did I ever convince myself I had any right to do this?

I turned and walked two steps back from the door and sat on the edge of the stoop with my face in my hands. Hauling back all the months of thinking I'd put into this.

It was reasonable thinking. I was there for a reason.

It's not like I hadn't known it would be risky. I'd just kept coming back to the fact that I had to do it anyway. Over and over, I just kept ending up there.

OK, I thought. I have to do it anyway. But just in that moment, I didn't get up.

Before I could, I heard Rachel's voice say, 'Angie?'

I jumped up and spun around and we looked right into each other's faces.

'Angie, what are you doing here? Did something happen to—'

'No! It's not an emergency. Nothing like that.'

'You're the last person I expected to see.'

'I know. I'm just surprising people all over the place today. Including myself.' I added that last part under my breath. But I think she heard.

'Are you here to see your aunt?'

'No. I'm here to talk to you.'

'Oh.'

I could see her surprise register. I think she was too polite to say, 'Why?' So for a moment she said nothing at all.

Then she said, 'Well, in a way that's good, because your aunt isn't home. She's out of town.'

'Out of town?' I think my tone made it clear that I found that amazing.

I walked the two steps back to her door, because I had something else to focus on now. Something safer.

'Yes, she's on her honeymoon.'

I felt my eyebrows go up. I said nothing, because the words would only have gotten tangled up.

'You didn't know she remarried?'

'No. I didn't. I'm kind of surprised, but I guess I don't really know why, come to think about it. She lost Charlie quite a while ago now. I guess everybody has a right to be happy.'

'You should come in.'

But I froze there for a moment more. I had a sudden terrible image that I'd walk into her living room and there'd be a man there. It was possible. Aunt Vi found someone. It sure wouldn't have been hard for Rachel.

'Look,' I said. 'It's not that I don't get that this is weird. And kind of rude. You didn't know I was coming, and I would hate it if somebody dropped in on me without calling like this. If this is a bad time, I'll just go away. I'll come back later. Or even in the morning. Whenever you say.'

Only, I realized, that plan had hinged on being able to stay at Aunt Vi's.

'It's not a bad time. I was just reading and I saw you through the window.'

I followed her into her living room and looked around. It looked completely different. More feminine now, with flowered curtains. And colors. And it wasn't cluttered, exactly, but it was pretty filled with stuff compared to Paul's house. Then again, just about every place was filled with stuff compared to Paul's.

'Have a seat,' she said. 'Can I get you something to drink? Milk, water, iced tea?'

'Iced tea would be nice. Thank you. If it's really no trouble.'

'It's really no trouble. Are you hungry?'

'No. Thank you. I just had pizza with my friend at the bookstore. But it was very nice of you to ask.'

She disappeared into the kitchen, and I fidgeted on the couch and tried to accept the fact that I was in it now, whether I liked it or not. I had passed the point of no return.

When she came back out, she stood over me and handed me a glass of iced tea and a coaster.

'Nellie?' she asked.

That completely threw me. I had no idea where it had come from, or why she'd said it, or how she knew. I swear I thought she was looking right through my skull and reading what was written inside.

'Why did you just say that name to me?'

'I wondered if that was your friend from the bookstore. The one you had pizza with.'

'Oh. Yes. You know her?'

'I go to that bookstore all the time. Usually every week.'

'Ah.'

I ran it around in my head a bit, and it made a degree of sense. It was less than a mile from her house. But it felt weird. Like the universe was lining up in some new way, and everyone I was connected to was connecting with everyone else, with no earthly reason why it should be that way.

She sat across from me, in an old-fashioned wing chair, and I tried to stop my head from spinning. I felt like I wanted to physically hold on to it. Like it might fall off, or fly away.

'I know this must be about Paul,' she said. 'Because that's the only thing that ties us together.'

'Yes. It is.'

'Is he all right?'

'He's no different than when you last saw him.'

'But you don't think that's all right?'

'Paul's in love with you,' I said. And then I just kept talking. To dull the echo of that huge piece of information. 'And he can't bring himself to tell you. So, no. I don't think he *is* all right. Look. He doesn't know I'm here. He'd be horrified if he knew. I'm kind of taking my life into my hands by doing this. But I don't think he ever will. Tell you, I mean. And I just can't get my head around the idea that a thing like that could go unsaid for ever. Here he is alone. He doesn't even have Rigby any more. And I'm not saying you two should be together, because what do I know? Only you two know that. But that's the thing. You *two*. It's a thing two people have to decide. But how can two people make a good decision when only one of them knows what's going on?'

I stopped. Breathed. Sneaked a look at her. She had a cup of tea on a saucer in her hand, and she was running the tip of her index finger back and forth on the handle. Looking where she was touching. I couldn't read anything by her face. She just looked lost in her own thoughts.

After what felt like a year, but was probably ten or twenty seconds, she said, 'How sure are you that what you're saying is right?'

'Positive. We talk about it.'

'That doesn't sound like Paul.'

'I know. I thought that, too. But we really do. I guess he finally had to talk to somebody. Did he really manage to keep it a secret from you all these years? I can't imagine that. I would think it would've come out in a million little ways.'

She sighed. She didn't look up from the cup.

'Not entirely secret. I knew when I met him how he felt. But so many years went by . . . Honestly? I don't know. I thought he either still loved me or didn't like me much at all any more. Because he always had these ways of holding us a little distant from each other. After

Dan died, I kept expecting him to say something. But that was two years ago. So I decided a long time ago that I was wrong.'

'You weren't wrong.'

'Well, why didn't he say? You say you talk to him. Did he tell you why?'

'He told me a reason. I'm not sure if it's the real one. He said it would be like gambling with the good friendship you two have. He said he has half of what he wants. But if he told you how he felt and you didn't feel the same, it would be so awkward and horrible for him, and then you might feel guilty for hurting him. And he worried he might lose your friendship. I need to explain why I'm doing this. I'm not the kind of person who does stuff like this. I don't want to be a person who meddles. But I've been thinking about it for six months. And I thought . . . Maybe this is something *he* can't do but *I* can. Because if I tell you how he feels, and you don't feel the same, nothing has to change. You can pretend this never happened. He won't be hurt, because he won't know. It's a huge gamble, but it made sense in my head. And I'm not asking you to say it's right. But . . . does it make sense in your head, too? Do you understand why I decided to come here?'

She looked up from her cup, but not at me. Out the window. That straight line of her long nose made her face different from everybody else's, but in a good way. I thought it was good, anyway.

'I think you care a great deal for Paul and want what's best for him,' she said.

'Do you think that really was the reason? What he told me? Sometimes I think he was just too scared, but he didn't want to admit that.'

'I think there can be more than one reason.'

'Oh. Right.'

Then I wondered why I hadn't thought of that.

'But I'm still not . . .' she began. She sounded like me all of a sudden. Like she couldn't get a thought to come out whole. 'I'm just . . . I don't want to seem that I don't trust you, Angie, and what you're saying. But I can't picture Paul telling you this huge thing.'

'He didn't. Exactly. It was sort of a thing I saw for myself.'

'How did you see it if I couldn't?'

'Because I knew what was happening when you weren't around and you didn't. He had this picture of you on the bookcase. The only picture of a person in the whole house. That I ever saw, anyway. And when you came to help him pack, he took it down.'

I watched wheels turn behind her eyes for a minute.

'And that's why you thought you'd already met me,' she said.

'Right. And he was giving me this look like, "Don't." So I didn't say anything. But then later, when he was in the new place, it was the first thing he unpacked. That picture. And he saw me notice it. And he said something about how this was the problem with having people around. You know. In his life. They notice things and start to know things about him. So I told him something about me, to make him feel better. And that's how we started talking about stuff like that out loud.'

I looked up at her, and watched her set her teacup on the end table. Then she dropped her head into her hands.

I waited for what felt like a long time.

Then I asked, 'Are you OK?'

'Yes and no. It's just . . . *that* sounds like Paul. What you just said. And now I think that what you're saying is right.'

I swallowed a couple of times, and decided this wasn't going well. It made my stomach weigh a hundred pounds.

'Is it really so terrible?'

She didn't answer for a long time. So long that, as I watched the sun come through her front window on a slant, lighting up little dust specks, I kept expecting to see the slant of the light change. I don't think it really did, though. I think time just stretched out.

'I'm sorry I upset you,' I said. I think my voice startled us both. 'I knew there was a chance this was the wrong thing to do. But I thought there was a bigger chance it was right. And good. And there was just no way to tell while I was sitting at home. It's like what Paul taught me about fishing. He said sometimes the fish are biting and sometimes they're not. I said, "How do you know?" He said, "You drop a baited hook in the water and see if they bite it." He said if there was a way to tell before you left the house, he'd bottle it and sell it to fishermen all over the world.'

She smiled just the tiniest bit. I thought maybe that was a good sign. But, if so, it was a small good sign.

I waited again for her to talk. I was beginning to think she'd forgotten how.

After a long wait, she said, 'All those years he didn't settle down with anybody else. I think I wanted to believe it wasn't my fault.'

'It *wasn't* your fault. It wasn't anybody's fault.'

'Maybe. But that's not the way it feels.'

'I'm sorry. I guess maybe this was wrong.'

'I don't know. Maybe not. The truth was the truth even before you told it to me. And, anyway, I think part of me already knew.'

'I hope you won't tell him I was ever here. I can't really stop you, I guess. But I really think it would be nice for him to not have to know.'

'I won't tell him,' she said. 'So he won't be embarrassed. And so he won't lose your friendship. Which I think has been a good thing for him.'

'I should go. I need to catch that last bus. I thought I could stay with Aunt Vi, but if she's gone . . . The last bus leaves at six.'

She looked at her watch.

'I'll make up my guest room for you,' she said.

'What time is it?'

'Twenty-five minutes after five. Even if I drive you, it's rush hour. You'll never make it.'

'I'm sorry for the inconvenience.'

'It's no inconvenience. Except . . . where are your mother and your sister?'

'Home.'

'You came here by yourself?'

'Yes, ma'am.'

'You don't need to call me ma'am. Rachel is fine.'

'Sorry. That's a bad habit of mine. I call all kinds of people ma'am whether they want me to or not. I think I just bend over too far to be polite.'

'You bought your own bus ticket and rode all this way alone?'

'Yes . . . Rachel.'

'How did you get here from downtown?'

'More buses. And some walking.'

'Why didn't you just call me on the phone?'

'Well. I didn't want to steal your phone number from Paul. And I didn't want to tell him I was about to talk to you. And I didn't know your last name . . .'

She gave me an odd look. Almost half amused.

'You don't know my last name?'

'No. How would I?'

'Do you know Paul's last name?'

'Sure. It's Inverness.'

'And so is mine.'

First, I swear, I still didn't get it. Then it hit me. And I hit myself. Literally. Smacked myself in the forehead with the palm of my hand. She was married to Paul's brother. Duh.

'I can't believe myself. That's just about the dumbest thing I ever did. But, honestly . . . even if I'd had your phone number . . . I don't think I would have said a thing like this over the phone. How could I? I needed to get on a bus and come all the way back here and sit in front of you and tell you to your face.'

'All right,' she said. 'Then I'd say making up the guest room is very little trouble compared to that.'

She served dinner late. Almost eight o'clock. Which was OK with me, because I'd had pizza pretty late in the afternoon. She made spaghetti with meat sauce, and it was good. She was a good cook.

We mostly talked about Rigby.

'I miss that dog so much,' I said. 'Don't tell anybody I said this. Because I know it would sound weird. But sometimes I think I miss her more than Paul does.'

'You don't. Nobody misses her more than Paul.'

'That makes sense in my head. But it feels like I do.'

'The inside of you misses her more than the outside of Paul lets on.'

'Oh. That makes sense, yeah. She was a really good friend of mine, though. I really don't have many friends. Paul and I have that in common.'

'You and Paul have a lot of things in common.'

'Really? What else?'

'You're both very smart. And very cautious with your thoughts and feelings. And you like to keep your pain on the inside where no one can get to it but you. And you have high standards. For yourself, and for everybody else. Paul really only had the one friend, before you. His dog. Imagine how hard that would have been for him. If you weren't there.'

'He has you.'

That fell pretty flat. Stopped the conversation in its tracks. It was obvious she wasn't going to say anything. So I did.

'I guess you don't feel the same way he does. If you did, I think you'd have said so by now. Or been a little happier. Or something.'

A pause, during which I was sure the pause was proving me right.

'It's not as simple as you make it sound, Angie. I don't know how I feel. For fifty-one years I've felt friendship for him. I don't know what will happen if I try to see him in a different light. It might take a while to figure that out.'

'I'm sorry. Seriously. I apologize. It's none of my business. Which I guess is a weird thing to say now. When I just made it my business. But it isn't. I came here so you'd know. Not so I'd know how it might turn out. I'll go back to that place now where it's none of my business. And I won't ask you about it again, or bring it up in any way. I promise.'

I expected her to say something about that, but she never did.

We ate without talking for a long time.

'I'll drive you to your bus in the morning,' she said.

'That's a very nice offer. Thank you. But it's awfully early. I hate to make you get up so early.'

'I get up every morning at four o'clock.'

'Really? Why? Oh. I'm sorry. That came out wrong. You can get up anytime you want. None of my business.'

'It's just very quiet at that hour. And it's my favorite

time to meditate. But I'm done by four thirty. So why not let me drive you?'

'Thank you. That would be very nice.'

There was a clock in the guest room, by my bed, and it ticked. At first I thought I'd never get to sleep with all that ticking. Then I woke up suddenly, and it was ten minutes to eleven. And I thought I could hear Rachel talking.

I got out of bed, and made my way in the dark to the wall between our rooms. Put my ear to the plaster. But I still couldn't make out words. It just sounded kind of buzzy. Impossible to really hear.

First I thought, She's calling my mom to rat me out. But she wouldn't do that so late at night. Of course, I hoped she wouldn't do it at all.

Then I thought, She called Paul to talk.

Or she's having a dream.

Or she talks to herself.

Part of me wanted to find out. Maybe go out in the hall, closer to her room. Listen at the door.

I didn't.

I went back to bed. Over and over I said to myself, It's none of my business. It's none of my business. It's none of my business.

I knew I'd probably never find out. But I really hoped she was talking to Paul.

Eventually I got back to sleep, but never for very long. I don't think I slept more than forty-five minutes at a stretch.

*

'You don't have to park and come in,' I said. 'I'll just jump out here. You've done enough. Believe me.'

She pulled into a loading zone, and shifted into park. Let the engine idle.

'You have your return ticket?'

'I do. Yes.'

'And enough money to get something to eat?'

'I had some change from the bus fare. Yeah.'

'I think you were right to come.'

I looked at her face, but she didn't look back. She was staring at her hands on the steering wheel. She had nice hands. Not like someone who was older at all.

'I was?'

'I think so. I feel like something was stuck for a long time and you knocked it loose. I have no idea where it will go from here, but I think anything is better than being stuck for fifty-one years.'

I took a deep breath, one that felt like it had been waiting for me to take it for a long time. I had no idea what to say. I don't think she did, either.

'I'll come visit soon,' she said.

'Good. That would be good. Thanks.'

I jumped out.

And started the long, slightly scary job of making my way back home.

Chapter Three

 **Unlocked**

By the time I walked home from the bus station, it was almost five in the afternoon. I opened the door with my key. Sophie was asleep – or at least, asleep-looking – in the middle of the rug. My mom was sitting at the kitchen table with her back to me.

'I'm home,' I said, kind of sing-songy. Like Ricky Ricardo telling Lucy he was back from the club.

Nothing. Not a movement. Not a word.

I have to admit that really iced me down. I knew she'd be mad, but I thought she'd be blustery, yelling-at-me mad. I didn't expect the great nothingness.

Then I saw what she had in front of her on the table. But I was hoping I was wrong. Because I was still hanging over by the door, not wanting to get closer to her.

I went closer. And it was just what I was hoping it wasn't. My father's wallet, watch and wedding ring were sitting on the table in front of my deadly silent mom.

'You went into my locked trunk? That's, like, the only privacy I get.'

'I don't think that's our biggest issue here, kiddo.'

'I had the key with me. How did you get in? Did you break the lock?'

I heard her say something in return, but I didn't hang around to make out what it was. I sprinted to the other end of the apartment. Around the room divider. The metal trunk was sitting on my bed, its lid wide open. Sophie could have been shredding my Himalayas book if she'd gotten it in her head to. I took a quick inventory, to be sure everything was still there. Everything that wasn't on the table in front of my mom, that is.

It all seemed to be there. But then I thought of Nellie's note. And then I couldn't breathe, until I remembered I'd taken it with me. At least, I thought I had. I plowed through zippered pocket after zippered pocket of my backpack, and when I wrapped my hand around it, that's when I let myself breathe again.

I flipped the lid of the trunk closed and took a good look at the lock. She'd broken it.

I stuck my head around the divider again.

'Nice,' I said. 'Now I have not one place in this whole house where I can keep anything safe.'

'I'm not letting you make me the bad guy here,' she said. Still deadly calm. 'I want to know where you were.'

I dropped my backpack on to the rug and shoved the note into my jeans pocket and walked to the table and sat. It hit me hard how tired I was.

'Well, I'm not going to tell you. Because I can't. Because it's somebody else's privacy involved. All I can tell you is that I had a chance to do something to help somebody, and I did.'

'*Where*, though? In what *location*?'

'I went back home.'

'Bad place for a girl your age.'

'I was a girl a lot younger than this in that city for a long time, and I survived to talk about it. Why did you break the lock on my trunk? How was that going to get me back?'

'I was looking for clues on where you might've gone. I figured you had some kind of secret. I thought you'd run off with some boy . . . or . . . person . . . and maybe I could find you.'

'I left you a note saying I'd be back today. How is that running off? And there's no . . . person. I'm not with anybody.'

She levered her chin in the direction of the objects on the table.

'Why were these in your trunk?'

'I've got a better question. Why are they in our house at all? You told me they were stolen.'

'You're trying to twist things back on to me again. How did they get in your trunk?'

I sat back. Folded my arms over my chest. Now I was getting pissed. And now the anger was making me extra icy and calm, too.

'I put them there.'

'Why?'

'So you'd eventually notice they were missing. And then you'd know that I know that a lot of what you told me about Dad was a lie. And then you'd have to tell me why we have the things you said got stolen off him that night, and what really happened. I wasn't stealing these things. You want them? Fine. Take them. They're yours. But tell me the story you should have told me all along.'

'It was a robbery.' But her icy calm had turned into more of an anxious defensive thing.

'With nothing stolen.'

'Attempted robbery.'

'Mom. All you have to do is type his name into a search engine and it brings up the newspaper stories.'

I expected her to say something. Maybe not much of a something. But something. 'Oh.' Or, 'Crap.' Or something.

Nothing.

'Did it have to do with the gambling?'

'Yes.'

'Then you should have told me that.'

'You were six.'

'So instead you told me he was just minding his own business. Like all you have to do to get murdered is just walk out on the street. You don't even have to make a bad choice to bring it on.'

'Well . . . you don't.'

'But what's going to scare a six-year-old most? I'd rather think he did something to bring it on. Something I could avoid doing. Instead of making me think the world is not only viciously violent but completely random.'

'It is,' she said.

I pushed the chair back, and the squeak made her jump. I got to my feet.

'This is getting us nowhere.'

I walked back to my little bedroom area and picked up my damaged trunk. I was halfway to the door with it when she tried to stop me with words.

'You do *not* walk out that door.'

My first urge was to keep going, but I stopped to challenge her instead.

'Or . . . ?'

'Let me tell you how it's going to be, kiddo. From now on you do not walk out that door unless I know where you're going. Or you relinquish all the rights you've earned over the years. I am the mother and you are the kid.'

'Really? Starting when?'

'Watch it, kiddo. Watch yourself. You're still under my roof.'

I set the trunk down at my feet.

'Your roof? How do you figure that? How did you earn us this roof? This is not your roof, this is Paul's roof, and the only reason you get to live under it is because of me. I got us this roof. Now let me tell *you* how it's going to be. If you ever invade my privacy again, I'm leaving home. I'm old enough to be an emancipated minor. I'll work and take care of myself and live someplace where something I own gets to be mine and only mine.'

Then I grabbed up the trunk again and walked out. It wasn't a very graceful exit, because I had to lean the trunk on the railing of the landing to close the door behind me. But she didn't say a word, or try to stop me.

But it did occur to me that she might have some words by the time I got back.

I hauled the trunk up Paul's back stairs and knocked.

'Angie?' he called through the door.

'Yeah, Paul, it's me.'

'Come in.'

I found him in the living room, playing solitaire on the coffee table.

'Hey,' I said.

'Where've you been? Your mom was a bit upset.'

'She didn't come up here, did she?'

'No, she just called on the phone and asked if I knew where you were. Which is marginally OK. What's that?'

'Oh. This. This is like the one scrap of privacy I've had for my entire life. And my mom broke the lock on it while I was gone. I was wondering if you could fix it. You said once a long time ago that you had a garage shop. You know. With tools, where you could make things.'

'Let's take a look at it.'

I set it on the rug, and he turned on the lamp on the end table, and leaned in and examined the damage.

'Can you fix it?'

'In practical terms, no. Almost everything can theoretically be fixed. But sometimes it requires parts. See this little metal piece right here? That snapped when she pried it. This is an old trunk, and the lock mechanism is something that was made specially for it. So I think you need a new trunk.'

'I spent my money.'

'Even your secret stash?'

'What do you think I was traveling on for the last two days?'

'Ah. Well. Does it have to be a trunk? Or does it just have to hold things and lock? I have some big wooden boxes out in the garage. A lot of different sizes. Part of a project I never got around to finishing.'

'But do they lock?'

'Any wooden box can lock. You just have to go to a hardware store and buy a hasp. I could put that on for you. And then you could lock it with a small padlock.'

'That might be good.'

'Come take a look at what I've got.'

So we walked down the back steps together and up the slope to the garage. He let us in through the door near the woodshed. Turned on the overhead light.

'I've got to get this cleaned up,' he said. 'So Rachel can get her car in.'

'She's coming for a visit?'

'She is. She called me and suggested we visit more often.'

'When did she call?'

'Last night. When you were gone.'

I swallowed the big excited-but-nervous thing and said nothing.

He headed for the far end of the garage, the shop

end, and I followed him. He pulled an old sheet off a big pile of stuff that turned out to be nice-looking pieces of lumber, wooden dowels . . . and big wooden boxes.

'Any of these look big enough?'

'This one would be great.'

I touched it. Ran my hands around the edges. It was heavy, dark wood, nicely finished. Smooth and rounded at the edges and corners. It was not as tall as my old trunk, but it was as wide, and almost as long.

'This would be perfect if you really don't mind parting with it.'

'Not doing anybody any good down here. Except maybe the spiders.'

'I'll walk down to the hardware store in the morning. I think I've got that much change left.'

But only because Rachel fed me dinner and breakfast and gave me a ride to the bus station. Of course, I didn't say so.

'So,' he said. 'Total state secret? Or are you dying to tell somebody where you've been? So long as that somebody's not your mother?'

I pointed straight up to remind him she was on the other side of the garage ceiling. I didn't know if she could hear through the floor, but I was in no mood to take chances.

He dusted off the big wooden box with a corner of the sheet, and handed it to me, and we headed upstairs.

When we were far enough away from the apartment, I said, 'It had to do with the . . . situation I was telling you about. Where I was a total coward. That situation kind of stayed on my mind since we talked about it. I wanted to make it right.'

Which was the truth. It just wasn't the whole truth.

'So, you saw her?' he asked, as we walked up the back stairs.

'I did.'

'Was it terrifying?'

'At first. It got a little easier as we went along.'

He opened the back door for me.

'And by the way,' I said, 'I think my mom knows. Because she said she thought I ran off with some boy, but then she changed "boy" to "person".'

He wrinkled his nose. 'Ugh. Yeah. That sounds like mom-speak for "I'm on to you." How do you think she figured it out?'

'Well, she's been waiting breathlessly for me to show some interest in boys. She must have noticed how far behind schedule I am. I just don't think it's that hard a guess. You know?'

'I guess our moms know us. Just set that box down here in the back bedroom and we can leave it here until you get the hardware. If you want, you can put your things from the trunk in it, and I'll guard it with my life until we get it locked up.'

'Thanks. But my mom's been plowing through it anyway.'

He looked into my face for a minute. I couldn't decide what he was thinking.

'Hungry?' he asked.

'Starving. I was hoping my mom would ask. But instead we just had this nasty fight.'

'Come sit in the kitchen. I'll cook. I'm hungry, too.'

I followed him in. Watching him. Tracking something in him that felt a little . . . different.

'You seem happy,' I said, and sat down at the table.

'Do I? How would some cold shrimp with cocktail sauce be for a snack? While I'm cooking?'

'It would be absolutely amazing.'

'Done. I just have to thaw them under running water for a couple of minutes.'

While he stood at the sink, doing that, he said, 'Happy. Yeah. I guess so. I just felt like . . . I'm not referencing this correctly. Rachel called last night. Like I said. It felt different. I can't explain it. It felt like something shifted. She didn't actually say anything different from before. But there's always this . . . I don't know. I don't want to say "wall". It's trite. But there's always some kind of structure that keeps us at a little bit of a distance from each other. And it's like she just stepped over it. Or something. Might be totally my imagination.'

'I don't think it is.'

He looked over his shoulder at me. Curious. But only mildly, I think.

'Why do you say that?'

'I don't know. Just an observation. We all go around saying we don't know where we stand with other people, because we don't know what they're thinking. Which is true. But we can *feel* where we stand with them. But then we get back into our heads and start second-guessing what we feel, and get ourselves all confused and tangled up again.'

'That's exactly what I did. I sat up most of the night deciding I only thought it was that way because I wanted it to be.'

'But you wanted it to be that way for fifty years, and you never thought it was until last night.'

He reached up into the cupboard and took down a fancy cut-glass . . . I didn't know what you'd call it. Like a cross between a bowl and a glass. Like something you'd use to serve ice cream or a parfait. If you were fancier than anybody at my house. He arranged about ten of these big shrimp with their tails hooked over the edge of the glass, and poured red cocktail sauce into the middle.

'I like it better your way,' he said, setting the glass in front of me. 'So I'm going with what you said. I felt like something was different because it was.'

I picked up a shrimp by its tail, bit off almost all of it, chewed three or four times, and sighed a very contented sigh.

'I feel bad about one thing, though,' he said. 'It doesn't feel fair. But if she's going to come up and visit more often, I'll be asking you and your family to scram more often. Might add up to an awful lot of camping.'

'It's OK. Some things are more important than others.'

I also knew that, if things worked out between the two of them, we'd be looking for a new place to live. Especially if I was right that Sophie was starting to revert to her old, pre-Rigby self again. Paul wouldn't want all that noise while he was trying to have a nice life with Rachel, and I didn't blame him.

And, also, I'd known it before I ever went down and talked to her. I knew, before I even started trying, that complete success would go hand in hand with our complete eviction.

But some things are more important than others.

By the time I got back upstairs, my mom and Sophie were in bed on the fold-out couch. They seemed to be asleep.

I breathed a sigh of relief, but a cautious one. My mom was not above sand-bagging me out of nowhere. It had happened before.

But I went into my little bed area, and changed into my pajamas, and nothing moved. So I figured she really was asleep.

It took a long time, because my head was such a whirl of thoughts, but eventually I got some sleep myself.

I woke with a start, feeling something touching my head.

I let out a little noise, and half sat up.

But then I heard my mom say, 'It's me, honey. It's only me.'

I lay back down again, and she stroked my hair some more. I looked at her shape in the moonlight and wondered how I'd gotten to be her honey again. It had been a long time since I'd been her honey. And I'd never been further from it than last night when we went to bed.

But I had no reason to ruin a decent moment. So I kept shut.

After a while she said, 'Andy knows more than I do. But I'll tell you what little I know.'

Andy was my dad's cousin. We hadn't seen him since my dad got killed. At least, I hadn't. Not once. This place in my gut tried to tell me I should tense up now. Because there was truth coming. But I never did. Because, whatever was coming, it just couldn't be any worse than what had been there all along.

Except . . .

'If he died some really bad way, don't tell me details about it. I don't want to know that part.'

'I thought you said you read the newspaper articles.'

'No. I didn't exactly say that. I said they came up in a search. I had a friend read them for me and spare me the details.'

'I'm relieved.'

'That bad, huh?' Then, fast, before she could answer, 'Never mind. I don't want to know. Just tell me anything you know about why.'

'He got himself into a big hole with a loan shark. I don't even know how big, because I tried not to ask. It scared me. And I got so mad at him. I couldn't figure out why he wouldn't just stop. He adored me, and he adored you, and I felt like we should be enough to make him stop. But then I talked to a therapist after he died, and I guess it's not that easy.'

'I didn't know you went to a therapist.'

'Went to one, and sent you to one.'

'I have no memory of that.'

'You only went about five times. That was all I could afford.'

'Anyway, go on with what you were saying.'

She sighed. Like she'd been hoping she'd never have to.

'I think if he were here right now, I'd be more understanding. I'd sure try to be, anyway. But I was *not* understanding at the time. I was really resentful. I don't want you to think he wasn't a good guy, your dad. He was. He wasn't a scumbag, or a loser. He was a nice guy, but it was like a sickness with him. Anyway, I started not really wanting to know how deep in he was. But after it happened, I talked to Andy to try to get some details. And the police talked to him, of course. I guess your dad told Andy he had a plan to try to get the money. Because if he didn't, they were going to break both his knees, and if that didn't work, I guess they'd made some kind of threat toward us. You know. His family. So . . . I don't know what the plan was, exactly. But I guess it had to do with double-crossing somebody you shouldn't mess with. And hopefully not getting caught. Andy said he didn't have all the details, but maybe he just didn't want the police to have all the details.'

'But he wanted the killers to get caught, right?'

'Yeah, but . . . I have a funny feeling if we knew the whole story it might not look so good for Andy, either. He might've gotten in some hot water, too. Anyway, I never really pushed him that hard for details. Because . . . what would the point have been? It's not like I needed to know how stupid a plan it was. Stupid enough to get him killed. That's all you really need to know about the quality of the plan.'

We didn't talk for a minute. I kept quiet, in case there was more. She was still stroking my hair. And it felt good. Not so much physically good. More like good that we could both be on the same side for a minute. Not always facing each other off like two sparring partners in a ring.

'I wish I'd known the gambling killed him,' I said. 'So I'd know to steer clear of it myself.'

'You're not a gambler.'

I could have argued. At first I wanted to. I wanted to get a little mad and say, See? You really don't know me at all. But I was so tired of us being mad at each other. It took so damn much energy. Besides. If she didn't know me, that was at least as much my fault as it was hers.

'If I handled it wrong,' she said, 'I apologize. It was a horrible time for me. It probably was a mistake. Probably everything I did around that time was backwards and wrong. But I was doing my best with what I had at the time. I hope you can understand that. I hope you can accept my apology.'

'I accept your apology.'

'I'll buy you a new trunk.'

'No, it's OK. Paul's got a big wooden box I can use. I just have to get a hasp and a padlock, and he'll put it on for me. It's a nice box.'

'Oh,' she said. 'OK.'

I could tell she would have liked it better if she could've solved the problem for me. She was probably getting tired of Paul being my go-to guy. But she didn't say anything more about that.

She stopped stroking my hair. We just sat that way for a time, in the little sliver of moonlight that came through the high window over my bed. I was thinking we felt done. But she wasn't leaving. So maybe not.

Then she said, 'You know I love you no matter what, right? Even if you're not anything like me. And no matter what you . . . I mean, no matter who you grow up to be. And how you . . .'

I waited, but she seemed to have run out of steam.

Not to argue with her, more to help her finish the thought, I said, 'Can we just say it out loud already? "Angie, I love you even if you're gay"?'

A strange little pause.

'Angie, I love you even if you're gay.'

'Thanks. I love you, too.'

She kissed me on the side of my temple.

Then she went back to bed.

The inside of my head felt a little heavy when I joined her at the breakfast table. I had a dull headache. I think I'd been missing too much sleep.

Sophie was sitting at the table, alone in her own little world, a sausage link flapping in one of her hands.

If nothing else, we'd been eating better.

'Scrambled eggs and sausage on the stove,' my mom said. Artificially cheerful.

'Oh,' I said.

I'm not sure why I'd bothered to sit down.

'Want me to get them for you?'

'No. I'll get up.'

'You look tired.'

'I am tired. I haven't slept straight through the night for days.'

'Oh. Sorry about that. Or, at least . . . my part in that. The last-night part. You sit. I'll bring you your breakfast for a change. Coffee?'

'Please.'

I watched Sophie for a minute, then fiddled with my fork for another one.

'Just to give you fair warning,' I said, 'I think we have another camping trip coming up soon.'

I expected an explosion of objections.

Instead I got a tiny little, 'Uh oh.'

'Uh oh what?'

'The queen is coming around a lot more often, isn't she?'

'*The queen*? Why in God's name would you call her that?'

'I don't know. I guess because everything grinds to a halt when Her Highness deigns to visit.'

I was more than a little stunned.

'Do you not like Rachel or something? Because I like her. A lot.'

A plate of eggs and sausage appeared in front of me. A mug of coffee followed. I spooned in sugar while I was waiting for her to answer.

She sat down with a grunt and then sighed.

'I don't even know her,' she said.

'Right. That's what I was just thinking. So where's all this bad-attitude stuff coming from all of a sudden?'

She sighed again.

I poured milk into my coffee, and took a big, long swallow. It went down just right. Tasted good, and felt good, and fit what I needed. Like a mild drug. Well. I guess that's what it was.

'It's just . . . I think she's interested in him,' she said. All whiney, like a teenager moping about dating problems.

'That would be great if she was.'

'Great? How would it be great? Sophie is getting fussier and louder every day, and every time Rachel comes to visit we have to clear out. Are you trying to tell me if she moves in we won't be moving out?'

'No. We probably would be.'

'So why is it great?'

'Because he's lonely.'

'I don't want to move! This place is rent-free!'

By the time she got to the word 'free', things had gotten a little screechy. Enough that, if I'd expected more, I'd have been tempted to put a hand over my mom-side ear.

I guess I didn't realize she'd been so panicky about it.

Then I wondered why *I* wasn't. Under the circumstances.

'He's been alone just about all his life. And now he doesn't even have his dog any more. He's almost sixty-eight. If this doesn't pan out for him, how many more chances do you think he'll get? He deserves to be happy, you know.'

'Well, excuse me for being more concerned for us than for him.'

But, honestly, I wasn't sure if I could excuse that in her. Considering everything he'd done for us.

'The point was to stay here and save money,' I said. 'So we can afford another place. Our own place. It would be nice to have a bedroom with a door that closes. This was always supposed to be temporary. And you said you've been saving money—'

'I have.'

'You said you could save a thousand a month.'

'Not that much.'

'But we're saving fifteen hundred a month over where we were before.'

'Life intervenes, kiddo.'

It was not the first time she'd said that. I hadn't liked it any of the other times, either.

'How much do we have?'

'A hair under twelve thousand.'

'Which is, like, half of what I thought. But at least it's enough for a down payment on something. I think.'

'You're forgetting two things, Angie. One of them is sitting right here at the table with you, eating link sausage. The other is that I have no credit. Which I've told you before. Every time you bring up buying instead of renting, I tell you that. And you always manage to conveniently forget.'

'I didn't forget.'

'You have some magic trick in your pocket I know nothing about?'

'Maybe.'

'And that would be . . . ?'

'That would be a friend who worked for forty-five years as a loan officer at a bank.'

She wrinkled her nose and forehead. Took a sip of coffee. Shook her head.

'I don't think it's a "who you know" kind of a proposition. More of a "how much you have".'

'I just thought he could give us some advice on how to get a loan.'

'I'm sure he will. He'll say, "Start with good credit."'

I shook my head and said nothing. I had that 'this is getting us nowhere' feeling again. It hit me that I got that feeling a lot around my mom. If it had been a day or two earlier, I might have jumped up and gone blasting away from the table in disgust. But that was getting old.

Besides. I was hungry.

Rachel showed up four days later. And only stayed two days.

On the day she left again, my mom had dropped me off at the apartment on her way to work. Partly because the Special Ed van still met Sophie there in the morning and dropped her off there in the afternoon. Partly because, if I hung out there during the day, I'd know when Rachel was gone, and whether we needed to camp another night. And it didn't matter if *I* was there.

They couldn't hear me up there, and it didn't change things for them at all.

It was Sophie. Sophie was the wild card.

I went upstairs and took a shower, and then poured myself some cereal. Before I even finished eating it, I heard Rachel's car pull out of the garage. I looked out the window, hoping they were both going somewhere.

It was just Rachel.

I sat back down at the table and tried to think whether it would be OK to ask Paul how it went. I never managed to figure that out. My logic just kept going around in circles. It also occurred to me that maybe she was just running to the store or something, and was coming back.

The phone rang. I nearly jumped out of my skin.

I grabbed it up on the second ring.

It was Paul.

'You're there,' he said. 'Great.'

'You sound happy.'

'I am happy. Why wouldn't I be happy?'

'I don't know. It was such a short visit.'

'Good one, though. Come fishing with me.'

'OK. Is there something to tell here? I mean, are you going to tell me what happened? I mean, *if* something happened. I'm not saying anything did. Just that . . . you sound really happy.'

'Meet me at the garage,' he said.

I did.

We packed up our gear, and drove to one of those tiny, cold mountain lakes.

But, while we were doing all that, he never told me what happened.

We were standing in a lake up to our waists – well, my waist – and had been for some time when he said, 'I think I feel weird talking about it.'

'So you're not going to tell me what happened?'

'I didn't say that. Probably I am. I just feel weird about it.'

'So what do you want me to do while I'm waiting? Just fish, and shut up? Or am I supposed to be trying to drag it out of you?'

'That's a good question. I'm not sure.'

I was looking at his face when he said it, and I laughed out loud. Then he wanted to know why, and I didn't know what to say. He didn't exactly *ask* why. Not out loud. He just gave me a look that I could tell meant he wanted to know. I thought it was interesting that we could do things like that without talking.

Here's the reason I laughed, if I could have put it into words at the time. Because when he was happy and excited, which he never had been before, that I knew of, he was sort of . . . adorable. But that's not the kind of thing you say to a sixty-seven-year-old grown man, even if you can wrap words around it while it's happening.

'We'll play twenty questions,' I said. 'Paul? Did something happen?'

'Yes. Not a huge something. Well. Yes. It was huge. But *you* might not think so. *Something* happened, but not *everything*. Does that make sense?'

'I've only asked one question so far.'

'She kissed me. I mean, we kissed. But *she* kissed *me*. I'm not saying I didn't kiss her back. Of course I did. But she was the one who kissed me. That's how it started.'

'When?'

'Last night.'

'And then . . . why did she leave?'

'We both just sort of . . . We talked about it. We didn't want to go rushing ahead. You know. Hurry things too much. We decided to go to our separate corners and see how we feel about what happened. I bet that sounds pathetic to you. Really old-fashioned. When you're sixteen, that must seem pathetic.'

'As a sixteen-year-old who has, pathetically, not yet been kissed, I'd be a fine one to judge.'

He threw his left arm around my shoulders – he needed the right one for the fishing pole – and pulled me in close to him and gave me a big smack on the forehead. Hard enough to bend my head back.

I laughed out loud again.

'Thank you, but that still doesn't count.'

'Of course it doesn't. I didn't mean for it to. If you think it's pathetic to never have been kissed, imagine if your first kiss was from me. Now that's pathetic.'

'I bet that's not what Rachel thought.'

'That's entirely different. Rachel is . . .'

Then he stopped talking to reel in a fish.

He pulled it up out of the water, and it twisted there on the end of the line, and he stood there in the lake and stared at it. Didn't try to get it in the landing net. Just watched it hanging there, like he hadn't expected any such thing to happen. That fish must have been hooked deep, because it couldn't capitalize on the opening.

Finally I opened the creel basket and held it right under his fish, and he lowered it in and then took the hook out.

'It's all about focus,' I said.

He cast back into the middle of the lake, and I put my rod between my knees so I wouldn't drop it. And then I threw my arms around him sideways, and gave him an awkward sideways hug, pinning his arms to his sides, and sloshing the lake a bit higher on to us.

'What was that for?' he asked, quite a bit after the fact.

'It's just nice to see you so happy.'

'Even though . . . ?'

He never finished the question. But it didn't matter, because I knew the finish of it anyway.

'Yes. Even though, if it works out, we'll be looking for a new place. It's still nice to see you so happy.'

We fished in silence for a few minutes.

Then he said, 'That's unusual. Most people think of themselves first. That's a pretty damn good friend.'

'Well, I'm glad you think so, because this pretty damn good friend is about to ask a pretty damn big favor. You know how I'm always looking at the real-estate ads in your paper? Well, I found something I want to look at. I was hoping you'd take me out there to see it. I know I told you I wouldn't need rides after I got my license. But I don't want to ask my mom if I can borrow her car, because I don't want her to know why yet, because she'll try to talk me out of going. Because she's totally down on the idea of buying something. She says we'd never make it work. That she doesn't have the credit.'

'Does she have a down payment?'

'Is twelve thousand dollars a down payment?'

'It might be.'

'Good. I've asked her twice before to go look at places with me, and she won't do it. I think it makes her feel degraded when they ask a bunch of money questions.'

'They don't.'

'They don't?'

'Not the seller. The bank you approach to handle the financing, now they'll ask questions. And the answers had better be on paper. But the seller or the real-estate agent just shows you the place.'

'Oh. Then I don't know why she won't go. I can't really go by myself. Even if I could get the car. Because I don't even think they'd show it to me. I mean, who shows real estate to a sixteen-year-old? But if we didn't happen to mention that we're not related . . .'

'That's not such a huge favor.'

'It's almost twenty miles outside of town.'

'I think I could manage that all the same. What do they want for it?'

'It's cheap.'

'How cheap?'

'Cheap enough that I don't want to tell you how cheap, because you'll say there has to be a catch.'

'Well,' he said. 'Only one way to find out. Let's give

the fish another half an hour and then we'll go see if there's a catch.'

We were driving out this little winding highway. Farther and farther from town. Paul was all lost in his own head, and I was just looking at the scenery. Even though it was nothing but trees.

You could do worse than trees.

'Why did this happen?' he asked. Just out of nowhere like that.

'Why did what happen?'

'This thing with Rachel. Why did it not happen for fifty years and then happen?'

I swallowed hard, and tried to get a bead on how he meant it. He seemed kind of intense, and I couldn't figure out if he was just being philosophical, or if he really thought there was something there to investigate.

'Well, forty-eight of those years she was married.'

'Forty-seven.'

'I think the point is still the same. Forty-seven years she was married, and the year before that she was a college woman and you were just a kid.'

'But why did it not happen in all this time since Dan died, and then suddenly happen? I still don't quite know how it happened.'

I sat very still in the passenger seat for a minute, and wondered how much I was willing to lie to cover my tracks. Not much, I think. I convinced myself that he was talking out loud. Not really asking me, like I would know. But even if it was a rhetorical question, I still felt like dirt for holding something back from Paul. Then I realized I'd been holding something back from him for a long time. And feeling like dirt a lot. But it was a decision I made before I talked to Rachel. There was no going back now.

'Wouldn't that come under the heading of looking a gift horse in the mouth?'

He peered through the windshield with that same furrow in his brow, that same faraway look in his eyes, for another half a minute or so. Then it broke like a fever and flew away.

'Yeah, I think you're right about that. I hope we weren't supposed to make an appointment. Did it say in the ad, "By appointment only"? Or, "Do not disturb occupant"? Or something along those lines?'

'I don't know. I'll look again.'

I pulled the listing out of my shirt pocket, where it had been for three days, changing shirts when I did. I unfolded it and read it from beginning to end for about the tenth time.

'Doesn't say.'

'Well, we've come this far. We can at least scope it out from a distance.'

There was a realtor's sign hanging on a wooden post at the intersection of the driveway and the highway. But I couldn't see a house at all. Just trees. But the trees looked nice. Too nice. It looked like a farm or a ranch, all out in the middle of nowhere and heavenly. Which meant we didn't belong there.

I was more sure than ever. There had to be a catch.

Paul took two color fliers out of a Plexiglas box mounted on the pole. Where I never would've thought to look.

'Here, take one of these,' he said.

I squinted at it in the sun, and it turned out to be a sheet of information about the property. It gave me a funny feeling in the pit of my stomach. Like I definitely didn't belong, and the realtor knew it, and the flier knew it, and the sign knew it. Even the post that held up the sign knew I didn't belong.

'Whoa,' he said. 'That *is* cheap. Well. Let's go see what the catch is.'

We walked down the dirt driveway together until a house peeked out from the trees. When we saw it, we both stopped in our tracks.

'Oh,' I said. 'That would be the catch, all right.'

It didn't even look like a place a person could live. The roof sagged, the porch sagged. The paint was half peeled away. Some of the windows were broken. You could look in and see nobody lived there. Nobody had lived there for a while.

'So much for worrying about disturbing the occupants,' he said.

'I guess we can go now. Sorry I wasted your time.'

'Now, wait. Now hold on a minute. Don't be so quick to run off.'

We just stood there for another minute, looking at it.

Then I said, 'Still not looking any better.'

'Well, no. It wouldn't. The only way it's going to look any better is if somebody puts hundreds of hours of work into it.'

'Are you saying I should still think about our buying it?'

'I don't know yet. I don't know.'

He walked up on to the porch, testing his weight first. I followed him. We looked through the windows. There was nothing inside but a few loose floorboards and a ton of dust.

'That's a lot of work,' I said.

'I'll grant you that. But your family never owned a home before. Sometimes young families get into a first home by taking one nobody else wants, and making it into something with sweat equity.'

'I have no idea what that is.'

'It's like elbow grease.'

'Excuse me?'

'Work. Good, hard work.'

'Oh. Why didn't you say so?'

'I did.'

'Oh. Right.'

'You'd have to get a home inspection. Make sure the foundation is in good shape and the floors are solid. Make sure the termites haven't eaten most of it away. If the basics are good, the rest is more or less cosmetic. Except you'd need new porch boards. And a new roof.'

'That can't be cheap.'

'True. So here's what you do. You go to the real-estate agent, and you say, "I'm interested in the house, but I'd need to put thousands into a new porch and roof, so you'll need to come down on the price."'

'And then she'll say, "Why do you think we priced it so low to begin with?"'

'Maybe. Depends on how long it sits on the market. And whether the seller is in a hurry.'

'You think that might work?'

He peeled a strip of paint off the windowsill and looked closely at the wood underneath. 'I think it's one of those things like whether the fish are biting.'

'Right,' I said. 'Got it.'

'I could show you how to replace the panes of glass in a window. That and new door locks and about forty man-hours of cleaning and you could live in it as is until the rains come. Don't get your hopes up, though. Don't make the assumption that no one wants it because it's ugly. Someone with money could swoop in here and take it for the land. Tear this thing down to its foundation and put up a modern three-story farmhouse in about six months.' He peered at the flier again. 'Oh, it's not that big. It's only two acres. That's odd. They must have subdivided it and sold off most of the original land. There must be a buffer of farmland and orchards between this place and the neighbors. Because there's no other house as far as the eye can see.' He cupped his hands around his mouth, tipped his head back, and bellowed, 'Hello! Can anybody hear me?'

We waited. But it didn't seem like anybody could.

'That's a big plus,' I said.

'Well, yeah. But you saw that coming, right? Isn't that

why you wanted to see the place? Because it was out in the middle of nowhere?'

'Um . . . no. I couldn't picture how many neighbors there would be. I wanted to see it because it was so cheap.'

'If you want, we'll stop by the realty office and get some details about it.'

'Yeah. Thanks.'

I looked up, instead of at the horrible house. Just to give my eyes a break. I thought I saw a few hanging pieces of fruit in some of the trees, but I couldn't tell what kind of fruit it was.

I thought about how it would feel to go to the realty office with Paul instead of going alone. It made me feel like I would be OK there. Like they had no right to laugh at me or chase me away. Then I realized it wasn't entirely because I wasn't even quite seventeen. It was because I was broke, and I figured they would know. That gave me a little glimpse into why my mom stayed away from places like that.

Almost like he was reading my mind, Paul said, 'Think you can get your mom to come out and see it?'

'That's going to be the tough part. She has so much resistance to buying.'

'Because of the credit? The loan?'

'I think so. I think she always feels like she's a phony, because she doesn't have good, responsible mom-answers to questions about money. So she tries to skate under the radar and not go where anybody might ask questions.'

'And a bank is not such a place. Maybe I could prep her, the way trial lawyers do with their witnesses.'

'I hope so. I hope there's something you can do to help her. Because we're really nowhere the way things stand now.'

In fact, the only difference between our current situation and the one we'd been in when we came up to the mountains was about twelve thousand dollars. Which was something. But only if she was willing to spend it on a house. Otherwise we'd go back to renting, and she'd dip into that money every month, because every month we'd come up short.

It's amazing how much time it takes to gather money, and how little time it takes for life to intervene.

'It used to be a working orchard,' I told my mom over dinner. 'Except this is only a little piece of it. They used to grow peaches and walnuts. And tomatoes, but all the vines are gone now. Now the trees are old and they don't produce much, and the land isn't worth much for farming. But here's the good part. It's more than a mile from the closest farmhouse of the closest neighbor. And the realtor lady says if I'm willing to climb trees, I'd probably get more peaches and walnuts in a year than three people could even eat.'

'I can't believe you're making me say this again,' she said.

Sophie started banging her fork on the table, with a little screech on each bang. Sometimes in rhythm, sometimes out of it.

I raised my voice to be heard over her.

'Paul even said he could prep you for the loan application the way trial lawyers do with their witnesses.'

She slapped her napkin down and glared at me in a way that made my face feel hot.

'Well, that's a little different, now, isn't it? Because all a witness has to do is talk. I have to produce pay stubs and tax returns. And I have to have more than just a down payment and a yes from a bank, which we'll never get. I'd have to come up with mortgage payments.'

Bang. Screech. Bang. Screech.

'You'll have to come up with rent anyway.'

'Kiddo. You're not listening to me. I don't make enough money to buy a house. I don't need a bank to tell me so. Now I'll thank you to not bring it up again.'

'Well, we'd better start looking,' I said. 'Because we may have to go somewhere. Not definitely, but it seems to be going that way. I just thought it would be nice to go someplace we could take Sophie along.'

'I'm looking into a placement for her.'

For a flash of a second I was filled with fight. I was going to lash out at my mom, and yell, and accuse her of caring more about her own fear of banks than she did about my sister. I opened my mouth, and the next thing I knew, I was just too tired. It washed over me and left me beached. I thought, What's the point? Why am I even fighting her? I've been fighting her for years. It wastes my energy, and things always turn out the same.

Just when I thought I'd ducked the drama by surrendering, my mom lost it with Sophie.

'Stop doing that!' she screamed. And I really mean screamed.

Sophie held perfectly still for a second or two, and then launched into full keening mode. My mom had to grab her up and carry her down to the car, the way she always did. So she could drive her around until she wailed herself voiceless, or to sleep.

'*That* was a rookie mistake,' I told the door a minute after it slammed.

 **Trust**

It was about three weeks after that, right before I turned seventeen, when my mom brought up the car. It was morning. I was lying on my bed reading, and she stuck her head around the divider. Which I never liked. I wanted her to treat that gap like a closed door. She more or less did, but mostly when it suited her.

'I've been thinking about your birthday,' she said.

'What about it?'

'How would you feel about having your own car?'

I put the book down. Narrowed my eyes at her. It was a good thing in theory. Almost too good. Maybe that's why something felt wrong.

'I'd feel great about it if we could afford that. But we can't.'

'If you can find a cheap transportation car for two or three thousand, I'll buy it for your birthday.'

'Out of our down-payment money.'

I watched the look on her face darken. She must have known we'd hit that wall early on. It seemed almost like a setup. An idea for her to break into that money in a way I couldn't object to, because what teenager says no to a car?

'No,' I said. 'I don't want a car if it's coming out of our down-payment money. I'd rather drive you to work and borrow the car and buy a house. Hell, I'd rather walk and take the bus everywhere and buy a house.'

'Kiddo, our money is not "down-payment money". Because we're not in the market to buy.'

'OK, then I don't want it if it comes out of our savings.'

She pulled in a big breath. For a minute, I thought she was going to light into me. But just then, we heard the honk of Sophie's Special Ed van.

'I'll walk her down,' she said. 'If you're going to drive me to work, better get dressed right now.'

I dropped my mom at the pharmacy, and then drove out to the property for sale. I'd been there alone one other time. But that time I'd only looked from the road.

This time I parked my mom's car in the driveway. And then, as I walked away from it, I looked back and realized I was ashamed of that car, and hoped nobody saw it there. Hoped the real-estate lady didn't come to show the place to anybody, because I didn't want to be the person who was driving that old clunker. Even though it matched the condition of the house. Still,

I was betting it wouldn't match the condition of the realtor's other clients.

I walked around the two acres. There were wire fences at the borders of the property. Not barbed wire. Just four strands of wire strung along wooden posts. The trees were planted in neat lines, and I walked up and down the orchard rows, thinking about the working farm days, imagining the voices of the pickers. I wondered how they got the high fruit out of those trees.

I singled out a tree that looked fairly easy to climb. It had a low intersection of big limbs. I took a running start, jumped up and got a hold on that intersection. Then I lost it again and landed on my feet in the dirt. I tried again, and this time I got a better hold, and got the sticky soles of my sneakers planted on the trunk, and pulled myself up so I was sitting in the crook of those limbs. Then I stood up. And looked up. And carefully climbed higher. I could see a peach, but when I got close to it, it was hard and a little green. So I climbed even higher. I came out into the sun above most of the leafy parts of the tree, and saw the mountains. I hadn't seen them from that property before, because the trees got in the way of the view.

I just stood there for a moment, holding on. Looking. Thinking I'd never stop loving those mountains. Then I wondered how they'd look if I'd just gotten back from trekking the circuit of teahouse trails around Annapurna, in the Himalayas. I decided they would look smaller and tamer, but still pretty.

I found a peach that looked ripe, so I leaned for it.

Carefully. I couldn't quite reach, so I pulled its branch closer. Grabbed the fruit and pulled, but it held. I twisted it on its stem. It came off in my hand.

I stood on that branch, holding tight with one hand, and looked at the mountains some more, and took a big bite of peach. It was juicy, and tasted like summer.

I started the climb down.

When I got back down to the intersection of limbs, I sat, and held the peach in my teeth so I could grab a limb with both hands. Then I swung out and dropped, and landed in the dirt on my feet with a whump sound, my sneakers kicking up little clouds of dry dirt. But I bit down without meaning to, and bit a piece out of the peach, which made the rest of it drop into the dirt.

'Crap,' I said out loud, my mouth full.

I almost thought of picking it up and trying to wash it somehow. But it had two bites out of it, and it was caked with brown dirt.

I left it and walked back to the house, chewing the one bite I still had.

The real-estate lady was there with a buyer. A man about fifty, who looked like he could write a check for the place if he wanted it.

I stopped cold when I saw them. Swallowed fast.

'May I help you?' the lady asked. A little coolness in her voice.

'I'm Angie. Remember I came in to see you with Paul Inverness?'

'Oh, yes. I do remember you now.'

'I was just leaving,' I said.

'Did you have more questions?'

'I wanted to know if the property was fenced. Because Paul's going to get a new dog, a puppy, and he won't be trained not to run off. Yet. So I told him I'd come see and then tell him.'

'He'd have to put a gate across the driveway,' she said.

'OK. I'll tell him.'

Then they were just looking at me, and there was nothing more to say. And neither one of them looked all that thrilled that I was there.

So I said, 'I was just leaving.' Again.

As I walked down the driveway, I heard the lady say, 'I do have some other interest in this property. As you can see.'

Then I knew that my being there was probably only going to put pressure on this buyer to make an offer faster. That chewed a little in my stomach, but I told myself to get over it. We weren't going to get the place anyway, so nothing was really lost.

But something felt lost.

Three days later Rachel came for another visit. Which I was kind of excited about, because I really wanted to know how that would go.

We didn't go camping, because my mom said she'd had it with camping. We went to that same motel where we'd stayed before.

The first night we were there, Sophie started screaming, and my mom had to drive her around for almost two hours before she went to sleep. By the time they got back it was after eleven, and I knew it would be hard for my mom to get to sleep until she wound down from that stress. And she had work in the morning. It all added up bad.

I took my life in my hands and brought it up again.

I said, 'Can you imagine how amazing it would be to live in a place that's so far from the neighbors nobody could even hear her? If she started to scream, we could just put in earplugs and let her wear herself down.'

'No place is that far from the neighbors.'

'This place I'm trying to get you to go see is. More than a mile from the closest house.'

'You're kidding.'

'I told you that already.'

'I thought that was just a figure of speech. You know. A mile away. I thought you just meant a long way away.'

'Yeah. Like an *actual mile*. Which is a long way.' The timing was right, and I could feel it. I was catching her in a worn-down moment. 'It couldn't hurt you to at least look at it.'

'OK, fine. Come by the pharmacy at noon and we'll go on my lunch hour. You can drive, and I'll eat on the way.'

Just before the last bend in the road, I got a little twist in my stomach. What if I saw something completely different from last time? A bunch of construction trucks in the driveway, or the 'For Sale' sign taken down?

Then I told myself that was stupid. It had only been a few days.

I looked over at my mom, who was in the passenger seat, wolfing down a sandwich. She had tuna salad on the corner of her mouth.

'What?' she said.

I pointed to the corner of my own mouth, and she wiped the salad off with a fresh tissue from the box at her feet.

We rounded the last bend.

The sign was still there. The driveway was still empty. But when we got closer, there was something on the sign that hadn't been there before. A strip of red, a few inches high and maybe a foot long. When we finally got close enough, I read it out loud.

'Sale pending.'

I stopped, right in the middle of the highway. Which didn't matter much, because there was nobody else on it.

'Shit,' I added. Without much energy.

'Just wasn't meant to be,' my mom said.

I said nothing. I was busy being stung. Because I'd thought it was.

'Well, that's two gallons of gas we'll never get back. Let's go, kiddo.'

Instead I pulled into the driveway. She probably thought I was turning around. Until I shifted into park and turned off the engine.

'What are we doing?'

'I just want to get a peach. I didn't really get one last time. I'll get two, and it can be your dessert.'

'Isn't that sort of . . . trespassing?'

'I don't see who it's going to hurt. By the time the sale goes through, those two peaches would be rotting on the ground anyway.'

I jumped out before she could say more. Trotted down the driveway, and around the house. Down a row between trees. I wanted to find the one I'd climbed last time, but it wasn't where I thought it was, and I didn't have much time.

I picked one that looked doable, and got a good running start. I jumped up, grabbed a limb, and planted my left sneaker.

It slipped.

I came down hard on my knee in the crook between two branches. I was wearing shorts, so there was nothing to protect the skin of my knee. But it was worse than that. My knee not only slammed the tree, but slipped off it again. So I sort of slid off the branch with all my weight on my knee. Next thing I knew I was in the dirt with my left ankle twisted painfully underneath me.

I looked at my knee. It felt completely numb. The skin was both scraped off and peeled back. Other than dirt and bark ground in, it was weirdly white. Like the size and scope of the thing hadn't hit it yet. Then dozens of little drops of blood sprang up, and became big drops of blood, and met each other, and formed a pool.

I had to fight back these stinging tears, which only made everything worse. That urge to cry when I get hurt unexpectedly is like crying when I'm mad. It takes a thing that's just plain bad and turns it into bad and embarrassing, both.

I got to my feet. Well, foot. By then the blood was running down my shin and on to my sneaker. I tested my weight on my left ankle, but it didn't go well. I hopped back to the car, using most of my energy to hold back those hot tears.

My mom had shifted over to the driver's seat. She didn't see me. She was looking off into the distance. I had to hop around to the passenger side and knock on the window. But then she couldn't see what was happening, because I was too close to the car. She gave me a shrug, like she didn't know why I didn't just get in.

I gave up on getting any help from her, opened the door, leaned in, and stuck my hand into the tissue box, grabbing about ten at once. I folded the stack in half and pressed it on to my knee to try to stop the bleeding.

Then I had to figure out how to lower myself on to the seat with only one hand, while standing on only one foot. Finally I gave up and just flopped down, refusing to say, Ouch. I picked up my bad leg with my free hand and put it in the car, then straightened out and closed the door.

'Did you hurt yourself?' my mom asked.

I wondered where she'd been for all that. Where she was now. I didn't ask.

'I just scraped my knee.'

'That must have been quite a scrape,' she said, pointing to the blood trail.

'I didn't have anything to press on it. Now that I do, it'll stop.'

She started the car and pulled out of the driveway
without saying much.

'Don't drop me at the motel,' I said. 'Drop me home.
We have more first-aid stuff there. And Paul will have
anything we don't.'

'You sure you're OK?'

'Nobody ever died of a skinned knee. That I know
of.'

'Too bad about that peach. I was looking forward to
that.'

'Yeah,' I said. 'Me, too.'

She pulled up at the bottom of Paul's driveway. Shifted
into park. I just sat there and stared at her. After a
bizarre length of staring time, she looked back.

'What?'

'Could you please drive me up the driveway? I twisted
my ankle.'

'You didn't tell me that. You just said you skinned
your knee.'

'Well. Now I'm telling you. I twisted my ankle.'

She shifted into reverse, backed up a little, and pulled
up the driveway. Drove me right up to the bottom of
the apartment stairs.

Rachel was standing on the stairs. Our stairs.

'Now, what's *she* doing?' my mom asked.

'I don't know. I'll find out. Just go back to work, OK?'

I opened the passenger door before she'd even completely stopped the car. When I looked up, Rachel was
standing over me.

'Could you give me a hand, please?' I asked her. 'I sort of hurt myself.'

'Of course.'

She nodded hello to my mom – they'd never been introduced, or spoken to each other – and took hold of my arm, and helped me out. I stood there at the bottom of our stairs, bent over so I could hold pressure on my knee, trying not to be obvious about how little weight I could put on that ankle. I waved goodbye to my mom in a way that made it clear I wanted her to go. She shook her head and backed down the driveway when she just as easily could have turned around.

I looked up at Rachel.

'I was out looking for you,' she said. 'I looked for you at the campground.'

'We're staying in a motel this time.'

'I was going upstairs to leave you a note. What happened?'

'Just a stupid accident. Just me being uncoordinated and not very athletic.'

'Let's get you upstairs.'

I had to wrap my left arm over her shoulders. Which made it hard, because she was tall and I wasn't. I had to reach up at a weird angle. Then she wrapped her arm around my waist. I had to give up on holding pressure on my knee. I had to just openly bleed.

While she was helping me up the stairs, I thought about my mom. Sitting on her butt in the car while I hopped around and found a way to get in. Granted, she probably hadn't known what was going on. But part of me felt like she should have. Like Rachel would have.

I unlocked the door with my key, and we avoided the rug and left a little trail of blood on the nice hardwood floor as she helped me into the bathroom.

'Sit on the edge of the tub,' she said. And she helped me get there. 'And wash it out as best you can. I'll go get Paul's first-aid kit.'

And I thought, See? Paul has a first-aid kit. Along with a flashlight for when the power goes out. It's just who he is. And who we're not.

I was sitting on the couch with my knee slung over the padded leather arm, an old towel under it to catch blood and peroxide. My foot was propped on a stack of pillows on a chair, so it was higher than my knee. Rachel had wrapped my ankle in an elastic bandage from Paul's first-aid kit. There was a plastic bag of ice draped over it.

She had her reading glasses on, and was studying my knee closely, holding a tweezers, trying to pick out any last shreds of bark.

'Ah!' I said, when she went after one. I tried hard to not say anything, every time. But some little sound always slipped out.

'I'm sorry,' she said.

'You have to stop being sorry.'

'I wish I didn't have to hurt you. But it's going to be hard to keep this from getting infected. Because of all the dirt and bark ground in. I just want to get out as much as I can. Brace yourself once more.'

This time all that came out was a breath. But it took some doing to hold it down to that. I had to sit on the pain, and hard.

I couldn't stop trembling. I could only remember one other time in my life when pain made me shivery. I didn't know why some pain did and some didn't. Something to do with how completely vulnerable it made me feel, I think. The peroxide she used to flush the wound in between tweezering was sending needles of pain through parts of my body it couldn't possibly be touching.

I looked at Rachel and got that feeling again that she would have been a good mother, and that things would have turned out better for me if I'd had more of a mother for a mother. This time I kept it to myself.

'Why were you looking for me?' I asked. 'What was the note about?'

Something dark came into her eyes, a cloud that pulled her back from me.

'Oh,' I said. 'It's something bad.'

'I'm so sorry, Angie. I made trouble for you. I didn't mean to. It was a stupid mistake.'

'Well, I can relate to stupid mistakes.'

I wondered why I was talking when I really wanted to hear what it was.

'I was tired last night, and sleepy. It was right before bed. Without thinking, I made reference to something you said when you came down to talk to me. Just an innocent little thing. About whether the fish are biting. And then of course he wanted to know when we talked, and about what, and why he didn't know.'

I felt that creepy tingling thing wash over my stomach. But it was so bad in there already. This new disaster didn't add all that much to the pile.

'What did you tell him?'

'As little as I could. But now he knows you came to talk to me. I didn't give a lot of details. I declined to answer some questions. But I didn't want to look straight into his face and lie to him.'

'I never meant for you to lie to him. *I* wouldn't, if he asked *me*.'

'Well, he will. I'm leaving you with cotton and the peroxide. Keep flushing it out for as long as you can stand. Then put a lot of this antibiotic ointment on it. And I'm leaving about five of these gauze pads and the roll of adhesive tape. You'll want to clean it and change the dressings once or twice a day.'

'Thanks.'

'I'm so sorry, Angie. I feel like I let you down.'

'I knew the risk.' I was in that place again. That belly-up place. All was lost. I was no longer trying to shield myself in any way. Everything sucked, and I accepted that. 'How upset is he?'

'Even more than I thought he would be. He doesn't put his trust in many people, so I think that's why this hit him hard. I'll keep trying to talk to him.'

She cleaned the blood off the floor before she let herself out and left me alone.

Usually I liked being alone. But this time it was too much aloneness.

Like I was alone in a lot more than just the apartment.

It was almost an hour before Paul came up. When I heard his footsteps on the stairs, I felt a strange sense of relief. Like when you're waiting for the executioner. It's one of those things. Better to just face it and be done.

He knocked, and I called out that it was open, and he should come in.

He looked down at me, half sitting, half lying on that couch, with my leg up, a saturated ball of cotton dripping peroxide down both sides of my knee and on to the towel. The sharp needles of pain punctuated the moment. I had no urge to defend myself. If he'd pulled out a knife, I might have let him stab me with it.

He didn't. He didn't yell, either. I remember half wishing he would.

'You went down and talked to Rachel?' It was only half a question.

For a minute I said nothing.

Then I said, 'Remember that first day I met you? I stomped over to your house and accused you of calling the police on us. You said when you do something, it's because you think it's the right thing to do. So, then, you wouldn't lie later and say you didn't. You'd say you did it, and why you did it. Yes, I went back to the old place and talked to Rachel. Because you made it clear you were never going to. And I wanted things to work out for you two.'

'Which they might not have. You could have messed things up big.'

'Apparently I did,' I said. 'But my thinking was that if *I* told her, then, if she didn't feel the same, she could just pretend I'd never said anything. And the two of you wouldn't have to be awkward around each other. And your friendship could keep going. Yes, I know it was dicey. I knew that all along. But I did it because I thought it was the right thing to do, even though I totally get why you're upset. I knew I was gambling our friendship.'

He stood staring down at me for another minute. I couldn't look at his face for long. Because I didn't recognize it. He still looked like Paul. But he wasn't the Paul I knew. He wasn't my friend. That Paul had gone away.

'How did you hurt yourself?' he asked.

'It's not important. It's stupid. I was trying to climb a tree. That property is gone. They sold it already. We lost that. Not that we ever really had it, but—'

'Look.' His voice was so flat it was scary. And sickening. 'I get that you did the wrong thing for the right reasons. But you broke a confidence. That was the most sensitive thing I ever shared with anyone and you took it to the most sensitive person involved. I get that you didn't do it as gossip or out of meanness, but it's just not something I feel I can forgive.'

Those last words made a sort of thump in my gut. I thought I was all surrendered in there, and nothing could pull me down another rung. Because there were no more rungs.

Wrong.

When I looked up, he was over at the door, his hand on the knob. His head was tilted down. He looked shorter. Like what was happening made him small.

'So,' I said. 'I guess we need to get out right now, then.'

He looked over at me. His eyes seemed confused and far away. Like he had to dust the inside of his head for cobwebs before he could answer.

'I told you when you moved in that if it didn't work out you could stay until you found a new place. So I'll stand behind my word on that. But as far as us being friends . . . my friends are people I can trust.'

Not to be mean, but I wondered who that was. Other than Rachel.

As if he could read my mind, he said, 'Not that I have a lot of friends. Now you know why. I won't be friends with anyone I can't trust, even if that means being friends with practically no one.'

It hit me how badly he must miss Rigby. Probably the only friend who ever completely made the cut.

'I hope this doesn't make a problem between you and Rachel. Things were just looking like they were going to work out. Don't let this ruin it. OK? Please.'

He leveled me with a look exactly like the ones he used to shoot through Aunt Vi's fence. 'What you still don't seem to understand is that things between me and Rachel are between me and Rachel.'

'Right. Got it. Sorry.'

Then he let himself out.

*

My mom got in a little after three. Opened the door with her key and then stood there looking down at me like I was only doing what I was doing – which was not much, by the way – to make her life more difficult.

'You didn't tell me you'd hurt yourself that bad.'

'You were kind of off somewhere.'

'Meaning what?'

'I don't know. You just seemed like your head was somewhere else.'

She put her hands on her hips the way she always did when it was time to defend. 'If the message here is that I didn't pay enough attention to you when you were hurt, you might want to look at the fact that I always ask if you're OK, and you always say you're fine. Like you want me to stay out of it.'

I thought about that for a minute and then said, 'That's true.'

It wasn't what she expected. It stopped the conversation completely.

After an awkward moment she said, 'Well. Come on.'

'Come on what?'

'Sophie will be home any minute, and then we have to go back to the motel.'

'Maybe not. We're sort of thrown out already. So maybe we can just stay here and shut up. I don't mean thrown out like we have to leave right now. But we're not invited to keep living here. So maybe it doesn't even matter.'

'What the hell happened, Angie?'

'It's kind of a long story. And I've had an incredibly crappy day. Can I tell it to you some other time?'

Rachel called at nine thirty that night.

My mom brought me the phone. Held her hand over the mouthpiece and said, 'It's for you. It's the queen.'

'I wish you wouldn't call her that. It really bugs me.'

She said nothing. Just handed me the phone.

'Rachel?' I asked.

'Yes,' she said. Like it hurt. Like that one word could shatter everything. 'I'm sorry if it's late to call. I hope I'm not waking anyone up at your house.'

I looked down at Sophie, sleeping curled up on the rug.

'No one's asleep except Sophie. And you didn't wake her. Why didn't you just come up?'

'I'm home. I'm not downstairs.'

'Oh, no.'

'It's all right. Paul and I will work it out. At least, I think we will. I think we've known each other too long to let anything come between us. It's you and Paul I'm worried about.'

I looked over at my mom, who was sitting at the kitchen table, her back artificially straight. Obviously listening. I had no way to get to any privacy. It wasn't worth hobbling outside. I gave up and let her hear.

'There is no me and Paul. He doesn't want to be friends any more. And I guess that's up to him.'

'Oh, dear. I was afraid of this. He may come around in time.'

'I don't think so. He might be civil to me at some point. But I think our friend days are over.'

'I'll keep talking to him about it. Maybe I can help.'

'That would be nice. But I'm not holding my breath or anything.'

'And if you had it to do over?'

'Excuse me?'

'The coming down to see me. And telling me. What if you had it to do over?'

'I'd do it again.'

'Even knowing it would cost you your living space and your friend?'

'I just feel like . . .' Then I stalled. I knew what I felt like. But not quite how to wrap words around it. I tried again. 'I feel like a love like that . . . one that's still the same after fifty years . . . I just don't think it should go to waste.'

'I'm going to tell him you said that,' she said.

When I got off the phone, my mom was staring at me.

'I've got plenty of time for a long story,' she said.

I sighed. 'I went back to Paul's old house and told Rachel how he felt about her. Which he had no idea I was going to do. But now he knows I did, and he's plenty pissed.'

A long silence. I looked up at her after a while.

'Oh,' I said. 'You look plenty pissed, too.'

I thought, Well, it's official. Everybody hates me. Except Rachel.

'You did that . . . knowing if it didn't work it would

make a God-awful mess and if it did work it would get us tossed out of here?'

I nodded.

'And you just told her you'd do the same thing again.'

'Way not to eavesdrop.'

'I don't understand that, Angie. I swear I just don't understand you at all.'

'I know you don't. Believe me. I know. But some of my favorite parts of me are the parts you don't understand. I don't mean to be hurtful. I'm not saying it in an angry way. I wish we fit together better, too. But I'm not going to change the best of me just because you don't get it.'

I waited for an answer, but it never came.

After a while I gave up and stopped waiting.

The following morning I slipped a note under Paul's back door. Despite the fact that there was walking and stair climbing involved. I just did it anyway.

It said, 'Will you please leave your newspapers on the back porch when you're done reading them? Because I want to look at the want ads for rentals.'

He never answered the note. But, after that, there was always a newspaper on the back porch by eight o'clock in the morning.

It was ten or eleven days later. I was sitting at the breakfast table with my mom. Sophie was flapping her hands in the air, but silently, ignoring her breakfast. I was reading the want ads, holding the paper with one hand, eating cereal with the other. It was only about seven thirty. The paper had shown up on Paul's back porch early.

'Any good rentals?' my mom asked.

She asked every morning, unless I read the paper after she was gone. I wondered why she didn't just trust me to tell her if I found something. It was a form of nervous small talk that made me uncomfortable.

'Well, that depends,' I said. 'In our price range?'

'What's the point of hearing about it if it's not?'

'Then, no. No good rentals.'

'You *are* reading "For Rent". Not "For Sale"? Right?'

'I'm reading both.'

'You're wasting your time, kiddo. We couldn't even afford that run-down place, and we'll never find anything that cheap again. Not around here. Face it. We're going back to the city. That's where you can live cheap, and that's where Sophie will be if we want to go see her.'

Before she even finished her speech, my eyes locked on a listing.

'Here's a place as cheap as that other one. Oh. Wait. It's the same place.'

I read all the details, and they couldn't possibly have been coincidence. It was even the same real-estate agent.

'Maybe it's a mistake,' I said. 'Maybe they ran the ad again by mistake.'

'Or maybe the sale fell through. But I'm not sure what difference it makes, kiddo, since we still have no credit. And now you don't even have that professional loan expert in your back pocket any more.'

'Oh. Right.' I ate three bites of cereal, chomping down too hard on my own molars. Then I said, 'Come by the real-estate office with me. We'll leave a little early for your work. I'll drive you.'

'Can you even walk on that ankle now?'

'Yeah. Pretty much. I can limp on it.'

'I doubt they'd be open that early.'

'Oh. Right. Lunch hour, then. I'll come get you.'

'To what end, kiddo?'

'I just want to know what happened. Why it's in the paper again. And I can't go in by myself. I don't think she'd take me very seriously if it was just me. I need a grown-up.'

She sipped her coffee, and I could see wheels turning.

'Make a deal with you,' she said. 'I'll go into that real-estate office with you today if you'll set a deadline to give up finding a place here and move back to the city. Two weeks, say.'

I hated that a lot. Because it was a bad gamble. Just the type I knew I was supposed to avoid. I was taking something flimsy and betting everything on it.

'Fine,' I said. 'Deal.'

It was a small office, all open space, with only four desks. Two of them had people behind them. A man I didn't know. And the lady I did.

She looked up at us. Squinted. I wished she didn't always look so put-together. I wished she could have been someone less intimidating to my mom.

'I know you, don't I?' she asked, looking at me.

'I was . . . we were interested in that property, that run-down house on the little orchard. I came in to see you with Paul Inverness. Remember?'

'Oh, yes,' she said, and got to her feet. And shook hands with my mom. Not with me. I thought that was weird. 'And this is your mother?'

'Right,' I said. 'That property was back in the paper this morning.'

'Yes, the sale fell through.'

'Fell through? What happened?'

'I can't give specifics about a prospective buyer's situation.'

'OK. Sure. I just . . . I mean, I don't even know what that would mean. What does it mean when a person tries to buy a house and it falls through? What can fall through about it?'

'Oh. In general.' She sat back down again. Like she'd already decided this wasn't worth much energy. 'Occasionally a buyer will just change his or her mind, but usually it's dollars and cents. Buyers may think they can come up with the down payment, or that their loan will be approved. But sometimes their thinking is too optimistic.'

I just stood there like a statue. Even though I knew I should talk. Because I'd just learned something that changed my world view. That buyer I saw, who looked like he could write a check for the place. He wasn't so different from us as I thought. Here I was thinking everybody had it together and everybody looked down on us. And a bunch of them were just wearing that on the outside. Just being too optimistic.

The real-estate lady got tired of waiting.

'If you think your grandfather is still interested, have him come see me.'

'Right,' I said.

My mom and I walked out into the bright summer sun.

'Now what did that accomplish?' she asked me as we stood blinking on the sidewalk.

'No idea.' Which was true. Housing-wise, I had no idea. But I'd gotten something else. Something I'd never expected. 'Did you hear what she said?'

'What about it?'

She signaled that we should walk and talk. We headed for the car. I was going slow on that ankle. I could barely keep up with her.

'That thing about how people are too optimistic.'

'Yeah? So?'

'Real-estate people see that all the time. All kinds of people try to buy houses when they may not have enough money or credit.'

'I'm not quite sure where you're heading with this.'

'You thought it was just us. Admit it. You thought every person who walks into a real-estate office or a bank is a qualified buyer. You thought they'd treat us like the only case they ever saw of somebody who might not be able to pull it off.'

No answer.

We reached the car in silence, and she got in and

opened the passenger door. I sat down, and put on my seat belt, wondering if I should press the issue further.

Just as she was pulling out of the space, she said, 'I might've thought that. Yeah.' Then, a block later, 'But I'm not really sure what it changes.'

I didn't answer. Because I wasn't sure, either. It changed something in me. But I wasn't sure it changed anything in my real-estate goals.

I more or less resigned myself to the fact that we were taking our newly found world view and moving it back down out of the mountains.

I dropped her at work and drove back to the apartment. I limped upstairs, leaning heavily on the railing. Got the newspaper off the table. Found a marking pen, and circled the listing. Drew three big arrows pointing to it. Underneath that, I wrote IT'S BACK, in big block letters.

Then I limped downstairs and slowly made my way up to Paul's back door. I left it on the porch, tucking one end under the door so it couldn't blow away.

I looked out the window an hour later, and it was gone. He'd taken it inside.

I sat on the edge of the couch for most of the day, hoping. Until it was time to pick up my mom.

Then I sat on the edge of the couch all evening, trying to hope less obviously.

But I didn't hear anything from Paul.

Two days after that, I was still more or less on the edge of the couch when I heard footsteps on the stairs. It was mid-afternoon, not quite time for my mom to be home. I ran – well, hobbled fast – over to the door so I could open it when he knocked.

But no knock ever happened.

Instead I watched as a note appeared under the door. Sealed in a lavender-colored envelope. I grabbed it up and sat back down on the couch with it, my hands shaking. I slaughtered the envelope getting it open.

It wasn't from Paul. It was from Rachel.

Everything fell and sagged in me. I knew then that I might as well slump back on the couch and breathe. Because that sudden change of heart I'd been counting on in him wasn't going to happen. I'd thought the fact that the house was back on the market might mean something to him. But, as I sat there, Rachel's note sagging on to my lap, still unread, I felt stupid for having thought so. I was the only one who cared about that ugly, run-down house. I had no idea why I'd ever expected anybody else to share my enthusiasm.

I lifted the note and read it.

It just said she was up visiting, and she wanted me to know. And that she'd try again to talk to him.

But I felt like I had a pretty good idea how that would turn out.

The following day, mid-morning, I walked into town.

It was a stupid thing to do, on a number of different levels.

First, my ankle wasn't really healed enough for that long a walk. My knee was partly scabbed over, partly still infected, and it hurt every time I bent it. And the whole point of the walk was what my mom called a fool's errand.

I'd gotten it in my head to go see that house one more time. To say goodbye before we left town. Except, underneath that, maybe to get another feel for whether I'd ever belonged there or not. Like maybe the answer could have changed.

Unfortunately, I hadn't thought of any of this before my mom left for work. And then, after she did, I just couldn't hold the idea back.

I was hobbling uphill toward town when a car pulled up beside me. I purposely didn't look. Because if a weird guy is following you in his car, you shouldn't encourage him.

'Angie,' I heard. In a voice that was very definitely Paul's.

He had his passenger window open, so I hobbled over and leaned on his car. I wanted to talk, but my heart was too thumpy, and I couldn't quite catch my breath. Because I didn't know if he was there to hurt me or to be nice to me, and I couldn't stand the waiting to find out.

'I've been looking for you,' he said.

'Why do people do that? All these people driving around trying to find me. Like I'm somebody important to find.' I was talking over my fear. Making very little sense. 'Last time it was to tell me bad news. Are you going to tell me bad news?'

'No,' he said.

So I opened the passenger door and got in.

We sat in absolute silence for a weird length of time.

Then I heard something move in the back seat. I whipped around to look. He had a dog back there. If you could call him that. He was more of a puppy, but at least half grown, and absolutely huge. Lying down, he filled the seat completely, from one door to the other. He was definitely a Great Dane. But not black like Rigby. An even silvery-gray color, like a Weimaraner. He was incredibly skinny. Painfully skinny. You could see every knob of his backbone. Every one of his ribs. When I looked at him, he turned his eyes away. His ears were long and uncropped.

'Oh, my God. You got a new dog.'

'I did.'

'Where did you get him? Him? Her?'

'Him. I went all the way to Sacramento to get him from a breed rescue group.'

'He's so skinny.'

'I know. They tried to fatten him up. Now I'm trying to fatten him up. But he has issues around food. It's like he's scared of it. He's scared of everything. Apparently he's been abused and neglected. But he'll come around.'

'What's his name?'

'Scout. That was his name when I got him. But I'm thinking I'll keep it. Because it's so different from Rigby. I think it's important to be clear that the new dog is completely different from the one you lost.'

'Scout.' I reached my hand out to him. He sat up fast to get out of the way.

'Give him time.'

'Does he let you touch him?'

'Barely. But he's getting better with me. Like his ears?'

'I do. Very much. Very handsome ears on the dog. Why were you looking for me? What did you want to tell me?'

I heard him pull in a long, deep breath and let it out again. I watched his hands tighten on the steering wheel, then relax. The whole thing seemed to take a long time. But I just waited.

'This morning . . .' he said.

And paused. And I could already tell this speech had been rehearsed.

'. . . I woke up very early. It was still dark. The wee small hours of the morning. And the love of my life . . . the woman I've loved since high school . . . was in my bed with me.'

He stopped, almost like he couldn't go on. I wanted to shout something about how wonderful that was. I didn't. I shut my mouth. For a change.

'I watched her sleeping for a long time. I don't even know how long. Could have been hours. And the same thought kept coming back. Over and over and over.'

Another long pause. Painful for me. But I waited.

'I thought, What kind of fool . . . what kind of *idiot* . . . would feel *anything* for the person who helped this happen . . . except gratitude?'

Tears sprang up, sudden. Just out of nowhere. I told them to go away. I clamped on them. But a few got loose. I didn't wipe them away again.

'I'm so sorry I hurt you with what I did,' I said.

'See, you're doing that thing again. Don't. You're doing that Angie thing where someone is trying to let you off the hook and you keep jumping back on it.'

'Oh. Sorry.'

We sat in silence for a time. I don't know how long of one. Scout shifted in the back seat and sighed a deep, sad sigh.

'That's so wonderful about you and Rachel,' I said. More silence. Then I said, 'Oh my God. You just told me another really sensitive personal secret.'

'Yes,' he said. 'The irony of that is not lost on me.'

'Was there something better I should've done? What would you have done?'

'I think I would have gone a different route. If I knew somebody who wasn't doing the right thing, I don't think I'd do it for them. I think I'd use more of a bayonet-at-the-back approach. Get behind them, see if I couldn't drive some action.'

'I have no idea what that would even look like.'

'I'll show you exactly what it looks like.'

He shifted into drive, and headed for town.

I didn't ask any questions.

I had a few. But I didn't ask them.

He pulled up in front of the pharmacy and cut the engine.

'Before I do this . . .' he said. 'If she had a house, could she be trusted to keep up the payments?'

'If she didn't, I would. I'd get a job and help.'

'That's what I needed to hear.'

He jumped out of the car and disappeared inside the pharmacy.

I looked back at Scout. 'What the hell?' I asked him.

A minute later Paul was there again with my mom in tow. He opened the passenger door.

'You sit in the back with the dog,' he told me. 'Don't try to pet him. He won't bite you, but it's best not to scare him.'

I got out, leaning most of my weight on my good ankle, and opened the back door. Scout jumped up into a sit. I eased into the back seat beside him, and he drew back against the door on the opposite side, pulling his paws in so they didn't touch any part of me. Treating me like I was a flow of molten lava coming almost all the way up to where he sat. I looked at him, and he looked away.

Then we were moving, and Paul was talking, more or less non-stop. But not to me. To my mom.

'You're not ashamed of the fact that you've never had a loan before. You take pride in being a first-time buyer. You're ready to move up to the middle class. You didn't try to buy in the past because you knew your own limitations. You didn't feel ready. Now you feel ready. It's not your fault that your income is low. You could work full-time, but your responsibility to your special-needs daughter comes first. That's why you work two-thirds-time instead of full-time. She's enrolled in Special Education in public school, so no extra expenses are incurred by her situation. Your older daughter is unusually mature and responsible, and is seventeen now. She's a good help to you. If you can wait until she's eighteen for her to work part-time and contribute, that would be preferable, but she's ready to step in at any time if more money is needed.'

'OK . . .' my mom said.

I had no idea how she'd gotten a break from work. I had no idea how hard he'd pushed her to get her to come. I had no idea if she was excited or intimidated. There was so much I didn't know.

'Let me do most of the talking. If I'm looking at the loan administrator, I'm carrying the dialogue. If he asks you a direct question, I'll turn to you. That's your signal to talk. Be direct. Be polite. Don't be subservient. Banks need to make loans. It's a big part of their income. His job is to get people into mortgages.'

'OK . . .' my mom said.

We pulled into the parking lot behind one of the two local banks. We all piled out. Except Scout. Paul cracked all four windows for the dog and then locked up.

'Heads up,' he said.

'What?' my mom asked, looking around.

'No. Literally. Hold your heads up.'

So we lifted our chins. And we followed Paul inside.

He led us straight to the desk of a guy I figured must be a loan administrator. He was young. Maybe thirties. Younger than my mom. I was hoping that would help. He had a beard, and, even though he was wearing a nice suit, he didn't look all that clean-cut. He wasn't too intimidating.

Paul shook hands with him, and introduced us. I listened to them talking, and my head was spinning, and I could have gotten anything wrong, but I got the impression that they had already talked earlier that morning.

'Have a seat,' the man said. Joseph Greely. I got that from Paul's introduction, and from the name plate on his desk. 'Let's see what we can get done. I have to tell you both, you're fortunate to have Mr Inverness advocating for you. We're here to make loans, and we love nothing more than to get people into houses. And we try to help as much as we can, in the interest of the first-time buyer. But, really, there's nothing as helpful to your situation as having an older, well-established person with great credit who's willing to co-sign for you. That's going to make all the difference.'

Silence. Absolute and utter silence. I was waiting for Paul to tell Mr Greely that he'd misunderstood. He never did.

'I'm sorry,' Mr Greely said. 'You look confused. Did you not know that?'

My mom opened her mouth to speak, but nothing came out.

'We do know that,' I said. 'We definitely know how lucky we are to have Paul's support.'

My mom walked to Paul's car like she was wandering in a dream. I purposely hung back, hoping Paul would stop and talk to me.

He did.

'Where's Rachel?' I asked. 'I can't believe you left her home alone. On your very first day . . . as . . . I mean . . . together.'

'I told her I had some important business to attend to. You got a problem with that?'

'Guess not.'

I was just about to throw my arms around him when he said, 'Do *not* get all mushy with me. Like that day at the lake.'

'*Me*? You were the one who started that. Kissing me on the forehead so hard you almost broke my neck.'

'That's entirely beside the point. Keep your head in the game. We've got a lot more work to do. Next we go by the real-estate office and put in a lowball offer.'

'Think they'll take less?'

'We don't know. We just know it's the next step. Just follow my lead, kid. I'll show you how it's done.'

Chapter Five

Where We Belong

I led her down the driveway by the arm, looking over now and then to make sure she wasn't peeking. Every time I looked her eyes were closed.

That's a lot of trust for my mom.

'Thank you for waiting,' I said. 'I know it must be very weird to buy a house you've never seen. And you must've thought I was plenty weird for asking you to. But it was really important to me to get it cleaned up first.'

I stopped in front of the house, and tugged her arm to cue her to stop.

'You can open your eyes now,' I said.

I watched her face, but I didn't know what to make of anything I saw there.

'Oh, honey,' she said, putting an arm around my shoulder. 'That is . . . so ugly.'

I burst out laughing. I couldn't help it. It was the way she said it. Like she was looking at a smelly old dog who she really loved in spite of himself.

'You should've seen it before I cleaned it up.'

'I hate to think. All those hours of work . . . all those weeks . . . that was all cleaning?'

'No. Not all. Mostly. There were a bunch of broken windows. Paul gave us windowpanes cut to fit. As a housewarming present. And new locks for the doors. Locking knobs and deadbolts, both. He installed those. He showed me how to replace window glass on the first one, and then I did all the rest myself. And he gave us a ladder. Turns out you're supposed to get fruit and nuts out of trees with a long, telescoping ladder. And somebody is supposed to hold it, or you're supposed to lash it to the tree. Turns out there isn't supposed to be any running or jumping involved at all. Who knew?'

'We're learning all kinds of new things, aren't we?'

'We are. Now that you've seen the bad news with your own eyes, how about some good news?'

'Shoot.'

'It has three bedrooms.'

'You are . . . *kidding* me!'

'I wouldn't kid. They're small. But there are three of them. Come on. I'll show you the inside. But first . . . the best news of all. Listen.'

We stood for a minute, side by side. Her arm still draped on my shoulder. Birds chirped, leaves rustled in the wind. Far away there was some kind of motor, but I couldn't tell if it was a loud car or a small plane. It never came close.

'I don't hear anything,' she said.

'That's the good news.'

'When we move in with Sophie it won't be this quiet.'

'But no one will care. Because no one but us will hear her.'

I waited a moment for her to take that in. Not that I hadn't tried to tell her. But it was different to hear it for yourself.

She gave my shoulder a squeeze. 'House, I forgive you for being ugly,' she said. 'In fact, you're looking better all the time.'

'It's not bad inside,' she said. 'It's really not. Once we get some furniture in it . . . Wait. We'll have to get some furniture. Where will we get furniture?'

'We'll figure it out. All the floorboards are nailed down now. And it's really not drafty. Not like you'd think. And now that the electricity is on, the heater works. Which we thought was really surprising.'

'Gas?'

'We don't get gas out here. There's a propane tank.'

'Oh. Propane.'

She wandered off to look around. First in the kitchen. Then I heard her footsteps heading for the back bedrooms, the back porch. I sat cross-legged on the wooden floorboards in a beam of sun through the orchard-side windows.

After a few minutes she came out and sat next to me, her arms hugging her knees.

'What day does Sophie get picked up here instead of there?' I asked her.

'Monday.'

'Good. Gives us all weekend to get our stuff in.'

'Seriously, kiddo? *Our* stuff? That won't take a weekend. Three trips, maybe.'

Then we sat without talking for a long time. I was getting the feel of the place. Letting it feel natural to be there. I think she was, too.

She put an arm over my shoulder again.

'You know,' she said. 'With Sophie still in the same school district . . . and the longer bus ride . . . and living in a place where she can scream till she's blue in the face with no problems . . . I could really take care of her myself. Mostly. You know. If you wanted to go to college.'

'Or Tibet.'

'Or both.'

'Right. College is important. I agree. Or both.'

'Wait. Tibet?'

I wondered where she'd been the first time around.

'Kind of a long story.'

She stroked my hair for a second or two.

'I'll make time,' she said.

THE END

Walk Me Home
Catherine Ryan Hyde

Two sisters,
One life-changing tragedy.

'You shouldn't trust anybody completely,' Jen says.
'Why not?'
'They're still just people. They can still let you down.'

Carly and her sister Jen are walking. Since their mother's sudden death, Carly has been left in charge, her faith in humanity shattered.

Terrified that the two will be separated, Carly wants to find the last person she trusted – their stepfather. But Jen holds a secret about him which could put them both at even more risk.

And so begins a journey neither girl could have anticipated. It's difficult, and dangerous, but also filled with the unexpected kindness of strangers. And some new relationships that hold the potential to change everything . . .

Don't Let Me Go
Catherine Ryan Hyde

*What if the only way to save your mother . . . is
to leave her?*

*"Remember how you said you'd always find me?
Well, don't ever forget that. Please."*

GRACE

Ten-year-old Grace knows that her mum loves her, but
her mum loves drugs too. There's only so long Grace can
fend off the 'woman from the county' who is threatening
to put her into care. Her only hope is . . .

BILLY

Grown-man Billy Shine hasn't left his apartment for
years. People scare him. And so day in, day out, he lives
a perfectly orchestrated, silent life within his four walls.
Until now . . .

THE PLAN

Grace bursts into Billy's life with a loud voice and a plan
to get her mum clean. But it won't be easy, because they
will have to confiscate the one thing her mum holds
most dear . . . they will have to kidnap Grace.